I0777275

Between Salt & Serenades

BETWEEN SALT & SERENADES

SERENADES

A LOVE X MAGIC NOVEL

MARISSA SERRAO

BROKEN WING PRESS
An imprint of Eighty-Eight Butterfly House

To my sister. The weight of the eldest child was one I never bore, but I am endlessly grateful for you paving paths I didn't know I needed until I reached them.

CONTENT WARNINGS

- Grief
- Physical pain
- Mild profanity
- Sexual situations
- Blood and mild body gore
- Previous loss of a loved one

PRONUNCIATION GUIDE

Names

Breena: BREE-nah
Cliodna- KLEE-na
Niven: NIH-vuhn
Sidra: SID-rah
Tetwin: TET-win
Tinelle: Tih-NELL
Zellia: TSEL- e-ah

Places

Barthoah: Bar-THO-ah
Dreslee: DRE-z-lee
Kilkov: Kill-CAH-v

CHAPTER ONE
THE SHELL AROUND HER NECK

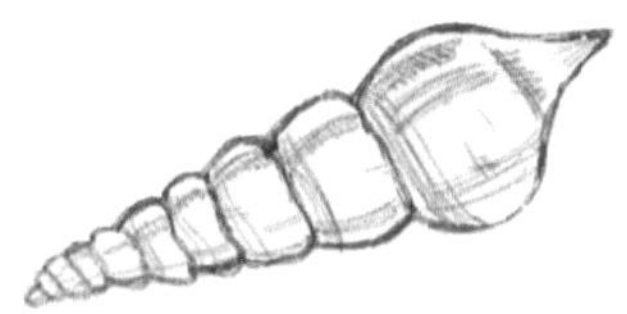

Being from the depths of the sea, you'd think I'd be frightened of the light and its ability to illuminate what we all tried not to see, the memories we tried to leave in the dark because it was too painful to do anything but. This was true for the rest of my pod, yes, but not me. I relished in the way the sun's rays pierced the surface of the water and fractured into a million stars of the sea. I cherished the way their energy heated the sand beneath me so I could forget I was a creature of the dark depths.

Here in the Kilkov, the seafloor rose to a natural plateau a hundred odd feet below the surface, the only place I could find peace in the light. It was my sanctuary of sorts, beyond the forest of kelp that hid my pod's territory from the larger creatures of the sea.

The Kilkov was the shallowest place in our territory, the place I would go when the darkness of the sea's depths weighed on me. It was where I could lie alone and stare up at the ripples on the surface that glimmered in the sun's rays like melted glass—or so I'd been told. I had never seen melted glass firsthand, just broken pieces and old bottles that had found their way to us like abandoned memories. My father, on the other hand, used to wield it, commanding the molten sand to bend to his will, shaping it into art that spoke to the souls of sea fae like us.

Of course, he kept his large and fragile pieces on land, fearing the rough sea would destroy his life's work. He only brought us small odds and ends to invite us into his world, such as thick glass shells less prone to damage. Zellia and I would safely tuck them away in marked locations in the sand, deep enough to not be swept away by the sea currents.

His remaining art had been destroyed in our war, abandoned, roaming the sea floor like his haunting spirit. Each time I saw a glimmer in the water, I dove down to the sand to collect it, wondering if, at one point, the glass was his.

I'd convinced myself that if I found every last fragment, he would finally be able to rest. Sometimes, I swore I was fighting for peace and a chance to move on from his death. Other times, I wondered if all I was doing was torturing my wounded heart. The wooden chest in my room filled halfway with glass fragments was a source of both pride and pain.

My back rested upon the sea floor, and I stared up at the surface of the water, lost in its constant, mesmerizing fluidity. I was thankful most of my pod was too fearful to come to the Kilkov, because that meant more peace for me. I didn't understand their hesitancy. Yes, it was hundreds of feet closer to the surface, but we were by no means close to land.

The fear wasn't always present. Long before I was born, my people used to purposely swim to the surface to find ships for an easy way back to land. The fishermen didn't mind the company, and the sirens didn't mind the clothes and food supplied to them for the journey ahead. Those journeys were how we ended up with so many hybrids, babies of both worlds, like my father had been. Only a few dozen remained of my pod, since many of them decided to remain on land with their families. Even more had been killed in the war, like my father had.

I wasn't stupid enough to go to the surface, but if I laid here in the Kilkov, I was safe from the greedy sailors who had forgotten how we were once cousins of the sea. Now, we were nothing but distant enemies, and I refused to get close enough to find myself in their grasp.

As I pressed my hips into the sand, I bent my tail up so the thinner flesh of my fin came between me and the sun, illuminating my opalescent scales. They shimmered with shades of pink and blue, bleeding into each other in a purple haze one could only see in the daytime. The light had a way of making everything down here far more beautiful, myself included.

The Kilkov was the sole place I allowed myself a morsel of happiness, knowing that when I went back down to the Dreslee, the weight of the entire sea would crush me once more.

"Sidra." The sweet voice echoed in my mind, yanking me from my thoughts. My tail fluttered as I sat up, burrowing my hands into the fine sediment below me. My neck cranked to find my sister peering over the ledge of the Kilkov at me. She remained in the safety of the deep, hanging on to the ledge with her two webbed hands. Her small face poked over the top, her ash blonde hair floating above her, glowing and hypnotic.

"Zellia?" I responded with a cocked head, taking in her scrunched face distorted with worry. I didn't need to open my mouth to ask my question, but the speculative words rang through her mind all the same. *"What's going on? What are you doing up here?"*

"It's Mom," she said in my mind, biting her trembling lower lip. My heart faltered, and my hands clenched a fistful of sand, allowing bits of broken shells to penetrate my palms. The sharp pain woke me from the peaceful daze I had stupidly allowed myself to slip into.

"What about her?" I snapped, all patience leaving me as my sister stared into my very soul.

"She gave her rations away again." She said the six words with haunting sadness, and my mind filled with her grief and despera-

tion. I could almost taste her emotions as present as my own, maybe even stronger. *"She needs food."*

"Have Xifi and Tetwin not come back from their hunt?" I peeled my eyes from her and peered into the kelp forest below. I searched for movement, but nothing stood out past the flow of the kelp as it swayed in its usual pattern, being pulled softly in and out by the rolling waves above.

"They have. Empty handed." Her grave face and the way her features pinched together reminded me so much of my father. Great waves, she was the spitting image of him.

"Again?" I gawked, surveying that all-too familiar face. How many times had they come back empty handed?

"Again. It has been months, Sid. We can't keep doing this. We need more than kelp and crustaceans. I think I may very well perish if I have to eat one more anemone," she all but whined, and my stomach lurched at the thought. I could almost taste the bitterness, feel the gooey texture between my teeth. Never again did I want to stoop to eating such a thing.

"Do you think we haven't been trying, Zel?" I didn't miss the way she gripped the ledge, as if her life depended on it. She wouldn't even swim up here, yet I knew why she had come to the Kilkov in search of me. I knew what this subtle ask truly was, though she would never admit it.

"No, it's not that. I know it's not your fault. It's just... When will this end? When will we be free from this hunger? I just want to go back to the way things were before—"

"We all do," I said, not wanting to hear it from her right now. *"I'll grab my spear. I'm going to take care of this."*

"Sid, you won't." Zellia's sharp nails dug into sand and rock, and she rose a little higher over the ledge, just enough for me to see the silver scales trailing over her shoulders.

"I will if it means I can keep this pod alive. What's left of us, at least," I said, my jaw clenching. Out of the three dozen sirens in our pod left, many of us were too young to remember the start of

the war. Most of us hadn't been alive, and those who survived were the young ones who had been kept hidden away in the deepest parts of the sea, far from cruel fishermen.

The water around me suddenly seemed too warm, too thick. I itched to dive back into the Dreslee and have the cooler waters wash over my skin and scales, cooling the heat accumulating under them.

"But none of the other hunters would dare cross the territory." Her eyes scrunched as if the sun had struck them. I hadn't said I was going past our territory, but she knew from the look in my eyes exactly what I'd meant when I said I'd take care of it. That looming truth was what she really wanted to ask of me all along.

"And that's exactly why we have nothing to eat!" I fought. The other twelve hunters hadn't attempted to leave the Dreslee, despite their need to save us all. We should have been working together, but somewhere along the way, a competition had formed to see who could feed the pod the best, who contributed the most. That person was rarely me these days, because I felt no need to compete, only to feed. Gone were the days of working together; first, we lost camaraderie with the sharks, then each other.

"At least bring one of the other hunters with you! Tetwin or Xifi maybe," Zellia begged.

"No. They've all been searching nonstop and need a break. It's my turn." I pushed off the sea floor and darted toward her. She turned to the side, making room for me as I dove off the ledge of the Kilkov. Zellia chased after me, a trail of bubbles behind her as she followed me. We swam through the forest of kelp, winding between the layers of slippery plants that protected the west side of our territory.

The cool water as I traveled deeper was a relief, but it was also a reminder of what I was: a creature of the deep sea, a predator made to protect these waters from those who didn't belong, from those who wished it harm. I was a hunter—a warrior—because if I wasn't, who would be?

Each family in the pod needed one designated hunter, and after my father died, I was the only one who could stomach it. So, here I was, on my way to the sunken ship we called home to grab my spear because I was my family's killer.

Zellia darted up ahead of me, clearing the forest of kelp we had resorted to eating when there was nothing else to fill our stomachs. Once I was in the clear, my view opened to an expanse of deep blue water and shady sand.

When I was young, the Dreslee was full of life—colorful fish zipped around, giant schools filled the empty spaces, octopuses came and went, and the smaller sharks were our allies, working with us in our shared hunt.

Now, my home was barren. Empty, dull, lifeless. Every cell in my body craved to see it as it was when I was a child, to relive those memories of chasing fish, of swimming alongside fierce predators as they taught me the beauty of the chase. The sharks were still around every now and again, but we no longer hunted together. Instead, it was a competition to see who could satisfy our hunger with the few fish that remained.

The sunken ship my pod called home loomed in the distance. The wooden vessel had been swallowed by the sea three years ago and was now tipped into the sand, partially lost to the sea floor. As I swam closer, I trailed my fingers over the sign that read "The Ever Wanderer". The paint was chipping, but we would never forget the ship's name or the reason it was here.

I swam through the entrance closest to my dwelling, passing my pod members who attempted to harvest crustaceans brave enough to enter the ship. I didn't care for socialization right now, swimming past everyone before someone could stop me to chat. Idle conversation would only delay the inevitable.

Once inside, I rifled through my spears, all made of different materials—bone, wood, cartilage, sunken metal—anything I could find on the seafloor that could be made into a weapon. I grabbed the bone spear with the sharpest tip, running my fingers along the swirling engravings my mother had insisted on adding for protection. I had about a dozen hand-whittled spears that looked just like the one in my hands, and over the years, I had broken twice that amount.

"Don't do this, Sid," Zellia begged as she swam through the room's entrance. We shared this area of the ship with our mother while the rest of the pod claimed their own sections of the wreck. It was our place to store our belongings and stay safe from predators while we slept. That was the extent of the time we spent here in The Ever Wanderer; the rest of our home was a wide expanse of sea and sand, and that was where we spent our days and learned the way of the siren.

"What else would you have me do?" I asked. *"You came to me on the Kilkov because you knew I was the only one who would cross the territory. Tell me this isn't what you want, and I won't go."*

She pressed her lips together, and the lack of her voice in my mind was all I needed. She didn't want me to go, but ultimately, she was too hungry to stop me—too desperate for what I was after to put up a real fight.

"Then it's settled."

Zellia rubbed her temples, as if the sound I had just echoed through her mind caused an instant headache, as if my leaving inflicted physical pain on her. Her eyes were dark in the ship, as was the rest of her, but even then, I could see the redness in them. Tears were for humans, but those red eyes of hers told the same story.

I swam to her and placed my free hand on her shoulder. I pressed my palm into her silvery scales and cocked my head at her. Zellia was more familiar with emotion, but after twenty-two years of knowing her, I had grown used to her red eyes and puckered lips.

I had learned not to hold the innocence of her sheltered youth against her. Her heart was soft, and my mother and I did everything to shield her from the realities of this world. I had four years on her, but they were all I needed for our upbringings to be vastly different. I was my father's daughter—a curious mind with a troubled tongue—but Zellia, she was my mother's. She closed her eyes to the truths of this world and lived in blissful unawareness of our reality. That was, until a few months ago, when food became so scarce that there was no possible way to ignore it. She was now living in the truth, choking on it, like we choked on the kelp we force-fed ourselves to survive.

"Everything will be okay," I said. *"You have everything you need right here."*

I pressed one of my palms to her chest, reminding her of what lay underneath. Looped around her neck was a spiral shell with a small glass bead dangling from the tip. It was the only piece left from our father, a small reminder of him and his sacrifice. My mother had given it to Zellia after he'd died. My sister was a healer, after all, and her job allowed the piece to remain safe around her neck. I, on the other hand, would never risk my life for something as trivial as jewelry. I had my box of glass, and that had to be enough.

"How do you know everything will be okay? Everything is—"

"Stop. I said everything will be okay, and so it will be. I promise you that. Have I ever broken a promise?"

Zellia shook her head, placing both her hands over mine. We stayed like that for a minute, silence in our minds but saying everything we needed to with our eyes. When she let me go, I dropped my hand from the shell around her neck.

"Tell Mom..." My words drifted off, the rest of what I wanted to say not willing to leave the comfort of my mind. *"You know what, I'll tell her when I'm back."*

I gripped the spear and gave her a nod before I darted out the door. I couldn't stare at her anymore or spend too much time thinking about what I was about to do. If I let my heart feel the fear of never seeing her again, I wouldn't leave. It was the same reason I wouldn't say goodbye to my mother. I'd see her and tell her just how much I loved her when I returned.

Swimming through the wreck, I didn't allow myself to make eye contact with a single soul. Xifi and Tetwin attempted to wave me down, but my eyes remained forward, oblivious to their calls.

Once I made it into the clearing and had nothing in my way but the distance between me and the end of our territory, I let my narrowed eyes relax. I fled with the tightness in my chest and let myself fall into the emptiness of my mind.

CHAPTER TWO
RAVENOUS AND THE ROPE

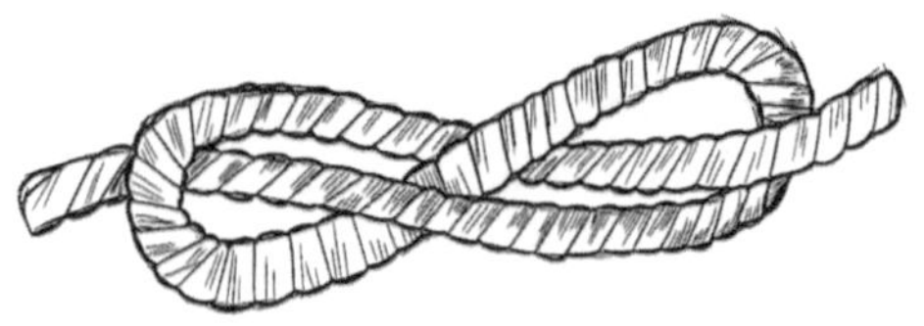

Hunger clawed at my belly as I darted through the water. I spent so much time thinking about how starving everyone else was, I forgot sometimes that I was just as ravenous.

As I approached the end of our territory, I stared out into the hazy distance. The area didn't look any different from where I had grown up, but would it feel different? Would the weight of the hungry pod lift from my shoulders, or would I drown in the fear of the unknown?

In the distance, something caught my eye. A flash of silver darted across my vision. My gut tightened, and my eyes focused on what was in the distance, as if there were nothing else in the entire sea.

Tiny air bubbles swirled around me with the force of my speed as I chased what was mine. My eyes narrowed into slits as I closed in on the fish. It was the first sizable one I had come across in months, and I ached for the meat on its bones to fuel me.

The fish crossed the threshold of our territory, but I didn't hesitate as I swam right up behind it. I swam and swam, tunnel vision on the tuna as it dashed away from me, taking me further from where I was supposed to be. I gripped the spear in my right hand, ready to strike when the time was right.

A dark streak in the corner of my eye stole my attention, and I took my line of sight off the fish as I scanned my environment. Blood pounded loudly in my ears, pulsing the water around me.

The dark creature was too large to be another tuna and too small to be one of us. I held my spear up, ready to take aim at the oncoming enemy. It was nothing but a blur in the distance for now, but it closed in on me quickly.

A shark?

No.

A slick, tan animal glided through the water, chasing after my prey.

A damned seal.

I lowered my spear but didn't drop my guard. If I was seeing a seal, then I was far closer to land than I should have been. I focused on my prey; I couldn't let myself think about how far out of my territory I had strayed.

As I grew closer, I slammed into the side of the seal, throwing it off course. I closed in on the tuna, close enough that I could smell it. I braced the spear in my hand, brought it above me, and shot it through the water, spiraling toward the fish. Just when I thought it was mine, the tuna slipped between two rocks, and my spear clattered against barnacle-covered stone.

I could almost hear the seal laughing at me, mocking my inability to make the kill. Another pang of hunger ravaged me, and I lunged toward the mammal with red hot anger. It slid out of the way with ease, and I crashed against the rocks, scratching my forearm in the process.

You're getting sloppy, Sid! Focus!

Diving deeper, I scooped my spear out of the sand on the seafloor. Rising above the rock once again, I stared out into the vast expanse of water. The seal hovered on the surface, taking a dangerous breath. If I was desperate enough, I would have ended that mammal's life—the thief of our fish. The other hunters would be disappointed in me for doing nothing more than swimming away, but I was determined to find food elsewhere. I couldn't waste any more time or energy on something that mattered so little.

I swam, fear clawing at the back of my mind that I was going too far too quickly. I stopped recognizing where I was long ago, but there *had* to be more fish out here somewhere. We had gone for months on kelp and crustaceans, and my muscles grew weak and sore.

The rumbles of my stomach shattered all rational thought, and I followed the curious animal as it bobbed in and out of the water, gliding in graceful, quick loops in the opposite direction of my home. To land.

I stayed far behind the creature, not wanting to give myself up but desperately needing a guide to food. We swam until we reached a translucent, grey wall.

Not a wall, no. A net.

I grew closer to better understand exactly what it was I was seeing. I grabbed hold of the net, looping my fingers through it to allow my aching body some much-needed rest. My stomach lurched as I saw movement through the material—a lot of it. It was a whole damned school of fish!

The seal slipped over the top of the massive, netted enclosure and dove into the swarm of fish. A limitless supply of food for the both of us. The mammal took several into its mouth, swallowing them whole.

This can't be real.

I rose to the surface, much like the seal did, and felt the air on my skin for the first time in over a year. I slipped back under the surface, the water feeling cool after the sun's rays had touched my skin and scales. Immediately upon re-entry, I was surrounded by a school of fish swimming in massive circles around me. My hand tightened on my spear, the fish around me oblivious to the fact that several of them would be my next meal, several more brought back for the pod.

As I prepared to take aim, the spear was knocked out of my hand by an unusual force. That same force closed in around me, a web of rope and tangles. Bubbles escaped my mouth as I thrashed violently, attempting to claw my way out of this unknown prison.

My tail struck something solid, and a strange noise echoed through the water in response. There were too many fish in my face, sharp scales cutting my skin and roughing up my own as we all were pushed together. The space between us grew smaller and smaller as the net that had been dipped into the enclosure was lifted through the water. By the time we broke the surface, I was scrambling for air, wiggling my way toward the edge so I could breathe.

My whole body was airborne, and the lack of salt water on my skin would have me transforming any second now. I felt the familiar, deep-rooted itch as though it was so far beneath my skin, the only way to rid myself of the discomfort was to shed it altogether. Memories of the pain that came with the transformation clawed at my mind and struck fear into my veins.

I'm far too weak for this!

My raw, exposed skin was thrashed by slimy scales rubbing against me in all the wrong directions. Without warning, the net dropped to the deck of the ship, and I stifled screams into my palm as my fins shed and my tail split in two. I choked down the tearing pain in every cell as the new skin wrapped my arms and evolving legs. Anguish blinded me, but I did my best to shake it off. I didn't have another choice.

Tangled in the half-opened net, my legs were buried by the rest of the catch. We were a flopping mess on the deck of the fishing vessel, and curious fishermen would be approaching any minute.

I gritted my teeth as I began pushing the slimy fish off the raw skin on my legs, further exposing myself to my surroundings.

Familiar whines and barks erupted through the air, and my

foot shot out on instinct, kicking the seal in the ribs to shut it up. The animal whined once more before falling silent.

Is it trying to get us killed?

I couldn't see the fishermen, but I knew they were around here somewhere. I closed my eyes, focusing on the sound of the waves as they splashed up against the side of the boat. They started mild, a soft patter against the wood of the ship. With a deep breath, the waves began to grow louder—more violent.

Shouts broke out as the ship began to rock, and I used the distraction to search for a way out. The weight of the fish pinned down the net, and I used my newly separated fingers to tear at it, but the rope didn't budge. Hissing, I threw my hands down on the wooden deck. My nails were dull and useless in this form.

I scanned the surrounding area through the holes in the net, and my eyes froze as a small metal spear with a wooden handle came into view. The tool sat upon a sodden wooden crate, almost in reach. I wiggled through the slime and scales left behind from both the fish and me until I could wrap my fingers around the wooden handle.

A groan left me as I secured the handle within my grip and pulled the tool from the crate. My eyes darted around for images of feet running toward me, but I saw nothing of the sort as I started sawing through the rope ensnaring me. There was no way in the dark depths that I was going to be caught bare in a pile of fish by these men. I'd die first.

My arm muscles cried in pain by the time the rope snapped under the blade's ferocity. I kicked fish off me as I crawled free of my entanglement along the ship's deck. The sheer weight of the creatures pinning down my human form made my ribs scream, but I kept going. When I found my freedom, I felt like nothing more than a flopping fish as my wet body plopped into the puddle of water pooling next to the net.

Peering over my shoulder, I watched as the fishermen attempted to catch their balance and hold on for dear life as a massive wave rocked the boat. The seal cried out, begging me to free it with its wide, dark eyes, but there was no time, and the sounds of its heavy body on the deck would give me away. It was me or the seal, and I was going to choose myself every single time.

My feet struck the ship deck, my bare toes spreading to stabilize myself as I found my bearings. I was too weak to jump back into the water; I'd never survive the transition back to my siren form. I needed clothes, and there was nothing else that mattered until I was dressed like one of *them*.

I snuck through the ship, the wind of the day wrapping around me like the clothes I sought. The commotion at the front of the ship calmed, and I picked up my pace, trying not to trip on my unsteady legs as I rushed to the back of the ship under the coverage of the storage area.

Escaping the harsh daylight penetrating my skin, I found shelter among barrels of rum, tangles of ropes, and a few trunks full of supplies. A shirt and cap were hung to dry over the back of one of the open trunks, and I grabbed the shirt, throwing it on over my wet hair. I twisted my long locks into a knot at the base of my neck and squeezed it into the brown leather cap.

Rifling through the trunk, I dampened the contents as I searched for pants and shoes. I pulled free a pair of slacks and a thin jacket. Throwing them on, the tightness in my chest eased as each new article of clothing covered more of me. I settled into the new attire, the slacks inches from the floor. I forgot how puny human men could be.

There was a creak behind me, and I spun to face the sound. My body thudded against something smooth and wet, and I stumbled back, my hand gripping my chest. Adrenaline coursed through me as my eyes landed on a figure before me. Thoughts of attack ran rampant through my mind as my blurred vision focused.

A woman with dark, soaked curls and wide brown eyes stared at me with a cocked head. She stood with her arms behind her back, her bare form exposed to me. She blinked as she took a step toward me, her eyes trailing my clothed body. Her hair dripped onto the floor, and the spotted pelt she held behind her back sent a wave of understanding through me.

"*You?*" I threw my hand up, motioning to the woman.

"You left me..." she seethed. "You left me with the fish. To die."

"Yeah, well you're the reason I'm in this mess." The hiss left my lips, my eyes narrowing on the woman. "You should've let me make that kill. You had no business being that far from land. Those are *our* fish."

How had I not known she was a selkie? The way she teased me and swam in mocking loops around me... I should've realized she wasn't a mere seal.

"I'm hungry. There's no fish near our land." She held her warm brown hand up to her bare belly.

"What are you talking about? Did you not see all those fish? We have nothing like that in the deep," I bit out.

"Yes, but we are not near my land. I traveled far for that tuna, despite the warnings of my people about getting too close to yours." She tossed me a disgusted glare. "There's no more fish in our cove. I had no choice."

"You have no fish?" I asked, my eyes darting through the crack in the door to where I saw a sliver of blue. As I peered into the water, I thought about all the times my kind killed hers for getting too close to our territory and stealing our food.

Have they also had nothing all along?

My eyes wandered over her bare skin once more and groaned. I didn't like this one bit, but if I left her here, in this state, we'd both be caught.

"You need to get dressed," I demanded, gritting my teeth together. "There's no clothing left back here. I took everything I could find. We'll have to take something off one of them."

Her eyes widened, and she peered through the crack in the door.

"From the humans?" Her lips peeled back, and sharpened canines poked over her bottom lip. I ran my tongue over my own teeth, but they were now blunt, human. The residual taste of blood remained in my mouth, my new teeth sore and slightly wiggly as they set into my raw gums. I peered down to her nails, but even in this form, mine were still longer than hers. I'd take the one advantage I had.

"Yes, from the humans," I said. "Just stay here."

I directed her to the back of the room, and she placed her pelt on one of the closed trunks. She rose to her tiptoes then took a seat upon it, dangling her legs off the side. She stared at me expectantly with the beautiful eyes of a selkie, dark, mysterious pools I could get lost in if I wasn't careful.

Creeping toward the cracked door, I placed my hands on it and poked my head through. The men hauled the now-still fish into baskets. There had to be twenty of them at least, all hustling around in their stupid little hats, stealing *our* food.

"Plug your ears and keep your eyes off me."

She nodded and shoved her pointer fingers into her ears, blocking out what was to come. She didn't need to be asked twice; the selkie was smart enough to listen the first time.

A piercing song escaped my lips, slithering through the crack in the door. As soon as the high-pitched frequency flowed out of me, the fishermen all stopped dead in their tracks. Their stillness turned to desperate curiosity. We were meant for this, luring in the humans, leading them to a certain death. I just never had the honor of this kind of hunt, not until this very moment.

The man I was targeting, the small one closest to me, wouldn't die by my hand today, not if I could help it. I didn't need a mess to clean up; I simply needed what he wore on his back.

Upon hearing my song, he dropped the fish in his hand and began shuffling toward me. His dark eyes were glazed yet eager— eager for me and my ability to allow him curious pleasure in every cell in his body. I would instill a need in him that wouldn't be quenched even after the end of my song.

I grabbed the bat they used to brutally kill the fish they caught and waited for him with it gripped in my hand. Once he was close enough, my lips fell shut, my song ended, and I pulled him through the crack in the door. Whacking him over the head with the wooden bat, his limp but still-living body hit the floor with a thud. His hat tumbled off his head, spilling auburn hair across the floor.

The fallen cap halted right at the bare feet of the woman, so she unplugged her ears and scooped it up. After analyzing me, she mimicked my look, twisting her curls into a bun and shoving the cap upon her head.

I slipped off his shoes and tossed them at her, socks and all. His feet thumped against the wooden floor of the ship one at a time. No part of me wanted to undress the man. I took one look at the selkie as she sat upon the trunk, expressing no discomfort in the way she exposed her chest to me. I knew she needed the clothes far more than he did. Our survival, *and my sanity*, depended on it.

CHAPTER THREE
HAVOC ON THE HULL

The woman donned the fisherman's damp white shirt and slacks, her hair tied-back, dripping down her spine. I rubbed my temple as my gaze dropped to her chest. It didn't matter if she dressed like a fisherman when her hardened nipples screamed that she didn't belong.

I glanced down at the opaque, navy-blue jacket I wore, and within the same breath, stripped out of it and tossed it at her. She missed the catch, and the jacket plopped onto the face of the sleeping man.

"Put that on," I demanded, straightening the wrinkled shirt that remained on my body. The fabric was thicker than hers and deep red, hiding what hid underneath.

"It's too hot to wear a jacket." She held the piece of clothing out distastefully.

"Well, apparently, it's too cold to wear white," I muttered. She peered down at her shirt, rolled her eyes, then plucked the jacket off the man's face.

"I'm sorry my body *offends* you. I didn't realize sirens were so... proper." She said "proper" with such utter distaste, as if there was a word she would have preferred, a more honest one.

"Your body did nothing of the sort. But if you look right now through the crack in that door, there is not a single soul like us on this vessel," I said, nodding toward the door. Her eyes followed my gaze as she let my words sink in.

"You mean they're all human?" she asked, clearly not understanding.

"I mean they're all *men*. Men presumably without the perfect pair of boobs," I mumbled under my breath.

"Perfect?" She cocked her head with a tiny smirk crossing her face. Her eyes trailed down my face, taking in every facial twitch.

"They're fine. Now, hide your pelt and let's go. We've got a ship to take over." I decided for her that she would be helping me on this journey. I had enough magic to sink this entire ship, but that wasn't what I was after. We already took their precious Ever Wanderer; we didn't need another sunken vessel.

"How do you know about my pelt?" she asked, slipping the navy jacket over her head. The baggy garment shielded her curves from suspicious eyes. All she needed to do now was keep her face down. There was no hiding her feminine features, the unmistakable beauty of a selkie. Her round eyes, colored cheeks, and plump lips all gave her the pretty, approachable look they all seemed to have.

Sirens were known for our captivating voices and the illusion of beauty, but we were creatures of the deep. We thrived in the darkness where light didn't touch our pale, scaled skin and gills.

"How do I know you need to hide your pelt?" I pulled my gaze off her lips and focussed. She nodded her head, pulling a sigh of boredom from me.

"I'm from the deep, but that doesn't mean I'm oblivious to the world. I know the way of the selkie-folk. So hide your skin and let's go!"

"I also know of the siren." She pursed her lips, as if I should have been embarrassed by this fact. "And fine, but I have to find a good spot."

Her eyes darted around the tiny storage area jammed packed with chests and wall hangings.

"Put your pelt over there, in the bottom of that chest. There's just a bunch of old rags, so there's little reason for them to look inside," I directed, motioning to the trunk. My fingers separated more than I was ever used to seeing. There was so much space between them now that the webs were gone. Staring down at them, I flipped my hands over to take them all in as she scoped out the trunk.

"Why don't you just go back to the water instead of going through all this trouble to disguise yourself?" she asked as she dug through the chest I'd pointed out. Pushing all the rags aside to make room for her pelt at the bottom, she hid her seal skin. A human man finding the skin of a selkie woman was the worst nightmare of the selkie-folk, and with good reason.

"I can't go back." My teeth ground against each other. "Can you transition again so soon?"

"Yes." She nodded her head, pointing down at her seal skin before burying it under the scraps of fabric. "As long as I have my pelt."

"Then why don't you leave? Swim back to your cove?"

"My home is too far from here. I need to rest for a few days before going back," she said, eyeing the chest where her pelt now resided. I also needed a few days—at least—before I would be strong enough to transform again, and we wouldn't make it on the boat for that long without getting caught. I need to go to land—I suppose we both did.

"Well, if we're stuck together on this ship, I guess I should know your name." I peered at her with narrowed eyes. "I'm Sidra Solei."

"I am Breena. Just Breena." A snarky smile passed over her lips before she dropped her expression all too soon.

"Well, this one won't be waking up for a while," I said, kicking the leg of the sleeping man. "We should probably use that to our advantage."

I crept toward the door, peaking my head through the crack. All the fish once on the deck were now gone, sorted into baskets. The fishermen's supply was bountiful, yet here they were, casting another net into the water and looking for more. My pod would have been satisfied for months with their last haul, but that was what humans did. They took and took until there was nothing left.

I hissed as I watched them toss another net into the water with a splash.

"Alright, lads, three more hauls, then we'll head back," a man with copper hair shouted.

Three more hauls?

I couldn't believe what I was hearing. I couldn't believe the greed. My kind and the humankind had not been friendly since well before I came into this world. When people spoke of human tendencies, they became no more than detached stories to me. Seeing it firsthand, I understood the rage that filled the veins of the pod elders. They were the ones who remembered. They were the ones who experienced the betrayal firsthand.

An uninvited heat grew in me as I thought of all the trapped souls I witnessed within the large aquatic enclosure. At first, my eyes were glazed over with hunger, but now, seeing their catch and knowing they planned to take so much more, I was fueled by far more than my aching belly.

How often do they come out to sea for these catches? Monthly? Weekly? Daily?

My eyes darted to the basket closest to the door. I was desperate to draw it close to me so I could refuel my body and steady my racing thoughts. I wouldn't be able to think rationally until the hunger was no longer altering my thoughts.

My gaze locked on the tempting basket and fish sitting in a small puddle, and my stomach growled with a furious need.

Lifting my hands in front of me, the water on the deck began to vibrate with my magic. The shimmery blue swirl only I could see mixed with the puddle and slipped under the basket. My magic caused the puddle to flicker and rise, pushing the basket closer to me, as if brought to shore by a rolling wave. The puddle met its end, spreading too thin to carry the basket any farther. I would have to close the distance myself.

I peered around, seeing if anyone was close by and if they would notice me stealing the fish from right under their noses. The men were too busy casting their nets into the water to bother looking my way. I could leave the safety of the room, grab the basket, and be back before any of them saw me.

I took a deep breath, steadying my nerves. As I took a step forward, a severe grip tightened around my wrist, halting my progress. My head swung around to see Breena standing no more than a foot behind me. How she snuck up on me, I had no idea.

"What?" I seethed, trying to yank my wrist from her. My slitted eyes refocused, the haze of hunger, the hunt, washing away. Her hand didn't budge, and neither did my arm. I felt cemented to her, and the bite of fear nipped at me as I realized she could snap my bones right here and now. This woman was a stronger opponent than I gave her credit for.

"Where are you going?" Her head tilted, seemingly unaware of what her grip was doing to me.

"What, are you worried you'll miss me?" I asked, pulling at her one more time, signifying I wanted my freedom, because I sure as depths wouldn't ask her for it.

"I'm worried you'll get us caught." She finally released me, and I pulled my sore wrist into my chest, rubbing it with my other hand. There was a red ring wrapped around my skin, the ghost of a handprint that would surely bruise later. Breena glanced at my arm and frowned, as if she found the marks she left on me unusual, as if confused by my apparent weakness.

"I won't get caught. I'm light on my feet, and what I'm after is no more than a few feet away," I said. "If you think about touching me like that again, don't."

Breena's eyes relaxed, and she took a step back. I spun on my heels before inspecting the ship's deck one last time and sneaking out of the room. I tilted my head downward and let the small lip of the hat shield my face as much as possible. At first glance, you would never know I wasn't one of them.

I grabbed the handle of the wooden basket and lifted it. I brought the fish-filled basket back with me to the room and shut the door behind me as Breena's eyes darted between me and the basket of fish. Staring at the contents, I saw the mixture of still fish of varying sizes.

Reaching into the basket, I grabbed the smallest one. I tossed it to her, and she didn't hesitate before swallowing it whole. In seconds, the selkie began choking, her face contorted and paling. I stared at her in horror as she coughed up the contents of her stomach, a mixture of scales and fins in a pile on the deck before her.

"What's the matter? Is this fish not up to your fancy selkie tastes?" Grabbing another one from within the basket, I turned it over in my hand to see if there was something off about it, or if the selkie had simply taken too much at once.

"Something is very wrong with that fish," she said, wiping her chin with the back of her hand. Her lips were contorted, and she twisted her body away from the remaining fish, as if seeing them would cause another bout of vomit. She smacked her lips together, hungry for more but hesitant to refill her stomach that had rejected the food.

I glanced down at the small fish in my hand before dropping it into my mouth. The second the salty creature touched my human tongue, my stomach clenched. The smell of it struck my nose, and nothing about the scent was right. I spit the fish back into the basket before it could slip down my throat. Setting the basket down, I turned my back to the contents within, unable to cast my eyes upon them without feeling a wave of nausea consume me.

I spit out the residual fishy taste that lingered in my mouth. "It's not the fish. It's us. I think we need to cook it or something. We need human food."

The selkie stared down at the regurgitated fish on the floor, realization setting in. Her jaw tightened before saying, "I don't eat fish in this form. None of us do. We hunt in the sea and eat in the sea, always."

"I've also only ever eaten raw fish in my siren form. It seems our needs are different above water. We need to find *their* food." I pointed to the man on the floor. "And we need water. Fresh water."

I smacked my lips together, the saltiness that remained on my tongue creating an urge only water could quench—the type of water I was not used to.

My eyes darted around the room for sustenance, though I hadn't recalled seeing any as I'd sought out clothing. If nothing was in here, we would need to get it from somewhere else. That meant getting closer to the humans or going to land with them. I wasn't sure which of the two options was more idiotic.

"They will get their fish and go back to their land, and that's what we will do too. Go to land," Breena said, trying to pull my attention back to her.

My head nodded slowly, thankful she reached the same conclusion. After the wrist grab, I wouldn't try to force her to do anything, not until I better understood what she could do.

"Alright. Well, we better start causing some chaos then." I wiped my cold, clammy hands down the borrowed slacks I wore.

"Chaos?" she asked, touching the hollow of her neck.

"Yeah, trouble. If we cause trouble, they won't be able to catch their three more hauls of fish, now, will they?" A tiny spark of excitement ignited in me, but I snuffed the spark out before it went up in flames. The last thing I needed was to let my emotions get the best of me. Feeling anything other than focus was a dangerous game. "They will eventually give up and go back to land, and we will go with them."

"Alright then," she agreed, a small curl escaping her cap with a bob of her head. "You'll use your siren call and kill them all?" she said in a tone that sounded more like a question.

"What? No, I'm not going to kill them all. I said 'cause trouble', not murder."

"But you're a killer." She spoke cut and dry, as if she knew me. Why this selkie was baffled I wouldn't immediately turn to murder was beyond me.

"I'm a hunter, just like you. There's a difference." My words were sharp as glass. I knew I had called myself a killer not too long ago, but the sentiment was different when it was coming from someone else's mouth. It was more official, solidified. "And how do you expect to get back to land to find food and water if we kill them all?"

"Good point, fish."

"Fish? Yeah, don't call me that." My face scrunched in response. I'd start calling her 'mammal' if she wanted to play that game. Her head tilted once more, and I allowed the irritation to roll off me like a bead of water on a boat.

I gathered myself, looking over at her and asking, "What can you do?"

Maybe the question was for my own selfish reasons, but I wouldn't let her know that.

"Do?" she asked.

"Yes. What are your... abilities?"

"I can swim and..." She trailed off, and then she turned to one of the barrels of rum. She looked it over once then wrapped her arms around it, lifting it off the wooden planks beneath her.

"And you're strong. Got it. Not sure how helpful that's going to be right now, but I'm sure we'll come up with something. I'll go out there and cause a distraction."

Turning on my heel, I stumbled on a wayward plank and

caught myself on the edge of the chest. I pointed and flexed my foot, still getting used to the separation of my tail. I couldn't remember the last time I had stared at my toes, what it felt like to have air on my entire skin, not just my back and tail when I went too close to the surface. Even then, I had a long, thin fin that ran down the length of my spine, but my back was now smooth, human.

I righted myself, slipped the shoes back on, then stepped over the man sprawled out on the floor. I peeked my head through the crack, watching the men as they bickered about needing new nets. When I was done with them, it wouldn't be an argument. If I had my way, all their precious nets would be destroyed and lost to the sea forever.

These sailors would've heard of the curses of the sea, and it was my job to ensure they knew just how real they were. Or make them think so, at least.

I could play all-powerful for the day, mimicking the Goddess of the Sea taking revenge on the humans for mistreating my creation. They prayed to the goddess for safe voyage and bountiful catches, but little did they know, the women of the sea, my people, were the ones they were praying to, and we hadn't answered their murmurs in decades. Today, they would get a taste of what they were missing. They would get a taste of the goddess and her wrath.

As they re-secured their net, I flicked my wrist, sending waves crashing over the side of the boat. The water slammed into the wood, spilling a frothy cap over the edge. They shouted as their shoes filled with water.

"The sea is mad today!" one of the men yelled out. Their grip on the net began to loosen as I continued to crash waves down upon them. Before the men could regain their composure, my mouth cracked open, and the sounds of seals in distress poured out of me. My mimicry magic caused a few men to run over to the other side of the boat to see what was going on. Little did they know, there was nothing but fierce waves on the port side to greet them.

Breena came up beside me, her head cocked. She strode forward, but I held my arm out to stop her.

"It's just me," I spoke, almost in a warning not to go any farther. My mouth opened again, and the soft whine of a seal slithered from my mouth to her ears, soft enough for only her to hear. Her face contorted, and her arm shot forward faster than I could move. She grabbed my cheeks, ending the cry of her kind.

"You tricked them?" she asked, her touch softening as she turned my face to the side.

I didn't pull away from her as I stared into her darkened eyes. "Yes. I can mimic the voices and sounds of other people and animals."

"Please stop. I don't need to hear it, real or not. Whales, birds —fine—but not my kind." Breena's voice trailed off, her attention leaving me, lost to some distant memory, or maybe it was her new reality that haunted her.

I slowly nodded my head, and in response, Breena's hand dropped from my face. The dim light of the storage room found her eyes once more, but I still saw the swirl of distress that lingered in them.

"What do you suppose we do next then?" I asked, my fingers finding my cheek. I ran my hand over its smooth surface, feeling the tickle of small baby hairs on my palm. It's not that Breena hurt me as much as she shocked me. The creature standing before me continued to throw me out of focus, and I didn't know what to make of it. I didn't know what to make of *her*.

Breena glanced around before lifting a barrel of rum and striding to the door. She threw it onto the deck, causing the wood to bust wide open, spilling their precious drink. A few men began slipping and falling in their own toxic poison.

I pulled Breena out of the doorway as some of the fishermen swung their heads to see where the barrel had come from.

"Great; now we have to get out of here," I muttered. "They're gonna come looking to see how their barrel managed to fly across the boat."

"Well, cause another wave then." She motioned to the sea with a look of determination. "And keep doing it. Don't give them the chance to make it over here."

Grunting at the selkie, I raised my arms, focusing on the white caps in the water. A swell rose, towering over the top of the boat and crashing down. Breena lifted yet another barrel and rolled it this time, as if the mad sea had pulled it free from storage.

As the boat rocked and groaned, Breena and I held onto ropes secured to the wall. The door to the storage room swung open, and before it had the chance to slam shut, another wave rocked the boat. Each time the door opened wide for us, we saw the men struggle to stand on the ship's deck.

One of the men was tossed overboard, shouting all the way down until a wave swallowed him whole. A few brave men leaned over the side of the boat, calling out for their fallen crewmate. I calmed the water for a moment, just long enough for them to fetch him with a flotation device. I let them work for it, though, rocking the boat each time they thought they had him.

Breena giggled behind me, the men's distress feeding some kind of wicked desire in her. I watched her for a quick, dangerous moment as she drew her fingers to her curved lips, eyes widening as they pulled the drenched man over the side of the boat. The heavy thump of his wet body hitting the deck stole my attention.

"Lads, good Gods, we've angered the Sea Goddess!" a man cried out, dropping to his knees in prayer. He pressed his forehead to the ship's deck, the mixture of water and rum threatening to drown him in his devotion if he didn't lift his head.

"A curse has been placed upon this great vessel!" a young, copper haired man shouted, pulling his crewmate up by the back of his shirt. The man on his knees gasped as his face resurfaced.

"You'll have to send me to the depths before throwing another net into this cursed water! Cut free that forsaken thing and let the Goddess have her creations once more," a third man called out, ripping his cap from his head, revealing a bald scalp dripping with sweat and sea water.

An excited bubble rose in my chest and popped as it reached my throat, leaving only fear and uncertainty.

We were going to land.

CHAPTER FOUR
GETTING UNDER HER SKIN

The men pulled their remaining net back to the safety of their vessel, giving in to our chaos and destruction. Breena plopped herself down on top of the closed lid of the trunk, a subtle grin finding its way onto her lips. A chuckle escaped her as she leaned back and rested her shoulders on the wooden planks behind her.

"Back to land they go," she said.

"And to land *we* go, I suppose," I said as I sat upon the chest across from her, trying to make myself comfortable despite the metal latches digging into my new, tender flesh.

"Have you been on land before?" she asked, casting an eye over me. Her gaze trailed the length of my legs and paused on my shoe-covered feet. Her attention to them had me slipping out of the shoes to free my raw feet. Dried bits of blood were crusted under my toenails and between my toes from my transformation. Her eyes squinted as she presumably noticed the rest of the dried crumbles, but she said nothing when she met my gaze again.

"Once as a child," I admitted. I didn't need to go into detail about how my father grew up on land, how his father was human. She didn't need to know that my dad taught me the way of the humans in case it was ever safe to return to land in my lifetime. He taught me to be one of them in hopes that things would get better for Zellia and me, that we would have the chance to experience all that he had on land. He taught me so I could someday know what it was like to walk among them without fear.

"I see. I have spent plenty of time on land in this form." She gestured to herself. "But I have never been to a human village. We are taught from a young age that while we are welcome on their land, it's too risky, too vulnerable."

"Yeah, I'm sure you *are* welcome," I grumbled. Selkies were known to be treated as esteemed guests in human villages. It was only the sirens who were treated with such utter hostility, all for reasons out of our control.

"We've never had a reason to go to war with the humans, but that doesn't mean we want to live amongst them," she said. "What caused your war with the humans?"

"You really don't know?" I asked, and when she shook her head, I scoffed at her ignorance.

"It wasn't always like this," I said. "It started when the number of hybrids in the pod outweighed the full-bloods. The difference between the hybrids and full-bloods is the hybrids feel no pain as they transition. It's an incredible advantage, but they also don't inherit the siren song, and without our song, we are more vulnerable to humans. Our song acts as a mask, a disguise that allows us to appear more beautiful."

"Without it, we appear as nothing but our true selves— monsters of the sea. The sailors were not keen on this version of us, so much so that they cast nets into the water to capture the hybrids and kill them. They believed them to be mistakes, but little did they know, the sirens they were killing were their responsibility, their doing."

"They killed their own children?" Breena asked, her face scrunched. She pulled her feet up onto the trunk and rested her cheek on her knee as she listened to my story.

"They did, and in return, my pod pulled a ship full of those same human sailors down into the depths of our sea, and we celebrated as they drowned. We now live in that very ship—the Ever Wander."

"The selkies—"

"Stayed out of it. As did the kelpies," I cut her off, my anger building once more. "While the sirens were being slaughtered, the other sea fae did nothing to stop it. The sharks and whales did more to protect us, circling boats, intimidating the humans, acting as a buffer to our pod. The sea fae didn't lift a finger. They all stayed in their corners of the world and minded their business as our numbers dwindled—as we died. Mothers. *Fathers.*"

Breena cleared her throat and straightened her jacket before saying, "Maybe if your kind didn't kill us—"

"Try again," I snapped. "Sirens didn't start killing selkies until after the hunger set in, about a hundred years after the war had started."

"Neither one of us were alive back then, and I don't intend on holding a grudge over something that had nothing to do with us," Breena said. She dropped her legs back down and crossed her arms over her chest. Her gaze dropped to my wrist. The sensitive skin was bruising, a ring of purple in the shape of her hand.

"It's too late for that,' I said. I covered up the bruise she left on me and hardened my gaze so when she looked at me, she knew just how I felt about that little mark, her unintentional claim.

"You're telling me that you will forever hold a grudge against me and all other selkies?" Breena asked, clicking her tongue in annoyance.

"I will," I promised. After a choppy wave hit the boat, I adjusted my position on the chest again, shoving a rag beneath me to serve as a buffer between my butt bones and the latch.

"That is downright pathetic." Breena was now the one scoffing.

"Excuse me?"

"Punish me all you want, but you are really going to hate all selkies for not getting involved in *your* war? Something that had nothing to do with us?"

"Yes, just as I am not forgiving the humans. While it was the sailors who did what they did, you really think the rest of the humans are any better? I have been there on land amongst them. You have no idea what it's like."

"And are you going to pretend human men don't steal selkie skins and force selkie women to become their wives and the mother of their children?" I asked. I knew I would strike a chord with my words, but I spoke them anyway. I would always sit in my anger, but I wanted to see hers.

"That's different." Breena gritted her teeth, her elongated canines poking out from behind peeled back lips.

"How?" I pushed myself off the chest, my bare feet striking the slick wood of the deck. My toes stung instantly, but it didn't stop me from taking a step toward Breena. She flinched, but her body remained where she sat on the chest. "The women of this sea are used and then tossed away when they are no longer convenient. You and I are the daughters of the sea, and it is our job to protect it against the predators who want to destroy it. You can't ignore what has been done."

"I'm not ignoring it! But can't I want peace? We have our cove, and we stay away. Our cove is protected, and that is enough for me," she said, eyes squinting.

"Protected?" I laugh. "You are starving just as we are. How much longer do you think the selkies can hide away in their cove when there is nothing to eat? How long before the kelpies start looking at you as their food source?"

"They wouldn't." Breena all but cowered under my words. She might be stronger than me, but I could crush her without lifting a finger. All I had to do was open my mouth. That was where my true gift lied.

"I wouldn't be too sure. Why don't you leave your family with them and find out? Oh, that's right, you already did leave them, didn't you?" I asked, sudden guilt piercing me as I thought of my own family and how I had chosen to leave them in hopes of saving them, just as Breena had.

"This is ridiculous. I will be returning home to my family as soon as rest finds me. And when we reach shore, fish...you better stay away from me."

"Or what, seal?" I asked, my guilt fleeing my body as Breena's threat left her lips.

"Or you will discover much more than a simple bruise around your wrist," she said, her voice stiffening, as if her vocal cords had turned as hard as the stone her kind sunbathed on.

I strode over to her and grabbed her by the face, forcing her to meet my eyes before saying, "You may be stronger than me, but I advise you to never forget that I control this sea. Even seals aren't immune to the wrath of the water."

My heart pounded in my head, blocking out all other sounds. Breena's eyes darkened as she glared at me under long lashes, her lips puckered by the strength of my fingers on her face. Her fists gripped the edge of the chest, and the wood she sat upon splintered and cracked.

"I haven't forgotten," she spat before she tilted her chin up with a swift movement, breaking my hold. My arm dropped back to my side, but my fist still held the tension of my annoyance.

"Find your rest, then," I demanded, taking a step back from her to help put out the fire between us.

"Like I would close my eyes around you."

"You think I plan to kill you in your sleep?" I laughed. "You insult me. I've already had so many chances to take you out. I don't need to wait until you're vulnerable to make a move. Now, shut your eyes and get some sleep."

"And what will you do?" Breena asked, her grip on the cracking trunk loosening.

"Watch."

Breena's mouth parted, and she said, "Excuse me?"

"The sailors, not you," I clarified before turning on my heel. I grabbed the scrap of fabric I had been sitting on and tossed it at her, not bothering to wait for her reaction before I strode to the door.

I had already rested too long. The waters were now smooth, and the men were well on their way back to land. It was only a matter of time before one of them wandered back here to the storage of the boat, and one of us had to be on guard when they did. I didn't trust Breena to know what to do in such a situation. She truly didn't understand the ways of the land, the ways of the humans.

I cracked open the door and peeked outside. Sailors mopped sticky rum off their deck while others prayed to the sea goddess for a safe return. Pride swelled in my chest, knowing these vicious men still feared the women of the sea.

After an hour or two of relative silence, the boat began to slow, and the voices of the men began to increase in number.

"Get up," I said, shaking Breena's shoulder. Her head fell off the hand she was resting it on and bobbed in front of her before she straightened her neck. She made an annoyed muffled sound as she stretched her back and batted her heavy eyes. "We must be getting close."

"There are kinder ways to wake someone," she mumbled, fighting a yawn.

"And there are worse ways," I said with a false smile. Her curls had sprung free in her sleep, so I motioned to her hat with my hand. She took the hint to tuck her hair back inside the cap and then straightened her stolen clothing.

"We need to make a plan for when we dock. Eventually, they will come back here to gather their things, and we need to make sure we are long gone before that happens," I said, my eyes darting to the door. I had kept watch as she slept, both on the door and the knocked-out man on the floor. He had made the strangest sounds for a few minutes, odd vibrations so loud that I feared I needed to knock him over the head once more. I was thankful he decided to end those irritating noises on his own. I wasn't sure how much a human skull could endure and what would happen if I hit him again.

"And how do you suppose we do that? Walk right off the ship?" she asked.

"Why not? We are dressed like them, and there's enough fishermen that we could try to hide in plain sight. We could cause one last distraction and get off this damn boat," I said.

"And what if we are caught? I'm sure they have some sort of routine for unloading the fish and whatnot. We will give ourselves away immediately when we don't do as they would," Breena said.

"I'm almost certain they do have a routine, but there is no way for us to know exactly what that is. I say we distract them and then make a run for it. There are too many of them for me to hypnotize at once, though, so we'll have to get creative again."

We *had* managed to manipulate them to shore.

"Fine," Breena said with a swift nod of her head.

The sound of thick rope hitting the deck brought my attention back to the door. I stuck my nose through the gap, seeing the fishermen hustle to tie up the ship.

Land.

"We're here," I whispered, watching as the sailors began tying knots in their rope to secure us to long wooden docks jutting out from the shoreline. I couldn't see much past that. I couldn't see the village or the village folk, but we would soon. We would be among them, just as I had when I was a child, and the humans, once again, would be none the wiser.

Breena hopped off the chest and tentatively came to stand next to me. She was quiet since our argument, and I couldn't tell if it was my words that had affected her, or if she simply couldn't be bothered to waste her breath on me. Her demeanor gave nothing away. The woman was warm by nature, but she certainly knew how to turn that warmth off when it suited her.

"Aye, mate, head to the back and grab another rope, will ya?" I heard someone shout. They weren't close enough to the door for me to see them, but I knew they would be here any minute.

"We need to get out of here!" I said, my adrenaline spiking when I looked down at the knocked-out man. Walking off the ship when they were distracted was one thing, but answering their questions on why their crewmate was unconscious was entirely different.

Breena spun on her heels and headed back to the chest she'd previously rested on.

"Where are you going?" I whispered. "We need to go, now!"

"My pelt. I need to grab my pelt," Breena said, making her way to the back of the storage room in panicked desperation.

"We can come back for it later, but right now, we have to leave. Let's go!" I said, all patience fleeing me.

Breena huffed, glanced back at the chest, and then grimaced as she rushed back over to me. I held the door open and all but pushed her out of the room. A man with a low whistle quickly approached, so I shoved Breena into a tight space between stacked crates and the outside wall of the storage room. I held my breath as I squeezed in next to her. We barely missed the man as he walked by.

Once the sailor was in the room, Breena tried to wiggle her way out, but I threw my arm up over her shoulder to halt her. Her head whipped to me, and I did nothing but flash her a warning glare.

"Aye! Aye, wake up mate," the sailor called from within the storage room, followed by a hearty thump.

"I suppose he found our mess," I whispered. Breena's chest heaved against mine as she waited for the man to reappear so she could try to escape me. Her skin was unexpectedly warm against mine, and for a quick moment, the sensation reminded me of sandy hugs as a child, the way the heated Kilkov water wrapped around me in a healing embrace.

My eyes focused on hers. I let my chest deflate so I had an excuse to take in another breath, to feel my chest press up against hers. She stared back at me, her eyes darting all over my face. Heat flooded my skin as our eyes locked. My arm over her shoulder didn't budge, even as the man exited the back room with a sack of ropes slung over one of his shoulders and his crewmate limply hanging from the other. He made his way back to his crew, but her body on mine was all my mind had the ability to focus on.

"Are you going to let me go?" Breena whispered, her breath tickling my face like a summer sea breeze. Her throat tensed as she waited for my answer.

"Do you want me to?" I asked before biting my tongue. I dropped my arm just as quickly as the words left my devious mouth.

What is wrong with you, Sid?

Breena's head cocked, and the ghost of a grin passed over her lips. She didn't move right away, frozen in place, pressed up against me. When she finally made her move, she took me by the wrist she'd previously claimed and led me out of our hiding place.

CHAPTER FIVE
AS THE AIR WE BREATHE

As the men rushed around, Breena and I snuck through the ship, ducking behind barrels and various equipment whenever someone came close to us. There were only three more steps until we were at the stairs to our next hiding spot.

When we were in the clear, Breena guided me down the stairs into the ship, the space illuminated by nothing more than light filtering through the lattice hatch on the ceiling. No one was down here, but I took my arm back from her just in case we ended up with unwanted company. I stayed in the well of the stairs so I could keep my eye on the men and their offloading routine. I analyzed the way they moved, talked, which items they took, which ones they left behind.

Not even a minute later, a few men filed into the storage room on the back of the vessel and began unloading their things. We could hear more than we could see, but my chest tightened as the sound of trunks scraping against the floor echoed below deck.

Breena began running up the steps before I could stop her. A puddle on the last step began to shimmer with swirling blue magic, and before she could take that last one, the water of the puddle shot up and created a blockade, tripping the selkie. She reached forward with both hands, fingers splayed as they hit the wooden stairs. I swore as I heard the floorboards groan under her sheer strength, a strength she surely would be thankful for, as it protected her face from the fall.

I grabbed her ankle as her foot kicked out. She tried to find her footing, but I flipped her onto her back and began tugging her down the stairs. Muffled screams vibrated against a second barrier of water that wrapped around her mouth as I pulled her into the safety of the shadows.

I scooped her into my arms before she thumped down two more steps. She writhed in my arms, ungrateful for my help, so I swung her from a cradled position to over my shoulder. I kicked the swinging door open, and as I did, I mimicked the jarring sound of squawking gulls over the ship to drown out our racket.

A human net was secured to the ceiling, stretching out from one wooden beam to another. I lifted Breena off my shoulder with a strained grunt and let her collapse into it. As her body settled into the makeshift resting place, her muffled screams grew louder, causing ripples in the water barrier over her mouth.

I leaned forward, grabbing onto the beam above me, and said, "I'm not going to give you your voice back until you quiet down. We've made it this far; you really want to be caught now?"

Breena's forehead tensed, but the sounds of resistance that once poured out of her ceased. The water wrapped around her mouth fell from her face and splashed onto her chest, shielded by the thin jacket.

"I need to get back up there," she seethed, sitting up in the net and bringing her face close to mine. "You and I both heard those trunks being moved around, and you know what's in one of them."

"I do, but I also know we are weak, and it's stupid to try to take on an entire crew of sailors right now. Not to mention, my kind is trying not to add fuel to the fire."

"I don't care about your kind and your stupid war!" Her shout caused the water on her jacket to vibrate once more. She peered down at my threat to silence her for the second time and shot me a grimace.

"Well, you should. The whole sea should. Does it seem like a coincidence to you that the fish are disappearing? You saw that giant enclosure in the water and what they were doing with the fish, keeping them in their false prison away from the sirens, the selkies," I said. "It may not be your war, but your time of pretending it doesn't impact you is over."

"Fine." Breena gripped the rope on either side of her. "But if my pelt is gone, you will pay for what you have done."

"I don't doubt it, selkie. I don't doubt *you*."

She shot me a surprised look and then processed my words before she spoke again. "Well, how long do you expect me to wait down here?"

"Not long at all. We need to get off this ship as soon as we can," I said, peering back toward the door. "Will you stay here while I scope things out?"

Breena stared up at me with her sharpened gaze before sighing and offering me a nod. I pushed myself off the beam and out of her face, making my way back over to the door. After one peek through the small crack, I ensured the coast was clear then slipped through. I crept up the stairs, my side pressed against the wall as I approached the railing. Peering through the gap of two wooden posts, I watched the feet of men as they scuffled along the ship deck.

"Let's go, laddies. We need to get these fish to our meeting spot." One of the men shouted, presumably the captain. He kicked rubbish that littered the floor after the mess Breena and I had caused.

The faint sound of Breena following me up the stairs didn't distract me from remaining on guard.

Of course she didn't stay put.

"They're leaving the ship," I whispered, watching as two dozen pairs of feet head toward the side of the boat.

"Well, let's go then." Breena prepared to launch herself up the stairs.

"No. Give it a minute."

Breena huffed but then settled onto a creaky wooden step. She propped her elbows up on the step above her and dropped her head back so the summer sun hit her face. She waited, just like that, until the last of the men exited the vessel. When the sound of nothing but sea birds and water lapping against the side of the boat hung in the air, her eyes flew open.

Breena flipped onto her belly and scrambled up the stairs. I followed after her, my eyes alert in case there was a straggler that had stayed behind. Breena darted to the storage room, making it to the door quicker than me, despite the length of my legs.

She swung open the door, and I followed behind, dragging my feet as she entered the room. We'd both heard the scraping of the trunks against the floor, and I couldn't imagine what she sought still remained. I stayed behind, holding my breath, hoping I was wrong.

A howl erupted through the air only a moment after she entered the room, sending a series of shivers up my spine and down my arms. I dropped my head with closed eyes and swiped my hand through the air, as if I was grabbing an imaginary fly. The mournful sound ended just as soon as it started.

When I pushed open the door, Breena was on all fours, her eyes wide and panicked. Tears poured out of her, but not a single sound left her mouth. As I walked into the room, her head swung toward me. She righted herself and grabbed her throat as she shot daggers at me with her fierce gaze.

"I'm sorry. I can't let you draw attention to us," I said, holding my hand out, my palm flat and facing the ceiling. Above the skin of my palm, an inky blue spark hovered above my hand. I'd covered her mouth earlier so the sounds of her resistant shouts didn't cause suspicion, but now, I selfishly couldn't bear hearing the haunting sound of her grief as it hit her that her pelt was in the hands of a man. Even a water barrier wouldn't be enough to shield the pain in her voice, so I took her voice all together.

Breena gripped at her throat, her red eyes swelling with tears. My stomach was raw, as if her pain had slithered its way into my pores and began rotting me from the inside out.

"Damn it," I groaned, reaching down and yanking her off her knees. I didn't hesitate as I pulled her into me. She pounded on my chest with the sides of her fists, resisting the embrace. The first hit knocked the air out of my lungs, but all I did was squeeze her harder.

Breena's silent sobs rocked me as she gave in, her arms falling limply to her side. Her face was hot as she buried it into the nape of my neck, making even her warm tears feel chilled as they rolled down my bare skin. The salt of them felt tingly on my neck, like a distant yearning to be fully encased in their salinity.

As she fell still, I placed my hand on her throat. One final sob escaped her as she pulled back from me, her face a swollen mess of snot and tears.

"This is your fault," she choked out. "I should have never listened to you."

The bite of her words was sharper than I expected, and I was used to disappointment. Each time I came back from a hunt with nothing, my pod all but killed me with their glares. Words of disapproval filled my head and overwhelmed my senses as they swam away from me, but here Breena stood before me, her eyes locked right on mine as she called me a failure. This time, I had no Kilkov to swim off to escape my shame. I had to stand here and take it.

"We will find your skin, I promise you," The words shocked even me as they left my lips.

"We?" Breena echoed.

"Yes." My confirmation caught us both off guard. I still had a family to feed, yet here I was, making promises to someone I barely knew, someone I owed no loyalty to.

What is wrong with me?

"We will find it together, you have my word," I found myself saying, as if my mouth and mind had two very different priorities.

"I don't know how much that means." Breena pushed herself off me.

I bobbed my head, understanding her distrust in me more than she could fathom. "That's fair. But let me prove you wrong."

"I suppose I have no other choice."

"You always have a choice." I bit my tongue as the stupid sentiment flew from my mouth. My words were the ultimate slap in her face, now more than ever.

"Not anymore." Breena turned from me and headed to the door with steps as heavy as stone. She tucked her hair back into her cap and disappeared under the light of the day. I tilted my face up to the ceiling and took in three centering breaths before I followed her.

I offered a hand to Breena to help her off the ship. She took it, squeezing a little too hard as she hopped over the large gap between the boat and the dock. She glanced down at the sea, tension held in her jaw. Without her pelt, she wouldn't be able to touch the water without being subjected to an immense amount of pain. She glanced down at the soft waves, eyes glazed over, frozen in place.

I lightly tugged on her hand to guide her down the dock, but she didn't budge. Her chest heaved, and the tear lines of her large eyes began to fill once more. Panic was written all over her face as she seemingly tried to process her new reality.

I stepped in closer, leaning down to her ear before saying, "I am as stubborn as the sea itself. If I tell you I will stop at nothing to find your pelt, then my words are as true as the air we breathe."

Breena took a step back from the edge of the dock, my words being the key to her imprisoned muscles. She bumped into my chest, but I took her in and guided her, one step at a time, away from the boat. She kept her eyes glued to her feet as we passed by the occasional fisherman. I avoided their eyes but kept my head up, focusing on the long dock that led to the human village.

My dry throat clenched as we grew closer, at the realization that our plan ended at getting off the boat. We needed food, water, and a change of clothes, I knew, but how to go about acquiring these items was a whole other challenge.

One step at a time. What's my next step?

My eyes fixed on the end of the dock, my heart pounding in my ears as we grew closer. When the wooden planks ended, the path carried out onto a winding pebbled path that bled into larger rocks that eventually turned into a mossy cliffside. There was no sand up here, merely stone I could picture seals sunbathing upon. I almost wanted to shield Breena's eyes so she couldn't be reminded of her home and her people, knowing she now had no way to get back to them.

The arm I had draped around the selkie found my side once more, but I still held her hand as I helped her transition her numbed body from the wooden planks to the path made of loose stone. The pebbles crunched under our weight as we followed a woman who bobbed down the winding path. In her hands, she carried a canvas bag full of shells clattering against each other as she walked. I wondered where she would take them, and if that place would offer us a solution to our predicament.

"Where are we going?" Breena asked what I was thinking. When I went to land with my father as a child, he had taken me and Zellia to his home away from the sea. I had no idea if it still existed, but if we were going to find food and a place to rest, that was going to be it.

"A place my father used to live," I admitted, unsure if it had been a poor choice to utter the words.

"Your father?" Breena's hand slipped from mine. "He's human?"

"A hybrid. If he was fully human, I wouldn't have my siren song, now would I?" I asked, ready to defend my father.

"I suppose not. Where is he now? Can he help us?" Hope spread across her face, as dangerous as an untameable fire.

My chest felt as if it was about to crack open and reveal my wounded heart as I said, "No, he can't."

"Well, why not? Is he back in the sea?"

Why can't she let this go?

"He's dead," I said flatly before striding forward, leaving her and her gaping mouth behind.

"Sid—"

"It's fine," I interrupted, desperately needing the conversation to change. I refocused on the woman carrying the shells, the sound they made as they rubbed against each other. I tuned out Breena as she apologized for pressing the matter.

At one point, this was my father's home. This was where he grew up and where he might've imagined raising his children if he'd fallen in love with another woman, one not of the sea. I glanced around, letting my hardened vision fade so I could see his home as he had, the place he'd loved as much as the sea.

Barthoah.

CHAPTER SIX
NEVER IN A MILLION YEARS, FISH

Breena and I made our way up a set of wooden steps that led directly into the human village of Barthoah. I kept my eyes out for fishermen and a familiar trunk, but we had no luck just yet.

The thought of fishermen reminded me of what I was wearing. I ripped off my cap and snuck it into a bush as we passed by. My scalp screamed with relief as my blonde hair untwisted and fell down my back. I scratched the skin on my head, running my fingers through the strands of my still-damp hair.

I caught Breena staring, her eyes following my hair as it unraveled and skimmed the top of my butt. She reached up and removed her cap as well, discarding it in a bush much like I had. She manually untwisted her hair, damp curls springing loose. It had been my first time seeing it since this morning, and back then, I had far more concerns than her beauty, as evident as it was.

"Lock and Leather should be up this way," I said, pointing to a cluster of stone buildings. It may have been a decade since being in Barthoah, but I would never forget the place we slept. I remember my first night on land as clear as day, the feeling of being heavy, weighed down under a pile of blankets.

"I know you said your father used to go to 'Lock and Leather', but what exactly is it?" Breena asked, not looking at me. Her gaze was focused ahead, taking in the buildings and the people walking in and out of them. She watched as a mother held her baby in front of a wooden cart, pointing at a stuffed creature made of wool.

"It's a place to sleep and eat. We'll be safe. We were always safe there."

As we approached a familiar building, my heart leapt. The old stone building sandwiched between two shops looked just as it had the last time I had been there, albeit its door had a fresh coat of indigo stain now. At the time, it had been a leather shop, but now, the wooden sign hanging in the doorway read: "The Wooden Apothecary".

"It's still here," I whispered under my breath, not concerned if Breena heard me or not. I opened the door to the building, and an older woman with a peg leg watering her plants offered us a soft smile. Breena stopped in her tracks to check out the hundreds of glass bottles lining the walls, but I pulled her by her forearm toward the back of the shop.

I pushed past the door with a sign tacked to it that read: "No Patrons". If my dad's place was still here, it would be right above this little shop. The place was a one bedroom for which he'd pay a percentage of the coin he'd earned from selling his glass pieces.

We ascended the groaning stairs and crossed the landing until we stood face to face with the door of my father's home.

"This is the one." Taking a deep breath, I turned the cool, copper knob.

Stuck.

I wiggled it again, with no luck. On the third time, I threw my body into it, and yet again, the door didn't budge.

"Let me." Breena placed her fingertips on the knob, and with a swift turn, the door clicked open. With a satisfied smile, she held out her hand to usher me inside.

Of course, she only used the tips of her fingers.

"Show off," I muttered as I entered the room.

Breena chuckled, but the sound seemed somewhat detached from her.

"There are so many *things* in here." Breena's gaze trailed over the many objects along the shelves and countertops. She stripped out of the light jacket and threw it on the floral-patterned settee.

"Yeah, humans are like that. They like to collect things. Little trophies, I think," I said.

"This is where your father lived on land? And these are all his?" she asked, pointing to the worn books and family portraits.

"It is." I took in the portraits of another family, as well as the absence of my father's precious art. "But these aren't his things."

Breena wandered over to the kitchen and grabbed onto one of the cabinet knobs. When she pulled it open, the entire door came right off its hinges. She turned to me, the cabinet door in her hand, and stared at me with a sheepish grin before saying, "I suppose this door wasn't locked."

Shaking my head, I walked over to where she stood in the tiny kitchen. I explored the contents of the cabinet for food, but there was nothing but different sized plates, for what reason, I was unsure. I scoured the rest of the kitchen until I found a sack of rice. Breena dropped the cabinet door and then tore the bag open. She took a handful of the small brown pieces, and I held my hand up to stop her, but she began pouring the grain into her mouth. Pieces of uncooked rice spilled from her hands and mouth as she began chewing, and they fell onto the floor like frozen rain.

I stood there with my arms crossed while I waited for her to realize it wasn't edible. Her face contorted with pain, and it sounded like all her teeth were breaking.

"Okay, enough! Spit that out, you dumb seal. It's inedible," I said after my entertainment quickly turned to annoyance. Hunger took over my mind, wielding control over the sharp words that escaped my mouth.

She glanced up at me, letting the crunchy pieces of rice fall from her parted lips.

Grabbing a glass from the cabinet and, filling it with water from the sink, I handed it to her. She took it from me greedily from where she sat on the floor, gulping it down much like she had the dry rice. Water leaked down the sides of her mouth, trailing down her neck and onto her chest, soaking her white shirt. I held my gaze on her face, not letting my eyes linger any lower.

Dark seas, why must she torture me like this? Does she even realize what she's doing to me?

I grabbed a glass, chugging the water within, feeling my throat rehydrate as the tepid fluid traveled to my empty belly.

"I'm not even going to attempt cooking that. We'd burn this whole place down," I said with a sigh. "I'm going to bed. The sooner I can rest and escape this nauseating hunger, the better. I fear what I may do if I stay awake any longer."

"What would you do?" Breena wiped her face with the back of her hand.

I glanced down at her but didn't offer her a response as I refilled my glass. I ran my hands under the water, enjoying the feel of it on my new skin. Once my glass was full, I dried my hands and left Breena on the floor.

I trailed my fingers over the bedroom dresser, realizing it wasn't the one I had carved my name into as a child. Everything about this place was different now, and it certainly didn't smell like him anymore.

Has it already been that long? Long enough to erase him from this place like the sea had?

Breena walked into the room with her wet shirt held off her stomach so the sodden fabric wasn't touching her. She looked up at me before saying, "It's not fun to be wet on land, is it?"

"No, it's not," I chuckled, pulling my hand from the dresser. "But I'm sure there are plenty of clothes here. We both need to change anyway. We reek of dead fish."

"I cannot return to the sea, but do you think I can submerge myself in water on land?" Breena pondered. "I would like to bathe eventually."

I kicked my shoes off and wiggled my toes before ridding myself of my socks as well. Breena watched me and followed my lead, stripping out of her pants, then her wet shirt.

I spun on my heel and yanked open the top drawer of the dresser as I blinked away the imagery she left me.

Not that I haven't seen all of her already.

"Here," I choked out, tossing a large shirt behind me. I tentatively stripped out of my own shirt, facing the wall, exposing my bare back to her.

"You're covered in blood. Whose is that?"

I dropped the shirt down my back, hiding my skin once more before facing her.

"It's mine. From my transformation," I said then resumed scouring the drawers for pants for the two of us.

"I didn't realize..." She trailed off.

"Didn't realize what?" I asked, my back still facing her.

"Our transition is pain free, and I know you said the same for hybrids, but I just didn't realize yours was so..." she paused again, "intense."

"I basically shed and grow all new skin, teeth, and nails simultaneously. Of course it's intense." I tossed a soft pair of leggings over my shoulder then stripped out of the grimy fisherman's slacks. Aware I was exposing my bare ass to her, I carefully climbed into the fresh new ones. Stabilizing myself on the dresser, I shoved down the flutter in my gut that came with the vulnerability of her eyes on me.

"Do you want me to help you wash that off?" Breena asked quietly. I slowly turned on my heels to examine her fatigued features.

"I don't need your pity. It's just," I paused, "how things work. I accepted that a long time ago."

"But that's not how it was for your father. He lived in two worlds, didn't have to choose."

"Until he did," I barked out, the residual flutters in my stomach squelched by her words. "And it got him killed. Are you done asking questions now?"

Breena made a soft, breathy sound as I shifted away from her, but she didn't respond. What was there to say anyway?

I grunted as I collapsed onto the bed centered between two windows. The mattress groaned under my weight, and I stifled my own moan as my body cried in relief. My spine stretched and settled into the firm mattress; Breena jostled me as she clumsily climbed in.

"What are you doing?" My head swung to look at her and I propped myself up on my sore elbows, ready to use my foot to kick her off the mattress.

"Going to sleep," she said between yawns as she got comfortable under the light-colored sheets. She pulled them up under her chin, her eyes fluttering closed.

"Not here, you're not. There's a perfectly good settee in the other room," I said loud enough to make Breena open her eyes. I yanked at the sheets to steal her comfort. The last thing I needed was her in this bed.

"The last surface I slept on was a trunk. I'm not sleeping on that lumpy thing you call a settee." She pulled the sheets back and held them with a firm grasp. We both knew I wasn't getting them back from her with that grip of hers.

"Well, at least you slept on the boat," I bit back. "If you recall, I watched your back so you could rest. Therefore, I'm taking the bed."

"Don't act like that was for me. You would have never trusted me enough to keep watch. You can stay here, I don't care, but I'm not leaving."

"Fine, but don't even think of sleeping on top of me. I've seen how you seals sleep." I faced away from Breena to make it easier to forget she was there and my mother and Zellia weren't. Swallowing hard, I tried to ignore the heat radiating from her under the sheets, wrapping around me, begging for my attention. I squeezed my eyes shut and thought of nothing but the icy waves of the winter to cool down my own heat accumulating in all the wrong places.

"Never in a million years, fish."

I woke to a clatter in the kitchen. I sat straight up in bed, my heart pounding as I realized where I was. Dreams found me, ones where I'd been back in the water and my brief time on land had all been but a terrible nightmare. I dreamt of an abundant sea and swimming in loops around a spotted shark as we chased little fishes, not out of competition for the last remaining resources, but out of companionship. It was bliss.

Clinking glass pulled me back into my reality. I threw off the sheets, swung my legs over the side of the bed, and made my way into the kitchen.

"What are you doing now?" I asked Breena as she hovered over the stove. Her hair dripped down her back, creating a patch of dark red fabric on the flowy dress she donned. I took a whiff of myself, and the stench that hit my nose was a swift reminder that I, too, needed to bathe.

I guess the fresh water didn't kill her.

"Didn't you learn your lesson last night that you can't eat raw rice?"

She dunked a wooden spoon into a pot and shoveled out a few scoops, dumping them into a ceramic bowl.

"It's not raw!" she said, shoving the warm bowl of wet rice into my hands. I peered around her to the stove and the pot sitting on top of it, both splattered with starchy water.

"You did not."

"I did!" Breena said with a smug smile, finding a spot to sit at a small wooden table by the window. She'd cracked open the window, letting a cool summer morning breeze into the room. I closed my eyes for a brief moment as the smell of the sea struck my nose.

A spoon clattered against the ceramic bowl, teasing my eyes back open. I sat down at the table across from her with my bowl of soupy rice.

"I found a little piece of paper in the bag with instructions, so I simply followed them. Or so I tried. I wasn't quite sure what the rice was supposed to look like when it was done, but I was too hungry to stay in bed and not try to feed us somehow."

"You can read?" I asked before taking my first bite. It was unflavored and not very pleasant, but neither of us were puking, so I'd take it over the raw fish any day.

"Of course. You think because I live on a secluded island and spend most of my time as a seal that I can't read and write?"

"That's exactly what I thought."

"Yet you can read, and you live on the bottom of the sea, far from shore."

"Fair enough," I said, then took another bite of the rice. "Listen, we need to find your pelt today so I can return home."

"I thought you needed a few days to rest. You made it sound like we had more time."

"Ideally, yes, I would take a week to rest, but I have a family to feed."

"Well, did you magically solve the issue of the fish being held captive by the humans while you were sleeping? Because as I recall, there are no fish left for you to bring them."

"Which is why I was going to find my way back to that net and get rid of it once and for all," I said.

"What happens if you get back into the sea tomorrow?" Breena scowled. "What happens to your body?"

I didn't answer, taking another spoonful of rice into my mouth. My eyes averted her gaze.

"More blood? More pain? Could you even survive that?"

"I don't know!" My voice rose. "But don't I need to try? What will happen to my mother and sister if I don't? They don't even know I'm still alive."

"What are their names?" Breena asked. She didn't even bat an eye at my commentary.

"What?" I asked, my teeth gnashing against each other.

Why did that matter right now?

"What are the names of your mother and sister?" she asked, elaborating further.

"Corrain and Zellia."

"Corrain and Zellia will suffer more if you push yourself by transitioning too early and never returning home than if you go home in a week, rested and alive."

"I have a brother I want to return home to as well, so I understand, but I don't think either of us have much choice in the matter right now. We need to stay, you just as much as me."

"Fine." I clipped the word short, because she had a point, and I absolutely hated it. I couldn't think of my sister for another second without feeling as though I would crumble in on myself. "Listen, as much as I loved this rice soup, I think we can do better."

I pushed my chair out and stood.

"Let's wash up and get out of here."

CHAPTER SEVEN
TEA FOR TWO

Breena strolled up to the stained-glass double doors and yanked them open, somehow keeping them on their hinges. A restrained breath left me as she let go of the handles and walked into the tea house, doors unharmed. I used my knuckle to keep the door closest to me open long enough for me to slip through the entry.

Inside the tea house, a soft, melodic harmony echoed across its pale stone walls. The pearlescence of the stone made it look as if the building itself had been crafted with pieces of abalone shell.

Large windows opened to a far-off view of the sea and the rocky cliffs that bled into it. Unfiltered light poured into the space, illuminating its patrons. As I grew closer to the counter, I began noticing something quite odd about the people waiting in line. One had suspiciously pointed ears, and another had pale skin just tinted enough to be considered green.

I glanced over to Breena to see if she'd noticed the same.

"Some of these humans are..." Breena trailed off, peering over her shoulder. "Odd."

"That's for sure. And I'm pretty sure it's because they're not.

Human, that is," I said, looking closer at the woman in front of me. She seemed human, all but those elf-like ears.

"You really think that...?" Breena trailed off again as we reached the front of the line. She placed her hands on the dark wooden counter, and the woman behind it stared at her expectantly.

"Just the two of you?" the woman finally asked, looking from Breena to me. We both nodded our heads, and the woman directed us to a small table near the third window.

She pulled a padded chair out for Breena, but I waved her away before she could do the same for me. I tugged the long, lacy skirt wrapped around my legs to the side before I sat. I'd stolen the thing out of the chest of drawers at my dad's old place after I'd bathed the blood and salt off my skin. I'd tied my damp hair back with a ribbon I'd found on the bathing chamber vanity and scoured the owner's clothes for something that would fit my long body. Breena had managed to find a pretty red dress that fit her perfectly, but I, on the other hand, had to make do with what I could find. The women's clothing was yet another reason the place had felt so much less like home, almost all familiarity stripped from it.

"Kylan will come over shortly to take your order. Enjoy your tea. I highly recommend the Enchanted Elderberry herbal tea!" the human woman said before setting off to her counter.

"That was rude," Breena mumbled as she adjusted herself in the blue chair.

"What was rude?"

"Never mind," she said, dismissing me with a wave of her hand. Her gaze settled on something in the horizon, and I shrugged her off, staring up at a slate board on the stone wall.

It read:

Specials:
Enchanted Elderberry Herbal Tea
Henri's Bourbon Black Tea

Vanilla Honey White Tea
Strawberry Shortcake
Shortbread Cookies

I decided to stick with the human's suggestion of the first tea on the list and then unfolded a leather booklet on the table. Inside it was a list of dozens of flavors of tea, along with a variety of food for various times of the day.

My eyes took in the foods listed under the "Breakfast" section. Upon realizing I didn't know what any of it meant, I settled on the first item, which happened to be the most simple: happy eggs and buttered brambleberry loaf.

Breena began itching her arm mindlessly, creating a reddish-brown patch on her skin, lined with ashen scratch marks.

"Stop that," I demanded. While her nails were dull, they still managed to damage her tender skin.

"Oh." Breena noticed the patch on her arm, as if she'd been too distracted by something outside and hadn't realized she was harming herself.

"I feel like I could crawl out of my skin, and this skin isn't supposed to shed, unlike yours," she sighed.

"I do too. We need to remember to drink water, and a lot of it. We have to keep our skin moist."

"Drinking water is so odd. Does the food on land not contain it? I don't understand why we must consume it. Water is not for drinking."

"Here it is. I hear the humans struggle to drink it too, so it's not just us. I think that's why they have this tea stuff. Flavored water to make it more palatable."

"I suppose," Breena said, distractedly thrumming her nails on the table.

"Hiya, I'm Kylan!" a chipper human chimed, making both Breena and me jump. "What can I get you today?"

"Oh, I haven't decided ye–"

"We'll take two elderberry teas and two of those happy eggs dishes," I said, cutting Breena off. Her head swung to me as her eyes squinted, but the Kylan human didn't seem to notice.

"Great choice. I'll have those out for you as soon as they're ready. The kitchen is usually pretty fast despite all the folks we get in here," they said with a too-big smile. "Can I get you anything else?"

"No," I said, looking them over. They wore an outfit made of loose canvas, and their hair was in an intricate knot atop their head. Kylan wore tiny tan shoes with a matching apron that had the words "Henri's Herb House" written across it in scrolling font.

"Well, I'll be at the front if you change your mind," Kylan said, their too-large smile wobbling. As soon as they made it across the tea house, Breena's eyes sharpened on me.

"Can you stop being so rude to that poor human?"

"What?" I asked. I wasn't sure what she was going on about now, but I *was* certain I'd never be able to please the selkie.

"It doesn't hurt to be a little kinder. Kylan has done nothing wrong. In fact, they're quite pleasant. So was that first human."

"Done nothing wrong? All of them have," I protested. I jut my hand out to the side of the table, motioning to the people of Henri's Herb House. Sure, some of them seemed suspiciously fae-like, but that didn't change the facts. Humans were the barnacles of the land.

"Because they were born human?" Breena asked with an elongated sigh. She acted as if she already knew what I was going to say.

"Exactly." I wondered why she even needed to ask.

"You need to learn to lighten up. You saw that we're not the only fae in this tea house. I doubt there are humans with green skin, and I'm pretty sure I saw someone with claws, so let's not judge too harshly, okay? This place is clearly not what you remembered."

"You're right about one thing." I gritted my teeth. Those two words weren't as hard for me to speak as they were for some, but saying them to her was utterly painful. "I don't recall Barthoah being like this when I was young. I'm not sure if I had been oblivious to it back then, or if this is all a recent development."

Breena itched her skin some more, and I pushed a carafe of water that sat off to the side of the table toward her. She took the jar with a sigh and held it up to her mouth, taking a big gulp.

"There are cups for that," I said, setting a little glass cup in front of her.

"Oh." Breena smiled sheepishly and took one of the glasses, sliding the other to me. She poured water into them, careful not to spill after her recent embarrassment.

Kylan had been correct, because no more than a few minutes later, they were back with two steamy cups of tea. When they set them down in front of us, a fruity aroma floated up from inside my porcelain cup and met my nose in a satisfying stream of warm air. I'm not sure if the scent of the elderberry was the cause of the heavily perfumed air, or if this tea had been as enchanted as the name suggested.

I doubted humans knew how to perform such acts, nor did I believe they would be okay with serving magic-infused foods in their shops and eateries. Had I gotten this all wrong as a child, or had the stories that had flown from my father's mouth all been but a tale to keep us away? He loved Barthoah; it didn't make any sense to hide something like this from Zellia and me.

"The tea smells amazing. Thank you, Kylan." Breena grabbed the sides of her boiling hot tea and held it up to her puckered lips.

"Careful! I'd let it sit for a few minutes before you go and burn your mouth. A burnt tongue is just no way to go through your day, trust me," they said with a nervous chuckle, eyeing Breena's cup of tea.

Breena said nothing as she set her cup back down on the tiny plate provided.

What was up with these land folk and all their different sized plates?

"Anyway, I poured the first one for you, but I'll bring over a teapot with your food so you can refill as you please. Enjoy!" Kylan said, not waiting for us to respond before they spun on their heels to speak with the auburn-haired family next to us.

Breena picked up a small spoon resting on her plate then glanced around the table at the odds and ends that sat upon it: a jar of honey, an ornate pot of sugar, and a bottle of unfamiliar dark liquid. The worn label read: Locally Tapped Birch Syrup.

She opened the pot of sugar and stuck her tiny spoon into it, scooping out a pile of brown granules. The selkie stuck out her tongue in focus as she held her spoon out and balanced the sugar all the way to her cup of steamy tea.

I watched the way she moved and focused, wondering if she used this tea and sugar to distract herself from her woes. She'd lost her pelt, after all, and it was in the possession of some human man we had no way of finding.

A small smile crossed Breena's lips as she made the spoon into her cup without spilling.

"Can you feel that the pelt is no longer in your possession?" I asked Breena over the chatter of the tea house. She didn't look up at me as she twirled that little spoon around in her cup of tea. I stared at the ripples forming as I waited for her to answer, wondering if I could control them, or if my magic only worked on salty seawater.

"I can, but I can also feel that this fisherman has not yet... claimed me. I feel no draw to him, and until I do, I don't know how we'll find him," Breena admitted, bringing my attention off her tea and back on to her. Her forehead creased as she met my gaze.

"He hasn't?" I asked. "Maybe this is a good thing. If he hasn't *claimed* you yet, it means he probably hasn't opened that trunk and found it. Now, we just need to find it before he does."

"Do you suppose we walk into everyone's homes in this village and look for the trunk?" Breena took her first sip of tea to try to hide her annoyance.

"Of course not..." I trailed off, having nothing else to offer her. Watching foamy waves as they crashed over sun-baked rocks, I debated whether I had gotten in over my head agreeing to help her. Fear crept up my neck at the thought that I would heal before finding her pelt. I didn't want to have to make the decision of staying or leaving her behind, because deep down, I already knew which choice I would make. Sitting across from her knowing that made my skin crawl.

The uncomfortable feeling reminded me to take a sip of water from the small glass next to my tea. First, I downed the disgusting, unflavored liquid, and then I went in for the flavored water that was warm and smelled of berries. The flavor of the tea swirled around my mouth, eliciting an immediate response from the side of my tongue. The drink was sweet, tangy, and utterly perfect as a cool gust of early summer breeze blew through the window we sat next to.

Kylan popped back over to the table as they tended to do, far too often if you asked me, and said, "Looks like you two have tried the tea. What do you think? We call it enchanted because it's infused with the love of this place. And trust me, there's a lot of it."

Love? Not real magic, but love? You've got to be kidding me.

My heart dropped as Kylan stared at me expectantly with a smile. They held a small wooden tray with two dishes and a tea pot sitting on top of it. I swallowed my mouthful of tea and scratched the back of my neck before saying, "Yeah, it's good."

Breena kicked me under the table, and I threw in a 'thanks' for good measure. Kylan took that as their sign to place the plates in front of us, along with a quilted square they rested near the edge of the table. They placed the teapot upon the square and cautioned us from touching the sides of it.

"Kylan?" I called out before they had the chance to walk away. "Do you know much about the fishermen of Barthoah?"

"Sure, it's a small village! What about them?" Their hazel eyes focused on me, their pupils so round, so human. I was sure if I looked in a mirror now, my blue eyes would look the same. A knot formed in my stomach at the mere thought.

I focused back on the task at hand as questions ran through my mind. I searched for the one that seemed the least creepy, but that task was difficult when asking for the address of strangers you wanted something from. I did my best.

"Where do they typically hang out?" I asked.

"Well, the best place to find a fisherman would be around the boats and docks, of course. But other than that, they like to hang out around town. They sure do love their sweets. If you head over to the Honey Spot this afternoon, I'm sure you'll find one of them over there."

"Honey Spot? Got it, thank you," I said, surprising myself when it came out naturally. And I had meant it, too.

When Kylan slipped off to help another table, I searched Breena's face for any sign of emotion, but she held her feelings close to her chest, giving me no indication if she found relief in Kylan's answer.

"Well?" I asked, hoping she would fill in the blanks.

"It's a start," Breena said with a nod. "We'll eat, and then we'll get started. It's not much to work with, but it's more than we had to go off yesterday."

What we would do once we found one of these fishermen was beyond me. Follow one home and sneak into his house in hopes we would find the trunk? It wasn't necessarily a good plan, that was for sure.

I nodded my head and dove into the plate of food in front of me. My stomach lurched as my first bite of happy eggs hit my stomach, triggering a monstrous need to consume everything in front of me. No words left me as I demolished every last morsel on my plate, almost licking it free of yolk and loaf crumbs. I didn't take time to determine the flavor, let alone if I liked the meal. It was edible, and that's all that mattered.

When my plate was clean, I peered over at Breena, who was licking her crumb-covered lips. Her plate was just as clean as mine, and I wondered if she had bothered chewing her food or merely choked it down like I had.

We'd consumed the food we needed, gathered a bit of information, and there was only one thing left to do.

Run.

"Is Kylan looking at us?" I asked Breena.

"No, why?" She glanced over at the counter where the human seemed to spend much of their time.

"Get ready to run, and please, for the love of all things salty, do not get caught."

"Run? Caught? What are you talking about?" Breena muttered, leaning in toward me.

"We have no coin. How else did you think this meal was going to end?"

"Kylan is a nice human. Can't we just—"

"No," I cut her off, not needing to know what she was going to say. Our only option was getting out of here and doing it fast. "Get ready to go in three."

"Oh, fine," Breena said, finishing off her cup of tea and wiping her face with the back of her hand. "Ready when you are."

I counted down from three, and the two of us launched out of our seats and beelined for the door. Surprisingly, neither of us tripped as we maneuvered through the customers and their tables. No one called after us as we made it through the double doors and out onto the street. We didn't slow as we rounded the building then flattened our backs against the rough stone of the shop. We were shaded by a mature tree's broad branches and sandwiched between the tea shop and the leather store next door. Breena dove behind their bin of trash, and I did not join her. I'd create my first tsunami and destroy this place before touching human garbage.

"Are we in the clear?" Breena said from her hiding place under a discarded wooden box. Her curls sprung out from under the cracked box as she peeked out.

This woman... She was going to be the death of me.

When the coast was clear, Breena and I crept out of the alley and hurried down the block, bypassing town shops and pedestrians.

"We need coin," Breena panted as we slowed. "I can't do this again."

"I couldn't agree more, but we don't have time for that now. We need to find a lead on this fisherman," I said. I peered over my shoulder to make sure no one from the tea house had found us. We couldn't linger here for long. Barthoah was too small not to recognize the faces of outsider thieves.

"Yeah, we do," Breena said. Her face hardened, and she stood straighter and adjusted her summer dress.

"I think we should split up to save time. I'll head to the dock, and you should find the Honey Spot," I said.

"Okay, and what will we do if we find a fisherman? Follow him by ourselves?"

"Just don't be stupid about it," I said with an impatient sigh. "Give him plenty of space and don't let him know you have interest in where he's going. The last thing we need is for you to go and get kidnapped."

"You could get kidnapped too, you know," Breena scoffed.

I stared at her, taking a quick step closer, as if she was my prey and I hadn't eaten in ages. My pupils adjusted from black spheres into inky slits, and she stumbled back with her hand on her chest. Her own eyes widened as she stared into mine—the eyes of a huntress.

"I didn't know you could do that on land." She pressed her palm flat against her heaving chest. I was aware just how frightening I could look, and that was exactly why I wasn't worried about being taken. That was why the cute one was being sent to check out a sweets store in town, and I was going to the docks.

I blinked my eyes, claiming rounded pupils once more, before saying, "They come out when I'm in a hunt. And rest assured, if a man tried to take me, I'd consider it a hunt."

"Well then, yes, I'll be careful." Breena cleared her throat and wiped a hand down her hip. "I'll follow from afar and gather any information I can find on them. We can meet by that big clock tower over there and come up with a plan based on whatever information we find."

"Meet me when the clock rings four times. Don't be late," I said. Breena nodded her head and turned on her heel to head down the street. Before she could make it too far, I yelled out, "And be careful!"

CHAPTER EIGHT
GRANDFISHY

I watched Breena, her head held stiffly as she wandered off alone into the sun kissed town. The flow of her dress was an odd juxtaposition to her posture, which grew ridged the second she'd taken a step away from me. I doubt it was I who made her comfortable, but more so my presence and my knowledge of who she is and where she came from that had her at ease.

She was headed into an area where no one knew her, and no one would be there to correct her when she inevitably began doing something odd and suspicious. I didn't want to separate and leave her to her own devices—depths knew she was out of her element —but I also needed time.

It had been a day since I was alone, and while that may have not seemed very long to most, it had been an eternity for me. I missed the Kilkov and craved the sunlight it afforded me. I peered up to the sky, careful not to look directly into the sun. It was a bright day in the village, with a spattering of wispy clouds. I desperately wanted to roll up my sleeves and feel the sun on my arms, but I feared my skin would burn in the midday summer rays.

I'd always watched the light dance across the water and found solace in its beauty and peace, but it was much different here on land—harsher. I missed the way the sea filtered it, but I couldn't pretend the strong rays of sun beating down upon the shiny green leaves of the trees, the dewy blades of grass, and the windows of the shops wasn't absolutely breathtaking. I noticed all the ways the sun lit up this world on my way to the docks.

Half of my focus was lost to the sun, and the other half was struggling to remember the task at hand.

Focus, Sid. Find a fisherman.

As I approached the docks, I stopped short and cut across the rocky landscape to find one flat enough to sit upon. Finding a large stone cast in shade, I took a seat from my new vantage point. From here, I could make out the docks and the massive fishing boats tied to them, all without having to squint into the brightness of the day.

I wasn't sure how much time had passed. I'd realized after a while that I was too far from town to hear the grand clock strike twice—or three times, I wasn't sure. I'd seen plenty of fishermen, but it was a specific type of fisherman I was after. I kept my eyes glued on the boat Breena and I had come to Barthoah on. Painted on the side of the vessel, the words "Indigo Tide" were scrolled across in cursive lettering. This was where we would get a clue as to where her pelt was.

Sending Breena off to the Honey Spot was a waste of her time. She had no way of knowing which fishermen were from the Indigo Tide, and even then, she didn't know the ship's name. Maybe I'd just wanted some peace and quiet. I tried to convince myself that there wasn't anything wrong with that, sending her away for my own selfish needs.

My eyes grew heavy staring at the ship with such intensity. I tried to keep my gaze off the water, as I didn't know what feelings would stir up in me if I allowed them to wander.

When the timing between my blinks shortened, I stood and shook myself out of the sleep that wanted to take hold of me. I began walking to get my blood flowing and then hopped from stone to stone, each one taking me closer to the sea.

My feet began to tingle when I stepped onto a large rock that had been misted by the salty sea. My cells instantly recognized it as my home, and they fought the morphing that would take place if I'd been consumed by the water.

I kept going, despite the rocks growing more and more slippery. A voice in my head shouted at me to go back to dry land, but the waves crashing down upon my feet were stealing my willpower. I lost focus on the Indigo Tide. The sea lured me in, as if it had its very own siren song. The hold this force of nature had on me was like nothing else I would ever experience, and I craved to be consumed by it, wrapped within its comforting embrace.

There wasn't much stopping me from calming the waves and diving into the water that called to me. I could feel my mother, Zellia, my pod. I could feel their hunger and their voices calling me back to them.

I could grab fish from within the humans' cruel net. I could take them back to my home and forget about this whole mess with Breena's pelt.

My hand twitched, and a dark blue swirl shimmered over the surface of the water. The white foamy caps that splashed upon the jagged rocks halted. The water around me calmed, and I took another step, then another. I hiked up the skirt I wore so it didn't get caught on one of the sharp stone spikes that jutted out around me.

When the water reached my thighs, the tingling sensation began to feel like razor blades being dragged down my skin. Panic shot through me as scales began tearing through my flesh down the back of my calves. My teeth ached and grew wiggly, knowing my jaw was minutes from releasing them all into the water and replacing them with the teeth of a siren—small, jagged and deadly sharp.

Scrambling back, I held my hand out in front of me, and the

water recessed, creating a wall around me so the sea was no longer tempting me forward, so it was no longer urging my body to change and become its monster once more.

Before anyone noticed what I was doing, I hopped from stone to stone, carrying myself back to the shore. I released the water, and it came crashing back down upon the land, nipping at my heels as I dragged myself away from it. The scales that had begun growing like barnacles drifted to the ground below, falling into the cracks between the stones, where they would be lost to the human world. New skin began growing on my legs once more, red, shiny, and tender.

As much as I wanted to see my family, I couldn't fathom the risk of never seeing them again because I was being stupid and impatient. Breena's words from this morning echoed in my mind as I took myself back to my spot in the shade, safe from the sea. Who knew what would've happened to me if I let the transition fully take hold.

I sat down once more, patting the new skin on my thighs to gently soothe the itching that came with regrowth. I pulled my knees into my chest and rested my cheek on one of them. Letting my gaze fall back on the Indigo Tide, I tried to remind myself why it was that I was here in the first place.

Movement caught my attention as a man stepped out of the vessel of interest. This man, I recognized him from our time on the ship. He was young, tall, with copper hair and arms that swung loosely as he walked. He was dressed head to toe in white and had a black bag hanging around his left shoulder. The human smiled at people as he passed them, and I wondered what kind of sick joke this was. Did he know he was trying to pull one over on everyone, or did he simply not realize? Or maybe the people around him were also in on it, all humans planning and plotting the destruction of my home. And doing it with a smile, no less.

The fisherman hopped off the end of the dock and took the path lined with short shrubs that would lead him into town. I stood and brushed loose pebbles off my skirt, giving him some time to distance himself before I followed. As I took my first step, my pupils turned to slits, and I stalked the man who would lead me to Breena's pelt.

A brass bell on the door chimed as I slinked into the shop. My eyes searched the entire room until they landed on the fisherman. I'd given him a few minutes' head start, kneeling in the street and pretending to adjust my slipper as I'd kept my eyes on the door. After I'd felt enough time had gone by, I'd found myself in a little market bustling with hungry humans.

The fisherman grabbed a paper-wrapped sandwich from a man he'd called Erwell then headed for the front door once more. I stared behind the counter at all the different types of foods I'd never seen before. I knew I would be hungry in the next few hours, and I wondered how Breena and I would go about acquiring food this time. I didn't think we could pull off what we had this morning again. We either needed to find another solution or eat what was left of the soggy rice Breena had cooked. I preferred not to do the latter.

The chime rang again as I left the market empty-handed. I hoped wherever the man was going next would prove to be more useful than the short sandwich adventure he'd just lead me on.

My head swiveled left, then right as I determined which direction he'd gone off in now. It didn't take me long to find him heading into yet another store, this time one called "Muliver's Glass Masterpieces".

I waited outside the door for a moment so as not to cause suspicion, wondering what the chances were that there were two glass blowing shops in Barthoah. Leaning on the stone building, I pretended to look at the pink flowers billowing out of the planter box next to me. When I felt I was in the clear, I gingerly opened the door to the shop in hopes I didn't draw attention with my entrance.

"Hello, sir," the sailor said as he approached the front counter. He glanced around at the art filling the place as he stuffed a wrapped sandwich into his jacket pocket. "I'm looking for a glass sailboat for my mother's birthday. Would you be able to discuss custom boat pieces with me?"

A gift for his mother?

It seemed like a rather sweet gesture for a man like him. A false man of the sea, that was.

"I sure can," the older man behind the counter said with a bob of his head, already moving to the other side of the counter.

I made my way to the opposite side of the store as them, doubting I was going to gather useful information on Breena's pelt while in a glass-blowing store. I didn't feel the need to listen to the two of them talk, but I positioned myself in the corner behind a glass case holding a few of the shop's larger pieces. From where I stood, I could keep my eye on the fisherman and the door, all without having to lift my head from behind the glass showcase.

The men spoke for a while, the older of the two making gestures towards different pieces of warped glass. He looked up at me a few times, to presumably check on how I was doing, but the fisherman didn't pay me any mind.

As I tuned out the muffled sounds of chatter, my attention was stolen by the colored glass. Inside the case, three large, blown pieces sat on carved wooden stands. The first one was a detailed depiction of an anchor layered in pesky barnacles, the next was a swirling blue wave, and the last was a shimmering fin of what looked to be a siren. I stared at the fin for a long moment, forgetting far too quickly why I was in the shop in the first place.

My eyes took in the detail of the work, and I wondered if the older gentleman had made this piece himself, or if there was someone in the back crafting the marvelous art of my people. They reminded me much of my father's work, and seeing these whole pieces of glass before me, not broken and roughed up by the sea, I realized everything I had within my chest at home was nothing compared to what I saw before me. While the fragments of art I had found scattered through the sea were a reminder—a beautiful torture—they had lost most of their luster, dulled by their time treading against sand and salt.

"Thank you, sir. I'll be back on Wednesday to pick it up. She's going to love it!" the fisherman from the Indigo Tide chirped to the shop owner as he made his way to the door. I cleared my throat, adjusted my skirt, and prepared to follow this man to yet another destination. A minute after he was gone, I attempted my exit.

As I put my hand on the doorknob to leave, a weary voice called out, "Miss?"

"I have to go!" I said, not turning around to look at the elderly gentleman behind the counter as I cracked open the door and took my first step out of the shop. My eyes remained glued on the back of the fisherman's head.

"You look just like him, you know."

I froze as the older man's voice hit the back of my head. My target grew farther and farther away as I debated whether I was curious enough about what this man was saying to let my only lead slip away. My hand held the door open, and I remained a statue in my mid-step position. The sailor pulled his sandwich out of his pocket and began eating it as I let him get away from me.

I slowly turned around, noticing the sound of my heart as it beat noticeably louder. I wonder if this mysterious shop owner could hear it.

"I look just like who?" I asked, my stomach rising into my throat. My gaze fell on his blue eyes and trailed down to the soft, knowing smile that lifted his full cheeks.

"Lock the door, will you? I want to show you something," he said. With his jolly smile, he didn't look very threatening, but I sure as depths wasn't about to lock myself in the room with him.

"I will not lock the door, and you're going to tell me something useful in the next five seconds before I walk out of here. I was kind of in the middle of something." My words cut like a sharp knife through the air.

"Oh, I'm sorry, I'm getting ahead of myself." His already pink cheeks began to redden. "I'm the owner of this shop, and I am the husband to Liselle... and the father to Sidven."

My blood froze in my veins when this stranger uttered my father's name.

He chuckled and said, "I told you, you look just like him."

"You're my father's... father?" I sputtered, looking him up and down. He looked human, that checked out. I looked closely and noticed that his eyes were ice blue. I always assumed my father had gotten that trait from his mother—a siren—not his human father. But as I took the rest of him in, he didn't share any other feature that resembled a creature of the deep. His smile was warm, his skin kissed by the sun and splattered with faint freckles and age spots, and his hair was a mixture of white and black. His face was full and jovial, and his eyes, while ice blue, were large and full of wonder.

"How did you know?" I asked. "You told me I look like him, but I look far less like him than my sister. What made you know for certain *I* was his daughter?"

"I'd heard Zellia took after him. Your father always said your face was straight from your mother. And he loved you dearly for it. All of you."

My stomach grew raw at the mention of my mother and sister. *He knew their names?*

"And I knew because you haven't changed all that much since you were a child, Sidra. You probably don't remember me from your visit when you were young, but do you remember this place? Well, you probably don't remember the shop, it has had some remodeling since then, and well, you weren't interested in the glass that had already been blown. You wanted to be in the back with your father and me, right in the heart of it all."

"The workshop," I murmured, half to myself, half to him.

"Ahh, so it's coming back to you. Now, will you lock that door and let me reignite those memories of yours? I too would like to speak of my son and his love for this place."

No words found me, but my fingers did find the lock on the door. I did as he asked and flipped the "open" sign over for good measure. When I turned around to face him, he was already on his way to the back. I maneuvered behind his counter and followed him to the workshop.

There were pieces, both finished and unfinished, scattered across a large metal table shoved at the back of the room. To the left of me, there was a cumbersome brick oven that had flickering embers still heating up the space, as if he had just finished up his work for the day. Windows lined one wall, letting in natural light that reflected off the metal shelves holding glistening art.

"When your father told me of his decision to return to the sea for good, I knew it was a mistake. His heart was too soft for the deep. He belonged here on land, but the three hearts that beat outside his chest belonged to the sea." He released a wobbly breath, picking up a palm sized piece of glass that had been sitting on a fire-scorched wooden table.

"You wanted him to choose the side of the humans?" It was hard to pay any mind to his workshop when this man was telling me my father had the soul of a human, that he belonged with them. The sharp pain in my chest wouldn't be mended by the distraction of melted glass, not this time.

"There's no 'human side' and 'siren side'. If you think that's the case, you don't know much of this war." The older man grimaced. He smoothed a rough thumb over the glass in his hand mindlessly as he brought his gaze up to meet mine.

I gritted my teeth, disappointment creeping through my chest like a poison as I said, "Most of what I know about this war is from my father. Are you calling him a liar?"

"Sidven wasn't a liar, but he did want you to remain in the sea. He didn't want his pain to pass to you."

"His pain?" I asked, wishing I had something to fiddle with as he had. In the sea, I would use smooth, thumb-sized stones. I'd picked up the nervous habit from my father, and it was clear who he'd picked it up from.

"Yes, the tear of the soul that comes with being of two worlds. If you stayed in the sea, fearing land, then you would never go through what he did."

"What, so you're trying to tell me he brought me here as a child as a warning? Told me stories just to spook me? I think you're forgetting that I live inside a ship we sunk during the war. I have lost half of my pod. Lost *him*," I said, anger pricking at my waterline.

"I'm not saying the war doesn't exist. I'm saying it's not what you thought it was. But I didn't want to get into all of that now. I can see I'm upsetting you, and I never meant to do that," he said, holding the piece of glass out to me. I took the smoothed oval, warmed by his hand, without a word. "I simply wanted to show you a familiar place. A place he loved. I hoped that you could learn to love it too, like you used to."

The clock struck four, and those four simple tunes filled me with an assortment of conflicting emotions.

Was I torn leaving this man, this hazily familiar place, and the answers I knew he held close to his chest?

Sadness was an emotion I reserved solely for my father, and here I was, spending it on someone else.

"I have to go," I whispered. "I have someone I need to meet."

"And here I wasted precious time talking about something so off putting. I'm sorry, Sidra. Won't you stay a little longer? I can make some tea and fix up some sandwiches for a late lunch. How does that sound? I have plenty of happy stories about Sidven." The crease between his eyes deepened.

"She'll be waiting for me, and I can't be late, or she'll worry." I knew Breena would think I abandoned her if I got there much past four o'clock. I was the one who told her not to be late, after all.

"I understand. Here, take this," he said, plopping a pouch of coins into the same hand as the worrying glass. "I'm not sure how you've been getting by, but I have a feeling it's not legal."

I took the coin pouch from him with a sideways smile and a one shoulder shrug before saying, "Thank you."

"Just do me a favor, will you?" he asked as I turned for the door. I stopped in my tracks and peered over my shoulder at the older man. "Come back and see me tomorrow?"

CHAPTER NINE
THE MEAD MISHAP

"What did you find?" I asked. My back was pressed up against the stone clock tower as I watched Breena walk down the cobblestone path toward me. Her hands were behind her back, holding something I couldn't see. I hadn't seen her most of the day, and as she approached, an unusual feeling snaked through my body. This feeling was far too similar to excitement for my liking, and I didn't know what to make of such a thing.

"Something called a sandwich! I got two. One for me, one for you," she said, a proud smile plastered to her face.

What is up with these people and their sandwiches?

"And how did you go about getting these?" The words from my grandfather about illegally acquiring food echoed in my head. I took one of the sandwiches from her anyway and motioned for her to sit on a bench near the tower. We both made ourselves comfortable and began unwrapping the paper packaging on our laps.

"Well, we don't really need to get into that." She lifted a slice of compressed bread and took a look at the contents of her sandwich before taking a bite.

I shook my head with a shrouded grin and peered into my own sandwich. I didn't know what half of the things inside it were, but the green leafy stuff looked way too similar to kelp for my liking. Breena seemed to be enjoying it, though, so I sucked it up and took a bite.

Definitely not kelp.

I now understood the sandwich situation. This thing was delicious.

"Did you find anything?" Breena asked. I swallowed my bite reluctantly and wiped a few crumbs from my mouth before responding to her.

"Yeah, I sat at the docks for a while, and I followed a fisherman from the boat we arrived on. It's called the Indigo Tide, by the way. I followed him into town and then to a few shops, but I lost him. I couldn't get any more information on him, but I know he'll be going back to one of the shops on Wednesday, so I'll be waiting for him when he does," I said, leaving out the part about meeting my dad's father and being unable to return to the sea. She didn't need to know that I had more reasons than one to stay on land for a little while. I'd let her feel guilty for keeping me here as punishment for getting me kidnapped by the fisherman in the first place.

"And when is Wednesday?"

"Four days from now. It's Saturday today."

"Okay, that's not too bad," she said before taking another bite of her sandwich. She chewed for a few minutes before saying, "I saw a fisherman at the Honey Spot."

The look on Breena's face paused my chewing. I lowered my sandwich into my lap and brushed the breadcrumbs off my hands as I waited for her to continue.

"I also followed him. I followed him out of the shop and to his home."

"You what?" I shouted, attracting the attention of nosey humans passing by. Breena swallowed and winced, keeping her eyes on her thighs.

"He didn't catch me."

"And what if he had?" I grew physically hot at the thought of her locked away in some man's home. A human man, at that.

"I could have broken every bone in his body." Breena met my eyes now, determination painted across her face. "I'm not a frail thing, you know."

"I know more than anyone here how true that is," I said, holding up my bruised wrist, a perfect handprint matching hers wrapping it. "But that doesn't mean you should follow a strange man back to his home. Alone. What if he'd been the one to have your pelt? Hmm?"

Her silence confirmed everything I suspected. "Yeah, you wouldn't have been able to break his bones then, would you?"

"No." Her lip curled over her sharp canines as she shook her head. I used my pointer finger under her chin to make her look at me.

"Don't give them a reason to keep you. Walking right into their home is all they need," I said, my cool skin clashing against her warmth. Why did I want to touch so much more than just her chin? I wanted—no, needed—to grab her by the face like I had on the ship and make her understand how her getting caught would have wrecked me.

Wrecked me? No, not wrecked me. It would have been irritating to say the least, but nothing she could ever do could wreck me. She was a selkie, a practical stranger. I reminded myself of exactly that.

"I know. I just... I just want to find my pelt already. It hurts to be away from it like this. My soul has been torn into two, and he hasn't even claimed it yet. Can you imagine what it will be like when he finds it in that trunk?"

"I can't, and I don't have to, because it's not going to happen. If he claims you, I will end his miserable life," I found myself saying, once again betrayed by my own mouth.

"Why would you do that?" she asked. Sea breeze blew a piece of her hair into her face, and I found myself tucking it behind her ear. Her shock at my touch made me drop my hand faster than my eyes could capture.

Why did I just do that? Stranger. She's basically a stranger, Sid. Remember that.

I grabbed hold of my sandwich and shoved the bread into my mouth, focusing my attention on the people who passed by. It took all my strength to ignore the odd feeling in my stomach that screamed at me, as if the entire thing had been full of excitable minnows.

When I swallowed, I covered my ass and said, "Because I want to return home too, you know. I made you a promise. I intend to keep it." I still couldn't meet her gaze, my face too hot, my palms too itchy. Was I ill?

"Well, then I guess I should be grateful you keep your promises," Breena said. "Or should it be the sea I should be thankful for? For making it too painful for you to return to it."

Breena motioned to my legs, and I crossed them to hide the raw patches of skin on my calves.

"I had to try," I said between gritted teeth, embarrassment flooding me. Clearly, I cared so little about her and her pelt that I couldn't even stay on land to help her. Her needs were never going to come before the needs of my family, and if my body had accepted the sea, I would be gone, back in the belly of the deep.

"Then I guess you understand why I had to try to find my pelt in that man's home. Because though there's a risk I could get hurt, the thought of not trying is so much worse." Breena made her point, and I hated that she had one in the first place.

"Okay." I spoke slowly, lowering the half-eaten sandwich into my lap. I'd begun talking before I had my mind sorted and took a long pause before resuming. "We'll keep separating like this every day to double our chances of finding your pelt sooner. We both know how to take care of ourselves, and I trust you'll do what you need to stay safe."

"I will. And I'm quite resourceful, if you haven't noticed."

Breena held up the remaining bites of her sandwich and wiggled her proud brows at me. A small chuckle slipped out of me, and I tried to suppress it with a cough.

Get it together, Sid.

"This sandwich is kind of dry," I said, "What do you say about getting out of here and going for a drink? I'd like to understand this obsession these humans seem to have with rum."

Swinging my legs off the side of the barstool, I eyed the glass bottles on the elongated wooden shelves across from me. The bottles had various labels stuck to them with varying lettering. My eyes trailed over the ones filled with amber liquid as I searched for the word 'rum'.

"What can I get you ladies?" a woman chimed from behind the counter. She had short, spiky blonde hair and a piece of silver metal looped through her nose. I stared at the piece of jewelry as Breena answered the woman.

"We'll take two rums, thank you," she said with a friendly smile. At what point did she decide she was going to be friendly to these people? She'd spent her whole life away from Barthoah, and here she was, with none of the fear or anger from this morning lingering in her voice.

"Two rums?" the woman asked with a chuckle, her eyes lingering a little too long on the selkie before her head swung to me. "Two shots coming right up. My name is Denivier, by the way. If you need anything, think twice about whether it's worth my time before you ask."

The woman's bluntness was stark in comparison to my recent company. I smiled at her, appreciative of a woman who spoke her mind. As she itched her ear, I noticed the tip of it extended well past my own, past any human's.

"Denivier..." I leaned in, eying up that ear of hers.

"Yes, I'm an elf." She grabbed a bottle off the shelf behind her, sloshing amber liquid against the sides of the glass. She brought it back over to the bar, her blonde brow raised as she met my curious gaze. "You did just hear what I said about wasting my time, right?"

She set the thick glass bottom of the bottle down on the counter as she grabbed two tiny glasses with her other hand. She poured the rum to the very top of each glass before placing them on the wooden countertop Breena and I leaned against.

"When I thought Barthoah was a village of humans, yeah, it felt worth it to ask," I shot back.

"Why did you think that? I haven't heard of an all-human village in this entire realm," she chuckled, her annoyance shifting to amusement. Breena and I shot each other a glance.

"Where are you both from? Either you were born yesterday, you live underground, or you haven't spent much time on land."

"I suppose one of those assumptions is accurate," I grunted. Glancing at the tiny cup in front of me, my head cocked to the side.

Why was it that the teacups here were far larger than the rum glasses?

"You do look a little pasty." That comment of hers pulled a laugh from Breena, who thoroughly enjoyed the woman's insult.

I tossed her a piercing glance and said, "Don't make me steal your voice again."

Breena rolled her eyes and didn't rush to end her laughter.

"Let me guess. You're from the sea, but you're not sun kissed enough to be a mermaid. And those cold eyes..." She trailed off. "I haven't seen eyes like that in a long time. Those are the eyes of a siren."

"And you?" she said to Breena, not giving me time to respond. "You have the eyes of a doe. You're cute, non-threatening. Your shoulders are darker than the rest of your skin, signifying you like to bathe in the sun. You're a selkie. A beautiful one, at that."

Breena dipped her chin, and I swore I saw her flutter her long lashes at the elf.

Was she flirting with her?

"Great. Now that we have done the completely improper thing of guessing what kind of fae we all are, can the two of you take your damn shots and let me tend to other customers? There's a fairy who needs a refill on her mead. Incomprehensible, right?"

I sighed and shooed the sassy woman away. She took my hand gesture as her release and sauntered over to the fairy at the end of the bar with a parted mouth. I could have gone as far as saying it was a smile.

Breena reached across the counter and pulled the two pours of rum toward us, giving one to me and taking the other one for herself.

"Well, my pasty siren," she said, stifling her laughter, "what do you say we see what this stuff is all about, hmm?"

I picked up my rum, sloshing a tiny bit of it over the lip of the glass, before clinking it against hers like I had seen the other patrons doing.

"Here goes nothing, my little doe-eyed selkie."

The two of us downed the contents of the glass in one sip, causing us both to gag and cough.

It burns. I panicked as the fire in my throat trickled down into my belly.

"For the love of all things salty! What is that?" I said, wiping the rum that dribbled off my chin with my thumb. Breena's eyes were teary and red, and she looked as if she had just downed poison, which, I guess she had.

"I feel like I'm going to die," she choked out. "People pay for this?"

"I'm not quite sure what all the fuss is about. Why do sailors live and die by this stuff?" I asked, annoyance dripping off my burning tongue.

Denivier walked over with a pitcher of what I assumed to be mead in her hand and asked, "Ready for another round?"

"Absolutely not. That was horrid," Breena all but spat. "Do you have anything—better?"

"Want some of this? It's wild berry mead. Might be more suited to your *fragile* tastes," Denivier said with yet another half smile. The way she took in Breena's face with quiet amusement had me clenching my fist around the tiny glass in my hand. I took a deep breath as the odd feeling hit my heart like a dark wave.

I slid the empty glass to her and muttered, "Why not?"

Denivier nodded her head, not peeling her eyes from Breena. Her dark gaze swam with lust, and Breena stared back at her, her large eyes pouring into the elven woman. Eventually, her stoic face broke, and Breena's lips lifted into a coquettish smile as she watched Denivier pour two goblets of mead.

My jaw clicked, and when my hand twitched, liquid sloshed out of the pitcher without control. Denivier let out a squeal as she was drenched in the alcohol, and she stumbled back from the counter. The mead continued to rush toward her as if it had a mind of its own, even after she spaced herself from it.

Breena's head swung to me, her eyes wide and disapproving. There was no hiding from either one of them that the mess was my own. I glanced down at my hand, droplets resting on the back of it from the mead mishap. With a little focus, I urged the stationary liquid to roll off my hand, and so it did.

Well, that answers that, I thought to myself. It was undeniable now that I had the ability to control more than the water in the sea. Mead was also on my list. I wondered what else I could do on land that I never knew I was capable of. A flutter of excitement flickered in me for all but a moment before Breena's disappointed glare squashed it.

"What was that?" Breena asked under her breath as Denivier excused herself to get cleaned up. The barmaid shot me a deadly glance as she ran a stained rag down her arms.

"An accident," I said in a neutral, unyielding tone.

"You can control mead?" She didn't look convinced by my claims of an accident as her forehead knitted.

"Apparently so. This is news to me too." My sharpened vision followed the elf as she ambled off into the back room of the pub.

Breena glanced from me to Denivier before saying, "Are you... jealous?"

"Jealous?" I scoffed. "Of what?"

"Oh, stop." Breena shoved my shoulder with a twinkle in her eye then rested the side of her cheek on her cupped palm. "You are so dense sometimes, you know that?"

"Dense? Excuse me?"

"Are you really so oblivious to your own feelings? You can't tell me Denivier didn't get under your skin, that if I went into that back room right now and made a move on her, you wouldn't control the rum in this place and shatter every bottle on that shelf?" she said, pointing to the long wooden slabs across from us.

"Shatter the bottles? For what, you going off with some random elf?"

"Yes. Touching her in the way you wish I would touch you," she said with one raised brow. My fist clenched, and the spill of mead on the counter began to shimmer and shake.

"Can you tell me that when I do this," she said in a low voice, reaching toward me with focused eyes locked on mine. Those rambunctious minnows in my stomach came back as she began trailing a finger down the length of my arm, stopping right at my wrist. The touch triggered memories of our chests pressed up against each other on the Indigo Tide, our breaths one, our warmed faces inches from one another. "That you feel nothing?"

"No, I feel something, alright. Annoyance." I ignored what she really meant, just as I ignored the reaction she pulled from my body with a mere touch of her finger. The pleased expression on her face wobbled before dropping all together.

"Great waves, Sid. You are relentless, insistent on maintaining this icy shell. You're not in the deep anymore; thaw out already." Her curls bounced as she shook her head, and her words pinged against my sensitive skin. I tried my hardest not to let them sink in, but that was exactly what she was talking about, wasn't it? My hard, unrelenting shell.

"What do you expect, Breena?"

"Can't you just enjoy the time we *do* have? Not everything needs to be so serious," she groaned. her gaze settling on the hand bracelet she'd given me the day we'd met.

"When I'm not serious, people die," I said with a clenched jaw, my voice dropping an octave. "When I give in, when I let go, horrible things happen. I can't live this life of being carefree that you so clearly want of me."

"It doesn't have to be that way." She reached back out toward me and wrapped her hand around my wrist once more. She didn't touch me in a manner that sought control, but one that begged for surrender.

"But it is," I said, wishing my words weren't true. "I'm here for a few more days, and then I'm never going to see that cute little face of yours again. Or those tempting fingers."

"That may be your truth now, but it doesn't always have to be. If you think you can't change your reality, you're not as clever as I thought you were."

When I didn't respond, she kept going. "Don't you want more? Don't you want to *be* more?"

"I didn't realize I wasn't enough." I leaned forward my chair to use the countertop as support.

"You are. Everyone else sees that but you. There's so much more out there than hunting and protecting. I want you to see that," she said. "Even if it's just for a little while."

She thinks I'm enough. I thought to myself as I surveyed her face laced with a fine focus.

Fuck.

"Give me that mead," I demanded, motioning to what was left

of the pitcher. A smile tugged at my lips as she slid it to me. I took the sticky mess by the handle and chugged its contents, the sweet liquid hitting my tongue in a satisfying explosion.

I did want more, but those thoughts were too dangerous to admit. The thought of returning to the sea soft and malleable terrified me. But sitting in front of this woman, seeing the candlelight of the pub flickering across her skin, it seemed impossible not to let go, not to give in.

"That's my girl." Breena chuckled then took the pitcher from me. Squeezing my thigh in proud encouragement, she had me cursing under my breath.

She is going to ruin me.

Breena took a chug of her own, finishing what was left of the mead. She wiped her hand across her lips, no coughs following.

"Oh, I love this." She released a giggle. "I think we need some more."

"That, little droplet, I agree on," I said, swiping my thumb across her cheek where a wayward droplet of pink mead rested. She leaned into my touch, and the gaze that met mine was one of need. I had never seen such a look directed at me, at least not one I was ever able to return.

As I pulled away, I popped my thumb in my mouth as Breena kept her eye trained fiercely on me. I needed a taste of her in any form I could get--even through a tiny drop of mead.

I waved a new barmaid over after I had disposed of the last and ordered us both a large goblet of wild berry mead. Breena and I sipped on it for hours, talking and giggling. With each sip, I felt my composure slip. With each sip, I felt my eyes linger a little too long on places they shouldn't. With each sip, it became more and more undeniable just how jealous I had been of Denivier's longing glances directed at the stunning woman next to me. I knew the next time someone looked at Breena the way I did, they would pay far more than the barmaid had. They would pay with blood.

CHAPTER TEN
SLEEP, LITTLE DROPLET

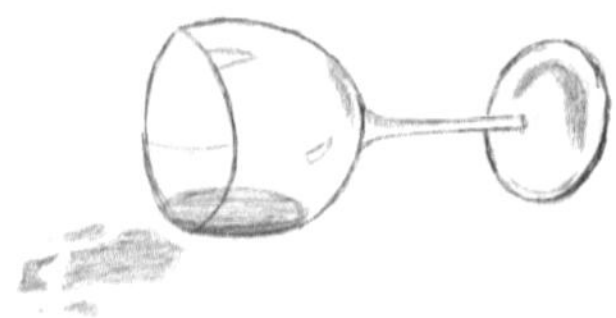

Breena and I stumbled up the stairs of the apartment, using the wall and each other to balance our wobbling bodies. Each touch of her hand was a shock to my senses, lightning striking across my sensitive skin. My tongue was numb from the mead, but my mind had never been more awake. I was aware of each of her breaths that danced across my skin, aware of the giggly smiles and trailing touches.

Great waves, this woman was a temptation hidden under the mask of innocence. She knew exactly what she was doing, always had. When I'd first met the selkie, I'd thought she had no clue the effect she had on me, but tonight, she'd made it clear. She'd known it all along, and she'd been basking in the enjoyment of my suffering—my crumbling restraint.

Pleasure twisted in her with each spontaneous touch from me that slipped past my defenses. The moments my brain shut off, my icy exterior slipped, and my body did what it longed to do. In those moments, she knew I was wrapped around her little finger like a string.

We stumbled into the apartment, the smell of starchy rice and old books flooding my senses.

"Thank goodness we brought food back with us," Breena said with a laugh as she set down a basket she'd swiped from the tavern's kitchen. "I hadn't realized how bad that rice was until I tried other types of human food."

"It was horrible," I chuckled in agreement. "Better than the raw fish, though."

"*Anything* is better than that raw fish," Breena said. "I fear when I take my seal form once again, I won't be able to swallow them down like I used to."

"That is if we can manage to take down the huge net. You know that's the first thing we have to do before returning to our families, right?" I asked, bringing the mood down as I always managed to do.

"I know. We find my pelt, return to the sea, and take down the enclosure. Then, and only then, do we go home," Breena said. "But until that time comes..."

She trailed off, causing everything in me to stir. Just one look from her sent shivers down my whole body because I knew the intention behind those big, brown eyes.

"Until that time comes, we don't take things too seriously?" I asked, pulling her in by the small of her back. She yelped as she collided against my chest. Her squeal melted into drunken laughter that reached the depths of her. I could feel the vibrations of it hitting her stomach as she pressed herself against me.

"Exactly." Breena's gaze wandered over my face before it dropped to my mouth. Her hand found the side of my face, and she cupped my cheek. I leaned into her touch, my eyes closing as I felt her warmth. I sank into her embrace, the shards of ice protecting my heart melting one by one, and I let them. I did nothing to stop the softness from consuming me, because that was what she begged of me. I was never willing to do it for myself, but *depths*, I would do it for her. That should scare me, but for some baffling reason, it didn't. Not tonight.

"Look at me," she demanded, her tone hardening. I did as she asked, my eyes blinking open. They focused on her and the way she drank me in. "Let go with me."

It was all the permission I needed. Slipping my hand to the back of her neck, I guided Breena's lips to mine. I tasted the sweet mead on her tongue as she let me in, allowing me to explore her.

She pulled back and took a breath before a devious smile crossed her face. She pushed me onto the settee with reduced strength, and I sank into the floral cushions. Staring at her expectantly, my lips cried for more of her. My entire body zinged, downright *demanding* more.

Breena crawled into my lap, a knee on each side of my hips. She stole more kisses, and I let her. I'd let this woman take whatever she wanted from me, because I wanted it just as badly.

"What am I going to do with you, siren?" she said as she pulled back from my mouth. We both caught our breaths, our chests heaving. She licked her lips, looking at me as if she could devour me whole, and somehow, I believed it.

"Whatever that wicked little mind of yours comes up with."

"Wicked?" she asked, a smile matching the word she spoke.

"You think I don't see the darkness that lurks within you? The spark that lights you when you use your strength? You could break me in more ways than one, little droplet."

"But the risk of it all makes it so much more fun." Her hips rocked forward as she pressed into me harder.

"I may be stronger, but you have more magic than either of us knows. You *are* magic. You are pure, raw power." She bent down and whispered into my ear, her words skating across my skin. "And I want to feel it."

"Are you sure about that? You might get a little... wet," I said, excitement prickling across my lower belly. No one told me I'd be able to use my magic on land, and now, it was mine to wield, mine to make this woman crumble.

"That, I'm counting on."

Using my foot, I knocked over the glass of water on the side table next to the settee, and it came clattering down. Water splashed us, and Breena yelped at its surprisingly cool temperature. I flicked my hand, and the spilled water began pooling on the settee before migrating toward us. It snaked up Breena's leg, and she watched as the trail of water slipped under her dress.

Her eyes bulged, and she held her bottom lip between her teeth. It was then I knew the water had reached her center. I watched her face light up, pleasure behind her eyes, satisfaction swelling in me that I was causing this reaction in her.

When I could no longer take the tease of watching, I pulled her in by the back of her neck and stifled her moan with my mouth.

This is release. This is freedom.

Breena grinded into my lap, and I could feel the water I used to elicit wicked pleasure in her soak through my skirt. I increased the vibrations through the water so I, too, felt my power. I never needed anything other than this. This right here was all I could ever ask for. I remembered that as each layer of our clothing was peeled off. I remembered it as my back hit the seat of the settee, stretching out for my selkie. And I remembered it as her kisses trailed down my body.

The water I used like a third hand intensified as the build between my thighs did. Breena could barely contain her moans, and at some point, both of us stopped trying to contain anything. We reveled in the unyielding pleasure until sweet release found us.

Water dropped to the floor, and Breena collapsed onto me. Nothing but heaving breaths and beating hearts filled my ears. After a minute, Breena propped her head up on her arms folded across my belly. Sweat beaded her hairline, and her smile reached her twinkling eyes.

A laugh poured out of her, and between heavy breaths, she said, "I've never been more thankful for water in my life."

Breena and I devoured summer soups and bread after washing up and throwing on some lounging clothes left behind by the previous owner. Exhaustion had overcome her, so she'd made her way to the bedchamber early. I, on the other hand, needed some time to relax before slipping into bed with her, and that was when I'd picked up *The Last of Elhain* and sank into the settee.

The book in my hands was one I'd never seen in my father's collection. I'd realized moments after entering the apartment that my father was no longer the owner of the place, but I hadn't told Breena. From the dust and empty cabinets, it was obvious the new owners had been gone for a while, and I hoped it would stay that way. There was no reason to freak her out.

It'd been silly of me to think this place would have still been full of my dad's belongings, that it would have smelled like him. He'd been gone for three years now, and every day, more of him was lost to this world as I was forced to stand by and witness his erasure.

Adjusting the blanket thrown over my lap to cover my toes, I took a deep breath and tried to recapture that feeling of release Breena had gifted me. And that was exactly what it had felt like—a gift. When had I ever been out of my mind for that long and smiled that much? When was the last time my chest released the tightness it always held?

These past few years had been a crushing weight that never let up. I always thought the pain of losing my father was going to ease with time, but then, the fish disappeared. We all had to endure a different kind of pain then, now a physical one.

Being on land, I was able to slip into a temporary amnesia where my problems didn't matter. I was able to throw myself into finding Breena's pelt, and instead of thinking about the next time I got to eat, I thought about the next time I got to see my grandfather.

Life had shifted in an instant the second I had run into that selkie, and more and more, it was hitting me that I was thankful for her trying to steal my fish. Because if she'd never been there, annoying me to my very core, I would be back in the Ever Wanderer, sitting in my guilt for having nothing to contribute to my pod.

The book slipped out of my hand, and I realized I had been caught back up in my mind once again. I scooped the dusty old thing off the floor and cracked it open to the page I'd been reading. Paper and water didn't go together well, so I hadn't read a book like this since I was a child. I'd missed the feeling of the paper in my hands, the way I got to go at my own pace instead of having to listen to our elders tell stories, as fascinating as they all were.

I refocused on the story of the princess, Elma, who searched for the last dragon in her kingdom. Running my fingers down the aged, burgundy spine, I allowed myself to get lost in someone else's world.

When my eyes grew heavy with sleep and mead, I rolled off the settee, placed the book on the side table, and left the blanket folded on the padded armrest.

The door to the bedchamber creaked as I pushed it open. Breena stirred and propped herself up under the thin summer blanket. The moonlight shining through the thin curtains cast a blue glow over her brown curls, illuminating her familiar figure.

"You're still awake?" I asked, concern finding its way into my tone. She'd come in here hours ago, and I thought for sure she would've been deep in a dreamland by now.

"I can't sleep." Her voice wobbled when she gripped the top of the sheets. Her face was swollen, and her cheeks shimmered in the dim light of the room.

"What's going on?" I noticed the way she rubbed the bottom of her nose with the back of her hand. Snot glistened on her skin, and I hardly doubted it was due to an illness.

"It's nothing," she said with a little sniffle. Reaching for the small table next to the bed, she grabbed an already-used hand-kerchief.

"Tell. Me. Now." I made my way to the side of the bed and nudged her over to make room for me. She scooted over, sniffling some more as she shimmied under the sheet across the bed. I climbed in after her and slid my arm under her cool pillow. The spot I rested my head on was warmed from her body, and her scent filled me with comfort despite her unease. Being here on land with Breena, I couldn't imagine never basking in this aroma again once I returned to the sea.

"It's stupid. I shouldn't be crying about it. It's just..." Breena trailed off and took a deep breath. "It's hard for me to sleep knowing my pelt is out there somewhere. And I hate that I have no idea what will become of it—or me. Here, I've been trying to get you to let go and not take things so seriously, and I'm a full-blown mess inside."

She released a tormented chuckle, a residual tear rolling down her cheek. I willed the thing away, unwilling to see the physical reminder of her pain. It evaporated into thin air, leaving a sparkle of salt behind that only I could see.

"It's not stupid. I would be more worried if you didn't care," I said. Zellia was the only person I'd ever had to comfort, and even then, she knew if she wanted more than an awkward pat on her scaled back and some mildly comforting words, she had to go else-where. My mother was far better with the feelings of others. I may have felt them as if they were my own, tortured by them, but that didn't mean I knew how to fix them or make them go away. Breena was no exception.

"I need this man, this captain, to be the one who has my pelt. At least we know where we can find him. I could survive a few more days if there was a guarantee my pelt was in his home and we could retrieve it soon enough. What I can't survive is the thought that—"

"Stop. While I can't guarantee he has it, I *can* guarantee that whoever does will not live long enough to attempt to claim you as their wife," I growled out, my eyes boring into the side of her face. She rolled over, giving me a better look at her red-rimmed eyes.

"You said that earlier. I don't believe you would go as far as to kill someone. Humans aren't fish, Sid. You can't hunt them."

"I can and I will if it means you can return to the sea to see your brother." Could she not see how much I'd given up staying here with her? What a waste it would all be if I left before she had exactly what she was after?

"Do you mean that?" she asked with a loud sniffle. It wasn't as cute as the last had been, but I wouldn't let her know otherwise.

"You know I mean it. Now, whether that's comforting to you is a different story entirely, but I mean it all the same."

"You don't even know his name, yet you'd be willing to risk it all so I could return to him," She didn't meet my eye. All she could do was run the back of her knuckles over the sand-colored sheets, as if the movement soothed her somehow.

"Because it's not about him—it's about you. If you said you needed to get home because you desperately missed the rock you sat upon, I would risk it all just the same."

She let out a snotty snort, and I took that as a victory. The tightness in my chest released me from its hold long enough for me to take a lung-filling breath, a cleansing one.

"I do also miss my rock," she said, sinking into me and the mattress further. "My brother's name is Niven. You may not care about him, but for some reason, I want you to."

"Then I will." I peered into her tired eyes. She perked up when my promise left my lips, and a lump in my throat formed, as if I had swallowed a rock. How was I able to give this woman hope? Relief? How did my words hold enough weight to possibly change the way her body poured into mine?

"Also, I meant it when I said I don't want you going around killing anyone, but I appreciate the sentiment." She spoke with a small chuckle in her voice, releasing some of the tension she'd been holding in her face.

"If I do recall, you were the one who called me a killer, who told me to drown all of the sailors while we were on the Indigo Tide." I thought back to her giggles as the fishermen struggled to stand against the waves powered by my magic.

"Well, that was different." A hint of a smirk danced at the corner of her mouth. That smile, *depths,* I didn't think I'd see it for the rest of the night.

"How so?" I asked, my head cocked on the pillow beneath me. Using the side of my arm, I fluffed the pillow up so I could get a better look at the woman next to me despite the dim lighting. Sirens could see in the dark, of course, shapes and figures that allowed us to maneuver through the night with ease. Tonight, though, I wanted to see more than just the shape of her. I wanted to see each twitch at the corner of her mouth, each time her eyes twinkled through her tears.

"I don't know. These humans, this place, it's kind of growing on me." Breena adjusted her hands so they were under the side of her face and the pressure of them on her skin pushed up her right cheek.

"It is, isn't it?" I asked, more to myself than her. Breena yawned and settled a little deeper into my side. Her grief-filled eyes grew sluggish in their blinks until she no longer tried to fight the fatigue.

"Mhm, except for that fisherman. He'll still pay, just not with his blood," she mumbled with her eyes closed, another yawn breaking up her speech. "Do you promise?"

I couldn't promise such a thing. If it came down to it, I had no qualms about relieving the man of his life if he attempted to claim the woman in my arms. She wasn't mine, and that was the whole point. She wasn't anyone's, and I'd kill that man to have it remain true.

"Sleep, little droplet," I cooed, stroking back the baby hairs that invaded her forehead. She was always beautiful, but in this state, it did more than drive me mad with desire. Her beauty shone from within, and the grief mixed with it made my very heart ache for her. "There are far better things to dream of than this."

When Breena's eyelashes began to flutter, I pursed my lips together and focused on what sleep would sound like: peace personified. A soft song flowed from my lips, swirling around Breena and sinking into her temples. The dark blue, shimmering magic penetrated her skin, her mind. I closed my own eyes as I continued to sing, and I thought of flat, warm rocks baking under the summer sun. I thought of the brilliant waves of the sea misting them, kelpies and selkies darting around in a perfect balance of peace and life. I thought of her home, what I imagined the cove looked like based on all she had told me of it.

When Breena's breaths deepened and she lost all awareness, I let my mind slip into a beautiful dreamscape full of music and freedom. I hoped that, if we slept close enough, we could live in each other's dreams, and I could keep her tears at bay there as well.

CHAPTER ELEVEN
SHORTBREAD AND SHORTCOMINGS

I woke to what I think was supposed to be a bowl of eggs on the side table next to me. Propped up against it was a fork and a well-loved recipe card for berry custard. I flipped the worn card over to discover a note from Breena scribbled on the back in crude lettering. It read:

Sid,
I'm out chasing down a lead on the docks and didn't want to wake you. Thank you for singing me to sleep last night. Your song felt like home...
Meet you at our spot on the fourth strike.
-Breena

"Felt like home," I repeated to myself out loud. As I did, my fingers found my lips, as if I could reabsorb the sentiment into my fingertips instead of letting it slip away into the morning air. Those three words replayed in my mind as I ate the watery eggs in bed and changed into a flowy white dress that hit my ankles instead of the floor where it was meant to.

Those three words replayed in my mind as I ambled through

town, taking in the scent of freshly baked bread and sea salt that lingered in the air where the village met the misty shoreline. They replayed in my mind as I walked through the doors of Muliver's Glass Masterpieces.

"Sidra! You came," my grandfather called out, that jolly smile of his spreading ear to ear. He scrambled off his stool behind the register and worked his way around the counter towards me.

"I suppose I did." I allowed the edge of my mouth to curl upward for a moment in hopes of easing the man's nerves.

"Come, the workshop is far more exciting than up here with all these knickknacks." He waved his hand dismissively at his work. When I nodded my head with yet another curl of my lips, he all but skipped to the front of his shop, where he flipped his sign over to "closed".

"You're not going to have much business if you keep flipping that sign over," I said, attempting to be charming, but instead, my words came out like a chastisement.

My grandfather directed me to the back with a nervous chuckle, dismissing the awkward interaction. I cleared my throat and followed him through the door behind the register.

He broke the tension by showing me the project he was working on. He'd prepped for a commissioned bowl and had already picked out the blue and white glass. He laid out the appropriate tools for turning the colored pieces into a cohesive unit, explaining what each tool was and its purpose in glassblowing. I'd been familiar with some of these tools from my father's many detailed stories about his work, but it was much different seeing them before me, having my grandfather place them in my hands.

My arms were speckled with raised bumps at the mere thought of a past version of my father using the same tools I now held in my hands. I'd been staring down at them, lost in my own world, when I realized his father had been talking to me, asking me a question.

"Hmm?" I mumbled, tearing my eyes from the metal clamps I gripped.

"Do you want to try?" His eyes flicked to the piece of curved metal in my hand. "If you're anything like your father, you'll be a natural."

I wanted to tell the man "No" and explain that I wasn't a natural at anything. I didn't want to disrespect my father's craft and taint my memories of it, but the way he stared at me expectantly dissolved my internal protests.

"Yes," I blurted before I could change my mind. "I'd love to."

"Alrighty then." He didn't fight his contagious smile as he tinkered with a piece of brass on the table. "You just made this old man real happy."

"Where do we start?" I asked, inspecting his shop with increasingly eager eyes.

"First, you're going to want to tie that long hair of yours back. My wife, your grandmother, used to like making a big bun right at the base of her neck. Don't want to catch yourself on fire, do you now?"

"I suppose not." I took a silky blue ribbon from his outstretched hand and began twisting my hair back the way he'd suggested. If anything, I could at least offer him nostalgia for the woman he loved.

"Ah, perfect. She was blonde like you, you know," he said with a big smile. I thought for a second that he was going to ask me to perform a twirl, but he simply took me in, his hands clasped in front of him. He seemed... proud. This man I barely knew stood before me looking proud, and all I'd done was tie my hair up. This kind of appreciation was only followed by love, and the feeling that filled me reminded me so much of my father's.

"Now these. May I?" the chipper man asked. He held out a pair of funky looking goggles with tinted lenses. I simply nodded my head and stepped forward so he could slide them onto my face. "There we go. Now you really look like Liselle."

When he took a step back, my vision was consumed by partial darkness, as if the sun had decided to depart early today. I cleared my throat, watched him through tinted glasses, and asked, "What next?"

"Now, we get to work! What're you looking to make?" he asked, leaning on his char-covered workbench.

I sat with his question, my mind running through the pieces of art he had in his shop. My mind went to the pieces my father had displayed in his apartment all those years ago, what he'd brought to the sea to show Zellia and me. I thought about what my sister had worn around her neck for years.

Her necklace was something I could never have as a hunter. I needed to be prepared in case of an attack, and that preparation didn't include jewelry that could get me killed. I hated that necklace of hers because it reminded me that she got to be a kid, and all I got was the weight of heavy responsibility.

I wasn't in the Dreslee right now, fighting for my people. No, I was here on land. The realization that I was free to wear whatever I wanted hit me, and it was the relief I didn't realize I needed.

"What about jewelry?" I asked, nerves fluttered through my stomach.

"Jewelry, huh? It's not what I typically do, but I guess you have no need for big glass pieces, do you now?" he said, more so to himself than me. He scanned his shelves and moved some things around, in search of, well, I wasn't sure. "Yeah, we can make you something small and lightweight, something wearable that you can easily take with you when you go back to the sea."

Back to the sea.

Why did those four words sit in my gut like a rock?

"Yeah. Sounds perfect."

"Alright then. Let's see what I've got." He went off into his storage room, making a racket as he dug through his things. When he came back, he held up a thin rope like the one tied around Zellia's neck. "I have an idea."

"Let's hear it." I fought a grin as I took in the excitement that bubbled up in him. He could barely contain his smile, but I didn't need to see his face to see this man's contentment. His voice said it all.

"I obviously haven't been to your home, but I've heard as much about it as a human could and, well, I know a thing or two about aquatic fashion," he said. "How about we make you a necklace? You can make the glass whatever color you'd like."

"A necklace?" I thought about it for a moment. Was I a fraud if I wore a pretty, dainty thing like my sister had? It wasn't uncommon for women in my pod to use the treasures they found in the sea to make themselves body decor, but I was never able to be one of those women. I had my chest of glass, and that was all I could allow myself.

"You're on land! Might as well have a bit of fun while you're here. What color would you like?" he asked. He held up a panel of sample glass pieces, so I shoved the protective glasses onto the top of my head so I could see the colors clearly. My eyes skimmed over various beautiful blues, hues of greens, and deep reds, but I didn't want something so obvious. I was about to scratch the whole idea and go for a ring instead when an opalescent piece of glass caught my eye. It was mostly clear but had hints of pearl running through it.

"This one," I said, tapping my nail on the seashell-inspired glass twice.

"Good choice. This one is gorgeous in the light. It will suit you well, little minnow."

I smiled at his little nickname and slid the protective glasses back over my eyes. He grabbed a pair for himself, and the two of us got to work. He showed me the ropes, blowing several swirling glass designs that resembled water droplets using spare pieces of glass from previous projects. He made sure I watched his every move, down to his glass cooling technique, and I took it all in without a second thought.

We'd only taken a brief break for shortbread cookies and tea in the little sitting area at the back of the workshop. I remember the melt-in-your-mouth cookies being my dad's favorite, but it had been so long since I'd had one, I completely forgot the taste. Not this time, though, that was for sure. I savored each little buttery bite as my grandfather told me stories of his son. He beamed with absolute pride, though, every once in a while, pain would slip into his voice.

When the conversation had died down, I'd decided to tell him about Breena. I'd caught him up on our predicament: how we'd gotten to land, why we were here, and why we hadn't been able to get back home.

"What a pairing. Well, I suppose your grandmother and I were too," he said when I was finally done talking.

"We're not a pair." I brushed shortbread crumbs off my hands by rubbing them together. The grease from the crumbs spread across my hands, making me even stickier. My grandfather handed me a hankie, and I took it with a sheepish grin. Eating on land was always so... messy.

"No, I suppose that's not what the kids are calling it these days. Mate?" he asked with a subtle tilt of his head. One of his large ears poked out from his white hair as his locks fell to the side.

I almost snorted the tea I had just taken into my mouth. This man was relentless. I shook my head, placed the porcelain cup onto the saucer on a small wooden table next to me, and reached for another cookie.

My eyes flicked to the oven, suddenly all too aware of the flames that danced over the stone walls marked by years of scorching touch.

"Yeah, we call it a mate these days, but you don't know Breena. She's, well... I'm still trying to figure her out," I admitted. I placed a hand on my hot cheek and averted my gaze.

"Alright, little minnow. I didn't mean to embarrass you. I just thought... Well, I just hoped you found yourself a partner, someone who loves you like I loved your grandmother and your father loved your mother. Because you stayed here to help her, well, I just thought..." He trailed off.

"He did love her, didn't he? My father," I said, diverting the conversation. Things were too new with Breena; it felt odd to speak whatever was going on between us into existence. Maybe part of me was scared that if I did, it would all be ripped away from me before it even began.

"He sure did," he said as his face dropped. The man who outlived his own son now had to live the rest of his days knowing he wasn't coming back. I choked on the lump in my throat, needing a distraction. I needed a different topic of conversation or to resume working on the necklace he'd wanted me to have.

"You know, the name of your store isn't very modest." I forced a chuckle out to release the tension building up in my windpipe.

"Oh, I'm aware," he said with a chuckle of his own. I wondered if his laugh was real, or if he also had to force out a lump in his throat before it transmuted into a sob. "Muliver was my father. He let me name his store when I was a wee lad, and at that age, everything he made was a masterpiece to me. When he passed and I took ownership of the shop, I didn't have the heart to change the name from 'Muliver's Glass Masterpieces.'

"The two of us made that sign hanging out front a long time ago. I couldn't imagine coming into the store each day and it not being there. This place is my life, my home, and until you stumbled in here, it was all I had left of my family. Funny how this place even brought me you."

"I assumed *your* name was Muliver," I admitted, trying not to let my embarrassment show.

"Your father never really mentioned us, did he?" he asked. I grew silent, watching as hurt passed through his eyes. "I guess I shouldn't be surprised. He never wanted to tempt you girls with any tether to land, didn't want to be the reason you chose to leave your mother behind. My name is Wallace, by the way. I know you probably don't want to call me Grandpa."

I ignored everything he said except for his name, but that didn't mean his words didn't sit in my gut. I didn't want to be the one to reconfirm his thoughts on my father, because the truth was, my father spoke of land often, just not the people he spent his time with. He all but erased his mother and father from my memory.

"Alright, Wallace. You can call me Sid."

"Ouch!" I yelped, pulling my hand back. My milky skin had turned an angry red from the sheer heat emanating from the blazing oven.

"Careful," Wallace said. He rushed over to me to take a look. Upon inspection, he clicked his tongue and ran a rag under cool water. When he pressed it to my skin, I let out an angry hiss. "When we wrap up here, you better get this hand of yours into the sea. It should heal you right up."

"I can't." I shook my head, taking the rag he had pressed against my skin. While it stung at first, the coolness of it was a quickly dissipating relief as my hot skin warmed the fabric. "Last time I went near the water, I almost passed out from the pain. I started shifting while only having my legs in the water."

"Take that cloth to the shoreline and wet it where the sea gets caught between the rocks. Press the wet rag to your palm, and that should do the trick. Fix you right up."

"Thank you. I'll bring it back," I said, motioning to the cream-colored fabric in my hands.

"Don't worry about it. I have more than I know what to do with," he said, motioning to the staircase with his thumb. Wallace lived upstairs, just as my father had lived above a local shop. The only difference was, Wallace owned his entire building. I suppose glass sales were good.

"I guess this is a good spot to end for the day," I said with a chuckle, still pressing the wet cloth to my palm. "I'm not a natural after all."

"Don't beat yourself up over it. You should have seen your father when he first started," Wallace said with a twinkle in his eyes. "He was an utter disaster. I was walking him down to the water at least once a day to heal some kind of burn or another."

"Really? I thought you said he was a natural." I glanced at the oven embedded into the workshop's far wall, fierce flames licking the stone with an insatiable hunger.

"A small fib," he said with a shrug. The small piece of glass at the end of the long metal pole resting on a stack of bricks was a warped, opalescent blob, but it had promise. Tomorrow would be better.

Tomorrow.

I guess sometime during my stay, I'd already decided there would be a tomorrow here in this quaint workshop with my human grandfather.

As I watched him clean up, I said, "By the way, that man I was in here watching the other day is a fisherman from the Indigo Tide."

I figured there was no point hiding that tidbit of information from him now. He was family, after all.

"Well, yes. He's the captain. Captain Rory. Is the Indigo Tide the ship you ladies came on?" *The captain? That scrawny little excuse for a fisherman is the captain of the Indigo Tide?*

"It is. I overheard *Rory* will return on Wednesday, and I'd like to be here when he does," I said. What I'd said had been more of a statement than a question, and I hoped he'd agree so I didn't have to turn the sentiment into a demand.

"What are you going to do? Shake him down for answers?" he asked. "He may not look like much, but the man does have a bit of influence in Barthoah. All the captains do."

"I wish a shakedown would solve this problem. I want to follow him home, find where he lives and if he's the one who took

Breena's pelt. Good chance if he's the captain, he's the one who took the chest home with him," I said, more to myself than him.

"Are you sure you want to go and do all that? What if he catches you?" Wallace asked. He sat down on the stool on the other side of me, closest to the oven. A bead of sweat rolled down his brow, and I wondered how he kept up his work in the dead of summer.

"It's worth the risk," I said with a shrug, watching that glistening bead of sweat as it tracked down his face, leaving a salty residue behind that he wouldn't be able to see.

"Says the woman who claims she doesn't have a mate," he said under his breath with a concealed smile. My grandfather knew all too well how fast a siren could fall, and he was going to keep rubbing that in until I had something to admit.

I rolled my eyes and shoved my shoulder into the older man, mumbling, "Cut it out. Can I be here on Wednesday or not?"

"Yeah, you can. And I'll do you one better. I'll ask the man for his address myself," he said with a lifted chin. A hint of mischief twinkled in his eye, and I wondered if my troublemaking streak came from him.

"Will you really get his address for us?" A shred of hope crept into my heart.

"That way, you girls can go together. Keep each other safe. I don't want you goin' and tryin' to do this on your own."

I jumped as the town's clock tower rang out four times. Breena's face flashed through my mind, as did a pang of guilt. Yet again, I'd spent an entire day stowed away in this workshop while she fought to find the answers she so desperately needed.

"I promise I won't," I said, meaning every word. I debated using his name, but something about that felt unnatural now. What I was about to say would be just as foreign, but in some odd way, it felt right. "Thanks... Grandpa."

CHAPTER TWELVE
CUCUMBER SANDWITCHES

Before meeting up with Breena, I'd stopped by the sea and wet the cloth my grandfather had given me with salty water. I'd stayed in the safety of the rocks, not ready to have my skin peeled off again so soon. When I pressed the damp rag to my palm, a burning relief washed over me. I held it there for several moments as I took in the misty horizon. It'd been a foggy day in Barthoah, and the nip of the festering breeze coming off the sea felt like home. I wondered if it felt like home to me in the same way the song I sang last night and the memories it evoked felt like home for Breena.

When I peeled the cloth off my hand, the bright red mark across my palm was now a faded pink. I pressed my curious pointer finger into the wound, and the tenderness that resided there just minutes ago had all but vanished. I supposed the sea did wonders for my skin and bones just as much as it could break and distort them. It was the sea's ever complicated sense of balance that had been impossible to ignore as the years passed me by.

"I thought I told you I'm not running out of a restaurant again," Breena whispered as she attempted to catch up to me. I headed for the large double doors in front of us, reading the entrance sign as I did. This eatery had been one I'd been eyeing since my first walk through the town center. The stone of the building was a faint pink, the windows laced with bits of colorful glass.

"And I told you we won't have to. I'll explain once we're inside, I promise," I said, noticing the way the light refracted off the beautiful pieces of glass as we approached. One of them projected a blue beam onto my arm, and for a split second, it made me miss seeing color on my skin. I missed the blueish purple scales that trailed up my arms and differentiated me from my sister's pale, pearlescent ones.

"Alright," Breena relented. "I'm trusting you, but you better not embarrass me like that again."

"I'll probably end up embarrassing you somehow, but not because we won't have the means to pay." I held open one of the double doors for her, tapping a nail on its thick wood.

"You're not going to be absolutely terrible to the people who serve us again, are you? I won't suffer through that again. I still feel bad for poor Kylan." Stopping in her tracks in the entryway, she demanded an answer from me before going inside.

"Absolutely terrible?" I asked. I hadn't been *that* bad. "I prefer to think I'm an acquired taste."

"No, you're just rude." Breena dug her shoulder into me as she walked past.

"I'll be kind, I promise," I said, promising this woman something for the second time in a few minutes. I felt like it was all I'd been doing since arriving on land, and it was about time I kept one of them. I would be more than kind; I would be an absolute delight.

Walking into the eatery after her, I let the door close softly behind me. As I stepped forward, sweet and savory aromas hit my nose: cinnamon tea, spiced rum, and I believe I detected a hint of fruity jelly. Strawberry, maybe?

The place was just as pleasant on the inside as it was on the outside. Light poured in from every angle but the far wall, where sounds emanated from the kitchen. Handcrafted figurines sat on wooden shelves that lined the wall closest to the door. When I looked closely enough, I even saw a ceramic mermaid—a more aesthetically pleasing choice than a siren I supposed.

"Hi, can I help you?" someone behind us asked. Breena whirled around to answer the man, but I beat her to it. When we both jumped to answer, he smoothed his hand down his smudged apron.

"Hello, sir! We'd like a table for just the two of us, please. Thank you oh so very much," I said with a large smile plastered across my face. This man screamed *human*, but I'd be kind to him all the same. A promise was a promise, and I supposed my grandfather was a human and he wasn't all that bad. He was the reason Breena and I were standing in this beautiful restaurant in the first place.

Breena's head swung to me as she narrowed her eyes suspiciously. I was doing exactly what she wanted, yet she still wasn't happy.

What did this woman want?

The man took us to a table by the front window, perfect for watching people passing by on the street. He set down two glasses of water and left us with a stiff parchment with the meal options for the day written on it. While Breena read off our options, I debated how I would tell her about my grandfather. I suppose it didn't matter to her; we would both be going our separate ways after this. Still, for some odd reason, I wanted her to know about him, and not just because we needed him for our plan on Wednesday. I wanted her to know about him in the way that Breena wanted to tell me her brother's name.

"So, are you going to tell me," Breena leaned in, "why we won't have to run this time?"

"We have coin now," I said, moving a glass cup over the wooden table toward me. I took a sip and peered out the window to a couple of children by the town fountain. "My grandfather gave it to us. He's also going to—"

"Your grandfather?" Breena asked. "Why didn't you tell me you have family here?"

I stared at her and sucked my lower lip into my mouth. I bit down and glanced up to the ceiling as I thought about how to explain this situation, how I'd been meeting up with him instead of helping her find her pelt.

"Because you didn't know about him," Breena answered for me. "Is this good news?"

"Yeah, I think it is. He's actually going to help us. He owns the glassblowing shop in town, and I ran into him when I was following the fisherman. When he saw me, he recognized me and, well, we got to talking. He gave me coin and told me to come back, so I did. I was there today. He told me the fisherman would return on Wednesday and that he is the captain of the Indigo Tide."

"He is?" Breena asked, her already large eyes widening.

"Yeah, and my grandfather has agreed to let the both of us go into his shop on Wednesday. He'll give us the man's address so we can get your pelt back once and for all. I was thinking that, even though my grandfather has the address covered, it would be good for us to go into the shop so you can get a sense of this captain. You think you'll be able to tell if he's the one if you get close enough to him? It would be nice to have some idea before breaking into the man's house."

"I won't be able to tell, but I still want to go." Breena twisted her hands on top of the table, and I slid her a glass of water to distract her anxious fingers. She mindlessly grabbed onto the glass, not taking a sip but also no longer fidgeting.

"You do?" I asked.

"I want to meet your family, and I want to make sure the captain doesn't get away in case your grandfather can't get his address. We will be the back-up plan," she said. I couldn't help but smile when Breena told me she wanted to meet my family; I didn't hear much else after that.

"Alright then, looks like we have a plan," I said with a bob of my head.

"It feels good to have direction. And did you say coin?" Breena asked. She propped her head up on the heels of her palms, her umber curls cascading around the warm skin of her face.

I laughed and said, "We do, in fact, have coin. I have enough to spoil you with..." I looked down at the sheet of paper on the table and read the first special off the list. "Cucumber sandwiches."

"I do love myself a sandwich, but I think you picked the most expensive thing they have here," Breena said, staring at the sheet with the meal options scrolled onto it in black ink. "Are you sure we don't have to run again? How many coins did your grandfather give you anyway?"

"We're not running," I said with a chuckle. "I think we deserve an expensive treat, don't you? If we have to acquire more coin somehow, we will. It's not like we don't have skills, you and me. How hard could it be to earn some coin?"

"I was hoping you'd say that. I suppose you have a point. My strength could come in handy down at the docks," Breena said. She set the parchment down and traced my face with her gaze.

"You're not getting a job on the docks," I said, no hint of emotion in my voice. My stoic face gave her no indication of the impact her words had on me, and I would maintain that protective wall as long as I could.

"Why not?" Breena asked. She tilted her chin to the side, and I attempted to ignore the way her forehead scrunched as a precursor to the disapproval I knew was sure to come.

"Being around sailors is what got you into trouble in the first place, remember?"

"You want me to hide from them to avoid their temptation? I have to hide instead of them changing their behavior—how does that make any sense?" she said, that crinkle in her brow deepening like I knew it was bound to do.

"Haven't you been doing that your whole life? This is your first time leaving your precious cove, is it not?" I pointed out the inconsistencies in her logic. Did she seriously not see the issue?

"I'm done hiding. This whole trip, despite it having a tragic start... Well, I regret nothing."

"How can you say that while your pelt is still out there somewhere?" I asked.

Breena sighed and rubbed her temple before saying, "I'm not happy it was taken. It tears me up inside—I shouldn't even have to explain that to you—but I can't imagine going home after all this and just forgetting about everything we've learned here, can you?"

"Are you asking if I'd come back to land?" Goosebumps rose over my skin, and I tried desperately to ignore my gut screaming at me. "Because the answer is no."

"Truly?" She propped her elbows up on the table, placing her fingers just below her trembling lips, as if to hold them still so I wouldn't notice. Foolish of her to think I would ever be oblivious to that mouth.

"Truly." The lie was a rock in my throat, but I wouldn't budge. How could I ever speak the words in my heart out loud? I didn't need those dangerous truths to be heard by the universe.

When the server came back, we ordered a tray full of cucumber sandwiches, along with a tea like what we had sipped on the other day. The only difference was, this time, it was cold and came in a tall glass instead of a teacup. I hadn't been sure if it'd been a mistake, but I liked the drink nonetheless. Plus, it was something I could get Breena to drink, so I'd take it as a win.

As we ate the refreshing little sandwich bites, I thought a lot about what Breena said. After returning to the sea, I shouldn't have wanted to come back to land. The truth was, since being here,

I hadn't had to kill anything. I hadn't had to worry about intruders invading our territory and what I'd be forced to do if they did. I was able to shove thoughts of the pod starving out my head for a few blissful hours of the day. Was it so wrong to not want to give that all up?

When Breena finished her cold tea, she pushed her water glass to me and said, "Do you think you could add bubbles to my water?"

"Bubbles? Sure, I can try," I said with a shrug, wondering where she'd gotten such an idea. I knew I could draw oxygen through the sea, but like most of my skills, I'd never practiced them on land. I wasn't sure what all was possible for me here yet.

Sure enough, when I placed my hands around her glass, I was able to churn the water enough that hundreds of tiny bubbles filled her water. They consistently rose to the surface and popped in fizzy harmony. It was a skill I never would have attempted without this odd request, but this wasn't the first time Breena had pushed my boundaries, and I had a feeling it wouldn't be the last.

Breena took a sip of the water, and a smile spread from one ear to the next before she could set her glass back down. She ran her tongue over her bottom lip, as if deciding exactly how she liked having those tiny bubbles popping in her mouth.

"Good?" I was eager to know what she was thinking, eager to think of something else entirely, something delightful like I had promised.

"You made my water actually drinkable!" Breena pushed the glass toward me so I could try for myself. I took a gulp for myself, and the air in the water instantly rose back up from my belly and erupted through my lips and nose.

"*Depths*," I cursed, slapping my hand over my mouth. The table of women in black summer dresses and pointy hats sitting next to us politely applauded my belch.

"I believe you have that coven's approval," Breena said with a giggle. I felt heat rising to my face when I glanced at another table and noticed the man there sneering at me.

"I think I'll leave the bubbly water for you." My hand was held over my chest, preparing for another round of rejected air I feared would come. "But if this gets you to drink more water, I will be your personal bubbler."

"Your magic is useful for more than one other thing, I suppose," Breena said, grabbing another square sandwich off the plate. The cucumber sandwiches stacked upon the plate were smaller than my palm, tea sized, someone called them. She bit into the soft bread, a firm crunch following.

"Mmm, and is that one other thing tricking sailors or making you scream?" I said as she finished up her bite. The crumbs gathered at the corner of her mouth tempted me to eat another tea sandwich. These green cucumber things were quite juicy and fresh, and I didn't mind them paired with the creamy substance slathered onto each slice of bread.

Breena choked on her bite and said, "I cannot believe you just said that in public."

"Well, I told you I'd embarrass you somehow. I can't be nice to the humans who work here *and* forgo embarrassing you at the same time. That requires a skill I don't possess."

"I thought you already covered the latter with your belch," she said. She eyed the sandwich-eating witches next to us, who were now no longer focused on us, but on a leatherback journal sitting upon their table. The paper was scribbled with all sorts of interesting and unfamiliar symbols and text, and I wondered where these women were hiding when I was a girl looking for magic on land.

"That embarrassed me more than you," I admitted with a crooked smile. "And what? Are you going to argue what my magic does to you?"

"I mean..." She trailed off, and the hand holding up her chin slid in front of her mouth to hide her smile from me. "I suppose I'll have to adjust my previous statement just a little bit."

"I want to hear how much you love it. No hiding behind your hand," I said.

Breena lowered her hands and clasped them in front of her. She sat up straight and said, "And I want world peace, but I know that won't happen."

I shook my head from across the table, loving the fire that coursed through her veins. I used to think stubbornness was the worst quality, and then I met Breena. I loved the way she challenged me and made me work hard for the things I wanted most, which, most of the time, was the stubborn selkie herself.

CHAPTER THIRTEEN
BOUND BY FLESH AND WATER

Breena ran her nails down her arm, creating ashen lines in her golden-brown complexion.

"Stop that." I pulled her hand away from her skin before she mindlessly called forth her own blood.

"Ugh! I'm so itchy. I can't *stand* being in this skin," Breena said, releasing a lungful of air. I gave her her hand back, and she sat on it quickly to avoid the gnawing temptation to scratch. "I've never been out of the water this long. Usually, I'll hang out on the shoreline and chat on the rocks with Niven or one of the other selkies for a bit, and then I'll head back to the water. I barely spend time on land, especially these days. I've been too busy trying to hunt."

"Have you drank water at all today?" I asked. Broken blood vessels were already showing under her damaged, irritated skin. They were nothing compared to the flesh tearing I endured when excess amounts of salt touched my skin, but that didn't mean I wanted to see her beautiful arms marred up by her own volition.

Breena glanced over her shoulder to the sink, where a glass sat untouched since I filled it this morning. I chuckled and retrieved the cup off the counter, filling it with bubbles like I had at the restaurant a couple days prior. Forcing it to her lips, she looked up at me as if I was forcing her to eat her own hand.

"Drink," I demanded. Breena gave in and took the glass with both hands. She didn't take her time sipping it, and the contents of the cup was drained in no more than a minute. "Good girl."

"It's disgusting, but not as bad with the bubbles in it."

"I'll make you tea next time. Now that we have a bit of coin, we can go shopping if you'd like. We can grab a few things to have around here other than the necessities we... acquired after our time in the tavern." I took the cup from her and held its thick glass bottom. The fresh water that had gathered beneath the glass would have stung if my grandpa's trick with the saltwater rag hadn't cleared up my burn.

Breena stared at me with a blank expression before her eyes fell into a cautious squint.

"What?" I traced her confused look with my own.

"It sounds like you want to settle right in. Are you sure you want to go and do all that?" she asked. "Tomorrow is Wednesday."

She didn't need to point out what was happening on Wednesday.

"You need to be comfortable while you're here, even if it's just for one more day. That's all," I said. I gripped the bottom of that glass as the lie pierced my throat like a blade. Had I realized it was a lie before I said it?

"Well, if that's the case, I need to be submerged in water. It's the only thing that's going to make my skin feel better. You can give me as many glasses of water as you want, but—"

I began walking away from her, not needing to hear whatever she was going to say next. Her words triggered an idea, and I had just the thing to fix this problem of hers.

"Sidra?" Breena asked.

I walked into the bathing chamber and headed straight for the clawfoot tub sitting smack dab in the center of the room. I yanked on the brass faucet, letting the tub fill with steamy water. There was a small table next to it full of glass jars, and I begged for one of them to be sea salt. If the sea in small doses could fix the burn on my palm, there was a good chance it would help Breena with her skin dryness.

As I waited for the large tub to fill, I tinkered with each one until I found exactly what I needed. I dumped the entire jar into the tub, knowing even then that it wouldn't compare to the salinity of the sea.

While the water filled the tub, I cracked open the bottom half of the window, allowing a cool breeze to meet my skin. The fresh air blew through the wispy white curtains, sending the scent of the sea with it. From the bathing chamber window, I couldn't see the water, but I could certainly hear it if I closed my eyes and listened carefully for its familiar lullaby.

I loved how crisp the nights in Barthoah were. After a long, warm day, nighttime was an escape from my beloved light. Night felt like swimming in the depths of the Dreslee after lounging in the Kilkov, a cold cleanse from the warmth. The break only made the return that much more pleasurable.

When the tub was three quarters full, I shut off the water. I heard Breena call after me again as I removed my clothing piece by piece—first the white dress, then the underlayers beneath it. I climbed into the water and relaxed into the belly of the giant tub.

I let myself sink down, my head slipping below the surface. My eyes fell shut, and the immediate silence of being surrounded by water filled my heart with longing for my home.

A muffled sound pulled me from the water, so I sat up and wiped the salty droplets out of my eyes. The warm bathwater had a slight zing like the sea did, but it was so faint, I had to close my eyes and focus to feel it.

"Sid?" Breena called again, and I realized now what the muffled sound had been.

"Oh, stop calling after me and just get in here," I said. My hands moved through the water, the warm liquid swimming through my fingers. The sensation was odd without webbing between them. There was less friction, less force. No wonder humans always seemed so pathetic once they hit the water. I always found their flailing hilariously entertaining.

After hearing a scramble in the other room, I waited expectantly for Breena's cute little face to appear in the doorway.

"What are you up to, siren?" she asked as she peered behind the door. Her gaze flicked to the surface of the water. When she met my stare, I made sure she knew I was aware of what those beautiful eyes of hers were doing. Her chin dipped, and the shy smile that spread across her lips lit a fire deep in my belly.

"You did say you wanted to be fully submerged, so I thought I'd join you." I splashed the water with my foot. Breena tilted her head before coming out from behind the door and shutting it behind her.

"You're taking this 'letting go' suggestion a little far, don't you think?" Breena asked with an amused smirk. She slowly made her way to the edge of the tub. Trailing her finger down the pristine porcelain, she met my eye with a mischievous grin.

"I don't think I've taken it far enough," I said, grabbing her hand before her finger could get another inch closer to me. She let out a surprised yelp as my bath-warmed skin met hers. I dipped her fingertips into the water to tease her in. She bit her lip, her eyes peering through the water to what remained hidden below.

"Well, it does seem like a pretty good solution to my problem. I can't keep scratching my arm."

"No," I whispered. "You really can't."

Breena lifted one foot and sank it right into the tub before doing the same with her other. She stood in the tub, her wet gown plastered to her legs, before she sank onto my lap. The remaining fabric of her dress puffed up with air, hitting me in the face. The water then consumed the fabric, and the entire dress clung to her like a second skin.

"I'm pretty sure you're not supposed to wear your dresses in the tub." I peered down at the deep pink fabric that wrapped around her breasts in the way my hands ached to.

"And I'm pretty sure you didn't ask me to remove it," she said with a cheeky smile.

"Fair enough."

Breena shifted off me to investigate the jars sitting on top of the small wooden table next to the tub. She picked up the empty jar with salt residue dusting the bottom. She motioned to it, and I explained to her how I'd put a bit of salt in the tub to help with her skin.

The glass jars clattered and clacked against each other as she continued to use her wet hands to sort through each one.

"What are you looking for?" I asked, playing with the hem of her soaked dress.

"Mmm, I don't know. Something fun." Her eyes didn't leave the labels, and she mumbled quietly to herself as she read them all. Finally, she picked one up and examined its contents. When she opened it, the jar slipped out of her hands, and the entire thing plopped right into the water, mysterious goo and all.

Breena gasped, and my hand shot out to catch the thing before it smashed against the bottom of the porcelain tub. I secured the jar in my hand, but when I pulled it out of the water, the only thing left inside was a bit of bath water and sudsy residue from whatever had been inside of it.

"Oops," Breena said with a guilty giggle. She took the jar from me and sniffed what was left of the mystery substance before setting it back on the table. "I have no idea what it was, but at least it smells good."

She laughed and leaned back into the water, submerging herself. She stayed under for a few minutes, her dress swirling in the water as it progressively grew more and more sudsy with her movement. Relaxing into the water with her, I attempted to keep my eyes off where her dress rose a little too high and where her skin met mine.

When she came up for a breath I knew she didn't need, she moved her flattened palm over the surface of the water and the many bubbles collecting on top of it.

"Have you ever seen so many bubbles?" she asked in amazement, the amount of fragile, iridescent spheres growing by the second. Breena couldn't contain her laughter, and I couldn't remember a time I had seen her so full of joy, or the last time I had been so infected by someone else's emotions. She wore her happiness with no shame or reservation, and the glow it gifted her highlighted her beauty more than I could have ever imagined.

For the love of all things salty, why this woman? Why this selkie?

I could only lie to myself for so long, and it was becoming increasingly difficult to pretend to be indifferent towards the amazing creature sitting on the other side of this tub. I had already given in once, and depths knew I would again.

I shook my head and cleared my throat before saying, "No, but I guess now we know what was in that jar."

Breena made a pile of the suds until there was enough foam for her to pick up. She lifted the mass of bubbles into the air, and it jiggled as she moved it suspiciously close to me.

"What do you think you're doing?" I asked, holding out a hand to prevent her from getting any closer. Her strength broke right past my defenses with nothing but a small push and a giggle until she was on my lap once more. She moved fast, and the next thing I knew, that pile of foam was on top of my head, spilling down my hair.

"Oh, you're mine now," I growled before blowing foam off my face as it began rolling down my forehead. It puffed up into the air, and Breena was distracted by the way it floated above us before beginning to fall back down to the water again. I used the moment of vulnerability to my advantage.

Blue shimmery swirls invisible to Breena began looping around her, pulling her off my lap with their magical tendrils. She glanced around, confused as she began moving her curious hands through the water that had seemingly come to life.

"Wha–"

Breena's back hit the side of the tub furthest from me. Her arms shot out, splashing water over the sides. The back of her hands slammed into the porcelain, water wrapped around each wrist like a bind. She sat there flustered, straightened curls glued to her wet neck, nothing but the tops of her breasts peeking out of the water.

"You—" Breena jostled against her restraints. Her pure strength was a challenge against my magic, and it flickered and pulsed with each yank. "That magic of yours is going to get you into trouble."

"And that's exactly why I use it," I said, leaning forward until I was on all fours in front of her. The top of my ass poked up through the water, cooling my bare skin. "You look ridiculous in that wet dress."

"You look..." Breena trailed off as her eyes roamed my face. "Fucking beautiful with your clothes on the floor."

I moved in until my face was inches from hers. A droplet of water hung from the tip of her nose, and I gently kissed it away. My mind was silent, no worries of being too forward, no worries about what it all meant. And then, it hit me like a tail fin to the gut.

"It's really not fair, is it?" I asked, the pain sitting within me, mixing with something much sweeter. The water should've been cooling off by now, so why did it feel so much hotter?

"What isn't?" Breena sank into her restraints, no longer using her strength to push against them. She simply accepted that I had her, and she was mine for now.

"You. Me," I breathed. "And the fact that what we have in this moment can never last, never be more than what it is here and now."

"You never know," Breena said with a weary grin. "This world has a weird way of ensuring everything happens as it's meant to. Now, stop worrying about the future and give me what you are so desperate to."

"Desperate?"

"Mmhm…" Breena hummed, staring down at my mouth while biting her own. Our breaths mixed as I brushed her lips against mine. I wouldn't tell her just how right she was, but I fully intended on showing her all the ways her mere presence tormented me.

I held my position in front of her with a ghost of a smirk. Breena leaned forward to meet my lips, but she wasn't going anywhere, not if my magic had anything to say about it. She let out a grunt of frustration, then a plea. Not to be released, but to be touched. Kissed. *Loved.*

"Kiss me," she begged against my mouth. Those words were all I needed to cave. I brought my lips to hers in a soft expression of release and downright desire.

I teased my hand up over the bodice of her dress and cupped her. My curious thumb slid over the hardened bead at the center of her breast, pulling a small cry from her lips. She gasped into my mouth as I repeated the motion, this time, more intentionally.

"Get me out of this thing," Breena demanded, her eyes mercilessly penetrating me.

"I don't know," I teased, moving the hem of her dress up her leg until it was bunched in my hand at the crease of her thigh. Her knees were on either side of me, and she held me there much like my magic held her wrists. "It's kind of growing on me. Reminds me of the day we met when you wore that scandalously thin white shirt, completely soaked and see through."

Breena released her bottom lip from between her sharp selkie teeth.

Those teeth. I wanted to feel them against my skin, scraping and carving her claim into me.

"And I insulted your fragile sensibilities," she said.

"No." I shook my head with a chuckle. "You broke my fragile concentration."

I kissed her again, deep and needy, and she returned it, her delicious lips devouring me like I knew she could. I was lost in the way her mouth fit perfectly against mine when her lips hardened and contorted. I pulled back from Breena right as a scream ripped through her, as if she were breaking from the inside out.

I dropped the restraints I had on her faster than I could blink. Breena's screams prickled across my skin and curdled my very soul. She curled in on herself, unable to breathe. She tried to suck in air, but sobs cut her off before she could pull in a breath.

"What happened?" I asked. "What happened?" I asked again when she didn't immediately respond. I pulled her into my lap, my arms, and cradled her. In no more than ten seconds, pain shot through every cell that was in contact with her. It seared into me, blinding me from the horrified look plastered across Breena's face as she scrambled away from me through the water.

I tried to free myself from her, but that damned dress took hold of my legs like kelp, keeping me close to her. I tore the skirt of her dress as I pulled away once more, pressing my back against the opposite side of the tub. I threw up a shield of water between us, not taking the risk again that our skin would come into contact.

"He has it." The words broke through Breena's sobs, and I threw myself against the shield between us. My spread hand pressed up against it, desperate to hold her, desperate to comfort her tormented heart. "He has my pelt."

CHAPTER FOURTEEN
AND WEDNESDAY IT IS

"What's this?" Breena's curious fingers left the grass we sat upon and reached toward me. Her warm skin met my cool chest as the tips of her fingers trailed along the glass hanging around my neck. As she did, she zapped me and pulled back just as fast as the pain sank into my skin. My stomach jumped, and Breena cradled her hand as if she was protecting her own child.

The two of us exchanged a look of confusion and hurt before I averted my gaze and focused on where the rocky cliffs dropped off into the sea. Neither of us wanted to think about what had happened last night and all that had followed. We definitely didn't want to speak about it, because if we spoke it into existence, we were acknowledging that the truth we'd been avoiding was already our reality.

The two of us wouldn't be able to touch without pain until her pelt was in her possession once more. This fact was more telling than either of us wanted to admit, because Breena had no problem brushing up against the man who served us breakfast this morning, or the kind stranger who gave her an encouraging shoulder pat during our walk to the cliffs. I watched as others touched her, waiting with bated breath to see if they would wither in pain, but they never did. Only I was affected by this fisherman captain claiming Breena, and it took longer than I liked to admit to understand why.

"Sidra?" Breena asked, keeping her hands away from me this time. She twisted them in her green cotton-covered lap, a look of worry passing over her face. As much as she tried to mask her emotions with an unconvincing smile, I could see right through her wobbling façade.

"Oh!" I lifted the necklace off my chest so she could see my creation in all its glory. I wanted her to see the way the sun hit the opalescent glass and sent shards of light dancing across my skin, to see if it awakened something in her as it did for me. "I, um, needed to clear my head last night, so I made it with my grandfather while you rested. Took a few tries, but I think I finally got the droplet design right."

"You made this?" Breena's eyes lit up, and her fingers twitched, as if she was eager to run her fingers over the glass again. "It's magnificent and... familiar."

The corner of her lip curled into a smile. Not a façade, but a real, genuine smile.

"Well, when he'd asked me what I wanted to make, maybe the image of a little droplet came to mind," I admitted, releasing an embarrassed chuckle. My face burned with each word I spoke, but Breena's eyes only wandered over my face with shrouded amusement.

She cleared her throat and stretched her tempted hand over her head before leaning back on it against the blanket. The top of her hand hung off into the grass, and she tickled the blades with her ever-moving fingers. "I'm sure you had all sorts of pieces like it that you left behind. Sirens can be quite creative in that way."

"Not quite." Stretching back on my own corner of the tartan blanket, I rolled my ankles. My feet were sore from our walk up the hilly landscape to find this place—a hidden slice of peace. "As a child, I used to make all sorts of stuff from the random odds and ends I found in the sea, but it doesn't make sense to do all that now. It hasn't for a while."

"What changed?" she asked. Her eyes flicked back down to my chest as she awaited a response.

"My dad started spending more time on land when my sister, Zellia, and I grew a little older. I planned on being a tinker forever, making things for my pod to trade, but I had to become my family's hunter in his absence." My lungs took in a deep breath full of the salty, seaside air, and I relished in the power of the scent and its ability to calm me.

"You had to?" When her eyes met mine once more, they were clouded with confusion.

"Every family in the pod needs to contribute to the bounty. You don't just feed your family, you feed all the families," I explained, realizing I hadn't spoken much about my people since being here on land with Breena. Was it bad that there was a reason for that? Was it bad that I was able to breathe easier each time they slipped my mind?

"And your father wasn't around to contribute enough?" She caught on quickly. Shade from a passing cloud afforded her brief relief from the sun, allowing her to relax her furrowed brow.

"Something like that. The elders put pressure on my mother, but I could see the weight his absence had on her, and I wasn't about to let her go off with a spear. She wasn't meant to be a hunter."

"Were you?" Breena asked yet another question, probing further into the things I'd rather keep buried in the safety of my mind.

"I'm good at it," I said with a shrug. My gaze drifted from her face and got lost somewhere along the horizon where the sea washed the sky.

"That wasn't my question." The string of words uttered from her mouth sent a wave of bumps down my arms. I may have hidden my truths from my pod, my family, and myself for so long, but Breena wouldn't let me do the same to her. She demanded my truth and all the painful thoughts I never wanted to face.

"I don't know anymore," I whispered, letting the air fill with nothing but the sound of waves crashing upon rock before I spoke again. "It doesn't matter, though."

"It should be allowed to matter," she said. "You don't allow yourself to dream of a different life, do you? You've simply accepted your fate."

I may have wanted to scream from the top of this cliff that I didn't want to pick up a spear again for the rest of my life, but what good would that do? If I didn't, my mother or Zellia would have to. Zellia was meant to save lives, not take them. And ever since my father's death, my mother had been far too fragile, of both the body and the mind.

"My grandfather's shop will be opening soon. We should get over there." I began gathering my things from the blanket, shoving them into the cloth bag I'd taken from my dad's old home.

Breena threw a corner of the blanket over my hands then took a deep breath and pressed her hands on top of the tartan fabric. I stilled, feeling the pressure from her body through the thin wool, even if I couldn't feel her skin on mine. She forced me to be still and sit with these feelings ravaging my gut. I closed my eyes, a prick of emotion stinging the corners of them.

Depths, when was the last time I let myself cry? When was the last time I allowed the flood of emotion to consume me instead of holding it back like the fish trapped on the other side of the humans' merciless net?

"What you want matters." Breena's firm tone, reconfirming and healing, made my walls crumble to dust. Silent tears tracked down my face, taking with them the notion that I had to sacrifice all my happiness for those I loved.

"I told you we could have some fun before we head over to the shop," I said with a pathetic chuckle that morphed into a hiccup. "This isn't very fun."

Breena shook her head and cupped her hands over mine through the blanket, "I didn't need to have fun. I needed to make sure you're taken care of too."

"What do you mean?" I asked with a sniffle. The sea, the breeze, the sun, and the cliff we sat upon all melted away until all that remained were Breena's intense eyes locked onto mine.

"You've been taking care of me since we've gotten here, but I should have been taking care of you too. I didn't realize you needed it, but I see it now, and I think you finally do too," Breena whispered. "Will you let me take care of you? Let me hold some of the weight that burdens you?"

"We're so close to getting your pelt back. It's Wednesday. We've been waiting for this. We can't get distracted now," I said, tempted to pull my hands out from under the blanket but not having the heart to do so. I didn't realize how much I would miss her touch once it was gone. It was as if she'd been ripped from me when I hadn't realized I ever had her.

"Then promise me something." Her eyes brimmed with tears as they bore into mine.

"What?" I asked, everything in me softening again. I forgot about her pelt, my family, the net, everything, and simply existed in her gaze.

"Promise you'll share yourself with me, your truths, your burdens, and your dreams. Share them with me tomorrow if it's all too much today."

I nodded my head, stiffening my muscles so I didn't collapse into her and give in to it all right this instant. Now that her offer— or demand, more like—had been put into the universe, I realized how badly I needed someone to tell me they had my back, that they cared about taking care of me just as much as I cared about taking care of them.

It was impossible to deny just how badly I needed her. It didn't matter that she was a selkie. It didn't matter that I got wrapped up in her mess, or that I had just met the woman. Despite it all, she knew me better than any creature on this planet, and I would sooner die than deny my feelings for this woman any longer. Tomorrow, Breena wouldn't be mine. No, she'd be free, but I sure as depths would be hers.

Earlier this morning, Breena and I had risen with the sun, but neither one of us had gotten much rest. The springs of the settee had dug into my back, and my legs had grown numb from trying to curl their length against myself, so my feet didn't hit the floor. I'd demanded that Breena take the bed. Since she'd cried out everything but her soul from her body, she had no fight left, and she'd accepted it without issue. She may have been able to stretch out, unlike me, but that didn't mean sleep had found her either.

When we found ourselves back at the apartment, I was tempted to curl up in that bed and let sleep take me, but there was far too much to be done. Breena and I both raided the chest of drawers for clothes as black as night. We found dark ribbons to tie our hair with and shoved it all into a bag for later. We wouldn't be here again until after we had Breena's pelt. Then, and only then, would I be curled up in her arms, drifting off into a peaceful dreamland free of controlling fishermen and breath-stealing pain.

"Have everything you need?" Breena asked from across the room. She tidied the top drawer that we'd left in disarray after our search for acceptable articles of clothing.

As I opened my mouth, a sound emanating from the other room halted any speech that would have followed.

"What was that?" Her big brown eyes fluttered with worry, and she dropped the top in her hand to crouch next to the bed.

"Hello?" a feminine voice called out. My jaw slackened, and Breena and I stared at each other in complete shock. "Who's there?"

"Someone's here," Breena hissed, her pointed teeth peeking

out behind curved lips. My heart pounded in my hallowed chest, and my eyes darted from her to the cracked window on the left side of the bed.

Great waves.

We were on the third story; surely, we'd survive a jump from this height, right?

As I shifted my weight to make my way toward the window, the creaky old floor betrayed me. The wooden planks groaned loudly enough to pull another distressed call from the woman at the door. This time, she admitted to having a weapon in her possession. Whether it was a lie fueled by fear or not, I didn't want to stay long enough to find out.

"The window," I whispered, pointing toward it with my chin. Breena nodded her head in understanding, but she didn't look confident in my suggestion by any means. She rose from her position next to the bed then pushed the glass of the window open as wide as it would allow.

Steps pounded down the hall and stopped when the woman in the other room said, "Roderick! There you are! The lock was broken and look at this mess. Someone was in our apartment. They still may be here..."

Breena didn't care about being quiet then. She pulled off the quilt on the bed, ran to me, and scooped me right off the ground like a swaddled baby.

My stomach rose into my throat as my arms were wrapped tight, useless, as she carried me like I was nothing but a child's stuffed toy. She squeezed the both of us through the window, stepping out onto the stone ledge as a man barged into the bedchamber, a dagger in hand.

A yelp ripped from my lips as Breena leapt from the stone ledge. I squinted my eyes closed, screaming a string of curses as we free-fell. My eyes flew back open when Breena's feet hit a gravely surface, and pain shot through me as my cheek hit her chest upon impact.

She set me down, and I scrambled from the quilt as if it was full of the angry hornets I encountered as a child. Swinging my head, I noticed we weren't on the street level. Breena and I stood on the roof of the building next door as the man, Roderick, shouted at us from the open window.

"We have to get out of here," I said, kicking the blanket aside. Breena and I climbed down the iron stairs on the side of the building until we found ourselves in an alley hidden from the sun. I threw my back against the stone wall, catching my breath.

Laughter erupted out of Breena's heaving chest and poured into the silence of the morning.

"What's so funny?" I asked with panting breaths, thankful we didn't have stairs in the sea. Those things were torture.

"How many times are we going to wind up in an alley, running from humans?"

"Hopefully, this is the last," I grumbled. At least she didn't dive into the trash to hide this time. "Do you have the bag?"

Breena showed me her back and the pack that was strapped around both her shoulders.

"Good. Let's get out of here. We have to get to my grandfather's store before the captain does."

When my knuckles rapped against the door of Muliver's Glass Masterpieces, the sound of clicking locks followed moments after. I suppose my grandfather had been waiting all morning for this moment as well.

"Girls, come in," he said, not flipping the "open" sign over just yet. I waved Breena in, careful not to follow her too closely. My grandfather watched with curious eyes as we maneuvered inside, a subtle smile creeping over his aged face. "Happy to see you both this morning."

"Mhmm. This is Breena. Breena, this is, uh, my grandfather. I supposed we won't pretend you both don't already know about each other," I said with an awkward grin. I wiped my damp brow with the back of my hand and swallowed what little moisture I had left in my dry throat.

"It's so lovely to finally meet you!" Breena chimed, beating him to the expected pleasantries. She wiped her sweaty palms down the length of her skirt before holding one out to him.

"Likewise." He removed his tweed hat before taking her hand. "Honored to meet the person responsible for the extra time I've gotten with my granddaughter."

When he glanced at us again, his white brows drew in, and he said, "Why don't I grab you both some water, and you can tell me what happened."

Old people always knew when something was wrong, didn't they?

When we caught him up to speed, the man simply laughed. That's right—he laughed, just as Breena had. What was wrong with these two?

"You've been staying at your dad's old place all this time?" he chuckled. "Polly and Roderick have lived there for years now. Just got back from their extended vacation in Cerys."

"Cerys? Where's that?" Breena asked, sipping on her glass of bubbly water. My grandfather was even so kind as to slice up an orange for her drink, which Breena was quite pleased by.

"Oh, you girls have so much to learn. Cerys is the next kingdom over, ruled by a long line of Dryad Queens," he said. Water didn't abide by kingdoms. Us sea fae had our territories, and that was that. People of the land had villages within kingdoms, within continents. It truly was too much to remember.

When the sound of a knock on the front door reached us in the workshop, my grandfather rose from the wooden stool he sat on with a stifled groan. "Anyway, you two girls stay put and make yourselves comfortable. I was supposed to open the shop about twenty minutes ago."

My grandfather disappeared to tend to his customer, and Breena and I settled into the workshop as we waited for the captain to show. I was grateful he hadn't come first thing in the morning, because it gave Breena and I time to slow our racing hearts and cool off from our run through the village on this summer day.

Wallace had promised to let us know when the captain was here, so the two of us could rest in the meantime. Breena and I slipped into a much-needed sleep, her curled up on a cushion on the ground, me slung across the leather armchair.

When the signal arrived, it came in the form of three knocks on my grandpa's register. Breena woke first, her eyes more alert than mine. I blinked away my grogginess while battling the adrenaline starting to course through my veins all in the same breath.

Breena rose from where she sat on the floor and made her way to the workshop door.

"Can you tell it's him?" I asked, wondering if she needed to see him to know, or if she had an innate feeling, just by being close to him.

"Even dead asleep, I felt him the second he walked into the shop." The warm brown of her skin fell into a sickly grey hue. "It's him."

I felt as if I had a mess of ropes and nets for organs, all bunched up and tangled inside me. Breena moved closer to the door with an odd look on her face. I watched her for a second, trying to figure out what she was doing when it hit me.

Launching myself off the leather chair, I beelined toward her. She was reaching for the handle of the door that would lead her right into the arms of that man.

Before she could turn the knob, I reached for her, a deadly mistake. The two of us stifled our own screams as pain took hold. Breena fought through it faster than I and went for the knob again.

"You can't." My hand slammed onto the wood of the door.

"Being this close to him... I don't know if I have a choice," Breena said, the whites of her eyes slowly turning pink. She batted the moisture rimming her eyes away before tearing her gaze from mine.

"You can fight it." I wanted, with everything in me, to be the one to pull her into my arms. Why did *my* touch have to threaten this man's hold on her? Why did *my* touch have to be what caused her pain? "Just a little longer."

"And then what? We follow him to his home? Get even closer to him and torture me even more?" Breena asked.

"I'm not trying to torture you," I choked out. "We are so close to getting your pelt back, so I can't let that captain see you right now, can't let him have you. We're so close. Please, just stay here with me."

"I wish I could, but it feels like every cell in my body is screaming at me to go to him. I'm sorry, Sid." Breena opened the door only a sliver, but I called on the water making up her body and the humidity in the summer air. My magic swirled around her waist before she could go anywhere. She was stronger than me, and though she couldn't see my shimmery blue magic, she could feel it like ropes around her waist, and she yanked on them, hard.

The little water I was working with wasn't a match for her own power. My magic faltered under her strength, and I begged her to stop fighting me. Sweat broke out on my hairline and dripped down into my eyes as I focused on maintaining my hold as I moved far enough to reach the sink.

I yanked on the handles on either side of the faucet as hard as I could, and water poured uncontrollably out the spigot. Water spilled onto the floor as if I had broken a dam, and soon enough, the liquid mingled with my waning magic, strengthening my hold on Breena. Water wrapped all around her, tightening her arms to her waist and her legs together until she fell to the floor.

Placing a pillow under her head, I apologized profusely as she fought against me. I was growing weak, her pure strength as much a rival as the first day I met her.

A chime rang out, and Breena sank into the floor, limp.

The door swung open a moment later, and my grandfather stood in the doorway, head tilting side to side as he saw Breena on the floor in front of him, water spilling out of the sink. My hold on Breena broke, and I too dropped to the floor.

"What is going on in here?" my grandfather called out. He ran to the sink to turn off the water before kneeling next to Breena to check on the girl splayed across the sodden floor, her green dress slick and twisted like seaweed.

I apologized weakly, and with a motion of my hands, every ounce of moisture on the tile floor began migrating toward the sink's drain.

"Did you get his address?" I asked, lifting my suddenly all-too-heavy head off the floor.

My grandfather held up a small piece of parchment, dabbled by droplets of sink water, and said, "I sure did."

CHAPTER FIFTEEN
BANDITS OF THE NIGHT

"How are we supposed to steal your pelt back from the sailor if you're going to run right into his arms the second we get close to him and his house?" I took a large, angry bite of porridge then resumed pacing the workshop floor. "I'm going on my own."

"Like depths you are," Breena said, pushing off the stool she'd been leaning against. Both of us had eaten and rested our weak and shaking bodies, but neither of us were back to our best selves, and I wasn't sure when we would again.

My grandfather sat on his leather chair in the corner of the room, silently watching the two of us go back and forth with anxious, twiddling thumbs.

"There are only two things that can break me from this innate urge to go to him. The first is the obvious answer of getting my pelt back, and the second... is, well, magic," Breena said, her voice deepening on the last word.

"What are you saying?" I paused my pacing and met her gaze for the first time in twenty minutes. I couldn't let those dark, mesmerizing pools influence the decision I had to make to keep her safe.

"I'm saying, can't you use your song to hypnotize me?" Her

eyes traced the details of my face, as if she was making up for lost time.

"No. We're not meant to use our song like that on fae." I'd known this since I was a little girl. No one used their song on fae unless it was for healing purposes or to help them, never to control them. That magic was reserved for the humans, and with good reason.

"Not meant to, or you can't?" Breena asked with too much air held in her chest, too much hope.

"Not meant to, but do you really want me in your mind like that? It's just another form of control over you," I said, weary of her willingness to fall under my spell, my song.

"Yes, but this time, it will be you, not him. This time, it's someone I know... someone I *trust*." Breena stood a mere foot away from me now. My heart thrummed wildly in my ears as I felt her warm exhale skate across my left arm. I couldn't have heard her right.

Did she just say "trust"?

"Trust? You trust me?" I asked, almost feeling silly as I reconfirmed. Of course that's not what she meant.

"I do." Breena lifted her chin, a defiant stance in contrast to her soft eyes. "I've had no choice but to trust you, siren."

I wonder if she too felt the pounding of an unsteady heart—a heart that longed for the words like the ones she spoke—but entirely unsure she would ever hear them in her lifetime. Sirens, we had community, our pod, and eventually, when we grew mature enough, we found a partner we were meant to mate with. Trust, love, or anything in that realm were not always a given, even between mated partners. It was only when we found someone truly fit for us that we loved and trusted, and it always seemed to come faster than expected.

"Well, I think it's settled then," my grandfather finally chimed in from where he hid in the corner of the room. He stood and brushed shortbread cookie pieces off his lap and onto the already dirty, albeit dry, workshop floor. His shoulders fell to a relaxed state for the first time since we arrived. "You'll both go together. Keep each other safe."

I cleared my throat and begged the heat rising in my face to fade. I took a step further into the workshop and away from Breena. I'd been smart earlier not to look into her eyes, but I'd slipped up, and oh, I'd slipped up badly. Not only had I looked into her eyes, but I allowed them to crack my walls, splinter them even further than they already had been. Another crack, and I'd undoubtedly be lost in her, unable to reel back, helpless in my descent into maddening lust for the woman before me.

Depths knew, lust wasn't the only thing I had to worry about. There were much stronger forces at play here that I wouldn't yet admit to.

"Your granddaughter has nothing to worry about," Breena said. She spoke to him, but her brown eyes rimmed with gold were trained on me. "No one will lay a hand on her."

Those stubborn minnows in my belly came to life as her unblinking eyes bore into me once again.

Great waves.

Breena slid the black wool sleeves up her arms to the crease of her elbows, a bead of sweat forming on her temple as she focused.

"Do you see anything?" I whispered as she pressed her face closer to the warped glass trimmed with hammered iron.

"No, nothing yet," she grunted as she tried to reposition herself, squatting on a windowsill between two planters.

"Well, do you *feel* anything?" I asked, hoping to get something out of her. I waited in the dewy grass, shadowed from the glow of the waning gibbous moon by a large rowan tree. The fisherman's cottage was nestled between rolling hills, the sea far from view, a surprising location, given his occupation. There were several homes scattered across the wild grasses and sporadic blooming flowers, the soft orange flicker of candlelight emanating from the one closest to us.

"No, it looks like he's not home. If he was anywhere in this cottage, I'd be able to sense his presence," Breena said. She waved me over, causing the lump in my throat that I had been trying to ignore to become unbearable. I knew what would come next, and I'd told Breena she would have to wait for the very last second before I caved and used my song against her. It was finally time.

"Are you sure you want to do this?" I said as I approached her, leaning against a planter and rubbing a waxy green leaf between my thumb and forefinger. She stilled my movement with her stare, bringing attention to my anxious fiddling. I glanced up at her, and my gaze immediately landed on her reflective eyes, sending the moon's light right back into the sky.

"Your eyes. They're beautiful." It was all I could manage, all I could think to say when this woman dripping with beauty stared back at me. She was crouched on the rocky windowsill, leaning against the window, one of her sharp teeth poking over her bottom lip, her eyes reflecting the night sky like a feral animal. Those teeth. I wanted to feel them against my skin, scraping and carving her claim on me. But she belonged to another, and the mere thought of it made me want to climb out of my skin.

This view of her reminded me of her seal form, her primal form, and something about seeing her like this finally gave me the courage I needed to do what I had to. She would get her pelt back. Tonight.

"Yes, I'm ready."

I pushed myself off the planter and positioned myself in front of her. Her bent knees were on either side of my chest, never touching me. I stretched my arm up toward her face but flinched back. My palm itched to nestle itself against her warm cheek despite my healing burn. All I could do was stare at the spot right beside her ear that I imagined I held.

"Are you?" I asked, delaying the inevitable so I had a few more moments to find the right hypnotic words. We needed to make sure she didn't go after the fisherman, but to do that, I needed to steal her freedom.

Breena nodded, but that wasn't good enough for me.

"I need you to say it," I demanded, and my jaw clicked like it always did when my tone dropped to my most serious.

"I'm ready," Breena whispered, not an ounce of fear or hesitation in her voice. When she noticed my hesitancy, she sighed and let her head fall to the side. "I know you can't touch me, but will you sing to me, siren? I want to feel you, and your songs touch my very soul."

I didn't respond, too lost to blatant shock, so she continued and said, "I remember it from the boat, you know? That day we first met. It wasn't meant for me then, but I want it to be for me now, like it was the other night. I want your song to wrap itself around me, weaving through me like you are undoubtedly already weaved into my heart."

My mouth went dry, and the only words my mind could fathom came in the way of music, an ancient language of song lost to all but the sirens. I wove myself into it, taking pieces of my heart, my soul, and transmuting them into pure energy.

The song started low in my belly as a mass of untapped energy. As it traveled through my body and up into my throat, so did that stubborn lump. When the sound of my song pierced the air, the hypnotic melody focused in on Breena and slithered into her ears, touching her in the only way I could. The second it did, Breena stilled.

"Close your eyes." My voice came out in long, mournful strokes, like black paint on a pristine canvas. Breena slowly blinked, and those big brown eyes of hers didn't open again.

When I knew she was well under my spell, those eerily melodic words of mine slipped out once more. "Your focus is on your pelt. Should the fisherman come home, you will not go to him. You will feel no pull from the link between you and the captain," I uttered.

Breena didn't move except for the slow tracing of her eyes behind her lids, back and forth, back and forth. I brushed a wayward curl out of her face, careful not to touch her skin, and let out a belly-emptying sigh.

"You will maintain your autonomy. Do you understand me?" I asked. Breena dipped her head, and when she straightened her neck, her glassy eyes stared back at me.

"That's good, my little droplet. Let's reclaim your freedom."

"You told me to maintain my autonomy," she whispered, her voice distant and hollow. "That wasn't the deal. What if—"

"What if nothing. This will work, I promise you," I said. I may have slipped in that little sentence, but those words didn't erase the ones before it. "Where to next?"

I nodded my chin forward, signaling it was time to move on. Breena squinted her eyes for all of one second before they softened, and her lashes fluttered. "We can go in through the back door."

My eyes flicked to the door that led to the stone patio. The space was beautifully illuminated by the moon, the wild, winding gardens surrounding the patio a satisfying juxtaposition to perfectly trimmed hedges. I could only imagine the beauty of the garden lit by the waking sun.

"After you." I motioned her forward, knowing the selkie didn't need my help getting off the window ledge. She'd jumped out of a window with me in her arms and a pack on her back, sticking the landing, no less.

Breena hopped down from the window's ledge then made her way up the stone patio steps. She was careful not to step on the moss growing out of the cracks until she was standing in front of the rear entrance of the quaint cottage. She placed her hand on the nob, and with one quick jerk, she broke the lock of the wooden door. With a satisfied smile, she pushed open the door and stepped into the home of the man who had stolen her pelt.

I followed shortly after her, lighting candles in her wake. I started with the stout beeswax candles clustered on a copper tray in the middle of a wooden dining table. When the orange glow lit up the space, Breena and I both glanced at each other. Her eyes were glazed over, but the confusion in them was clear as day.

"Are you sure this is the place?" Breena said. I nodded and handed her the parchment my grandfather had scribbled the man's address onto, wondering the same thing myself. My eyes trailed over to the corner of the room, where a rocking chair padded with a round tweed pillow sat under an oil painting of a rabbit in a rolling meadow. A copper kettle sat on the wood-burning stove, and next to it were two hearty mugs dipped in a frosty glaze.

The scent of lavender and dried orange peel hit my nose as we made our way past the kitchen into the first bedchamber of the surprisingly cozy cottage. Twine draped from one side of the room to the next, and bundles of lavender and other dried herbs were hung across it with clothing pins. Paintings of rabbits, dried herbs, and tea... The man lived with his mother, surely.

Breena's vision flicked back and forth along the floor, not paying any mind to what hung on the ceiling. She threw open the closet door and just about dove inside when she noticed a chest pushed to the back under a pile of tartan blankets.

The blankets were tossed aside, but before she could break the lock on the box, her head perked up. "He's here."

"He's what?" I hissed and spun around. Sure enough, the front door of the cottage clicked open. I could barely hear the sound of his shoes tapping along the wooden floors over the sound of my heart. Tucking myself behind the bedchamber door, I threw my back against the wall. Breena closed the closet door with herself inside, leaving only a tiny crack to see out of.

My head tilted back as his steps grew closer and closer, and I sucked in oxygen like it was my first time breathing.

What do I do? What do I do?

Think, Sidra!

Should I jump out and attack the man? Demand he give up the pelt? Wait for him to leave and tear this place apart until we found it on our own? The passing seconds felt like an eternity, yet not nearly enough time all at once.

The last thing I needed was for him to find Breena, right here in his very home, but could I really let him get away?

The footsteps grew louder, closer.

I promised Breena I wouldn't let anyone take her. I promised her so many things... including killing the man who took her pelt. But more recently, I promised I wouldn't spill his blood, and the latter sat better with me. I was not who I was in the sea. I was not my family's killer, not here.

I sucked in a breath, squeezed my eyes together, and let my mind fall still. When the fisherman rounded the corner, he pushed open the door with a loud creak. The door squeezed me closer to the wall so the knob was pressing into my tense belly. I gripped on to it, and in one sweeping motion, I pushed it out in front of me and slammed the door shut.

Breena yelped from within the closet, and the young fisherman yowled like a street cat. His hands were thrown up over his head, and his knee rose up in front of him like he aimed to kick me but couldn't commit.

"Where is it?" I yelled at the man. His shaggy copper hair fell into his eyes, and he was too stunned to push it back. All he could do was blink, and he did so rapidly. "Where is the selkie skin?"

"The what?" the man yelled back, but not as loud as I had been. His voice was weak, shaking, nothing like what I heard from him on the Indigo Tide. This man was a fisherman, a captain, and he cowered before me like he had seen the Sea Goddess herself.

I blinked away my slitted pupils and straightened my spine before the man soiled himself.

Great waves, this is the captain I've been preparing myself for?

"The pelt. Where is it?" I asked again, losing my patience but not my edge. My eyes flicked to the closet door still ajar. I noticed a piece of curly brown hair poking through the crack, and I willed Breena through our hypnotic link to stay inside and away from the man in front of me. "Give it to me now, and no harm will come to you."

"And my mother? Will you spare her like you promised?" His voice wobbled as he clutched the hem of his shirt with white knuckles.

"Your mother? I don't give a shit about your mother," I barked. When I saw the tears rimming his soft green eyes, I cleared my throat and let my scowl fall. Fish didn't beg. Fish didn't cry for their family and plead for their safety.

What am I doing?

I stared into his watery eyes, trying to find a lick of malice to keep the fire in me going, but all I felt from him was sorrow and pain. The single tear rolling down his freckled cheek was enough to wash away the rage in my gut and put out the fire within me for good.

"Yes, I will spare her. I'm not here to hurt you," I admitted, realizing this man wasn't here to hurt us either. I called for Breena, who hesitantly crawled out of his closet on all fours. When she lifted her head, her glowing eyes made the fisherman flinch. He reached for the candlestick on the table next to him, but he didn't take his eyes off the selkie as he lit it.

"It's yours, isn't it?" He held the lit flame above Breena so the light cascaded down upon her. The glow of her irises was drowned out by the candlelight, and all that remained were her large, friendly eyes, brown and full of warmth.

She stood, straightened her black sweater, and said with cool, even words, "It is. And I'd like it back."

"I thought it was a rag at first. I thought nothing of it when I found it at the bottom of the trunk, but when I touched it, I saw you," he said. He cleared his throat and continued. "I saw flashes, bits and pieces of your life, but I didn't know what it all meant, except that I was meant to find you. I just didn't expect to find you in my closet, or with a siren."

"Do you have it here, in this cottage?" Breena asked, eyeing the trunk in the closet. I didn't blame her for disregarding everything else he'd said. I'd do the same if the man held the only thing keeping me from the sea.

"It's in the trunk in the closet, the one you presumably already found. Here..." He dug around in his pocket before stretching his arm out toward her, not moving his legs, as if he didn't want to be anywhere near Breena. "Go ahead. I don't want to touch it again. Those memories are your own."

Breena took the metal key into her hand with a cocked head and then turned back to the trunk. She knelt by it, tracing her hands along the metal caps on the corners before she stuck the key into the slot and turned it. When she dug around through the rags and pulled out her pelt, tears fell freely from her eyes.

I rushed over to her. I wasn't sure if it was safe or not, but I didn't care. I grabbed the sides of her face and planted the biggest kiss on her cheek. When no pain followed, my kisses moved to her forehead, her nose, all the places I had been tempted to touch but couldn't. A giggly sob poured out of her, but she silenced herself with my lips. She pulled me into her, her pelt sandwiched between us as we fell onto the pile of discarded blankets.

Admittedly, I'd forgotten about the man until the floorboard wined under his shifting weight. I pulled myself off Breena, but not before sneaking in one final kiss. I climbed to my feet and helped her up until we were standing side by side. The side of my arm pressed into the side of hers so not a mere centimeter kept us apart.

"Thank you, captain, for giving her pelt back so freely," I said, noticing the way the candlelight lit up his features. I hadn't thought about the fact that while Breena and I had been able to see him upon his entrance though the dark, the same couldn't have been said for him. The man came home to creatures in the dark screaming at him to return the skin he'd stolen. I'd forgive his tears for now.

"When I marry, it won't be because my husband or wife didn't have a choice in the matter. And from what I can see, your heart is already with another," he said to Breena with a coy smile.

"Something like that," she said, pressing herself harder into my side.

"What I don't understand is how your skin wound up in my chest. Or your pelt in my trunk, I should say," he said, his laugh awkward but real.

"That's a long story," I said. "And I have some questions of my own. Do you have cookies, perchance?"

"And tea," he said with a bob of his head. "But I have my mother's birthday celebration to get to. I only came back to the house because I'd forgotten her gift. Why don't you both come back tomorrow for tea and cookies, and we can talk. There's much to discuss."

Breena and I shared a glance, and she nodded first.

"Splendid. It's settled, then," he said, brushing one of his large hands down his slacks. His chest deflated, and his shoulders fell for the first time since I jumped out from behind his bedchamber door. I knew the man *had* to be drenched in his own sweat, if not other bodily fluids. "Oh, and next time, I ask that you use the front door."

CHAPTER SIXTEEN
BURNT COOKIES AND HIDDEN TRUTHS

With more pressing matters to attend to, Breena and I were admittedly late to Rory's house for tea. Thanks to my grandfather's spare room, we'd finally been able to stretch out in a bed again, yet somehow, I'd wound up just as curled up as I'd been on the settee. This time, though, it was because I was curled up in her arms. We hadn't spent all that much time sleeping, or talking for that matter, and for that, I was left feeling both in the clouds... and exhausted.

With Breena's pelt back, I was able to break our hypnotic link without having to worry about what kind of pull Rory would unknowingly have on her. So, when we'd showed up at his door approximately an hour late, the feelings that consumed me were not of fear and hatred, but anticipation and curiosity.

Did I trust the captain? Certainly not. But was I scared of him? Never again.

Rory welcomed us into his home that his mother didn't reside in like I'd originally suspected. He sat us down in his sitting room and scuttled off to make a second batch of tea because, apparently, the first one had grown cold in our absence.

When he came back and handed us both a steaming cup of dark tea, we'd accepted and took it as our cue to start talking about our time thus far in Barthoah and how we'd come to get here.

After Breena and I took turns telling him all we thought he needed to know, I leaned back in the settee he'd assigned us and said, "We've told you our story, so I believe it's time for you to start sharing yours, starting with an explanation of that massive net off the coast of Barthoah," I said. "Where you captured us, might I add."

I grumbled under my breath, but Rory barely spared me a glance, staring off into the kitchen and sniffing the fragrant air.

"Ah! I forgot the cookies." Rory sprang from his seat and ran off into the kitchen, ignoring my question. Whether it was intentional or not, I didn't care. The result was the same, and I was still no closer to finding the truth.

"Fisherman..." I called in a warning tone. "Don't hold back."

The man glanced over his shoulder at me as he pulled a stone tray from the oven. I wasn't beyond hypnotizing this man and digging around in that little mind of his for the information I sought. The only reason I was attempting to play nice was for Breena's sake.

A sigh echoed from the other room, but Rory no longer faced me as he pulled a maroon plate from one of his cabinets.

"My father commissioned the Indigo Tide before I was born and started his very own fishing company here in Barthoah. I've been in the business since I was a lad, out on the open seas with my father," Rory started as he transferred the cookies to the small plate. He peered down at the pile of treats, as if he wasn't sure he could wait till he was seated to eat one. "When he passed, he put the Indio Tide and his seaside cottage in my name. Back then, we took what we needed and no more. Yes, the war had already started, long before either you or I existed, but things as a child were just..."

"Different?" I asked, knowing all too well what he meant. As a child, we were both untouched by the war. It had its looming presence over me in the sea, and I'm sure over him while he was sailing with his father. But back then, my father was alive and our pod wasn't starving, and I'm sure life for Rory was far simpler.

"Yeah, that's one way to put it. Back then, I wasn't forced to destroy the very place I love."

"What do you mean by 'forced'?" Breena asked. She made herself comfortable on the settee, burying her back into the overstuffed cotton pillow behind her.

"Do you think I want to drain the sea of its resources? For the past few years, we have been overfishing and then some. As a fisherman, I have always seen it as my job to fish just enough to feed the people of Barthoah, but never more than that. Never enough for fish to go to waste or to have a negative impact on the sea. I resent what my father's business has become, what *I* have turned it into," the fisherman said. He set the plate down on a table situated between us and the settee. When he finally sat, the tartan furniture groaned as he settled into it.

"You're the captain. Aren't you the one giving the orders?" I asked. Rory leaned back and ran his large, calloused hand over his stubbly chin.

"If only it was that simple," he said with a half-hearted chuckle, moving his hand to scratch the back of his neck. "You know, I'm surprised you don't know more about this, being a siren and all. You are a siren, right?"

"I am. What do I have to do with it?" I asked. Breena stared at the side of my face, and I was thankful I no longer had to rely on longing gazes to feel her on my skin. I kept my eyes fixed on Rory but stretched my fingers around Breena's thigh and gave her a squeeze. She was warm even though her skin was only covered by a thin cotton dress. "I didn't tell people to put up a net and steal all the fish in the sea. What are you even doing with all those fish, anyway?"

"You may not have anything to do with the nets and overfishing, but your people do. Never made any sense to me. You're killing yourselves, don't you realize? We move so many fish from those enclosures every single day, it's only a matter of time before—"

"Enclosures, plural? My people? What are you talking about?" I sputtered. My other hand clenched against my thigh in a tight fist. I tried to hide that it shook, but Breena placed her hand on mine anyway. The fact that she was able to keep it there without causing either one of us insufferable pain calmed me in itself.

"The hybrids," he said with a scrunched face. "They are the ones who put up the nets. And yes, there is more than one netted enclosure. Far more."

"That's not possible. The humans started this war between us, and they wanted to finish it by starving us out because you're all a bunch of cowards! Can't even come to the sea and do it your-selves," I barked at the man before me, who shifted as if he wasn't sure if he should cross his legs or not. I'd been waiting three years to finally get in front of a human again so I could tear them apart for what they did to my father, my pod, my home. Here *Rory* was, and I didn't want to harm him. I wanted to tell him to sit up and have a little confidence. How was I supposed to avenge my pod and sea when the person responsible for stealing the fish was, well, *Rory*?

"We agree on one thing: the humans did start the original war, and for that, I'm deeply sorry. The fishermen's backlash over their hybrid children back then never sat right with me. But I suppose these days, the hybrids are the ones who want you dead, not the fishermen. Why, I don't know. They keep their secrets closely guarded," Rory said.

When I took my time to answer, he picked his mug off the side table and took a long pull. He closed his eyes as he enjoyed his warm tea, and I heard the clatter of Breena picking her mug up as well. I suppose he did make the beverage look quite tasty on this chilly morning.

I stared at the gentle steam rising from the fisherman's mug as I contemplated his words. It wasn't impossible to think the hybrids could have planned the nets, as they knew better than anyone how that would impact the sea fae. But the question was, why? And was I really supposed to believe the humans were innocent in this?

Not likely.

"Even if I did believe you that the hybrids were the ones behind this, why would you listen to them and go against your own wishes? What do they have on you?" I asked.

"Everything." As he set his mug down, a solemn expression plastered itself across his sun-tanned face. "They may be half of what you are, but that doesn't make them weak. My mother is only breathing because they allow it."

I dropped both my gaze and my tone and said, "That's why you asked me to spare your mother. You thought I was one of them."

"Do they visit you often? Threaten you and your family?" Breena asked. As her question left her lips, it hit me: of course, they threatened him. They didn't have the skill to take what they wanted. None of these hybrids would have their song. Try as they might to use the language of our people, the sound that emanated from their throats would never bend the fisherman's will.

"Often enough to not let me forget why I'm going against my values and draining the sea of its very lifeforce. If I could retire from this life as a fisherman and move on to just about any other vocation, I would. That's why I don't live by the sea anymore," he said. "The mere sight of it makes me sick these days; I could drown in my own guilt. But the life of my mother has to be worth all of this mess, this death and pain."

"One person in exchange for the entire sea," I grumbled, my jaw clicking.

"Wouldn't you do the same?" His gaze flicked to Breena, and then he stared down to where our hands met, and for the first time, I understood this human man. He knew of sacrifice, as did I.

He also knew what he wasn't willing to sacrifice, and I too was beginning to understand my own limits, where I drew my line in the sand.

I cleared my throat and thought it best to move past our little side conversation. Knowing about his mother and what he would and wouldn't give up wasn't going to help me take down these nets or the hybrids who put them there.

"Tell me more about the hybrids," I demanded. "Most of the hybrids in my pod left years ago or were killed by your kind. Human fishermen."

"They've taken up a home here on land over the past decade, though I couldn't tell you where that home is. They never come around town, and they only visit me here after dark. Their words come in the way of demand, and they make each one of those demands short and to the point. The one who leads them wastes no breath on me."

"Interesting. They've formed a new pod here on land. Tell me about this leader of theirs. Because whoever it was certainly wasn't a leader of my pod," I said.

"Her name is Tinelle, though I haven't yet met with her, only her little henchwomen."

Breena stole my attention as she rubbed her hand up my arm, as if to warm my chilled skin. The bumps that covered my flesh soon after caused me to finally relent. I picked up the mug Rory had offered off the table and peered inside. The liquid within was the darkest tea I had ever seen, like the sea under the stars. As I pulled the ceramic cup away from my lips and swallowed the steamy drink, Breena asked, "Do you know her?"

"Tinelle? I've never heard of this hybrid. She must have grown up here on land, or at least she's been here a very long time."

"So you really have no idea what their motivations are for setting up the nets and stealing the fish? The hybrids, I mean," Breena said.

Rory answered this time. "No. All I know is what they have demanded of us. My men and I have set up enclosures all along the coast on their behalf, twenty-three of them in total, all massive, all trapping the sea's creatures within their rope walls. We deliver fish to a neutral site for the hybrids, keep a portion for Barthoah, and then sell the rest to nearby inland villages, giving the hybrids almost all the profit. Even then, there are far too many fish. So much waste, I..." The fisherman cleared his throat and shook his head. "I dread the day my future children have to bear witness to what we have done, the irreparable damage to our home, your home. I'm not sure what awaits me after I perish, but I know it will be my own form of tort—"

"Alright, alright," I said, holding my hand up. "Save the wallowing self-pity for someone who cares. If you really feel as poorly about it as you claim, then you will help us right your wrongs."

"I won't risk my mother's life."

"How old is she? You're human, most likely in your twenties, so surely, she is close to death. Is she really worth destroying the sea for?" I asked. Breena dropped my hand and nudged me with her elbow, muttering words of disapproval in my direction.

"She's only sixty-two, and yes, she's worth it," he said, annoyance slipping into his tone.

"Well, how about this? You help us, and we'll promise to protect your mother," Breena said. "You can have the chance to make the sea a beautiful place again, a place you can be proud to share with your future children."

"You would protect my mother? How can I guarantee your plan will work and I won't get burned in the process?"

"If protecting your mother means we can go after the hybrids for what they've done, we will certainly do it. Nothing is a guarantee, fisherman, but if we don't succeed, we lose our family too. You can trust we have just as much at stake."

Rory pondered Breena's offer for a long moment before he leaned back in his chair, crossed his ankles, and said, "What do you need me to do?"

The plate of cookies was gone before the three of us had come up with anything resembling a plan. Rory had refilled our mugs three times, and I was starting to feel an odd buzz in my chest, and my speech flowed way faster than normal. The burst of energy seemed to have hit Breena and Rory too, because the three of us were babbling over each other in an excitable flurry.

"How many days do we have before the hybrids notice you're betraying them?" I asked all at once. I could hear the pounding of my quickening heartbeat in my head, and I spoke louder to drown out the insufferable noise. The sensation reminded me of when I was on a hunt, the adrenaline that coursed through my veins to encourage me to push harder.

"I'd give it five days," Rory said. He still sat on the same settee, but he sank into it more now. Not in a way that was lazy or slouched, but one that said he trusted us not to murder him right here in his very home.

Did he say five days?

"I'm expected to ask my weak and starved pod to transition and come to land to fight the hybrids with nothing but a five-day notice? That's absurd," I said. Transitioning into my siren form and then again back into my human form all within one week was downright stupid, yet I sat there considering it. At least my pod would only have to transform once, but I, on the other hand, would be risking my life before even making it to the fight.

Rory nodded, and Breena bit her lip, staring at the side of my face as if she begged for me to look at her. I couldn't let her see the gears churning in my mind.

"Five days it is," I agreed, though my mind was screaming at me in protest.

"Are you sure, Sidra? Surely, we can get a message to your pod another way," Breena said. I wondered if she thought of the blood that had smeared my back and was crusted between my toes as she stared at me with her bottom lip pulled between her teeth.

"Not a way they'll trust. I have to go. And if I only have five days, so be it."

"It's settled, then." Rory slapped his knees with his palms. "You'll both return to the sea."

"I didn't imagine when I finally found my pelt and was able to return to the Selkie Cove that I would be expected to ask my family to fight on behalf of the sirens. With the help of the human fisherman who stole my pelt, no less," Breena mumbled.

"Stole? You put your skin in my chest, and I just so happened to move it to an undisclosed second location without your knowledge," Rory said. "But I didn't even know you existed, or that either of you were aboard my ship."

"Well, yeah. I know that *now*. But my point still stands."

"That it does," I reconfirmed, giving her thigh another squeeze. I finally gave her the eye contact she had been looking for, and when I did, I was filled with the warmth of her large, brown eyes. She batted her dark eyelashes at me, and I had never been so thankful for the woman. She was willing to go back to her pod and ask her family and the rest of the selkies to fight on behalf of the sirens, but more importantly, on behalf of the sea.

"And my mother?" Rory asked, breaking the unspoken moment between me and Breena.

"She can stay with my grandfather. The hybrids won't know where to find her." I pulled my gaze from Breena to focus on Rory once more.

"Who is your grandfather?" Rory asked, fidgeting the moment his mother came up.

"Wallace from Muliver's Glass Ma—"

"Your grandfather is a human? Wouldn't that make you a—"

"No," I interrupted him right back. "I may not be a complete full blood, but I'm not a hybrid either. Not that there's anything inherently wrong with them. Just maybe... *these* hybrids," I said, referring to the peculiar pod of hybrids forming on land. Fishermen's intolerance of the hybrids is what got us all in this mess in the first place. I wasn't about to let Rory continue down the same path so many others had.

"Well, I suppose we have differing views on that."

"My father was a hybrid, and he was a good man. If anything, he had more of an appreciation for land and the humans than most sea fae," I said. "Let's get something clear. Hybrids in general are not your enemy—the ones threatening your mother are."

"I suppose. What's the difference between hybrids and full bloods anyway? Except being more human, of course."

"You don't even understand us, yet you're quick to label the hybrids your enemy?" I scoffed.

"And you've done the same for the humans," Rory said, his tone sharpening as his eyes did.

"Alright, alright," Breena finally chimed in. "And the selkies are guilty of their own mistakes, but aren't we all here to try to put that behind us? To create change to benefit all three of our kinds?"

Rory cleared his throat, and I released the rotting air filling my chest.

"Hybrids feel no pain when they transition from siren form to human form, but they also don't have the siren song—our most powerful tool," I said.

"And you feel pain and have your song?"

"A gift and a curse," I admitted. "Wallace may be human, but I exhibit all the traits of a full blood. He has been around sirens long enough to understand our ways. She'll be in good hands."

"And he makes the most delicious shortbread!" Breena mused. She stared down at the plate before us scattered with buttery crumbs before continuing with quick speech. "Not that yours weren't wonderful, of course."

"They were a little burnt," Rory said before releasing a quick chuckle.

"A little bit," Breena said, relaxing her shoulders.

"Burnt cookies aside, have we come to an agreement?" I asked.

Breena nodded her head with a quick smile. When my gaze met Rory's, he too nodded then said, "We have ourselves a deal."

CHAPTER SEVENTEEN
ALL ABOARD THE INDIGO TIDE

I couldn't bring myself to say goodbye to my grandfather, but I held the opalescent pendant we'd made together as Rory threw ropes off the port side of the Indigo Tide. They each landed on the dock with a thud until all ropes securing us to the docks of Barthoah were no longer holding us back. We were free to venture off into the sea at last.

The last time we boarded the Indigo Tide, it had been against our will, but now, here we were, climbing aboard the same fisherman's boat of our own volition.

Breena walked across the ship's wooden floorboards with her pelt hugged close to her chest. I wondered if she too was terrified of what she would find when she finally returned home. We may have only been gone a little over a week, but a lot could happen in that length of time, enough time for starvation to take those we love.

"Take us to the closest netted enclosure first," I said once Rory had pushed off a dock post. When he got behind the captain's wheel and wrapped both hands around it, his knuckles turned white.

"Why?" His question clipped short, as if this conversation was his last priority, an afterthought.

"My pod will need all the strength they can get, and I'm sure the selkies will too. We can't return empty-handed, especially if we are asking them to come to land."

Breena confirmed then settled down with her pelt on top of a stack of crates. Her feet dangled as she swung them mindlessly. She stared out into the horizon, the mist of the day dampening her sun-kissed cheeks.

I joined her on the crates, putting my weight onto them slowly in case I sent us both right through the wooden panels. They groaned beneath us but held up as I took my seat. I sat hip to hip with Breena, yet my feet had no problem finding their place on the ground, whereas hers were a few inches shy.

"You don't have to ask me twice. I'm more than happy to return fish to both your homes," he said, looking into my eyes for the first time since we boarded the Indigo Tide.

"Thank you," I said. The sentiment came out less painful than it once had.

"Breena, I'm going to need you to give me some general direction to your home. I figured we'd drop you off first. You do live on land, yes?" Rory asked.

"I live beyond the Great Aisle of Rocks," she said with a lifted chin, pride flashing in her large eyes. She still stared off into the distance, as if she could see her home from here and needed to keep her eyes locked onto the location so she would never lose track of it again.

"The Great Aisle of Rocks? I can't sail my ship through that. We would tear up the haul on those jagged boulders. That place is a death sentence," Rory said, gripping the ship's wheel even harder somehow.

"That's kind of the point," Breena said. "Drop me off just before the first layer of rock and I will travel the rest of the way myself. We made Selkie Cove our home for a reason."

"That's fair enough. I'd also choose a place humans couldn't reach me," Rory grumbled. "Especially after what I've learned of your pelt and how it felt when I picked it up."

"You mean when you claimed me?" she asked with a tilted head, analyzing the way Rory's face twisted in response.

"Can we not call it that?" Rory said as he stared off into the choppy water ahead of us. "Breena, I hope you realize I would have never touched your pelt had I known what would happen. I truly thought it was just a rag."

"So you've told me. A few times." Breena leaned back in her spot, running her gaze over Rory's features, trying to suppress a smile as she said, "I accept your apology, captain. Just don't tell me you thought my pelt was a rag again, or we're going to have a problem."

"Oh, I didn't mean it looked—"

"Rory, I'm just teasing you." Breena's face lifted, and her mouth finally cracked into a smile. She followed it up with a laugh that sounded like relief personified.

"Right. I'm sorry, I'm just extra... tense right now," Rory admitted with a weak smile. I shot him a look that told him to go on. "A little over a week back, my crew and I had a miserable journey. The waves came at us with a vengeance only the Sea Goddess herself could be responsible for. Each time I've returned to the sea since, I've been on edge, wondering when she'll show herself again."

Breena and I looked at each other and broke out in a fit of laughter. The salty sea air entered my lungs upon a sharp inhale and released with each choppy chuckle. The feeling reverberated through my chest and caused a mild ache in my belly where my muscles contracted. We didn't laugh this way in the sea, and the action was foreign to me, yet so right all at once.

"Yeah, about that..." I trailed off, a laugh lingering in my throat. I cleared it before I continued.

"What could you possibly be laughing about?" His head

swung to me specifically, and he looked me up and down. "It's unsettling to see you happy."

"Breena and I—*we* were the Sea Goddess you feared," I said, motioning between Breena and me.

"How do you mean?"

With a flick of my wrist, the water around us began to stir, lifting into waves that lapped up the sides of the ship and splashed over the rails. White foam rolled across the deck until it struck the top of Rory's leather boots.

He stared at his wet boots in quiet astonishment before his head slowly cranked to me again.

"I almost lost one of my men, and you had the rest of them praying to whichever god would listen!"

"Yes, it was quite hilarious," I mused, a little proud of myself, of both of us, for the scene we'd caused.

"Hilarious? You could have killed us!" His mouth gaped open, and I couldn't tell if he wanted to laugh or scream in relief. I don't think Rory knew either.

"I could have, yes, but I didn't. We didn't." I motioned to Breena, who still held on to her smile. "We had to get you back to land somehow."

"Yeah, that was one way to do it." His mouth finally melted into a smirk, and he gestured to Breena as he asked, "And what is it that you can do?"

"Well, I may have disposed of your precious rum. Sorry about that. It's not until we went to the Barthoah tavern that I discovered how costly the drink is."

"You tossed our rum?" he grumbled. "That was imported from the lower isles, you know."

"I didn't, but I do now. It's not very good, though, is it?"

Rory muttered something about us being ridiculous all while shaking his head. "I'd say you owe me, but... let's just call it even, aye? And are you telling me the Sea Goddess isn't real? That I've been praying to no one for safe passage my whole life?"

"I'm not about to tell you what's real and what's not. She may very well exist. What I *will* tell you is that my pod has been mimicking her since the start of our war, striking fear into the hearts of fishermen and trying to keep them out of our waters. No goddess has ever condemned us for our actions. Maybe she gets a kick out of it, or maybe the closest thing to a Sea Goddess you'll get is... us."

Rory let the words I spoke sink into his tender human brain, shaking his head in astonishment. "I can't believe this. All this time."

"All this time," I repeated back at him.

His gaze drifted off somewhere in the distance as he said, "It's a bit of a journey; you two should rest up. There's hammocks downstairs. Feel free to head below deck and make yourself comfortable. I'll call down to you when we approach the net. We'll stop by the one closest to the cove to better preserve the catch."

"You'll be okay up here?" Breena asked.

"As long as no one throws around my barrels, I'll be fine," he said with a little snicker.

Breena and I headed below deck and found ourselves in one of those human nets Rory called a hammock. I fell into the same one I'd put her in the day we'd met, and she crawled in shortly after. She rested her cheek upon my chest as she curled into my side. My hand stroked her back as I settled into her with a deep exhale.

"Five days," Breena whispered against the bare skin on my upper chest. Her warm breath tickled my neck. "Five days without you, and I feel like I just got you back."

"Are you nervous to see Niven?" I asked, thinking about how it would feel to see my own sibling. Five days was nothing in the grand scheme of things, but hadn't I only known Breena a few days longer? Isn't that how long it had taken to flip my entire reality on its head? Who knew where we would be in another five days.

"Are you nervous to see your mother and Zellia?" she asked in response to my question. I let my silence answer her. What was there to say that wouldn't form a pit in my stomach for the duration of our travels?

Breena and I sat in that silence for a long while until we both drifted off to sleep, guided by the rocking waves of the sea.

Rory hauled up a net full of fish and dumped the creatures into a large basket. He did this a second time, filling a basket next to the first: one for the Cove, one for the Dreslee. The fish flopped around, their mouths gaping open and closed as their gills flooded with air. I gathered the water that poured onto the deck and borrowed a bit extra from the sea. I created a dome of water over the two baskets to keep the fish alive and breathing until we made it to the Cove.

Breena and Rory both took turns poking the large bubble of water in quiet astonishment. Each time they did, I had to concentrate a little harder to keep my magic together, but I wouldn't tell them that, not only for my pride, but also because I saw no point in ruining their fun.

I stared at Rory as the two of them giggled like children. My eyes flicked back to the water and the netted enclosure he'd so easily captured dozens of fish from.

Twenty-three. There were twenty-three other enclosures, just like the one our ship bobbed next to. When my gaze focused back on Rory, I said, "Have you ever thought about cutting the nets? Or releasing a haul of fish for every catch you make?"

Rory stood straight and dropped his dampened hand to his side. His eyes lost their sheen, dulling and darkening as he said, "I've never attempted to cut one of the nets, but yes, early on, I did 'drop' a few catches here and there. You could never be too careful publicly doing anything noticeably... purposeful. You never know where the hybrids have eyes, who they have under their control."

"You don't trust your crew?" I asked. "And why did you stop 'dropping' your catches?"

Rory made his way back to his captain's wheel, rubbing his stubbly chin. He ran his thumb along the curved wood grain, his once proper posture drooping.

"I used to trust them, but not so much anymore, hence why the three of us are alone today," he said. "And I stopped because while I was saving a few fish here and there, it wasn't worth putting my mother and the safety of my crew's families at risk. If I drained the nets, there were less fish for our catches. The hybrids weren't satisfied with the number of fish we were hauling in each day, and well, that's when their threats became more of a reality for all of us."

"What did they do?" Breena asked, finding her spot once more on the stack of crates.

"Let's just say someone's brother was relieved of a thumb," Rory said with a wince.

"A thumb? Depths, they could have at least picked another finger," I said. Breena shot me a look that told me I was being insensitive again, so I pressed my lips together and blew a healthy amount of air from my nose.

"Well, it's just the three of us now…" Breena trailed off. "Neither one of us will tell Tinelle if you just so happen to damage the net. Permanently render it useless, even."

Rory's unconvinced expression had me building on Breena's argument before he could open his mouth. I tried to keep my tone neutral, but I heard the bitter sound of desperation slip into my speech as I said, "We're coming back in five days; surely you could get enough fish from the other twenty-two netted enclosures in that time. No one will even notice. You could probably even destroy three or four on your way back to Barthoah. We'll get the rest when we've secured our reinforcements."

Rory pondered both of our words for a minute then mumbled something to himself and wandered off to the ship's built-in fish prepping station. He swiped a large knife out of a wooden toolbox with shark-like, serrated metal teeth. The captain held it out handle side up and asked, "Which one of you wants to do the honors?"

Breena stuck her hand out and grabbed the wooden end of the knife before I could do anything about it. "It causes me no pain, and we're close enough to my home. I'll go."

She pressed both her pelt and the knife flat against her chest, as if the two items were the singular most important things to her. Why did I want to be nestled among them more than anything?

"Breena..." I trailed off, my throat tightening before I could get anything else out.

"Tell me in five days," she whispered, just loud enough that I could hear her over the sea winds and squawking birds overhead. Rory meandered away and pretended to fiddle with some odds and ends out of earshot. Paying him no mind, I stared into Breena's telling eyes, wondering how I was ever going to permanently say goodbye. This goodbye may be temporary, but what about the next? What happened when the nets were gone and the hybrids were dealt with?

"Breena, I—"

She silenced my wobbling words with a kiss. I leaned into her, all my worries vanishing. The thoughts that had plagued my mind just a minute ago were now faint whispers trapped somewhere in my mind, but they wouldn't take hold of me now. Now, she had me, and while she did, I was untouchable from my own self-doubt. I was untouchable from anything other than her, and great waves, did it feel right.

When she pulled away, I felt an odd sound bubble out of my throat, like a plea that died on my lips. My chest constricted, as if she had sucked all the air out of my lungs, and I couldn't remember how to fill them once more. I wasn't sure if Breena felt no ache in her heart, or if she was simply a master of deceit as she smiled back at me. A bittersweet emptiness rang through me, no matter her truth.

"Five days," she said again before taking a step back from me. "Tell Rory I'll see him soon, and thank him for me."

"I will." I nodded my head feverishly. "Please be careful."

"Always," Breena said, "And Sid?"

"Yeah?"

"I'm relieved Rory took me home first. Hearing the stifled screams that ripped from deep within you the first time I saw you transform was enough to last me an entire lifetime and then some. I simply cannot see you... I..."

"You don't have to," I whispered in a depraved, aching tone I hadn't heard come from my lips in years. Breena looked at me one last time then turned her back to me. She stared out into the sea for a heartbeat, slipped both sleeves of her dress over her shoulders, and let the airy fabric drop to the sodden deck. She leaped off the side, knife and pelt in hand, and didn't rise back to the surface for what felt like an eternity.

I scooped her dress up and held it close to my chest, much like she did her pelt. I suppose both of them were a part of us, a physical manifestation of the heart that beat outside of our chests.

I called Rory over to watch Breena with me as she slashed and sawed at the enclosure. She was magnificent, half-transitioned, utilizing her human upper half and swimming with ease with the help of her seal tail. As ropes loosened and frayed, creatures of all sizes flooded through gaps in the net, pushing their way in a frenzy to freedom. She continued until the entire inhumane enclosure was drained. Only then did she pop her head out of the water.

Her arm broke the surface, and she flung Rory's knife with a little smirk on her face, spraying sea water through the air around her. The blade end sank into the side of the Indigo Tide, just below where Rory and I stood. The captain shook his head and uttered his disapproval as he yanked it free.

"I'd have preferred if she just kept it," he grumbled.

"What use does a seal have for a knife?" I asked but kept my eyes on her. She waved at us then disappeared under the rippling water once more. When she next broke the surface, all parts of her human form were a distant memory replaced by a selkie indistinguishable from a natural-born seal. Most of her was blocked by swarming fish, but I did manage to see her swallow a few of the smaller creatures she'd just freed before darting off.

"Have you ever seen a selkie half-transitioned like that?" Rory asked.

"Never. But she was spectacular," I breathed.

"She really was. And you're next. Are you ready for that?"

"No," I groaned, his words breaking me from my trance. Rory's words sat there right next to Breena's in my mind, growing and warping with each passing moment. "But I have to be."

"Just think about the fact that you get to see your family. It should help with the pain," he offered.

"Thanks, human, who has never known the pain of transitioning. I'll give that try," I said with a distracted grunt, still staring out into the sea, as if I could still see Breena as she swam off toward the jagged rocks in the distance.

"Tell me about them," Rory said. I eyed the man as he got the ship moving once more. He flashed me a crooked grin as he caught me watching.

The two of us talked about my family for the duration of our travels, distracting me from the impending pain of returning home, both physical and mental. When we approached the Dreslee, both of us fell into a deep silence for longer than I'd like to admit.

Rory was the first to speak, and when he did, he asked, "What if I need to contact you in the next five days?"

"You can't, and neither can Breena," I admitted, twisting my hands on top of my lap. "But I can contact you. Keep a bonnet shell on you. If something goes wrong, you'll know."

"We'll be able to talk through the shells?" Rory sputtered. His disbelief took form in an uncertain smile that dropped into a gaped mouth.

"Of course not, don't be dense," I said. "The shell will grow warm, as if it had been baking in the summer sun. That will be your sign to meet me back here."

"That's not as fun, but it makes more sense." He closed his mouth once more, no longer looking like a suffocating fish.

I shook my head at him and unclasped the necklace my grandfather and I had made together from around my neck.

"Will you keep this safe for me until I get back?" I asked, holding it out to him.

"You should hold onto it." He took the necklace from me anyway then motioned for me to turn around, and hesitantly, I did. He resecured the necklace around my neck, careful not to catch any of my hair, then uttered the words, "There. Perfect."

"You're going to get me in trouble for this, you know." I faced him with my palm pressed onto the pendant.

"I think you're resourceful enough not to let them know about it. Not until you're ready," he said.

"Who says I ever will be?" I fiddled with the glass in my fingers, watching as the pearlescent streaks reflected the sunlight like my grandpa said they would.

Rory stared at me, his hair flopping to the side. An all-knowing smile spread across his face, and he clasped my hand in his as he said, "I thought you were a goddess of the sea? You will be."

"Thank you, Rory," I said. "For just, I don't know, being kind. Being... nothing like I thought you'd be."

"I'm happy to have shattered your expectations," he said, giving me a little nudge. It was what I needed to carry myself to the side of the ship. I motioned to the two baskets of fish surrounded in their gelatinous water spheres. Since Breena and her clan got an entire netted enclosure, we figured it was only fair I took both baskets home.

"Will you do the honors?" I asked. "Just give me a few

minutes. The last thing I need is a bunch of fish dropped on top of me mid-transition."

He nodded his head, and with that confirmation, I dove into the sea, dress and all.

Once I hit the water, I managed to take one deep breath before the itching began. The sensation started as a mild irritation and quickly grew into slicing pain across my whole body. I lost all concentration of the globes of water I'd created over the fish, and I felt the exact moment my magic failed me. White splotches clouded my vision as I lost myself to the all-consuming pain. Pressure grew along my back, where new fins would inevitably rip through the thin summer dress I still wore.

Out of nowhere, a man's voice echoed in my mind. I couldn't make it out at first, the sounds of my own screams bubbling through the water, but I tried to focus in on the sound anyway.

"Think about your family."

Rory's words became clear in my mind, and it momentarily drew me out of my haze. I pictured Zellia's sweet face as the skin on my legs began to melt together into a fleshy, scaly mess. I thought of my mother carving protection symbols into my spears as my teeth began falling out with each scream, only to be replaced by smaller, sharper ones. I saw my father walking through Barthoah as spiny fins cut through the skin on my back, my elbows, my ears, my fingers. Images of my grandfather blowing glass pendants flooded my mind as my dull human nails were replaced by razor-sharp talons. And I heard Breena giggling in bed next to me when the skin on my neck and ribs split into gills.

A large, dark shadow covered me, and I peered skyward to see a round object balancing on the edge of the ship. I darted out of the way as fast as I could in the tattered dress as wiggling fish began hitting the surface.

CHAPTER EIGHTEEN
OH, HOW I'VE MISSED YOU

Breena

Rocks jut out all around me, but the threat wasn't anything I wasn't used to. The Selkie Cove was the only home I'd ever known before discovering Barthoah. While Sid may have never left her territory, I knew the pathway through the jagged rock and violent currents like I'd been made for this journey.

I cut through the choppy water with my powerful hind flippers, dodging obstacles and fighting the currents that threatened to send me headfirst into stone.

After sawing through the netted enclosure and freeing hundreds—thousands—of fish and other sea creatures, I'd pulled the rest of my pelt up so I was in full seal form. As beautiful as I felt half transitioned, I'd needed the strength that came along with being a seal.

As I swam, the intense push and pull of the water released into a soft ebb and flow, and the rocks on either side of me rounded and divided, as if they were welcoming me home.

I broke the surface and peered up at the seaside cliffs forming a circle around me, the rocky landscape never feeling so much like an embrace as it did now. My heart fluttered as I swam closer, diving back under the water and darting in between the legs of two kelpies as they butted heads. One of their midnight-green tails wrapped around my flipper as I swam past them, so I gave them a gentle nudge with my nose. The creature with the upper half of a horse and the lower half of a mer-person freed me, and I dashed away.

The deeper into the cove I swam, the shallower and lighter the water became. I suspected it would take a day or two to start seeing most of the fish re-enter the cove, while some would never attempt to cross the rapids. There were a few, however, that had followed me through, using the path I swam as guidance. I'd let those fish be, but I'd certainly grabbed a few to eat after I first transitioned.

Niven, where are you?

Not only did I want to see my brother after being gone for what felt like months, but I also wanted to show him what I'd brought back with me. Niven was my older brother, and I didn't often like to admit it, but he was wiser too, given the number of years he had on me. My parents had passed on at different times in my life, my father taken by an orca and my mother from an unshakable illness. Niven had stepped up and raised me after their untimely deaths when I'd been far too young to say goodbye.

While true seals had a dozen or more pups in their lifetime, us selkies were more like the humans, as we only had a few. My parents had been gone for well over a decade, and only Niven and I remained. He was a father, a brother, and a best friend all in one. I'd missed sitting upon sun-warmed rocks with him, chatting about nonsense and watching young seals trying, and failing, to catch birds. So, when I needed to find him, our spot on the rocks was the first place I went.

Swimming past spotted and speckled seals, I watched for Niven's distinctive silvery pattern. When I approached the shore-line, I thrust myself out of the water onto the closest rock. My blubber cushioned my landing as always, and I waddled across sea salt-sprayed stone in search of him.

Water droplets clung to my whiskers, reminding me of Sid's little name for me. Shaking them off, I attempted to put the beautiful siren out of my mind. I had a mission, and how could I risk everything by allowing my thoughts to be consumed by her? I knew just how easily they could.

"Breena?"

I swung my head to see a brown-haired man with the silvery tail of a seal wave his two arms above him.

Niven!

Moving faster, I scooted over stones that grew progressively warmer and dryer as I continued. Seals and selkies alike chuffed and barked at me as I clumsily trampled their flippers, but I paid them no mind. When Niven was so close I could smell his distinct scent of driftwood and salt, I peeled my pelt over my face and arms, just enough that I could pull him into a tight hug.

"I knew it was you." My brother's embrace wasn't one I'd longed for while on land, but now that I had it, I didn't want him to let go, not so soon.

When he finally did, I flopped back onto the flat rock behind me, the contours in it so familiar and comforting that I cried out, "Oh, how I've missed you!"

"I've missed you too," Niven chuckled. "Where have you been?"

"I was talking to my rock. Don't be ridiculous, Niv," I said with an eye roll. He slapped my tail with his own and shook his head. I released pent up air in the form of a laugh, relieved to be home, relieved to be on my rock next to my brother, and relieved to have something to offer him—to everyone.

Sitting up, both of our smiling faces faded as a more potent reality struck me, the entire reason I'd come back home in the first place.

"What is it?" he asked, his voice deepening.

I took my time talking, but hours later, he knew almost every-thing, starting with how I'd arrived in Barthoah, of course, and why I'd needed to stay. I gushed about Sidra, and while he made some rather distasteful faces when he found out she was a siren, he said nothing on the matter. Niven knew me well enough to know if I was smiling over someone, they must be alright.

He'd never known me to have partners, and for the longest time, I wasn't sure I ever would. Seals mated for life, and I didn't take that lightly, even if my whole relationship with Sidra started by me telling her *not* to take things so seriously. Because as much as I thought I was serious, there had never been someone as stoic as her.

There was nothing as satisfying and fulfilling to me as watching her unravel day by day, a new wall crumbled, a new layer shed. Watching her fall into her own embrace of who she once was was the most beautiful transition I'd ever witnessed. I would never stop being honored that she allowed me to be there with her while all the old parts of her started shining through once more, taking over the icy, hardened parts she no longer needed.

My cheeks warmed as I felt Niven's attentive eyes on me. He cocked his head and said, "There's something you've yet to tell me. I know you. You're holding back."

He was right, of course. There was something I'd yet to admit: I needed him and many of the other selkies to come to land with me to fight on the behalf of sea fae known to be our enemies.

"There is. And before you react poorly, please, just hear me out," I said, analyzing the warm, freckled skin tightening over his features.

"Tell me, Breena. What is it?" He shifted on the rock beneath us. My flipper nudged his own in a way that said everything would be alright, and then I told him. I told him all about the netted enclosures and the pod of land hybrids. I told him why I'd come home and how Sidra was asking the same from her pod as I was of our clan.

He shook his head almost the entire time I spoke, so I softened the blow when I said, "When the fisherman, Rory, dropped me off on his boat just short of the first layer of rocks, I cut one of the hybrid's enclosures and freed the creatures within it. There's some in the cove right now, and more are most likely on their way."

Niven's face lifted, and a bit of color returned to his face.

"You let me bake on this hot rock with you for hours while fish swim about our cove? Are you mad?" he asked, placing his large hands on either side of my shoulders and giving me a good shake. "Let's go! This conversation can wait."

Niven began pulling his pelt over his human flesh until none of it remained. He morphed into a silvery seal with speckles and oval rings then scooted off to the water's edge. Though I was no longer hungry, I followed him to the water, guilt overcoming me that I hadn't thought to tell him, or anyone else, about the fish first. I knew as soon as I did, there would be a frenzy.

I kept the news of the fish to myself as I dove into the water after Niven. My clan, the true seals, and the kelpies would all find fish soon enough. For now, all I could do was watch my brother joyfully swim in spirals and loops on his way to have his first proper meal in, well, I wasn't sure how long.

"You don't understand, I need to talk with them now! Don't you realize how important this is?" I asked, walking down the shore with my pelt wrapped around me like a tiny, furry dress. Niven's was firmly secured around his waist the way most of the men, and plenty of the women, wore it. "It's not just about the sirens. These netted enclosures are taking *our* food too, Niven. Sitting by and doing nothing will be the death of us all. We have the privilege of growing legs and walking away from the sea, but what about the sea fae who can't? What about the sharks, and the orc—"

"The orcas? You're going to try to sell me on this by saying the orcas need our help?" Niven's jaw locked, and I cursed myself for my poor choice of words.

My toes dug into the sand beneath us, and I was thankful for the soft surface after the long day lounging upon our stones. Niven and I meandered around the sandy area, a private place to talk about such sensitive matters. The selkies in our clan rarely journeyed this far to the small strip of sand just outside the cove.

I smacked my lips, peered over at Niven, and said, "I know what they do to our kind, what one did to Dad, but the sea is imbalanced. Every single one of us, from the clams to the whales, is important. If *all* of us are to survive, we need to work with the sirens and end this horrible war."

"You sound like Mom, you know. She cared about this sea down to the last mollusk. I do too, you know; we just go about things differently," Niven said.

"Well, maybe it's finally time we get on the same page. The clan leaders won't listen to me if even *you* don't believe in me."

"I believe in you, Breena, always, but I couldn't blindly have your back and follow you to a human-infested land if I didn't have my questions answered first. If I didn't, I wouldn't understand the situation fully. Haven't I always told you to be armed with a question or two?"

"You have," I admitted with a sigh. "So does this mean you'll come with me to speak to the clan leaders?"

"I will, but not today."

"Well, why not?" My pacing halted, and I buried my toes in the sand, refusing to move from my very spot. My eyes were glued on my brother, his chest deflated when he finally met my gaze.

"We're reaching the end of pupping season," Niven said. "The leaders have their hands full with finding care for abandoned baby seals, and one of them has had a child of their own."

"Aila gave birth?" I asked. "I haven't been gone that long, yet I feel like I've missed so much."

"She has. A boy," Niven said with a soft smile. I knew he was eager to have his own one day. He'd forgone finding a mate because, for some reason, the man felt like he was still responsible for raising me. Maybe when I left, he would finally find someone and have a life of his own. He deserved that more than almost anyone I knew. "And it's a busy time of year, Breena. You know how it is. I promise I'll get something set up with them; it's just going to take a few days."

"Okay, but I'm trusting you with this, Niven. Please don't let me down." Flashing him a warning glare, I started pulling my buried feet free from the sand.

"Have I ever?" he asked, his hand over his chest, eyes wide.

"Yes! You're not perfect, you know." I gave him a weak shove. I'd grown used to being gentle with Sidra but forgot my brother's strength was a match for my own. When he flashed me a "That's all you've got?" stare, I shoved him a little harder, loving that I didn't need to hold back with my own kind. Sirens were so fragile with their light, thin bones. It was so cute.

"Are you coming?" Niven said as he stepped onto the path leading to our small village, a village that was nothing like Barthoah. The cluster of stone buildings didn't have a name; it was simply the heart of the cove. There were buildings for learning, healing, sleeping, and arts, and that was pretty much all we needed. We spent most of our days with a tail, whether we were fully transitioned or not, so there was no use for anything fancier than what we had.

Casting my gaze over to my brother, I said, "I'll meet up with you later. I think I'm going to hang out here for a little while longer."

"Suit yourself. Just be back to the cove before nightfall, please," he said, concern flickering in his eyes for the briefest of seconds before he straightened his posture.

"Yeah, yeah." I waved him off with a small grin. The man was ever the protector.

When would he realize I no longer need one?

CHAPTER NINETEEN
SWIMMING WITH THE SHARKS

As fish swam past me, leaving a trail of bubbles in their wake, my gaze traced up my scaled tail. Being so close to the light, my tail was brighter, with vibrant hues of blue and pink that melted into purple. Shreds of white fabric floated around my tail, as if I'd gotten caught in the sails of a sunken boat.

My gaze landed on my hands and the translucent skin laced between my fingers from knuckle to knuckle. The light from the sun flashed off my new nails, which stretched far beyond where the old ones ever did. These talons were deadly sharp, made to cut through flesh and bone. So, when I ran my pointer finger from the top of my bodice and down the length of the dress, the fabric split into two with no fight.

I watched the ruined dress sink into the depths, slowly growing closer and closer to the seafloor below as if something lurking under the sand beckoned it. Before I crossed over into our territory and into the Dreslee, I unhooked my necklace and palmed it.

When every reminder of my time of land was out of sight, I dashed forward, chasing lingering fish further and further into my home. As I dove deeper, the water grew colder, reminding me just how far from the sun I'd been all these years. The color of the water down here was an otherworldly blue, as deep as the night sky.

The Ever Wanderer was nothing but a hazy smear in the distance. I could feel my stomach in my throat as I wondered how Breena was faring. Was she darting through the water with the kelpies and other selkies, or was she already basking along the rocky shoreline, catching Niven up on her adventures in Barthoah?

I wondered then how much I would tell Zellia and my mother of my time on land and what all I would keep to myself. There was no time to decide, though, because out of nowhere, a flash of white streaked across my vision. There was no mistaking who it was, but my eyes didn't get to focus on her before she was already in my arms.

"Zellia!" I pulled my sister closer to my chest, squishing her flat against me, like if I hugged her hard enough, I would absorb her into my very soul. I clutched my pendant in my hand, careful not to drop it amid my excitement.

"Sid, you're alive!" her sweet voice echoed through my mind a little too loudly. She pulled back to take me all in, and only then did I see her face clearly. A single bubble fled my mouth as I gawked at her. Had her cheeks been that sunken in when I'd left, or had I grown accustomed to the starvation written plainly across the faces of those I loved?

"Where have you been?" she asked when I'd done nothing but stare at her. *"We all thought you were dead!"*

"Not dead, just on land. It's a long story, but I ended up in Barthoah, Zel." I'd let that sliver of information sink in before I bombarded her with anything additional.

Now, it was Zellia's turn to stare.

"Barthoah? The village where Dad grew up?" she asked. I nodded and finally let go of her arm.

"Take me to Mom, and I'll tell you both everything." I'd known when the words left my mouth that they had been a lie, but my mom and Zellia didn't need to know about that little fib. What

good would telling them about my relationship with Breena do? What good was it to tell Zellia about a secret family member she would never be able to meet?

"Wait a second. You brought fish, didn't you? Oh my gosh, there's so many!" Zellia's eyes went wild as she followed one of the larger fish with her eyes. If you didn't know any better, you'd think Zellia was the hunter of the family as her pupils stretched into focused slits.

"I may have brought a few gifts. Come on, let's go tell Tetwin and Xifi," I said.

Zellia led me into the Ever Wanderer, and as she did, sirens we passed placed their hands on me. They bowed their heads as I swam, someone placing their palm on my shoulder as someone else pressed the pads of their fingers into my tail fin.

Didn't think I'd be missed so much, I thought to myself as I flashed everyone half smiles. When we arrived at our little spot of the Ever Wanderer, I found my mom running her hands over my box of glass.

"Mom!" I called out into her mind, darting toward her.

"Sidra? Is that really you?" she asked, confusion written plainly across her face. My mother was slow to close the distance between us, her mossy tail flicking back and forth with apprehension. Squinting her sky-blue eyes at me, she placed her shaking hand on my cheek as soon as she could reach me.

"I'm truly here." I set my free hand on top of hers, my other hand remaining loyal to the pendant it gripped.

"And she has a lot to tell us apparently," Zellia said. *"She has been on land."*

"Land?" my mother echoed.

"Barthoah, to be exact," Zellia continued, playing with the ends of her silvery blonde hair as she waited for our mother's reaction. Mom's face dropped, as did her hand on my face. The area she'd once held was now cold, the sting of her disapproval that much more intense.

"It's not what you think, Mom. I had no choice. I left the Dreslee to find food, and when I did, I was scooped up by a fishing vessel."

Zellia's gasp cut me off, and my mother's mildly aged face morphed into an immovable stone.

"You were captured?" they asked at once, both in their own tone. Zellia's was borderline excited while my mom's was a mix of horror and disbelief.

"I cut myself free of their net and hid on their ship until they returned to land. I snuck off the vessel before anyone noticed me and found myself in Barthoah. There was no way I would risk transitioning again so soon, so I stayed in the village until I felt strong enough to come back. I'm sorry I was gone so long, but I had no other choice but to wait."

"What was it like? It's been ages since we've been!" Zellia asked, but my mother's deadly stare under sand-colored brows silenced her.

"Mom, it's not like I intentionally left. I would have never gone to land and left the pod if I'd had the choice."

My mother's face finally softened, and when it did, her gaze dropped to my hand. I gripped the pendant tighter, but it was already too late. She reached forward and looped the rope of the necklace around her finger. Upon her tug and pursed lips, I dropped the glass piece that was pressed into my skin.

"Zellia, please leave. We will catch up with you later," my mother said as she stared down at the necklace with dagger-like vision.

"I'm not leaving. Despite how you treat me, I'm not a child." Zellia fixed her tail fin into the sand scattered across the bottom of the ship. Sometimes, I had to remind myself that she'd been alive for two decades. I knew my mom forgot this even more than I did.

She ignored my younger sister as hurt burrowed deep into her expression. I knew my mother all too well to think she was truly mad at me. She was terrified. After coming back from land, I understood her more than I ever had. I understood why both of my parents hid the truth about land—because they knew what it was like to have Barthoah tear a family apart. The last thing my mother needed was to lose another love of her life to the land, be it a mate or a daughter.

I realized I'd been back for all of two minutes, and I was already following in their footsteps, hiding the truth from Zellia.

"I got that exactly where you think I did." I motioned to the necklace in my mother's hand. The muscle in her jaw ticked, and the whites of her eyes grew pink. If we'd been on land, I knew that was when tears would have trickled down her face.

"Where? Someone tell me what I'm missing," Zellia said.

"Zel, do you remember going to Barthoah?" I asked. *"Depths, you truly were a child then. I wouldn't blame you if you didn't."*

Zellia bit her lip and squinted her eyes, like if she focused enough, memories of Barthoah would come flooding back to her. While sirens had impeccable memories, even we didn't have minds of steel.

"A bit, but it's foggy," she admitted, playing with the fin on her elbow the way she always did when she was nervous. *"I remember Dad's place, seeing the sea from the shoreline, which was an odd sight, and of course, Dad's other home..."*

"His workshop," my mother said.

I nodded, and my eyes flicked down to what lay in my mother's hands.

"More like our grandfather's workshop," I corrected her, meeting Zellia's intense gaze.

"Our what?" my sister asked, her fingers curling inward, just shy of a fist.

"I told you I had a lot to catch you up on," I said with a sheepish smile. I wasn't yet convinced telling her was the right thing to do, but I knew my parents wouldn't have. Something about that told me I was ending some sort of cycle of lies, and that in itself allowed me to hold my chin high as I told her every little detail of my talks with our grandfather. I told her both sweet and bitter

truths and watched as the pink in my mother's eyes deepened to crimson red.

When I was done answering Zellia's endless stream of questions, my mother finally spoke. She held out the necklace to me and said, "*You better hide this in that box of yours. Add it to the collection of glass from the men who we'll never see again.*"

My mother had been quick to make me a new spear. I'd been in the Dresslee for three days, and yet life seemed to settle back into place far quicker than I ever imagined it would. Why had I thought if I came back for only five days, it'd feel like I was just a guest, not a permanent resident once more?

The truth was, I barely needed the spear. Tetwin and the other hunters had been so invigorated by the plentiful fish, that for the first time in a long time, we didn't all need to hunt. For the first time in what felt like forever, they'd actually caught enough fish to go around.

I happily left my spears in the Ever Wanderer, and for brief, blissful moments, I let myself believe everything about my return home could be permanent. I allowed myself to forget that this fish would soon run out.

The fish Rory had dumped over the Dreslee wouldn't stick around forever, and even if they did, there were only so many. I'd give it a day before we were left with nothing once more, especially at the rate people were eating.

The council of elders knew I'd been responsible for the return of fish. They had scouts looking out for me, Zellia being one. She hadn't been the only one to see me chase dozens of fish through the Dreslee.

After this, it didn't take long for the council to summon me. My mother and Zellia had escorted me to the three stone pillars at the far edge of the kelp forest for support. The four elders who remained led the council discussion regarding the circumstances of my return. I'd been honest when I'd told them the fish came because I'd convinced a fisherman to help me. While I'd led them to believe hypnosis was at play to dim their anger, most of them still had questions.

I, of course, knew that there would be a big request coming from my lips, but I hadn't found a way to let them know the fish weren't here to stay. I hadn't let them in on the fact that I needed as many sirens as possible to help me defeat the responsible hybrids in Barthoah. Depths, they still didn't know the hybrids were involved in our hunger and suffering in the first place. The name "Tinelle" had been one I'd only spoken above sea level.

"*Sid,*" a familiar voice called. Zellia hung off the edge of the Kilkov the way she always had. The last time I'd seen her like this was the day I unknowingly left for Barthoah. With no fat left in her once-round cheeks, she seemed so much older than when I'd left. Surely, time moved faster down here.

"*Zel, I've been captured by fishermen, and it wasn't all so bad. Won't you join me up here?*" I knew of her hesitancy to get too close to the surface, but no fisherman would bother to throw a net into these empty waters, not when twenty-three netted enclosures existed.

Even if one did, maybe I'd ask them to drop me off at the Selkie Cove on their way back to land. Three days had already been far too many without Breena.

"*Maybe next time. I came because there's something I wanted to show you.*"

"*What is it?*" I asked.

"*Just come with me. You'll see!*" she giggled. Ever since we were young, Zellia loved surprises. She'd loved surprising people far more than being surprised, but my parents and I always played along. Her laughter was too infectious to go to waste.

I chased her out of the Kilkov, and she giggled in my mind the entire way back to the Dreslee.

"Okay, okay. We both know you're faster than me. There's no need to show off," Zellia said.

I slowed and flipped onto my back so she was facing me. Zellia rolled her eyes, her chest heavy with fatigue. Cocking her head to the side, she stared at me far longer than anyone should. Her gaze was penetrating, as if she was analyzing every part of me.

"What?" I asked when her gaze began to freak me out. *"Why did you bring me back to the Ever Wanderer, Zel?"*

"Sorry, I just… I don't know." She averted her gaze. *"You haven't chased me in ages. Haven't laughed with me since—"*

She didn't need to finish her sentence. We both knew she was talking about my father's death. I didn't reply; I just returned her stare and waited for the right thing to say to enter my mind. Surely, if I stared back at her long enough, something would come to me.

Zellia continued and said, *"It's nice. I've missed you."*

"I was only gone for a week," I said with a half smile.

"Not really. You haven't been here, haven't been yourself in years. Even before Dad died, you turned into this icy version of who you once were. I'm not sure what happened on land, but I'm thankful for it. You've only been home for three days, and yet I've talked to you more than I have in years. I feel like I have my sister back."

My mouth went dry, which was a very unusual thing to occur in the sea. If I didn't have words for her before, I really didn't have them now. My heart ached for her and all the time we lost. My heart ached that she probably felt like her sister had died long before her father had.

"I feel more like myself too," I said. *"With the fish being back, it's like a weight has been lifted off my shoulders. But Zellia, I have to tell you…"*

"Look!" Zellia shouted, a loud sound pinging off the inside of my skull. Holding my temple, my head swung in the direction of her outstretched pointer finger.

Off in the distance, a grey figure glided gracefully through the water. My heart leapt as my immediate thought was Breena, but that hope was fleeting as the figure came closer and into focus.

"They're back," I whispered. I admired the magnificent creature from afar, my muscles locking up when I tried to swim closer.

"What are you waiting for? This is why I brought you down here."

I'd always had a close relationship with the sharks. They'd been my preferred hunting companions at a time when there was enough fish to go around. They didn't understand the competition of the sirens to hunt the most or the fastest, much like I hadn't. We had quiet hunts where they corralled our prey, and I finished the job with my spear. We shared whatever we caught that day, and the rest went to my pod.

I hadn't known if I had my mother's protection symbols carved into the whale bone of my spears to thank, or if it was the sharks, but I hadn't been injured a single time when I hunted with them. The same could not be said for hunting with Xifi and Tetwin.

I'd longed for my hunting partners to return to the Dreslee, but at this point, I feared they no longer knew who I was. Zellia took hold of my scaled back and gave me a shove through the water in their direction. I used the momentum to keep swimming, growing closer and closer to my old friend, or maybe it would be a new one. I couldn't tell from this distance.

A low hum vibrated out of my throat, and the shark changed course and headed straight for me. As it got closer, I analyzed its markings, both the natural ones from birth and the ones it had acquired over time. When I saw the small rake marks across the left side of her dorsal fin, I knew.

"Mai," I said, knowing the mature shark wouldn't understand me in the traditional sense. The name slipped through my mind anyway, excited to see my old friend.

I swam right up to her, all reservations lost in the current. When I darted toward her, she matched my energy, my speed. We met in a collision of scratchy scales, but neither of us seemed to mind. I ran my hand down her as I swam in a loop around her thick body.

Zellia approached much slower than I had. Her relationship with the other predators of the sea was causal at best. Most sirens who didn't partake in the hunt didn't go out of their way to commune with our neighbors, but it was inevitable as a hunter. Together, we pushed the boundaries of the Dreslee border. Sometimes, Mai would trail just past the border to egg me on, but I never let her or any of the others sway me. Even when the fish started disappearing and their visits became more infrequent. Even when the idea of escaping the Dreslee seemed all too tempting.

As I gripped on to Mai's dorsal fin, she took off at maximum speed. I flicked my tail behind her to boost us even more, and the sea became a blur of blues and greens. I allowed my eyes to shut, and I rested my cheek on her back, soaking in the sensation of the water rushing through my hair and over my skin.

My heart swelled as I allowed myself to mentally slip into a time before the hunger, before the death. My heart and mind were lost to the moment, and I took one more leap toward finding myself again.

CHAPTER TWENTY
PUPPING SEASON

Breena

Four days had passed since I'd first returned home. I hadn't realized four days would be quite so difficult without Sidra's presence, but part of me was thankful that each day dragged on, thankful that my heart was sore in her absence, that it longed for the unique love only she'd gifted me.

Every day I was in the Selkie Cove confirmed what my heart screamed every time our eyes locked, every time her skin brushed mine, every time she whispered sweet words meant for my ears only.

I wondered how she was faring in the deep as I swam nervous, impatient circles around one of my favorite kelpies, Isobel. She nipped at my hair, and I returned the favor by tugging at her slimy, blue-green mane. I'd always wondered what it would be like to swim in my human form and ride on the back of a kelpie, like a human on a horse. Alas, I never worked up the courage to flail around butt-naked as I attempted to maneuver in the water without a tail or flippers. How humans kept their head above water at all never failed to shock me.

I'd embarrassed myself in front of my clan more than enough over the years, so I would hang onto whatever pride I had left and pass on the flailing today. Instead, I wrapped my arms around Isobel's neck, my tail fluttering along with her as she brought me back to the shoreline.

When I hopped onto a slick stone, I thanked the kelpie by tossing her a brittlestar I peeled off the rock next to me. She caught the little treat between her teeth and offered me a muffled neigh before swimming off. Starfish didn't have the best texture, I'd be the first to admit, but just as quickly as fish had flooded the cove only days ago, they were already disappearing. We had one day of blissful normalcy, but each day after, the fish became harder to find, as if they'd been drawn away to some distant region of the sea.

"There you are!" Niven said from a few rocks over. "I've been looking all over for you! The clan leaders are ready to meet with you now."

"Thank goodness!" I grumbled. "Did it take the fish disappearing again for them to want to speak with me?"

"That could have had something to do with it." Niven offered me a tight smile. I simply shook my head and let him lead the way.

The clan leaders sat around a roaring fire, Aila with a seal pup on one arm and a selkie infant on the other. The woman was the head of the clan, though important matters were run by all six leaders, each with a different responsibility and area of expertise. Her new son suckled on her as she motioned for us to sit. I didn't hesitate to find a good log to share with Niven.

"Breena, Niven. I understand you share the concerns of many. It's no secret the return of the fish was a temporary luxury we were not fortunate enough to retain." Aila cleared her throat. The woman was dressed in a spotted tan pelt around her waist, long, braided hair covering one of her rich, brown shoulders. Secured to her hair were wooden charms hand-carved out of driftwood. "Please, tell us why yours stand above the rest."

I explained the situation to them, and Niven only jumped in when it seemed like I was losing my crowd. Why any of them would be disinterested in what I had to say was beyond me. Anger, I understood, fear too, but indifference? Incomprehensible.

"How was it that you were able to bring so many fish to the cove?" one of the leaders asked. The man named Arran tucked long, sun-kissed blond hair behind one of his ears. It was long, as most selkie men's hair was, but his was fine and tangled at the ends with crusted salt.

Ah, so one of them was listening to me.

"I cut one of twenty-three netted enclosures, the one closest to the cove. These areas are not mere fishermen's nets; they are large enough to hold three whales." If they were stupid enough to enter one as I had, I thought to myself. "So you can imagine the sheer number of creatures freed when their imprisonment was destroyed."

"And why is it that they all seemed to have disappeared once more?" Aila asked.

"That, I don't know for certain. It's one of the many reasons I need reinforcements when I return to Barthoah. I can't confront the hybrids alone."

"You keep saying 'I', but we all know you mean 'we'. You and the siren," a woman named Blair chimed in, a sneer painted across her face as clear as day. The fire illuminated her sharp features and turned down mouth, and my stomach tightened at her mention of Sidra.

As my mouth gaped, Aila held up her hand to silence us all. "As you're aware, it's pupping and molting season. As this is our most vulnerable season, I simply do not know how you expect us to extend any of our limited resources to this cause. It is a cause that impacts us all deeply, I understand. If you came to us in a month, maybe two, we might have been able to fulfill your requests, but we simply cannot up and leave tomorrow."

"We have vulnerable pups scattered across the beach that have just started weaning from their mothers. We need to focus on our responsibilities at home before we can tread off to distant places and expend precious energy waging war. I hope you understand."

I wanted to say I didn't understand. I wanted to say they were being selfish, but the fact of the matter was, we all knew the survival rates of pups. We all knew what would happen if we fled to Barthoah. I knew this, but still, I couldn't help but think about the bigger picture. What would happen to the pups once their mothers' milk was no longer there for them to suckle? What fish would they eat then?

My fists balled in my lap, and tears stung my eyes from the mix of anger and hot, dry smoke from the fire. Niven placed a heavy hand on my shoulder, and the pure weight of it calmed my torn, twisted soul. I squeezed my eyes shut and nodded my head, not in defeat, but in understanding.

I knew what I needed to do.

CHAPTER TWENTY-ONE
THE BUBBLE OF LIFE

It'd been a day since I'd seen a fish. Shortly after Mai paid the Dreslee a visit, we worked together to catch her a nice haddock. I'd let her have the fish in its entirety because not only did she need it more than I did, but I was also biding my time until I was back on land. My mouth watered for sandwiches and shortbread, not fish guts.

My grandfather's words of my soul being torn into two stayed with me over these few days, haunting me each night as I curled up with Zellia in our sunken ship and attempted to sleep. I tried to distract myself with all my favorite places in the sea, yet I still couldn't shake those stubborn words loose.

I missed that silly old man, and I missed the way Breena was so committed to living and loving this life despite everything we'd been through. I missed the way she made me feel more like myself than I had in years.

Now that my pod had fish in their stomachs to fuel them, I had to stop delaying the inevitable. Earlier this morning, I'd forced myself to get off my tail fin and request an audience with the elders about the hybrids and their potential plans. Rory said we had five days until Tinelle noticed something was off with the nets. While I trusted that Rory's mother could find safety with my grandfather in his shop, it had already been four days, and my thoughts were beginning to sour.

This afternoon, I would meet with what remained of the elders by our sacred pillars at the edge of the kelp forest. Our people had been meeting in that same location for centuries, debating politics and planning war strategies. Today would be no different.

I waited with a knot in my stomach for the elders to accept my request to reconvene. Nothing else made sense but to distract myself with the things that brought me peace.

I ran my hands over the metal chest in the Ever Wanderer then popped open its lid. Sitting on top of the pile of broken glass was my pendant, the rope swaying in the water above the rest of the chest's contents. The piece of jewelry called to me, and I obliged with little fight. Slipping my pointer finger through the rope, I pulled it from the chest. Before closing the lid, I removed a small hand mirror my mother had gifted me when I'd turned twenty-four.

Propping the mirror up on a wood ledge, I watched myself in the tarnished silver as I fastened the jewelry around my neck. When I peered into the reflective surface, I was overtaken by the sight of my sister's reflection staring back at me: high cheekbones, long blonde hair, piercing blue eyes, and that pretty pendant. My hand found the piece of glass, and I held it close to my chest as my eyes fell closed.

An odd sound rang out in the distance, and my eyes flung back open. One thing about the Dreslee: it was almost always quiet. So when I heard a weird "thump" coming from outside the Ever Wanderer, I swam over to a crack in the side of the ship and pressed my face against it. I hung onto the wood as I tried to get a good look at whatever was out there. After a moment of adjusting and finding the right angle, I saw where the unusual sounds were coming from.

At first, I thought only one or two sirens had gathered, but then, I noticed even more joined the group.

Had the elders motioned to convene early?

No, that couldn't be. They would never meet in the open like that, especially when we had the sacred pillars. We always met at the pillars.

When I tilted my head, I saw Tetwin in the front of the ever-expanding group. He held a spear in his hands, and he flashed it in a warning motion. My neck ached as I held the most awkward position, but I had to know what was happening. It wasn't until I saw a similar grey shadow, taunting and agile, that I understood.

Breena.

Pushing myself off the wooden wall, I fled the ship as fast as my body would carry me. Black rimmed my vision as I maneuvered past sunken objects and oblivious sirens, trying to get to Breena before Tetwin made a costly mistake.

Swimming through the entrance of the ship, I darted toward the crowd. I saw a clearing above everyone's heads, so I propelled myself upward and thrust my tail harder than I ever had. I had to get to my selkie.

Great waves, did she not understand how stupid this was? How dangerous?

"Breena!" I called out, unsure if she would be able to hear me from this distance, unsure if she would be able to hear me at all, or if our communication underwater would be like that of Mai and I.

When Breena seemed like she didn't notice me at all, I tried something else and rang out into the mind of my fellow hunter, *"Tetwin!"*

His head swung to me, the sight of slitted pupils though his bright green eyes making my stomach lurch.

"Stay back, Sidra. You may have been the one to find the pod food, but I'll be the one to keep it safe!" he shouted into my mind, leaving me wincing as I barreled toward him.

"No!" A scream ripped through me. I pushed my limits as I

darted forward, but it was already too late. Tetwin raised his spear as Breena swam closer, the muscles in his forearm rippling as his grip tightened. Before I could grab the back of his weapon, the sharpened bone carved with symbols of death left his hand and spiraled through the water.

I pushed a wave of water at the spear, but I'd been too far away. The bone spiraled a hundred yards and struck Breena right in the gut.

Pushing another wave of water, I aimed at Tetwin to buy myself a few extra seconds. The hunter was tossed to the side of the growing crowd, and I used his distraction to my advantage. He righted himself and swam back to his place in the front of the group like its false leader.

I sandwiched myself between him and his prey.

Tetwin only had one spear on him, but I was well aware of the weapons held by the sirens behind him. Xifi pushed his own spear toward Tetwin and said, *"Finish that fish-stealing pest. I bet it's the reason the fish are all but gone again."*

I threw up my hands, continuing to move toward Breena, though now, I relied solely on subtle movements from my tail fin to propel me backward as I stared at the amassing pod. I could smell her blood in the water, see the diluted red of it spread around me, but I couldn't see her. I couldn't see if she still held up her head, or if she was already lost to me. Tetwin had always had shitty aim, but I had seen his spear strike her gut clear as day.

"No, she's not!" I yelled back, ready to defend her against my own kind if I had to. *"I can explain, just please, put down the spear."*

"She?" Xifi called out, a look of disgust plastered onto his face as he peered past me to the wounded seal.

"You know her? You're protecting the very creature stealing our food?" Tetwin asked. Out of the corner of my eye, I saw my mother and Zellia swim up to the front of the group, but I didn't dare meet their anxious stares.

Tetwin lowered the spear he gripped in his giant, webbed hand down. My eyes surveyed his body language and flickering pupils and took his easing stance as an opportunity to turn my back on him. When I finally swam the remaining distance to Breena, she was limp in the water, floating in a crimson haze.

"Breena!" I called out again, not caring if anyone else could hear me. She didn't lift her head, didn't so much as open her eyes. I pulled her speckled grey and brown body into my arms, holding her close to my chest.

"Zellia, help me!" I cried out into my sister's mind. I had to focus my scattered thoughts to direct the communication only to her. I wouldn't give one of the hunters a chance to grab her if I could help it.

She is a healer. She can fix this. She can fix this.

Within seconds, Zellia was by my side. She would have only been able to get to me that fast if she'd already been on her way when I called. My shattering heart swelled for the briefest of moments before focusing all my attention back on Breena.

"I'm here, I'm here. What do you need, Sid?" my sister asked in a rush, her gaze darting from me to the seal I gripped in my arms.

"Help her, please. Please save her!" Fumbling with Breena's slippery wound, I begged Zellia. I knew better than to pull the spear from her stomach, but seeing it inside her broke me.

That cursed thing needed to be obliterated.

I clenched my hand in the water next to me, bending and constricting it until the pressure around the spear was too much for the bone to withstand. The section carved with the death symbols broke away, and as it slowly sank farther from Breena, my chest loosened.

"Sid, I don't know how to heal a seal. It's not fae. I-I-" Zellia began stuttering, but I cut her off.

"She is! She's fae." It was only then I realized that little confession wasn't just to Zellia. Anyone in hearing distance now knew exactly what Breena was: not a mere fish stealing seal, but a selkie whose kind left us sirens to die in our war.

"This is the hunter you have all been praising?" Tetwin boomed to the crowd behind us. *"The one who holds a slain enemy in her arms, weeping over it like a pathetic child?"*

"Air. She needs air," Zellia said to solely me. She tuned out Tetwin as she analyzed the seal shifter. *"I don't know how long she has been underwater, but seals can only hold their breath for an hour and a half. She'll need to go to the surface."*

We were far too deep.

Think, Sidra!

The next thing I knew, Tetwin was pulling at my shoulder, forcing me to face him. Zellia took Breena from me as I was ripped away from them both by the much larger hunter.

"The one who wears jewelry like tinker or healer," he continued, pulling the pendant from around my neck. The rope snapped in two, and he held up the dangling pieces for the pod to see. *"This is who you put your trust in to feed your family? Someone with such little regard for her own duty?"*

He dropped the pendant, but I didn't move as I watched it slowly sink to the seafloor, growing smaller and smaller as it did. I should have stuck up for myself, done something, but after meeting his cold, competitive stare, I turned my back to him and my pod once more. He and his ego weren't worth it, especially not as Breena was dying in Zellia's arms a mere foot away.

Tetwin grabbed my arm and pushed me out of his way. He reached for Breena, who was being cradled by my brave younger sister. When I realized he was going for the broken spear protruding out of Breena, I acted without thought. Our nails were always sharpest after a transition, and I used that to my advantage. I raked my fingers across his back, pulling forth trails of scarlet through the water.

Tetwin's back arched, his body responding to the shock of the sharp, stinging pain of a siren scratch.

"The next fae to touch that selkie dies!" I warned the two dozen sirens in front of me, almost the entire pod paid witness to my

treachery. The shock written across their faces was palpable as the remaining traces of Tetwin's blood washed away from my nails in the water.

"She has come here because the selkie clans are starving just as we are. There are no fish remaining in their hidden coves. When I went to land, the two of us worked together to amass all that fish you've been enjoying these past few days. If you haven't noticed, those fish are all but gone once more, but she is not to blame."

Finding myself by Breena's side once again, Zellia was already assessing her wound. I took the selkie from my sister to free up her hands. Peering down at Breena, her large, dark eyes were hidden from me. My throat tightened, and I blinked my eyes rapidly, though I knew no tears would come.

Wake up! I begged her in my mind, because I knew it was no use saying it aloud.

"Then who is to blame?" One of the elders swam forward and brushed a bleeding Tetwin aside. I peered at the elder named Donia as she approached us. The muted oranges of her scales were a stark contrast to her long, silver hair swirling around her as she slowed a few feet away.

The siren wore the shell and spear emblem of the elders on a sash tied from her shoulder to her hip. The sheer green material of the sash flowed with her as she moved.

Preparing to catch the entire pod off guard with two simple words, I held my head high and channeled to everyone as I said, *"The hybrids."*

Laying Breena down in the sand, I gathered every ounce of grace I could muster to avoid jostling her. The broken spear jut from her gut, but it'd been wrapped in seaweed to transport her to the Kilkov. While the trip from the Ever Wanderer typically took ten minutes, traveling slowly with her in my arms took closer to thirty.

By the time I arrived at the Kilkov, I was surprised I was able to hold her at all.

Once she was nestled into the warm sand, I stopped fighting the shaking from taking hold of my arms. Breena was the strong one, not me. I wanted so badly to shake her, wishing it would be that simple to wake the selkie. Alas, shaking her would do nothing but worsen her injury.

The Dreslee was too deep, the oxygen particles too widely dispersed. Here in the Kilkov, bubbles of oxygen littered the water from the waves above, but also from the kelp forest that exhaled the lifeforce I needed for Breena.

Closing my eyes, I imagined drawing oxygen through the water, moving water particles aside so the oxygen would flow in my direction, like what I'd done for the fish out of water. This time, my selkie was the one who didn't belong. She belonged in her cove, by the surface, not thousands of feet below sea level, where there was less oxygen and the weight of the water was crushing her fragile mammalian body.

When I opened my eyes, I saw a bubble forming around her mouth, her nose. The bubble continued to grow until the air engulfed her entire head. I knew mammals of the sea could hold their breath even unconsciously, but it was only a matter of time until her brain needed oxygen. My solution was temporary at best. I needed my sister to do the rest. She was the only one of the healers I trusted to save Breena's life. As it was, I was already sending out prayers to a potentially imaginary Sea Goddess to help protect her.

When we were aboard the Indigo Tide, I'd laughed at the men as they groveled on the wet deck of their ship, on their hands and knees in the mixture of sea water and rum. They begged their Goddess for aid, and thinking back, I pitied them for their stupidity. Now, I found myself doing the same, hoping the sirens and their tricks weren't the closest thing to Gods of the sea. I prayed that Cliodna, the daughter of the Sea God, would hear me.

As I waited for Zellia to arrive with her supplies, I prepared my wish for the Goddess. I placed a pearl in a double shell and tied it with a thinned strand of kelp. While humans tossed their wishes into the waves, I tossed mine off the edge of the Kilkov, thinking of Breena the entire time it drifted downward.

Just shortly after folding my tail to sit at Breena's side, Zellia returned with a basket woven of sea grasses. Baskets made by sea fae were long and narrow, with a small opening to avoid losing our belongings as we propelled ourselves through the water. My mother had always been quite good at the craft, and she even spent her free time making them for trade.

Zellia placed her basket on the ledge of the Kilkov then rubbed the back of her neck with her newly free hand. Her breathing quickened as her eyes roved over Breena from her protected position on the other side of the ledge. Finally giving in for the first time in her sheltered life, she fluttered her tail enough to lift her above the plateau. I stared at her as she entered the Kilkov, getting closer to the surface than she had in years. She was stunning up here, her white scales shimmering hues of both silver and gold. Looking at her, it was almost easy to forget why she was here in the first place, why she was facing her deepest fears.

"Thank you, Zel," I said, watching the way she grabbed her basket and tentatively brought it to Breena's side. She sat opposite of me, Breena the cucumber in our sandwich.

"If fishermen come, you owe me," she said with a scowl. Zellia glanced above us to the rocking waves of the surface. We were still a hundred feet under those waves, but that was nothing to a creature of the deep.

"Could be good for you. You're due for an adventure." It was all the joking I could manage as I held Breena's speckled flipper.

Zellia grunted in response, but then she tilted her head, and her eyes softened.

"What is it?" I asked. There were plenty of reasons to be

solemn right in front of me, but Zellia's expression told me this worry was something different.

"Mother found me as I was gathering supplies." She started fiddling around in her basket, pulling out a sealed shell that she thrummed her long nails against. *"The council convened without you. It was a closed meeting at the pillars to discuss what you told the pod about the land hybrids... and that fisherman."*

"They've made a decision?" I asked. She averted my gaze as she cracked the shell open and poured the gooey contents onto Breena's wound. She pressed the goo down into Breena around the edge of the spear before it had the chance to dilute and wash away.

"They did."

The way she stared at my hands as if she wished to hold them made acid rise into my throat. I knew what was coming even before she continued. It was written all over my sister's face.

"Tell me. Don't make me wait, Zel," I begged.

"They're not sending anyone to land." She pulled her bottom lip between her teeth and began freeing the seaweed from around the spear. As she did, scarlet blood leached out of Breena's wound. Zellia motioned for me to press into Breena's stomach, and I did despite my fuzzy mind.

"No one?" I had a feeling they would stick me with Tetwin and maybe two other hunters and say that was all they could manage, but *no one*? Did they not care who died? Who starved because they wouldn't do anything to help solve the problem?

"I'm sorry, Sid. I know you wanted—"

"Screw what I want! We need this! We need this to survive, don't they see that?" I fought, trying to keep my hands steady despite the intense urge to punch the water around me.

"We can still go! You and I," Zellia said as she grabbed another shell from her basket. She nudged my hands out of the way so she could pull another poor, gooey creature out of its home. When the tan goop with black streaks landed on Breena's skin, my sister rubbed it into her, stopping the blood as quickly

as it came. My heart felt like that sad blob: a helpless, crushed mess.

"Zellia..." My hands fiddled in my lap, wishing I had something productive to do with them. I sat and watched as my sister took care of Breena, but what good was I?

My gaze settled on Zellia as she worked, and depths, was she good at what she did. She was meant to be a healer. She wasn't meant to come with me to land, especially not to wage war with the hybrids.

"I know I'm not very fast or strong, but I have skills you don't," she said. *"You need me there, just like you need me now with Breena."*

"You healing someone in the safety of our home is your job. It's what you're used to. You coming to land for the first time in over a decade and helping end a war is an entirely different thing," I said, watching as she prepped to remove the spear from Breena's gut.

"You're going, and peacekeeper isn't your job," Zellia said in the sassy tone she always put on when she wasn't getting what she wanted. My jaw clicked and tensed as I stared at her.

"And that is exactly the problem here, Zel. You think I'm going there to keep the peace. I'm going there to do my job. To hunt."

"You won't." She paused what she'd been doing for the first time since she arrived at the Kilkov. Her gaze darted across my face as she held the end of the jagged spear in her hand.

"I will. Those hybrids are starting their own pod on land, with one goal in mind: destroy the sea. I don't understand why, but they are managing to do exactly that. A friendly conversation isn't going to solve this problem."

"It did with the fisherman. Plus, these are our people. You can't hunt them all down," she said, her blonde brows pulling together. *"I mean, you can, but you shouldn't."*

"Another reason you can't come. You only want to see the good in people, but that can get you killed here and on land. You should know that to be true, but Mom and Dad kept you so... protected," I

said. I wasn't here to hurt my sister's feelings, but if it was between that and permanently losing her, I'd crush her heart all day. My eyes flicked down to Breena so I could avoid seeing the pink creeping into Zellia's eyes.

"We can talk about this later. Breena needs you right now, and that's all that matters."

"Right," she whispered. *"Hold Breena steady. It's time to remove the spear."*

CHAPTER TWENTY-TWO
HIDING IN THE KILKOV

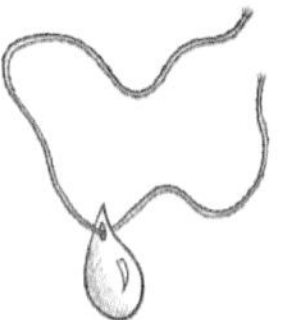

Zellia returned to the Kilkov as often as she could between her other duties as a healer. She'd been getting more and more comfortable hanging around my favorite place, until it seemed as if she'd never had a problem with the sunny plateau in the first place. When she arrived this time, she handed me two crustaceans and three pieces of seaweed. At first, I'd assumed they were for Breena's treatment, and then I realized they were meant for me. To eat.

Wonderful.

"Quite the hunter," I muttered.

"You know as well as I do that there's not much else. Xifi's sister spotted a black scabbardfish today, though, so that's something," Zellia said, picking at a crustacean she'd presumably brought for herself.

"Not much meat on their bones." After analyzing the offering, I wrapped one of the crustaceans up in a piece of seaweed. As I ate it, I thought of happy eggs with brambleberry loaf.

Has the food on land ruined me forever?

"How's Breena doing?" She peered down at the spotted seal, who remained as still and asleep as she had for the past day. Her

wound was wrapped, and the bleeding hadn't returned, thankfully.

"She's been making some odd sounds in her sleep, but Zel, I'm tired, and my magic is waning. You have to wake her. I can't keep drawing in oxygen like this, but if I don't, she'll—"

"Have you slept?" Zellia cut me off and scooted across the sand to be in front of me. She then grabbed my head and pulled down my bottom eyelids with her thumbs.

"Zel—"

"Leave. Go to the Ever Wanderer and rest. I will take care of her and make sure she gets all the oxygen she needs."

"I couldn't even if I wanted to. Mom doesn't want to see me, and neither does anyone else," I admitted. I'd hurt one of my own to save a selkie. Though I had just earned the favor of the pod through the brief return of the fish, that favor was a distant memory, now replaced by images of me slicing Tetwin across the back, making bold statements of a new pod ashore, and claiming a selkie as my protected guest.

"Mom will come around. She's more mad you put yourself at risk than anything. Don't tell her I said this, but I think part of her is relieved you found someone worth protecting, even if she is a selkie."

My response was lost in my mind as I watched Breena stir.

"Zel, will you please wake her?" I asked again. *"I understand why you sang her to sleep, but the spear is out of her now, and you already used your song to close her wound. I can't keep her here much longer. Every hour Breena is here, she's at risk of drowning or someone taking it upon themselves to eliminate her supposed threat."*

"Her wounds will heal faster down here with my magic, the power of the salt, and my song. And she will heal faster if I keep her asleep."

"Yes, but we've been back in the sea for five days already." If there was a time to tell my sister I would be heading back to land, now was as good as any.

"Okay, and?"

"I promised the fisherman, Rory, that we would return in five days, and I intend on keeping that promise, especially now. It's not safe for her here."

"So, what? You'll swim back to land and drag her with you?"

"No, I'd never do that," I said and picked up a bonnet shell, cupping it in my palm. *"Did I mention the fisherman is the captain of his own ship?"*

"You're going to bring that fisherman back here again? Sidra!" she exclaimed. *"It was bad enough that you showed him our location the last time, and you want to do it again? I wouldn't be surprised if Tetwin gathered the hunters to take down Rory's ship the moment it arrives."*

"Maybe, if it means I'll be gone, they won't care."

Zellia shook her head at me and shoved my shoulder. Grabbing the shell from my hand, she held it up so I couldn't reach like she used to when we were children.

"Promise me this isn't going to get you killed."

"I promise. Rory is, well, he's..." I thought for a moment. *"A good person. Not just a good human being, but a good being in general. You'd approve."*

Zellia sighed and handed the shell back to me. Her grip on it was tight, and I had to fight with her to take the shell back for a second, but she gave it back all the same.

"If you must go, I will wake Breena. But Sidra, if you don't take me with you, there's no knowing what will happen to her. She was stabbed. You're not forgetting that, right?"

"Of course I'm not."

How could I? The memory of the death-marked spear striking her played on a constant loop in my mind.

Zellia nodded then moved around to the other side of Breena. She did a final evaluation of her wound before she started the process of waking the selkie. While she prepped, I held that bonnet shell and set my intention. The object grew warm in my hands as I thought of Rory, imagining him with his legs crossed, sipping tea in a rocking chair in his cottage. I pictured a tartan pillow behind his lower back, the framed painting of a rabbit above him.

When the shell cooled, I knew he'd received my signal. Now, all we could do was wait for him and his Indigo Tide.

"Come hold her flipper so you're by her side when she wakes. I may need you to help me keep her still," Zellia said. I listened to every little demand she made about where to hold the seal and what to do when she woke.

Zellia bent over Breena, blocking out the sun as she leaned closer. Her lips parted, and a sound only Breena could hear swirled around her and snaked into her mind. I could lull someone to sleep with my song like any good full blood, but what Zellia was doing was a completely different skill, more specialized. She could sing her patients into a state of unconsciousness and keep them unconscious as long as she wanted. Eventually, the strain of the magic would fatigue her, but she could keep her patients asleep during healing procedures and well after, so as to speed up their recovery and keep them from consciously experiencing pain.

When Zellia finished her song, Breena seized, and Zellia had to grab her other fin to keep her still. I moved in closer as Breena went limp again then began to shimmer.

"What's happening?" I asked.

"I'm not sure," Zellia was not too proud to admit.

"What do you—"

Words evaporated from my mind as Breena's eyes flew open and her shimmering skin began to grow loose and peel. I was too stunned to make sense of what I was witnessing until curly brown hair and a familiar face appeared behind that of a seal, as if Breena had been wearing a mask the entire time. Breena wiggled toned arms out of the flippers we held until her upper half appeared human once more.

It wasn't until then that she met my gaze, and when she did, a thousand minnows swarmed my belly. Zellia backed up as I moved in closer. My webbed hand found the back of Breena's head, and I held the half-transitioned selkie in my shaking arms.

My mind flooded with a hundred reasons why I was happy to see her and a hundred more about why I was infuriated she'd put herself in danger by coming here. Breena stared at me, not hearing a single one of those reasons.

Depths, even if she could remain here with me in the Dreslee, I'd never be able to speak with her again. What kind of existence was that, constantly being tortured with the inability to tell the woman of my desires all the ways I saw her beauty, inside and out?

My free hand found her cheek, and I cupped it before bending my entire upper half across hers. I blinked my eyes for a moment, knowing she'd see the pink streaking them once I pulled away, but a voice in my head told me that showing a little emotion didn't matter. So, I folded further in on myself and let all the thoughts and feelings I'd been holding back erupt.

Breena's hand found my back, and she stroked my scales in a soothing repetition. I stayed clear of her wound but got as close to her as I possibly could, feeling the need to engulf her so I could never risk losing her again, not without losing myself in the process.

Eventually, I sat back up and peered down at Breena once more. When she'd transitioned, she'd lost the air bubble around her head, and she'd need oxygen again soon.

"Can I take her to the surface? Is she well enough to handle it?"

"The surface? No, Sid, you can't." Zellia shook her head at me from the edge of the Kilkov.

"Because Breena can't, or because you don't want me to?"

"Does it matter?"

"Of course it matters!"

"Yes, you can. Her wound is sealed, but be careful not to knock off her bandages," Zellia pleaded.

"Thank you, Zel. I think we'll need a minute—"

"I'm already out of here!" Zellia cut me off with a flushed face,

backing away. Before she dove off the side of the Kilkov, she turned back. *"Be careful, Sid."*

With that, my sister was gone, and only Breena and I remained. I pushed back her wayward hair and pointed up to the sky. Breena peered up weakly and then nodded her head. She draped her arm over my shoulder, and I looped my arm around her back as I guided her up to the surface. Her skin glowed the closer we got, though her brown complexion had lost a bit of its luster from the lack of blood in her system. The mere thought of how much she'd lost made my stomach churn.

When our heads broke the surface, I slowly took in air while Breena sucked in a lungful. I could barely get a word in before her lips were on mine. There was nothing on this planet that would have stopped me from returning her kisses. My tail moved side to side to keep both our heads above water as I showed her all the ways I missed her with my lips. Water dribbled down our faces as I pulled her closer into me. It wasn't until she let out an involuntary hiss and grabbed at her wound that I pulled back.

I whispered a dozen apologies, but all she did was run her nails over my shoulder as she breathlessly said, "It's not quite the welcome I'd been expecting, getting stabbed and all."

Resting my hand under her chin, I brushed away the water beads forming there.

"What *were* you expecting, little droplet? You know of our past just as well as I do."

"I know, but I had to take the risk. I had to find you and tell you that our fish are already gone. There was no reason for me to stick around in the cove for any longer, not when I knew Rory's mother could be at risk." She grunted as a wave smacked her in the back of the head, jostling her weakened body. I propped her up even more, so the tops of her shoulders were exposed. My tail fin would burn in pain before I let her chin dip back below the water. She was in enough discomfort as it was.

"The fish have all but disappeared from the Dreslee as well," I admitted. "Rory should already be on his way here. If he listened to my instructions, that is."

"Bonnet shell?"

"Yeah. I know he received my message, but there's no saying when he'll arrive," I said, my eyes drifting back to her lips.

"Hopefully soon. I'm starving."

I was too, but not in the way she meant. I refocused on her words, then her eyes, and said, "Have you not been eating? How many days have you been out of fish?"

"I have, I have," she chuckled, making herself wince in the process. "I've been stabbed in the stomach, though. I'm pretty sure everything I've eaten over the past few days escaped out of the hole in my gut."

"I don't think that's how it works," I laughed, relieved to see she was in good spirits despite being attacked in enemy territory.

"Well, I suppose it's all the blood loss," she said with a faint smile. My own smile faded, and I held her just a little bit tighter.

"How are you feeling?"

"My body has been better, but my heart is happy to see you. Was that your sister with us down there?" she asked, motioning her chin below to the Kilkov. I peered into the water below, though I knew Zellia was long gone now. She could handle blood, but apparently, seeing her sister in love made her squeamish.

"Zellia, yeah. She's the one who healed you."

She leaned forward and whispered against my lips, "But I know it was you who kept me breathing. In more ways than one."

My arms were too fatigued to reach out of the water and cup one of her cute little cheeks like I'd wanted to, so I nestled my face into her neck. Water splashed me in the face, but I could feel her heat on my skin, feel the pulse in her throat. That was all that mattered.

"I have your bubbly water to thank, I suppose. Drawing oxygen through the water is a lost art. We don't have too many visitors in need of it these days." I finally pulled back to take in the sight of her once more.

"I suppose not." Her eyes were starting to droop with fatigue, and the corner of her mouth formed a lazy curve.

"You need rest. Are you ready to go back down?"

Breena simply nodded her head, her energy fading quicker than I imagined it would. With one final kiss, I began to descend. Once both of our heads were a few feet under the water, my body screamed with relief.

We heard the sounds of a groaning wooden ship over the Dreslee a few hours later. Zellia returned to the Kilkov promptly to say her goodbyes and ensure Breena was ready for travel. She replaced her seaweed bandages and sang a healing song to lessen her inflammation. Though they couldn't speak, Breena mouthed "Thank you" to Zellia in her air bubble. I wasn't sure Zellia would recognize the words, as she hadn't seen words spoken since she was a child. I telepathically communicated Breena's thanks to my sister, just to be safe. Zellia returned the sentiment by taking one of Breena's hands and giving it a squeeze.

If our lives had been different, I believed they would have become fast friends. A piece of my heart ached that this hidden hope was equally as unlikely to come to fruition as Rory suddenly sprouting gills.

"Make sure she knows I'm happy I got to meet her, despite the circumstances," Zellia said. *"Oh, and I have something for you."*

Zellia swam over to the basket she'd left near the edge of the Kilkov and reached inside. After digging around for a second, she pulled out a pearlescent glass pendant with a broken rope dangling from it. She removed the rope, placed it in her basket, and swam back over to me with a proud smile.

"You found it!"

"I did." She placed the pendant in my palm then reached for her own. My sister removed the necklace my dad had given her as a child and freed it of its rope. She took the pendant back out of my hands and looped the rope through it to make it whole once more. I remained silent as she ushered me to lift my hair, I simply did as she asked. When the pendant hit my chest, secured around my neck once more, I felt my eyes grow pink with emotion.

"Zellia, I can't," I said, holding the pendant off my chest, as if to rip it back off.

"Yes, you can. It's your turn, Sid." Zellia placed her hand on top of mine and lowered it. *"I'll be fine without mine for a little while."*

"Thank you for everything," I said, my throat tightening.

"Just promise me something?" A sparkle in her brilliant eyes.

"Anything."

"If you won't let me come with you, promise me this won't be the last time we see each other," she begged, the sparkle in her eyes just a moment ago dulling.

"It won't. I will see you again, I swear it." I pulled her in for a hug then tilted my chin up to the massive shadow on the surface. *"But it's time for us to go. Please tell Mom I'll see her soon."*

Zellia nodded her head in a silent agreement. I took that as my sign that it was time to scoop up Breena and get to the Indigo Tide before any of the hunters did something stupid.

I dipped my arms under Breena and into the warm sand until I was cradling her. She threw her arm over my shoulder and met my nervous gaze as I hoisted her off the seafloor. She gave me a swift nod, as if to tell me we were doing the right thing, that it was time to return to Barthoah. And so that's exactly what we would do.

As Breena and I swam through the Dreslee, we remained close to the surface to avoid any unwanted attention. I knew curious and resentful members of the pod would be looking up at us, watching as we boarded the ship, but as long as they stayed out of our way, they could watch as much as they pleased. I was beyond caring what they thought of me.

When we grew closer, I saw movement around the wooden hull of the ship. My stomach clenched, and my grip on Breena constricted as the image of five hunters armed with spears came into view.

"*Get out of our way, Tetwin,*" I warned. Shooting daggers at him with my eyes, I assessed his deep red scales as his tail fin thrashed and flicked angrily.

"*Run back into the arms of our enemies, little hunter, but don't you dare forget for a second what you are!*" Tetwin shouted after Breena and me, echoing the thoughts of many as they peered up to the bottom of the Indigo Tide. I stopped swimming for all but a second to shout into the minds of every siren I could manage to communicate with.

"*You know nothing of our real enemy! You might not want to discover the truth, so I'll let you wallow in the ways of our past while I uncover our present and pave the way for our future!*"

Xifi's mouth gaped as he stared between Tetwin and me. Tetwin's face remained immovable for now, but when all the fish returned, I would prove to him everything I had been meaning to. I didn't care to see the look on his face then, because my mental imagery of him realizing he was wrong was already satisfying. I knew that moment would come soon enough.

I made a promise to myself right then and there that I would never waste my time or energy on someone who didn't deserve it again. What I would do was board the ship of my human friend with my second heart beating right beside me.

"*I advise you to let us board this ship in peace. I think there's been enough inter-pod violence for one week, yes?*" I peered over my shoulder at the five warriors, a scowl written across each of their faces. Once Tetwin backed off, the other hunters began to do the same. It wasn't until then that I turned my backs on them and broke the surface of the water.

"Hello there!" Rory shouted from the sunny skies above, as if he'd been the Sun Goddess herself. "Need a hand?"

"I never thought I'd ask this, but will you please scoop us up with your net, fisherman?" I asked with a crooked smile, trying not to look down at who lurked beneath the ship.

"Will do! Everything alright down there?" he called out.

"Could be better! A rush would be appreciated." My eyes darted below us. I didn't fully trust the hunters not to change their mind at any moment.

"I'll grab you ladies in just a moment."

"Just be careful, okay? Breena is injured," I shouted when I lost sight of his jovial face.

A net plopped in the water the next second, and I swam into it with Breena in my arms before it closed. I'd been so focused on Breena's injury, I'd forgotten what would happen when this net lifted out of the sea. My teeth gritted against each other, and my heartrate quickened as the net began closing in around us.

"It's going to be okay," Breena croaked out. "You are the strongest person I've ever met."

She grabbed my hand as we began rising out of the water.

The pain found me swiftly, and Breena dropped my hand as I began to thrash and scream. *Depths, I need to get out of this net.*

I needed to be freed before I hurt Breena with my talons or boney spinal fins.

"Hurry it up, Rory!" Breena called out in a weak shout, her beautiful eyes widening.

"I'm being gentle!" he called back.

"Be less gentle. Hurry it up, man!" she said, more frantic this time.

"Close your eyes," I begged. "I don't want you to—" A scream ripped out of me as we landed on the deck, cutting me off from my pleas to Breena. "I don't want you to se—"

Breena nodded frantically, tears spilling out of her eyes as she squeezed them shut. She stuck her fingers in her ears and blocked out the sounds of my shrieks as my skin began shredding and pulling.

Rory rushed over and began pulling the top of the net apart, freeing both Breena and me. He scooped her up as my blood splashed upon her seal tail, and he wiped her clean before she could open her eyes once more.

The fisherman gave me my space but watched me intently as he laid Breena down on a pile of rags. He offered words of encouragement, reminding me of my family, but all I could think of was the two beings I shared this ship deck with. It wasn't until a second set of screams rang through the air that my mind quieted.

Zellia.

CHAPTER TWENTY-THREE
LAND HO!

"Zellia!" I shouted out. "Zellia, is that you?"

"Sid!" she screeched, pain ripping through her fragmented calls. "It's me. I'm-I'm sorry!"

"Rory, please find her," I groaned as I rolled face first onto the net-covered deck. I focused on my breathing, not letting the pain consume me. My sister needed me too much. "And bring some clothes!"

Rory frantically ripped the shirt off his back and grabbed a handful of rags, then scrambled in the direction of my sister's screams.

"What were you thinking?" I yelled moments later through the throbbing in my temple as Rory and Zellia came into view. My sister was in his arms, his shirt working as a dress, rags wrapping her lower half. She was a scaly fucking mess, and if I wasn't so weak, I would have flung a host of creative curses at the girl to let her know just how I felt about her grand plan of sneaking aboard the ship.

"I couldn't let you leave without me. I couldn't let you do this on your own. You and Breena both need me, but you're too stubborn to see that," she said through horse vocal cords. Her words grew more faint as she spoke, and her limp legs smeared in blood dangled from Rory's arms. As much as he tried, the look of sheer panic couldn't be hidden from his face as he set her down near Breena.

"Sorry to interrupt this reunion, but I-I'm bleeding," Breena said. The seaweed that once wrapped her skin was dangling uselessly off her hip. The wound on her stomach had reopened, and her shaking hand hovered above it, as if she was unsure if she should put pressure on it or not. Rory rushed over to the selkie with a rag in his hand, ready to stop the slow crimson flow.

"Don't you dare put that dirty thing on her!" Zellia's voice was firm for the first time since she boarded the ship. She grunted as she sat up and began crawling a few feet across the wet deck. Her new toes scraped across the wood, and she stuck her tongue out in concentration.

"I need you all to stop bloodying yourselves. I finally got all the rum off my deck. Do you know how annoying a sticky deck is?" Rory's gaze chaotically flicked to each of us.

"Rory, I need you to shut your mouth and get these women a glass of water, okay?" I said.

"This isn't a tavern, lass. We drink from the flask around here," he chuffed, reaching into a crate nearby. Rory handed Zellia his waterskin as she settled down next to Breena, and she gulped it greedily.

When Zellia passed it off to Breena with panting breaths, Breena gave Rory a weary smile and said," Do you happen to have any citrus slices on board? Sid is in no condition to bubble this water."

I snorted as Rory gawked at Breena.

"You sea women are killing me. I don't have any feckin' citrus slices aboard my fishing vessel, you'd be correct. Not in the habit of staying aboard the Indigo Tide long enough to fall ill with scurvy." Rory ran a large hand through his hair, and I thought for a moment that he might rip out a few of his copper strands.

"Alright, alright, we're going to give the poor fisherman a heart disaster," I said to the women with a warning smile. I motioned for Breena to toss me the waterskin after she was done with it, but as she was winding her arm back, Rory took it from her and walked it over to me.

"I suppose all three of us are already enough of a mess. We don't need another person to join us. *Someone* needs to get us back to land," Breena grunted. Rory wiped his sweat-sliced face on the collar of his shirt and shook his head at us.

"We haven't formally met yet. I'm Zellia," my sister said to Breena. She sat by her side, her eyes continuously flicking toward her oozing wound. Rory took a step back from all of us and found his place behind the wheel.

"It's nice to finally meet you. Thank you for taking care of me. I really do appreciate it," Breena said. "Is it too much to ask for your help again?"

"Not at all. It's why I'm here," Zellia said, taking her hand. "Listen, what I'm about to do is going to hurt. Do I have your permission to sing you to sleep so you won't feel it?"

"You may, but first..." Breena peeked around Zellia to find my gaze. Her eyes were watery, and for a moment, everyone else disappeared. "I'm sorry I closed my eyes."

"I'm glad you did, little droplet. Now, get better. We have a sea to save when you wake." No part of me wanted her to see me in pain either; not because I felt like I needed to be strong in front of her, but because I couldn't bear the watery look in her eyes that she gave me now.

Breena wiped those beautifully haunting eyes, nodded her head, then gave Zellia her permission. Letting my head fall back onto the heaping net behind me, I momentarily shut my eyes. Zellia began working, allowing me to hear her song on land for the first time. The sounds flowed from her mouth in stunning harmony without the distortion of the water, sending chills up my arms.

When Zellia was done, Breena was unconscious with a cauterized wound. I peeled my eyes open and said, "Thanks, Zel. We should find some rest too. Will you wake us when we're there, captain?"

"I can do that," he confirmed.

I stared at my sister, who watched a sleeping Breena. Her eyes trailed over her features, taking her in from all angles, from her beautiful textured hair to the tips of her spotted fins. Breena still hadn't fully transitioned back into her human form, but I suspected she didn't want to irritate her wound further. Her body had already been through so much today.

Zellia smiled at me sheepishly when she caught me watching her. She hadn't spoken to me much, and though I'd heard her voice in my mind a million times, I wanted her to speak aloud to me. There was something so different about the way words were spoken into the air on land. It was almost as if the sounds lingered a little longer instead of immediately fading into the rest of your mind's chatter, as they so often did when spoken telepathically.

Zellia cocked her head to the side, and I realized I was still watching her. I simply gave her a soft smile and drifted off into a much-needed rest.

I woke to the sounds of hushed muttering. The sun had lowered in the sky, and a misty evening settled in.

"She'll stay unconscious until I wake her," I heard Zellia say. "She should remain asleep until tomorrow. Her skin won't heal right if I have to cauterize it a third time."

"So we'll move her while she's asleep, then," Rory said, leaning on his captain's wheel as he peered down at a disheveled Zellia. She still wore his shirt, but she now had one of the rags from earlier tied around her waist like a short skirt. Her bright blonde hair was knotted, with bits of silver scales crusted into it.

I sat up and fought a yawn as I mumbled, "And how do you suppose we do that?"

"I have a trunk." Rory glanced over Zellia's shoulder to where I sat in crumpled netting.

"First, you stole her skin and took it back to your home in your trunk, and now you want to take the entire selkie?" I teased with a croaking voice. "You fishermen are so greedy."

"Oh, am I now?" Rory smirked. "I think I've made up for it, Sid."

"Since when did we get on nickname terms?"

Rory gave me a once over and then shook his head with a shrouded smile.

"Captain, what did you say about this trunk of yours?" Zellia asked. "Is it actually big enough to hold her without further injury?"

"If we take everything out of it, it sure is," he said.

"Are you actually considering his idea, Zel?" My face scrunched as I imagined Breena jammed into a box brimming with humidity. I'd assumed Rory was messing with us, but here Zellia was, taking his suggestion seriously.

"Well..." She trailed off. "I'm not really seeing any other way to get her off this ship. Rory says we'll be there any minute now, and not only is Breena unconscious, but she still has her seal tail. I know I haven't been to land in awhile, but I suspect we would draw a little too much attention carrying her through town. Am I wrong?"

I stood and let out a deep sigh as I stretched my weak and stiff body. Peering out onto the horizon, Barthoah's coastline came into view, as I had suspected. Glancing down at Breena as she slept on the deck, I felt guilty that I hadn't had the energy to carry her below deck to the hammocks that resided there. I could have at least made Rory do it.

Thinking back to earlier today, everything that happened was a distorted blur, as if nothing had happened at all. From the moment we'd gotten into the net until now, everything we'd done and said felt like a weird dream.

Staring back out to the expanding view of the rocky shoreline, I said, "I can't believe I'm about to say this, but I see your point."

Rory and I had emptied the trunk together as Zellia tried to clean herself off a bit with a bucket of sea water. When everything was out of the chest but a layer of fabric at the bottom, we worked together to pick Breena up and gently place her inside.

I barely breathed the entire time Breena was in the trunk. As we walked down the docks and through town, I went back and forth between yelling at Rory to slow down when I felt we were jostling her too much and telling him to speed up so we could get her out of there as fast as possible.

I'd made Zellia and Rory stop for a break once we made it out of town and into a meadow clearing. We placed the trunk down in soft grass, and I opened the lip up to adjust Breena and fan her sweat slicken face. When we finally arrived at his cottage, my legs were burning, and my back felt all but broken.

We carried her to a spare bedchamber where she could continue resting and healing in the comfort of a safe, cozy bed. Zellia used a damp cloth to clean Breena's exposed human skin, but we both felt it best to leave her tail alone for the time being. When I first saw her half transitioned, I'd thought she was the most magnificent sight I'd ever laid my eyes on. Now, seeing her tail poke out from under the sheets, the feeling of wonder I once had looking at her shifted to deep-rooted worry.

Zellia and I eventually left Breena to take care of ourselves. We both bathed, dressed, and shoveled human food down our throats. Before Rory left again, he pulled out a dress his neighbor dropped off for him to mend, and Zellia took the upgrade from the rags very willingly, despite the unflattering cut of the black fabric.

"How are you feeling? You seem good," I asked my sister as she finished up her strawberry porridge. She looked at me with a mouth full and nodded her head.

Her throat bobbed. "Surprisingly, I feel fine. Better than you look."

"Thanks for that," I chuckled, digging my shoulder into hers. She laughed as she scraped her metal spoon against the sides of her ceramic bowl for residual porridge and bits of berry.

"Where did you send Rory off to again?"

"You know those netted enclosures I told you about?" I asked. She nodded with a focused gaze. "Breena cut one when we left land, freeing everything inside it. We did it with the intention that we'd see those creatures slowly making their way into the Dreslee and the Selkie Cove. The opposite seems to be true, and we need to figure out why that is."

He'd left almost as soon as we got Breena in bed, not wanting to waste time when his mother was still at risk. Sure, she was safe with my grandfather, but even I saw the risks in drawing out our investigation into the hybrids.

A high-pitched whistle sent Zellia jumping out of her chair. I rose from the wooden table and headed to the stove to silence the disruptive noise.

"Want some tea?" I asked, removing the copper kettle from the small stove flame. Zellia shrugged in indifference, her hand over her chest as if to slow her racing heart. She'd yet to sit back down, but I poured her a cup anyway. I brought it back over to the table with a small plate of shortbread, disregarding the fact that we had both just eaten more than enough.

"Smells good, lass. Make any for me?"

I cranked my head to see Rory amble through the front door. He closed the wooden slab behind him then braced himself on the wall as he removed his boots one at a time.

"No. What did you find?" I turned back to my cup of tea and gestured to Zellia to sit, but she still stared at the fisherman, following his movements with her gaze.

Rory rubbed his brow with the heel of his palm and dropped his shoulders. His eyes flicked over to Zellia, as if he'd just noticed she was in the room. The fisherman cleared his throat, adjusted his posture, and said, "I'll see about picking you up a few dresses tomorrow, Zellia. That old hag's garments just won't do."

"Hag? What a lovely thing to say about your neighbor," I spoke into my tea before Zellia had the chance to speak.

"I mean no disrespect," Rory chuckled. "Greta is an actual hag. An elder witch."

"You know a witch?" Zellia asked in awe, smoothing her palm over the wrinkly old fabric hanging from her hips.

"Of course! We have a coven that resides here in Barthoah. Amazing women. Great hats." Rory's lips curled back into a pleasant smile. Sometimes, it was impossible to give the man a hard time. He reminded me of Mai—relaxed, unproblematic, but occasionally skittish.

"Wow. I... well—"

When Zellia couldn't get her words out, I knew exactly what she was thinking. I'd been right where she was, so I smiled and said, "It's a lot different here than you expected, isn't it?

"You can say that again," Zellia muttered then faced Rory. "Are all humans kind to fae, or are you the exception?"

"I wouldn't say we're *all* kind to fae, no, but I'd like to think most of us are. But look, I'm not going to stand here and pretend like there hasn't been a violent history between the sirens and the humans. To our general population's understanding, though, we dissolved our tension years ago. The sinking of the Ever Wanderer was the final straw for humans and sirens alike. I'm sure I don't need to tell you that a lot of lives were lost on both sides." Rory set his bag down on the rocking chair and cleared his throat. My stomach flipped inside out at his mention of the Ever Wanderer, and I didn't miss Zellia's nervous gaze shifting toward me.

"That's when your elders came to land to settle matters once and for all. Since then, we thought we were living in times of peace. It has been years, so what I don't understand is, why are the sirens still fighting a one-sided, imaginary war?" he asked.

"Imaginary," I scoffed. "You're lucky I like you, fisherman. Say that to the wrong siren, and you'll lose your life."

"Noted," Rory said. "I had no intention on bringing it up with the hybrids, that's for certain."

"And I suppose they're the ones to blame, aren't they? You more than anyone should know our war isn't imaginary *or* one-sided. It may have not been your idea to drain the sea of its fish, but you sure are making your impact, whether you're proud of it or not."

Rory flinched, and his mouth gaped as if he was about to stand up for himself but thought better of it.

"We were also under the impression that we'd reached an agreement of peace years ago, until the fish started disappearing. We had no one but the humans to blame, since it was you humans who were steering the ships and tossing nets into the water. What did you expect us to do, to think? Our hatred has remained as strong as ever," I said.

"Rightfully so, I admit." Rory cleared his throat and eyed over my tea.

"I think we can all agree that both sides are guilty of their own grievances, but all three of us know better now," Zellia said, grabbing a shortbread cookie off the plate and handing one to Rory. "What did you find out while on your ship, captain?"

Rory took the buttery cookie and flashed Zellia a soft smile. My eyes darted from him, to her, to the cookie, and back at him again. They narrowed, but my mouth remained closed.

"Nothing but bad news, I'm afraid. The nets are intact again," he admitted, coming to take a seat with us at the wooden table littered with empty bowls of food. He took in the sight but said nothing about us raiding his kitchen. "I thought I must have gone to the wrong enclosure—got turned around somehow—but after I visited the third net, I knew what I was seeing."

"Intact? How?" I sputtered. When we'd left the enclosure,

Breena had sawed right through the rope netting. We'd watched the frayed pieces as they sank through the water.

"I don't know how else to explain it, but I think the enclosures are enchanted. I'd always wondered how they managed to hold so many creatures and why the fish seemed drawn to them but I never wanted to spend my time concerned with the horrible things. My own guilt, I admit."

"I wanted to test my theory, so I used one of my smaller nets and relocated a few fish outside of the enclosures. I sat and watched as the fish swam right back inside their former prison. Swam right *through* the net," he continued, his skin flushed.

"The nets are enchanted?" I said under my breath. "The fish can swim into them but not out. Did you try cutting them again?"

Rory cracked his knuckles and released a heavy breath as he said, "That had been my next move. The darn thing just shimmered and reappeared whole again a few minutes later, like I'd never severed it in the first place."

"Sid..." Zellia's pink lips quivered until she placed a steadying hand on top of them.

"Yeah, I know," I reached for her free hand and gave it a squeeze. The lump forming in my throat matched her weary expression.

Rory raised his hand just past his shoulder and said, "I don't read minds. What are you thinking?"

"The netted enclosures are massive, and there's twenty-three of them. Making mass enchantments like that takes major skill and power. In order to keep up that many, there must be more hybrids working on this than we'd ever imagined," I said.

"The hybrids have orchestrated this illusion of war under all our noses," Zellia said with narrowed blue eyes. "The question is: why? And where have they been hiding?"

"Our elders have no interest in aiding us, but we have someone who might," I said, biting my lip.

"Who?" Zellia and Rory asked simultaneously.

"Our grandfather."

CHAPTER TWENTY-FOUR
DO YA LIKE SAUSAGE?

Rory wandered into the kitchen with a ceramic mug teetering in his left hand. He rubbed his eyes with his free fist, letting a yawn sneak out in the process.

"Doin' okay this mornin'?" he asked with that lazy lilt of his.

"Yeah, are *you*?" I eyed over his slovenly appearance and weary expression.

"There's no fatigue a bit of fresh sea breeze can't fix." He took a sip of his still-steaming tea. I'd only been in the kitchen for a few minutes, and I wondered how long he'd been up, or if he'd even slept at all. From the darkened circles under his eyes, it seemed unlikely rest had found him.

"Except you need to remain here with Breena while Zellia and I head to our grandfather's shop. That fresh sea breeze will have to wait," I said, patting the man on one of his slouched shoulders.

"Mmm?" The muffled sound came from the other room, where Zellia reluctantly sat up on the settee and stretched out her spine. Her hair, while now free of scales and slime, was reminiscent of a straw bird's nest. She wiped at her drool-coated chin and smoothed out the black witch's dress that laid crumpled in her lap. It was odd seeing her like this—dwelling on land as if she'd been born human. I wondered if she felt equally as perplexed as she watched me maneuver around Rory's tiny cottage.

"Sid, it's far too early to be awake. Couldn't you be any quieter?" my sister's voice echoed in my mind. At first, I thought nothing of the sound, but when I attempted a response, I realized my mind was blank. There were no words to send back to her, just gibberish and stray thoughts.

My head swung around to glance at Rory, and I asked, "Did you hear that?"

"Your sister's downright musical yawn?" he asked, transfixed on my sister's ratty appearance.

He didn't hear her.

"Zel?" I asked. "Say that again."

"Couldn't you be any quieter?" she asked again, as if to confirm that's what she'd said the first time. She ran her parted fingers through her hair like a thick comb, smoothing out the bits that stuck out until her hair was silky and straight once more.

"But you said it in my mind the first time, you know that, right?"

"I did?" she asked, her head cocking.

"You didn't realize?"

"I think I'm too tired and hungry to realize much of anything. Can you not talk in people's minds on land like in the sea?"

"No, never," I admitted then attempted to reach her again. Nothing. "Interesting. I suppose we haven't tested everything you can do on land yet. I shouldn't have assumed we would have the same magic. We never did in the sea, either."

Sure, our magic was similar. Anyone full blood, or close to it, had standard siren magic, but all our skills varied slightly. Mine made it easier to hunt, and Zellia's was great for healing. I suppose now it was time to figure out what it meant for her on land.

"Rory, will you fix Zellia something to eat while she messes around with her magic a bit? Make sure she doesn't... I don't know, break anything." My back turned to my sister as I spoke.

"I'm going to go check on Breena and get myself together for the day."

"She's not going to accidentally kill me or anything, will she?" he asked, his eyes darting from my sister to me.

"How should I know?" A devious smile crept onto my face as I made my way out of the kitchen.

"Do ya like sausage?" I heard Rory nervously ask Zellia as I entered his spare bedchamber.

Breena laid unmoving on the bed. If I hadn't known otherwise, I'd think she looked perfectly at peace. I sat on the edge of the mattress closest to her and reached for her hand. While my songs couldn't heal or wake her like Zellia's could, I could certainly sing the lullaby I'd crafted for her the week earlier. My eyes fell closed, and I envisioned flat, warm rocks misted by the sea. I could almost hear the gulls in my mind as my lips parted.

There was no way for me to know what was going on in that mind of hers, but I could at least make her slumber more restful. I could make her feel at home as she slept in this strange bed.

When my song was over, my aching body found some relief, and I hoped Breena's had too. I stripped out of the evening gown and threw on the white dress I'd donned a few days earlier. Zellia wasn't the only one in need of a new dress. Breena and I had a bag jammed with a few items from my dad's old place, but nothing to call our own except the pendant around my neck and the tail Breena couldn't seem to rid herself of.

I crept around the corner when I was sufficiently ready for the day. I'd overheard Rory explaining what sausage was, and I didn't miss Zellia's horrified expression. I chuckled under my breath as I watched the pair from afar. Rory set a glass of water and a cup of tea in front of her, and she stared down at her hands, presumably wondering what she was still capable of here on land.

Within seconds, the water erupted out of her glass, and piping hot tea began bubbling over the sides of the ceramic mug. The wooden chair she'd been sitting in scraped across the floor as she stood to dodge her own mess.

With a flick of my wrist, every last droplet of water and tea began slithering from the floor, up a leg of the table, and back into their appropriate vessels. Zellia flashed me a sheepish grin as I leaned on the wall across the room.

"You have some work to do," I said with a laugh.

"I'll get there, don't you worry."

Zellia's eyes flicked back to the cups, and as she raised her hands to try again, I said, "There'll be time for that later. We've got places to be."

The brass bell rang out as we walked into our grandfather's shop, but I could barely hear its chime over Zellia's excited babbling. While we waited at his front desk for him to appear, Zellia's eyes hopped from one glass piece to the next with a small, amused grin.

Even though this visit was a family affair, I wished Breena was here with us. Zellia would only be on land for so long, and I wanted the important people in my life to know each other, to love each other just as I loved them.

When a few minutes passed and our grandfather still hadn't come out from his workshop, I called out his name. When that did nothing either, I grabbed Zellia's hand and gently guided her behind his counter, saying, "Let's go."

I called out for him again as I pushed open his workshop door, his name coming out as a question this time.

"Oh, hey ya! Look who's back!" Our grandfather climbed down from a creaky wooden ladder with a pail in his left hand. "I'd been wondering if I was gonna see you again."

Zellia stood next to me, rocking on her heels with her hands clasped in front of her, waiting to be noticed. When our grandfather fully descended from the ladder and faced us, he froze in his tracks.

"Well, would you look at that," he gawked, slowly setting his pail down to the floor beside him. Zellia flashed a shy smile, and her hand made a small, quick gesture, as if to say hello. All her excitement from earlier flew out the window, and she stood almost frozen next to me, letting her apparent nerves take hold of her body. "You're a spitting image of your older sister, Zellia."

"You know my name?" she asked, her beautiful face puzzled.

"Of course I do! How could I forget you? You're my youngest grandchild, after all," he said, a jolly smile rounding his already plump cheeks.

"Do you... do you mind if I hug you? Is that strange? I—"

"I would love that." My grandfather cut her off. Zellia took a hesitant step forward then threw her arms over the man. He returned the embrace, albeit with less gusto than she had. Before the moment passed, I ran forward and joined in on the hug, squeezing them both between my still-weak arms.

I should have felt embarrassed, and maybe a small part of me did, but the part of me that was overwhelmed by joy and love had far more of a hold on me. So, I held on to those I loved just a little longer, long enough for laughter to bubble up in each of us.

"Well, isn't this lovely," an unfamiliar woman's voice echoed through the workshop. "I'm just going to excuse myself. Why don't I grab you all a bite to eat? Yeah, that sounds good. I'll go do that."

Zellia loosened her hold on our grandfather, and I lifted my head to peer over her shoulder. An older woman stood before us, her face pleasant and round. She offered us a jerky wave and started heading for the door.

"You're Rory's mother?" I asked, pulling away fully from my sister and grandfather.

"I sure am." She stopped just as she reached the doorway. The woman clutched her coin purse in front of her and rocked forward onto her toes before rocking back onto her heels once more. "The name's Evina. Nice to finally meet you girls."

"Nice to meet you too, Evina. I'm Sidra, and this is my sister Zellia," I said. "Are you sure you don't want to stay?"

"Oh no, don't be silly. I'll let the three of you catch up. I'm sure there's much to discuss," she said, pushing copper hair behind one of her ears.

"You're staying here for a reason, though." The meaning behind my words lingered in the air between us.

"You're right about that," she said after several dramatic blinks. "But I won't be gone long. I'm simply going to walk a few stores down for a little treat to go with a bit of tea."

"She's not a prisoner, little minnow," my grandpa said with a chuckle. "Evina will be okay in town for a few minutes. It's a very public place, and the hybrids aren't very public people."

"I suppose so," I said, offering Rory's mother a weak smile. I didn't want the woman going and getting herself hurt in the name of snacks, not when the hybrids could be after her.

"A treat would be lovely!" Zellia blurted. If my curious sister stayed here in Barthoah any longer, the food of the sea would be ruined for her forever. I really should have been feeding her bland foods like soupy rice and plain oats. We didn't *both* need to be terribly torn apart, our hearts—and stomachs—having two homes. My heart was torn between the sea and land enough for the two of us.

"Alrighty, then. I'll see the three of you later," Evina said before disappearing out the workshop door. As I listened to the sound of her steps as she padded off, Zellia flashed our grandfather a curious look shadowed by the faintest hint of doubt. I'd been where she was now, standing in front of a man claiming to be family, having no idea how to interact with him or what to say.

As much as I wanted to give the two of them a moment to

connect and get to know each other, I battled with time and how little remained. If all went well with the hybrids, there would be time later for quaint conversation and buttery fingers from cookies.

"Seeing both of my granddaughters in the same room brings me great joy, but am I wrong to assume something... not ideal has occurred?"

"You could say that." Bitterness seeped into my words. "I went back to the Dreslee for a few days to amass our pod and convince them to come to land. The only one willing to join, though, came against my wishes. And you're staring right at her."

Zellia shot me a sharp look, but then her face softened like butter as she gave our grandfather a sheepish smile.

"Ah, so I have *two* rebellious granddaughters then," he said with a soft chuckle. "Why did you want your pod to come to land? I don't want to imagine what would have happened if the elders agreed to your request."

My head jerked back at his mention of our elders before I remembered he'd known about them since long before Zellia or I were even born. He'd had peeks into our world for decades, and that was the whole reason we were here in the first place. His knowledge.

"We need to stop the hybrids somehow. Because the elders denied us, we're gonna need your help to do it." Zellia's sheepish-ness had faded, and what remained was one of the hidden sides to my sister I'd been trying to coax out for years: her strength.

"Well, in that case, why don't you girls sit down, and we'll see what we can figure out together, hmm?" He gestured to the eclectic sitting area nestled in the corner of the workshop.

We all took our places, settling into leather armchairs and petite settees. We explained everything that occurred during my time in the sea, the information we'd gathered from Rory, and our most recent discovery: the enchanted enclosures. Our grandfather remained silent as he absorbed our words, his face twisting with various emotions each time we told him something rather shocking. By the time Zellia and I were done talking, the man looked as though he'd cycled through every emotion his body was capable of.

"It has been a busy week then." He mustered a weary smile, though his wrinkled forehead was written with a very different story.

"That's for sure." I straightened my spine and spoke clearly. "Please tell me you know something that will help us.

"I may know where these hybrids of yours are laying low."

Zellia shot me a look of hope, and I was hesitant to return it. I did, however, lean forward in my seat until I was just one step away from standing.

"I'm not sure if the place I speak of is still around, but there used to be a congregation spot for sirens on land. Your father would frequent it during long stints in Barthoah. The place was built as a safe haven for sirens to rehydrate their skin in saltwater pools hidden within the rocky caves just out of town."

"You think that's where they've been hiding?" I said as a question, though I knew his theory was sound. If there was a place hidden away on land for sirens, that had to be where the hybrids were dwelling. Especially now, since my pod no longer returned to land, we'd be none the wiser of their existence, or their growing numbers.

"Sounds likely to me," Zellia chimed in. Wallace nodded his head, his face unmoving.

"What are you thinking?" I asked, evaluating his aged features.

"If that is where they've been hiding, you're likely walking right into a trap."

"Mmm. Unless they don't realize we're against them," I said, turning to my sister. "Zellia and I have been lying to our parents for years. I think we could put on a performance for the hybrids for one afternoon. Don't you, Zel?"

Zellia's lips drew in and then parted, as if she was about to protest my claims. Then, a sneaky smirk lifted the corners of her mouth, and she bowed her head in agreement.

"I'm in."

CHAPTER TWENTY-FIVE
INTO THE DRAGON'S DEN

Zellia and I stood outside the cave entrance, seeing the flicker of light emanating from within. Her chin pointed toward me, and the briefest look of uncertainty flashed across her bright blue eyes. The emotion was as fleeting as my sudden doubt. Hers was replaced by hardened, narrowed eyes in the form of determination, and mine sank deep into my bones before settling into resolve.

She reached for my hand, and the two of us took our first step forward across crushed rock. The thin soles of our slippers ground dusty pebbles into the cave floor below us as we sank farther and farther into the depths of the cave. The humidity of the day cooled into crisp air, and the sound of crashing waves behind us melted into a soft trickle up ahead.

The light within grew brighter as we walked, and my ears picked up the faintest sound of music pinging off the rock walls in distorted, eerie moans. Our gazes crossed again now that we had the confirmation we sought. The caves were inhabited.

We approached the end of the tunnel and stared off at where our path broke into two. I squeezed Zellia's hand before I dropped it and stooped down. Under our feet, the rock was now damp. I took several steps forward to where the wet stone dipped and water trickled through the subtle depression in the floor.

"This way," I whispered, following the water to where the tunnel branched to the right.

It wasn't long after that the tunnel opened into a large room dotted with several silver pools. A dozen heads turned in our direction as Zellia and I stood with our arms hanging awkwardly at our sides, having nothing to offer our audience but our presence.

The cave dwellers lounged around the pools, some fully submerged, others hanging off rocks or dipping no more than their tails into the shimmering water. *Tails.*

My eyes frantically scanned the woman closest to me, and my heart leapt as I saw scaled fins, webbed fingers, and a deadly sharp set of teeth as she sneered at me.

There you are.

Understanding flickered in Zellia's eyes too, but neither of us made a move.

An older woman padded barefoot toward us. She was wrapped in wispy, sage green fabric, and she used a gnarled wooden stick to support her weight. As I listened to the clacking of wood across stone, it dawned on me for the first time how hard the harsh pull of land must have been on the bodies of elder sirens.

"Welcome," she crooned. We took a few steps forward to shorten the woman's journey, aware that every eye in the room was on us. When we stopped in front of her, the older woman reached up toward my face and pulled down my lower eyelid with her thumb. The sudden touch made my pupils flicker, and the woman hummed in satisfaction.

I straightened my neck to pull away from her invasive hand, but she'd already moved on, hitting Zellia in the ankle with her cane. Zellia didn't hold back a hiss as the wood struck her outer ankle bone.

"Very good," the woman mused then smacked her lips. She

took a step back, as if to signify her inspection was done. "What are your names?"

"Sidra, and that's Zellia," I said. My chin pointed toward my sister, and I did my very best to keep a hiss out of my own tone. My patience for this woman was growing thinner with each passing moment, but I was all too aware of the hushed chatter that surrounded us.

"Do forgive our weariness of an unfamiliar presence. It's not often that we get visitors. But we're always happy to welcome new sirens to our sanctuary," she croaked. I wondered what a song would sound like coming from that rough throat of hers, if she had a song at all.

"Of course. As sirens, we can never be too careful in times like this," I said, digging my fingernails into my palms to hide the nerves boiling up from all the wandering gazes in this place.

"No, we cannot," she said. "Well, do come in. I'll let one of our younger inhabitants give you girls a tour. My old bones can't keep me upright for very long these days. Isla?"

The woman motioned a brunette with milky-white skin forward. Isla, I presumed, pushed herself off a raised bed of rock lined with velvety cushions. A fragile smile was painted onto her pretty lips, resembling the porcelain doll I'd seen once as a child.

"Ladies, welcome to our home on land," she said, spreading her arms to the side. She motioned to the cavern that was lit by cracks in the ceiling, revealing the light of the summer day. The brilliant rays illuminated small waterfalls trickling down the rock into shimmering pools carved out of the stone floor. In the dry areas, sirens lounged on cushions and nibbled on various snacks being passed around on silver trays. The place was an odd mixture of primal and opulent, like a dragon's den, complete with a shiny treasure.

"It's beautiful," Zellia whispered under her breath, as if to not draw more attention.

"It is. Do you mind showing us around?" I asked, hoping to

take advantage of Isla's hospitality, whether it was a façade or not. I refused to go back to Rory's cottage without answers. Knowing these caves were occupied was only a small piece of the puzzle. We still didn't know if these were the hybrids we sought, or if we had been wrong about so much more than we'd originally thought.

"Of course. I'm happy to show you any area open to guests. Follow me." Isla gestured us forward with her long, slender fingers, as if we were sailors and she was beckoning us to the sea. The woman sent chills up my arms, and not in the way Breena did.

"There's more to the caves than what we see now?" I asked, my vision dancing around the open area in front of me. I thought back to the fork in the path that Zellia and I had stumbled upon. We'd chosen to go right, but what lay hidden beyond the left path?

"Certainly." She gave a weak smile and walked forward, not looking back to see if Zellia and I would follow. "Living quarters and such. The basics."

Taking a look around, I had to assume their living quarters would be anything but basic. Had they raided a castle? Or was this all bought with the fish from our sea—the evidence of profit from selling their abundance to neighboring villages?

My skin grew hot just taking in the wealth lining the walls of this place. This *had to* be it. These *had* to be the sirens wreaking havoc on Barthoah and the sea. And if that was true, it dawned on me that Tinelle was here somewhere. We just had to find her.

"You know, I just realized I forgot to ask the woman who first greeted us what her name was." I kept my face neutral, not giving Isla any more reasons not to trust our intentions. Our stranger status already did enough.

Isla looked pointedly at me before saying, "Do you know why sirens come here? Why we first inhabited these caves hundreds of years ago?"

"As a safe haven?" Zellia asked. I kept my eyes trained on Isla and watched her lips twitch as I waited for her to answer the question she so conveniently didn't hear.

"No. We didn't need a safe haven back then because we had no predators. We *were* the predators, you see. It wasn't safety we were after; it was health and comfort. Community. Sirens living on land would come to these pools to hydrate their drying skin and spend time amongst our kind, full bloods and hybrids alike. See, we have something for every siren, so we can all find comfort here.

"Over here are the salt pools with the salinity emulating the sea. The natural waterfalls continue to refill them to keep the water flowing. These are for hybrids who don't worry about the implications of their transition." she said. "And over here, we have the diluted pool for the full bloods. One of our many rules is that full bloods stick to their designated pool. Everything flows better that way, you see."

"Why are these pools for only the full bloods?" Zellia asked.

"The salinity is reduced enough that the water is still hydrating and healing, but it's not intense enough to send someone into transition. Full-blood transitions are rather unpalatable and uncleanly. We ask that those activities be reserved for the sea, not these pools. No one likes cleaning blood and flesh off the floor. The only exception is if a full blood acquires a blood stone. But as we all know, their cost is beyond what most would pay."

Blood stone?

Zellia and I both shot each other a look, but neither of us commented on this interesting tidbit. We'd grown up thinking blood stones were a myth. They weren't natural by any means, but crystals soaked in the blood of a witch during her moon cycle. When worn, they allowed full blood sirens to transition without pain like a hybrid could, but they retained their ability to sing their song.

Blood stones were a dream, a dangerous one at that. I'd given up hope that they'd existed long ago. I'd hoped my father would have done anything to acquire three so we could return to land with him for visits, so he didn't have to keep leaving us behind. I figured since he never had, they must have been a myth.

When neither of us responded, Isla clasped her hands in front of her and said, "Which pools will you ladies be soaking in today?"

"Oh, we didn't really—"

"Nonsense." Isla interrupted. "I'll have someone fetch you anything you may have forgotten. No reason not to enjoy the pools while you're here."

"Well, I suppose we will need two bathing cloths. And towels," I said, my eyes locked on Zellia instead of Isla. My sister gave me a reassuring head nod, and that small gesture allowed my clenched hands to relax.

"Full bloods, then," Isla said with an amused twinkle in her eyes. It had been the first time since we arrived that she looked genuinely interested in our presence. "I'll have what you need shortly. In the meantime, please, make yourselves comfortable. Help yourselves to something to eat and drink. We pride ourselves on our extensive wine collection."

Snacks and wine?

Our visit was far from what I'd mentally prepared myself for, and I could tell from Zellia's bemused expression that I wasn't alone.

"Thank you, Isla," I said.

The woman nodded and wandered off. Zellia's lips parted, but then she paused, as if she'd rather I spoke first. I dipped my chin down and leaned into her.

"This is our opening," I whispered. "If we're going to find anything out, we better do it now."

"Agreed. Let's head over to the full-salt pools and have a little chat with the hybrids. I doubt Isla will want to see us by the wrong pools with our messy peeling flesh and all, so we better be quick about it."

Zellia dipped her toe into the salty pool, the lounging hybrids keeping their eyes trained on her. Her lips twisted, and then she dunked the rest of her foot inside. When small scales began ripping through her toes, she pulled it back and forced a smile to smother a wince. The person next to her stared at Zellia's partially-transitioned foot.

"The water is... a nice temperature," Zellia said to the curly haired hybrid still staring at her. "Do you swim here often?"

I shook my head, watching the awkward interaction unfold. A chuckle slipped from my lips as I turned on my heels and headed to the opposite side of the pool from Zellia. There was a woman perched on the ledge, sipping on wine, gliding her teal tail back and forth through the water.

She craned her slender neck toward me and said, "You're new here."

"I am. My name is Sidra." I analyzed the way she could sit so peacefully before me, half in and half out of the water. I craved what she had, craved the freedom to come and go as I pleased without risking my life in the process.

"Maisie. It's good to see an unfamiliar face. It gets so... stale around here."

"Stale?" I asked, looking over both my shoulders to make sure we were looking at the same view.

"Stale probably isn't the right word to use," she said with a shrug, casting an eye over the surface of the water she frequently disrupted with her fins. "I'm more tired than anything."

"Shouldn't the water help with the fatigue and dryness?" I asked, watching as she manipulated the surface of the water with the tip of her tail fin.

"Mmm, I suppose it should." The hybrid's shoulders were slumped to one side, all her weight on her propped arm. Her webbed hand was stretched over the stone, sharp nails tapping mindlessly on the stone.

"Why are you so tired then? Do they put you to work around here? I'm sure a place like this requires a lot of upkeep."

"Like you wouldn't believe. But everything comes with a price. It's nothing you won't discover for yourself soon enough," she leaned in and whispered, "If you're not careful."

"What do you mean by—"

"Sidra. Zellia," Isla's voice echoed from behind me. "I have what you asked for. Why don't the two of you meet me by the diluted pool? It's much more suited for your needs."

Maisie's blue eyes flickered, and she remained close to me as she spoke low into my hair, "Remember what I said."

"Come along," Isla said, placing her fingers on my lower back and ushering me forward before I had the chance to reply to Maisie. I looked over my shoulder at the woman as I was steered away, wiggling my fingers in the air to say goodbye. Zellia trailed behind us, holding a glass of wine and munching on who knows what.

"Ah, here we are. Much better," Isla said with a proud smile as she halted in front of an unoccupied pool. Out of all the pools in the cavern, this was the only one no one lounged in or around, the only one that had been diluted.

Are we the only full bloods here?

"I'll leave your things right here. If you'd like to get changed, there are a few dressing screens over there," she said. Her finger lazily pointed to no particular location in the distance. "Do let me know if you need anything. We like everyone's experience here to be one of comfort."

"That's very kind, thank you, Isla. I think we are more than fine for now," I said. "But, before we go, there is one thing."

Isla said nothing, but one of her dark brows lifted.

"Why are we the only ones enjoying this particular pool?" I asked.

"Oh, you won't be for long," she said then snapped her fingers. "Maisie, please come here."

"But..." Maisie said, glancing around her, as if to find something to ground her to her spot on the damp stone.

"Now, please." Isla's tight lips drew into a line. "You've been quite chatty with our guests today, so it's your turn."

Maisie bowed her head then swung her tail out of the water. Within seconds, her teal tail began to split, and human legs formed. Maisie looked so unbothered by her transition; I couldn't help but gawk at her. No screams, no blood or tearing flesh.

The new skin on Maisie's feet carried her toward us until she stood no more than a foot from the water's edge. She stared down into the water, and for a second, she looked as if she saw her entire future in its ripples.

"Thank you. And now you are not alone," Isla said. "Off I go. Enjoy."

Zellia and I thanked the woman again, and when she was gone, I felt as though I could breathe again. The woman had a way of sucking out all the oxygen in the room, and I couldn't quite place my finger on why that was.

Scooping up the bathing clothes Isla had left for us, I handed one to Zellia, and we went off in the general direction the woman had pointed us in. From a distance, I watched an unmoving Maisie. She kept looking down into that water until Isla came back over to her. The two of them started bickering, but I couldn't hear them from where I stood by the dressing screens.

When Zellia and I both came out from behind the screens, our dresses were balled up under our arms. All that remained were cotton swaths of fabric covering the parts of us that our scales did when we were fully transitioned.

"This place has amazing food, but it kind of gives me the creeps," Zellia muttered before taking a sip of wine. I stole the glass from her, polishing it off. She didn't even complain—we both required liquid courage.

When we got back over to the diluted pool, Maisie was already inside. She forwent the bathing cloth Zellia and I donned and sat shoulder deep in the water. Zellia and I climbed into the tepid water and settled in next to her.

"I'm happy to see you again so soon," I said to break the tension. "Why is it that Isla wanted you to join us?"

"And why didn't you want to?" Zellia tacked on. She moved her palms over the surface of the water, back and forth, before lifting one of her hands and peering at her skin. Her teeth clamped over her bottom lip, and she squinted to get a better look.

"Oh, it's not your company I didn't want. I-I was just comfortable where I was, that's all. I prefer being in my siren form, you know. Silly since I'm on land, I realize, but you know how things are."

"I don't think I do," I admitted, leaning back onto the stone behind me.

"Well, as I said, it's nothing you won't understand soon enough."

"That's not ominous or anything," Zellia uttered under her breath. I jabbed her with my elbow then gave Maisie a friendly smile.

Glancing around the pool, my eyes trailed over the stone ledge and the little etchings carved into it. A curious finger ran over the one closest to me, and I realized it had been a familiar symbol. It may not have been carved into my own spears, but I'd seen it on Xifi's. I'd once asked him what the symbol meant, and he'd explained it was a rune almost lost to the sirens throughout history. The rune was one of old magic.

It made sense to see the etchings here, I supposed, seeing as the caverns had been around for hundreds of years. There was probably all sorts of magic hidden in the caverns and tunnels that I'd never laid eyes on. My finger dug into the etching, and I wondered why this rune was etched into this particular pool.

Glancing up to see Maisie following my finger, she looked as if the movement was going to make her sick, but when I watched her closely, I realized the sheen on her forehead continued to grow, even as her eyes darted away.

"You're not a full blood. Why are you really here, Maisie?" I asked.

Her eyes focused on something in the distance, staying off mine and Zellia's. "The hybrid pools get so busy sometimes."

"You were just in one."

"Yes, well, I suppose Isla wanted me to give you a warm welcome. What better way than to keep you company," she said, pulling her gaze from the cave's exit to finally look at me. "I noticed you keep rubbing your finger along that rune. Do you know what it means?"

"Yes. I just don't understand why it's in this pool."

"What does it mean?" Zellia asked. She no longer played with the water, too busy scratching at her irritated palms.

"It's a type of thievery rune," I explained. "Xifi used to carve one similar into his spears when the fish first started disappearing. He swore it helped him catch what little remained before the sharks could."

"Thievery? That's a rudimentary take on it," the hybrid said, biting the insides of her cheeks before she could open her mouth again. It wasn't until I noticed the odd stinging in my skin, in my cells, that I started to understand. Maisie's hesitancy coming into this pool, Isla's very specifically worded requests, and the odd tightness in Zellia's face...

"She said it was your turn."

Maisie's throat bobbed, and she rubbed her lips together before her bottom lip jutted out. She wouldn't answer me, but her face said it all. I lifted my hands out of the pool and watched as the water I attempted to pull jiggled then splashed back to the surface, as if it had weighed far too much to make it all the way to my cupped palms.

"Zellia," I said, my heart quickening. "Talk to me, but don't use your mouth."

"*W...w...wh...y?*" The garbled question rang into my mind, as broken as my own magic. My eyes narrowed in on a very nervous-looking Maisie, and everything I suspected fell into place.

"Not thievery. Harvesting," I said, my jaw clicking as I did.

Maisie moved to make a run for it, but I slammed my heel on top of her foot, grinding my bone into her precious tendons. She squirmed and hissed, but I stared her dead in the eye, using every residual drop of magic I could muster as I sang in a low hum only she could hear.

A horrendous voice left my lips, dark and sticky as I said, "You will forget this entire conversation. Should anyone ask, we enjoyed a peaceful silence as we all relaxed."

"Sid..." Zellia trailed off. "You did not just—"

I released a dazed Maisie and grabbed Zellia's hand, shooting her a warning glare until she fell deadly silent.

"They're stealing our magic. We've gotta get out of here," I said, pulling my sister through the water until she was standing. "Keep your head down, and don't act suspicious."

Zellia did as I asked while both of us crawled out of the pool. A hypnotized Maisie gave us a confused wave goodbye as we exited the dangerous water, but I didn't wave back. Glancing around the cavern, no one watched Zellia and I as we made our way to the opening in the stone wall. It wasn't until we slipped into the cool darkness of the tunnels that I allowed myself to breathe.

CHAPTER TWENTY-SIX
BREENA EATS A SANDWICH

Zellia woke Breena a few hours earlier, noticing her wound had been healing far better than expected. We had returned from the caves three days ago, and with our magic waning, Zellia had to rely on good old-fashioned healing to clean up Breena's wound and inspect her a final time.

When Zellia finally woke Breena with her song, she stayed in the room for only a few minutes to make sure Breena's vitals were stable. Only then did she escape, giving us a moment alone.

I laid with the selkie as she groggily woke, stroking her hair and teasing her senses. She suddenly blinked furiously, and when she attempted to spring right out of the bed, I was there to gently press her back to the sheets.

"Woah, you don't even have legs yet," I chuckled. "Why don't you transition before you try running around the room."

Breena peered up at me, almost dazed, then threw the sheets off herself to reveal her seal tail. She dipped her chin as an embarrassed smile spread across her stunning features. "I suppose you have a point."

Soon after, Breena shed what remained of her pelt, and she hugged it tightly to her chest as we cuddled in bed. I caught her up on everything she'd missed over the past few days, inspecting her face carefully as I spoke to ensure my words weren't overwhelming her.

"I know I shouldn't have done it, but what else was I supposed to do?" I asked, placing my cheek on the cool pillow to get a better look at Breena. "Maisie would have told everyone I was aware of what they were up to in those caves."

"You did the right thing. This is war, Sid. Even though we never expected it to be with sea fae, with your own people, we have to do what we must to protect the sea." She grabbed my hand with a newfound strength. Well, her strength had always been there, but after her injury, I'd be lying if I said her lack of it hadn't frightened me. I was relieved to feel the tendons in my hand crunch in her grip once more.

"Hypnotizing fae twice in one month was never a part of my plan. I haven't even had the chance to do it on a human yet!" My hands shook in the air and then fell to the mattress with a dramatic thump. Breena chuckled and rolled her eyes at me, but I simply sighed and resumed my position on her arm.

"You never answered me earlier. How are you feeling?" I asked.

"Well, you had much more exciting discoveries," Breena said. "I feel great, but I need a damned sandwich."

A laugh erupted from a low place in my belly. "I could arrange that. But are you sure a sandwich is what you want right now?"

Playing with the hem of her nightgown, the silky feel of the fabric sent shocks of excitement through my fingertips.

"Maybe not...." Breena's grin slid into something more demanding, and I returned it in the form of kisses. I didn't need a medical sign-off to know Breena was more than ready for me.

Placing my palm flat on her stomach, I indicated she was to stay right where she was, despite the path of destruction my kisses took as they lowered down to her core. Breena did exactly as I asked, surrendering to me when I knew there was nothing she wanted more than to flip me onto my back and take control.

I kept reminding her how good she was doing until the death grip she had on the sheets relaxed, and a final moan slipped from her lips.

"And how are you feeling now?" I peeked up from my position between her thighs, a curious brow inching up the left side of my forehead.

"Mad you didn't wake me sooner. My dreams are far more boring than my reality right here with you," she said, pulling me up for more kisses.

Rory knocked on the door, and the two of us sprung from the bed. I tossed her the night slip I'd worn just hours earlier and called out to Rory as she clothed herself. "Be there in a minute!"

When Breena was appropriately dressed, Rory popped into the room to give Breena two brass keys.

"Happy to see you're awake. And look at that," he said, peering to the floor. "You have feet again." Breena wiggled her toes proudly, pulling more chuckles from Rory until he motioned to the keys. "They're for the chest in the closet. You hold the only two keys that can unlock it."

She needed a safe place to keep her pelt after all, and what was more fitting than the very chest that had brought us to the fisherman in the first place?

Breena thanked Rory, and he let us be. Breena did the honors and opened the closet door to find the chest waiting for her on the wood floor. She stared down at her pelt for a while before finally placing the seal skin inside the chest and locking it up with one of the two keys.

She gave the other to me.

Staring down at the key in my hand, a prick of tears bit at my waterline. I whispered, "Are you sure?"

"As sure as I'll ever be." She grabbed both of my hands and kissed the backs of them. Then, she pressed them together so I could feel the cool metal between them and the weight of what that little key had meant to me, to both of us. "I trust you with all of me, Sid—today, tomorrow, and every moment after."

Swallowing down the emotion rising in my throat, I slipped it into a little pocket sewn into my dress. Once my hands were free again, they wandered to Breena's face. My thumb traced the faint freckles on her cheeks, and I peered down into those mesmerizing brown eyes.

Her lips pouted then parted, but I kissed her words away, not being able to handle any more sweet promises. Part of me wanted to drown in pretty sentiments, yet there was the reasonable, weary side of me that screamed somewhere in my mind. The voice reverberated off the sides of my skull, reminding me that we were merely days away from returning home.

"Let's get you a sandwich," I said when I pulled away from her supple lips.

"Will you feed it to me in the sun?" Breena stuck out her foot from under her night dress. "I need to feel it on my skin. I won't fully be healed until I do."

"Well then, what are you waiting for? The sun awaits you." I ushered her out the door, patting the key in my pocket to ensure I still had the precious piece of brass.

The two of us wandered outside and sat upon the bench positioned on Rory's front porch. Breena flattened her feet on the warm stone and closed her eyes to take in the mild summer day. Birds chirped in nearby roan trees, and a vibrant orange butterfly landed upon Breena's umber curls. I wouldn't dare disturb her; she found her slice of peace this morning, and even this dainty flying creature could sense that.

Zellia came out only long enough to drop off a plate of sandwiches and a stack of cookies my grandfather had brought over for Breena. We thanked my sister and dove right into the goodies.

The selkie hummed as she took a bite, and then she paused. "These aren't Rory's cookies; these are your grandfathers. When did he come by?" Breena wiped the corner of her mouth and waited for my response with a crease between her eyes.

"Last night. He came by a few times over the past few days, bringing a treat with him each visit, in case you'd been woken." Brushing my fingers across her arm, I paused at a small, lighter patch on her skin. I circled the beautiful mark with my thumb, wondering how many unique little marks she wore.

"Three days," Breena whispered, her chin tucking closer to her neck, as if to protect herself from this news.

"Zellia and I needed to heal too, so you didn't miss out on much! When we returned from the caves, our magic was all but depleted."

"I supposed I'm simply caught up on rest, right?" Breena said, her cheeks rounding as her lips pulled into a weary grin. "How is your magic now?"

We've been regaining it, but could you have imagined if we'd soaked in that pool much longer? It makes me wonder how long the hybrids are forced to sit in the diluted pools, their magic being stripped from them by the harvesting runes carved into the stone. The water was like pin pricks on my skin, and I'd just assumed the sensation was because of the salt. I'd been too distracted by the hybrid and trying to pull information from her to understand what was going on."

"I can't believe they take turns having their magic taken, and all for what?" she asked, though we both knew it wasn't a question I could answer. I did have a theory, but it wasn't something I was willing to voice until Breena had at least wiped the sleep from her eyes and had something to eat that was more substantial than buttery shortbread and tea sandwiches.

"Will you tell me something?" Breena sat back on the bench and crossed her legs at the ankle. She began swinging them when I took more than a second to answer, restlessness already finding her.

"Anything."

"Will you be able to return to your pod?" Her question was

like shards of ice to my bloodstream. This morning, I'd been in my head about how the two of us could never work, but there Breena sat, reminding me of the state in which I had left my home.

"I'm not sure." Shaking my head, I released a deep breath and admitted one of my deepest fears. "I'm not sure if they will accept me back, even if we break the nets and free the fish. I feel as though I could single handedly save the entire sea, and they still wouldn't accept me back after raising a hand to Tetwin."

"Well, you know if they don't, you always have a place with me. I know Selkie Cove isn't really set up for sirens, but—"

"You would bring me with you?" I cut her off, my heart stilling in my chest.

"Of course, Sid. Do you think I want to leave you behind?" she asked, planting her feet firmly on the ground and pouring all of herself into me with a single look. "Your pod may have turned their backs on you, but I will always be here to help you build a new one. Me, Rory, your grandfather, and of course, Zellia too. *We* are your pod, even if by the end of the week, we're all in different places."

I tipped over, curling into Breena and resting my head in her lap. She held my head, playing with the long strands of my hair, sending chills through my body in a way I cherished like no other.

"I don't know what scares me more: not being accepted back, or admitting I don't know if I want to go back." The whisper left my lips, and as I stared at the rose bushes in front of us, I knew I'd never be able to unsay those words. Breena's hand paused, hovering just above my temple.

I could still feel the pieces of my hair tangled into her fingers as she said, "What if I said I didn't want you to?"

All the air in my lungs left me, and for a moment, it was impossible for me to fill them once more. I sat upright, meeting Breena's gaze with a certain intensity I didn't think existed outside of a hunt.

"Would you stay with me? Here, on land?" My mouth felt numb, my lips moving of their own accord.

"For how long?" Breena asked, tucking her plump bottom lip between her teeth.

"I don't know, but what I do know for certain is that I never want to leave your side." My voice wavered but kept pushing through my tight vocal cords and the tears threatening to unleash themselves. It didn't matter. The only thing that did was right in front of me, staring at me, waiting for me to continue with bated breath.

"Whether it is at sea or on land, I don't want to go back to the way things were. Breena, you have changed me, every cell in my body, and I have never felt more myself. I have never loved another being the way I love you, and depths, I'll be damned if I let you slip between my fingers."

"Sid..." Breena trailed off, her eyes wide. For a moment, her frozen features had me spiraling through potential outcomes my confidence had not allowed me to consider. "I love you with everything I have and then some. I don't care where we go, so long as I have you."

She threw herself at me, and I caught her oh so willingly. The two of us lost ourselves in each other, salty tears wetting both our cheeks. A beautiful relief washed over me, releasing doubts, worries, and everything in between. Everything I had ever wanted was right here in my arms, and great waves, I would savor every moment.

Breena and I strode back into the cottage, new invigoration fueling us. It was easy to drag your feet on a project when you weren't excited about the outcome. Now that Breena and I had both admitted the very last thing we wanted was to split up after defeating the hybrids, I felt a sudden sense of urgency to bring those caverns and their harmful magic to the ground.

When we entered the living space, I noticed Zellia curled up on the settee under a thin blanket. Rory sat on the settee next to her, handing my sister a cup of black tea. The two of them clinked their mugs together before taking a sip.

Holding my hand out, I halted Breena before we disrupted the moment. I blinked twice, my eyes adjusting to what I was seeing. Zellia was smiling, as was Rory. They were two fish in a shell, chatting and sipping their drinks. Was this my sister's first slice of normalcy since the fish disappeared, since our father died?

The selfish part of me wanted to hang onto this moment forever. If Zellia could have a happy life on land too, was it all that bad of me to ask her to stay?

No, I can't.

My poor mother's heart would surely shatter.

And my mother, well, she would die before making a home for herself on land.

"Oh, Sid! Look at this," Zellia exclaimed when she noticed us standing in the entryway. Rory smirked and handed her a red rose with perfect, velvety petals. She sucked in a breath, and when she blew it back out, it came in the form of a sickening, horrible melody.

Breena and I winced, but somehow, Rory looked excited, proud, even. What were the two of them up to?

A gasp ripped from Breena before I had the chance to digest what I saw. Zellia held out that once-beautiful rose that was now black with rot. A crumpled petal broke off, and Rory caught it as it floated toward the floor.

"Turns out my healing songs work both ways!" Zellia's excited giggles etched themselves into my brain, even if her happiness stemmed from killing a flower with her very voice.

"Well, that's handy," I said, unsure what the correct response was in this situation. "How did you discover you could do that?"

"It was Rory's idea. He has seen your magic firsthand and all the ways you've gotten creative with it. We figured my magic was expansive too, so we started pushing my boundaries. I've broken a few things, but it was worth it! I can actually help you in those caverns now, Sid, not just wait around in case someone gets injured."

All I wanted to do was tell my younger sister she was being ridiculous, that this was a terrible idea, but that's not what I would tell her. She sat in front of me as a grown woman, and a powerful one at that. I wouldn't continue to baby her, when all she'd ever wanted was to be taken seriously and treated like the adult we all too often forgot she was.

I swallowed my fear. "This is perfect, Zel. Good job. We're going to need every advantage when we head back to those caves."

Breena ran her fingers over my lower back, as if she knew just how hard it was for me to get those words out. I gave her a soft smile, and she once again reconfirmed everything I already knew.

I fucking love this woman.

"We've been thinking a lot over the past few days about how we can get rid of the netted enclosures once and for all," Rory said. His large hands twisted in his lap. "We know they are enchanted somehow, right?"

"Right. An enchantment that requires a whole lot of magic...." I trailed off, gears churning in my mind. "Magic they're harvesting at the cave."

Zellia nodded her head like she knew what I'd say. "We've been thinking the same thing. Do you assume the netted enclosures would disappear upon the destruction of the runes?"

I sat down across from Zellia and Rory, Breena right behind me. My arms crossed over my chest when I said, "I'm not sure how else they would have found the magic to be able to do such a large-scale enchantment. They've essentially blocked all fish off from the rest of the sea. These runes *have* to be how they're doing it."

I'd been suspicious of those harvesting runes the second I saw them, and now, all the loose pieces and fragments of knowledge were fitting together in my mind.

"There's only one way to find out."

CHAPTER TWENTY-SEVEN
THE CIRCLE OF CHANTING PUPPETS

"How much destruction are we really prepared to create?" Rory asked as we trekked down the beach, the light from the moon and stars coating us in liquid silver. We'd spent the rest of the day prior debating potential plans, and we had a vague idea of what we wanted to do. I held that left path in my mind, the one Zellia and I hadn't taken last time we were in the caves. As we wandered across the shoreline, I couldn't help but run scenarios through my mind about what we'd find on the other end of the unknown path.

"The caves have been around for hundreds of years; I'd almost feel guilty destroying them," Rory spoke again when us women were too silent for his liking. I wondered if Zellia and Breena were stuck in their minds as much as I was.

"Rory, you can't even use the caves and you still don't want to see them ruined?" Zellia asked, being careful where she stepped along the sandy shoreline scattered with broken shells.

"Well, we all agree the hybrids can't stay in Barthoah after what they've done, correct?" Rory asked. He cranked his head behind him to look at us, seeking validation we were all on the same page.

"Correct." I dipped my head then peered over to Breena to see her doing the same, almost in complete synchronicity with me. I ached to reach over and hold my cute little selkie. I wanted to wrap her in my arms and take her away from the madness of the day, of this entire week. She deserves peace, and I hoped with every ounce of positivity I could muster that by the end of the day, I could give that to her. If all went according to plan today, we could achieve success and rid ourselves of these pesky runes and netted enclosures.

"So we should be preserving the caves for sirens—who *aren't* thumb chopping, family threatening villains," Rory said, his husky voice pulling me from my internal ramblings.

"Sirens *will* still need a safe place to soak after all of this is said and done," Zellia said.

"As will selkies!" Breena added. I reached for her hand and stroked the back of it with my thumb. The caves were beautiful, and the thought of them being preserved as a place for all the sea fae on land to come and soak their skin warmed my heart. I imagined Breena and I sipping tea as we lounged in the salty pools together, and for some reason, I knew that mental image was going to stick with me. Maybe Rory was onto something.

"It's settled, then," I said. "We try to preserve as much of the cave as possible. But the runes in the full-blood pool need to be destroyed."

Rory reached into the satchel slung around his shoulder and pulled out three daggers, holding one out to me first. I stared down at the object, the sun glinting off the polished blade, and said, "What's that for?"

"Protecting yourself. You should all have one." Rory thrusted it forward, but I dismissed the weapon with a wave of my hand.

"I appreciate the sentiment, captain, but I'll be quite fine without one," I said with a smirk, the humor in his gesture easing some of the pressure in my chest. While the pool had weakened my magic, after a few days of not using the power residing in me, I was able to recover quite quickly. My eyes shot to the waves creeping up the shoreline, and with a twitch of my fingers, the salty water rolled out to greet Rory at his boots.

Before him, a tool mimicking what he held in his hands formed from the seawater. He bent down and scooped up the water dagger with curious fingers. His head fell to the side as he was able to lift the molded water off the ground and swipe it through the air, as if it was made of wood and steel.

"Not bad," he chuckled. With that admission, the water suddenly exploded in his hand, soaking the front of his tunic and canvas bag. He threw his head back in shock, but before anger could set in, I pulled the water molecules off his clothing so the man wouldn't enter the caves dripping wet.

"Alright, alright. I get it. You don't need a dagger." He held his hands up in surrender, an impressed grin finding its way into his features. He gestured toward the other women, but they too passed on his offer. At least the man would be plenty armed if it came down to it. Every part of me hoped those deadly things would remain right where he left them, in the safety of his satchel.

"Ever the show-off, Sid," Zellia laughed and shook her head at me. Her bright expression vanished as soon as it came, and she let out a dramatic huff and groan, dragging her feet in the sand as we walked. "This trip feels even longer than last time. My feet are killing me."

"We'll be there soon. Traveling by foot is hard at first, but you'll get used to it." Thinking back to when I'd first arrived in Barthoah, I recall being so surprised at how much walking would be needed to get from place to place. While I was in the sea, I rarely thought or complained about how far anything was because it was all an easy swim—until I left our territory, that was.

Zellia sighed and peered out into the distant waves of the sea. "I won't need to get used to it. I'll be back in the water soon enough."

I'd forgotten I was still holding Breena's hand until I felt her thumb stroke me in soothing patterns. I focused on the calming sensations she sent through me and banished any anxiety that came as a side effect to that one simple sentence Zellia spoke. My sister never intended to drive an emotional sword through my gut; depths, she didn't even know I planned to stay on land. For all I knew, she could have assumed I'd be swimming right alongside her on the way back to the Dreslee. I knew all of this, yet the sentiment stung all the same.

It'd been one day since Breena and I decided to stay on land together, and I hadn't regretted that decision for a fraction of a second, but that didn't mean I hadn't been dreading telling my sister. As I watched her stare longingly at the waves lapping up the shore, I decided I would tell her as soon as this mess was taken care of. No more waiting.

Up ahead, the rocky formations that bled into the sand grew taller, an unmistakable presence along the cliffside.

"We're here."

The four of us moved through the caves like sharks in the night, silent and deadly. Breena and I crept along with our backs tight to the tunnel walls as Rory and Zellia followed closely behind. Candles flickered up ahead, and somehow, this place looked even more magical at night. The glow of the candles threw strange shadows that danced along the stone in rhythmic patterns, smooth and hypnotic.

"To the left," I instructed upon reaching the same fork in the path Zellia and I had the last time we made a visit to the caves. We all hoped to find sleeping quarters and nothing more menacing lurking in the shadows of the mysterious path.

My feet halted, and a distracted Rory almost came barreling into me. He let out a soft grunt as Zellia threw her arm across his chest to keep him from knocking me over and whispered, "What is it?"

"I hear something up ahead." I kept my voice as low as I could. Closing my eyes, I listened again, more intently this time.

There it was again. Singing, maybe?

"I hear it too," Breena said, glancing over to me before venturing forward again. We traveled toward the sound, and as we grew closer, we began to decipher that the odd, off-tune sound was definitely a song, just not very well sung.

The song of a hybrid.

Reaching the end of the tunnel, the path before us splintered off yet again. I turned left once more toward the terrible singing and a flickering orange glow.

I motioned for the others to halt then pressed my back against the wall right where it funneled into an opening. An intricate tapestry was draped across it, but there was a gap next to me where the fabric puckered.

Drip, drip, drip.

A repetitive sound mixed with the echoing song, and I noticed a small puddle forming near my foot. I glanced up to see water droplets falling from the ceiling, one by one. Gesturing to the others to watch their step, I peeled back the tapestry a meager inch to get a better look inside.

A woman with winter-blue eyes sat on a stool facing away from me, brushing her tangled hair as she stared into a tarnished mirror. I stared at her reflection, noticing familiar features that pinched as she let out her sorrowful song.

Maisie?

Watching her, she wiped salty tears from her eyes and set the brush down on a small, wobbly table. I had to pull the tapestry back a tad more to get a better look at her as she crawled into a straw bed tucked into the corner. The mattress was raised by no more than a few pallets of wood and squeaked under her weight as she climbed under thin sheets.

Grabbing Breena's hand, I pulled her forward to take my spot in the entryway, hidden behind the thick tapestry. Breena watched for a few moments then turned back to me and whispered. "She's crying."

I nodded in response then took a step back, avoiding the water to rejoin Zellia and Rory.

"The hybrid we spoke to the other day is in that room. She won't remember Zellia and me, but I have a gut feeling she has more information, and she'll be willing to share it," I murmured. "Get ready to move in on her. Rory, you got the ropes?"

He said nothing as he pulled the ropes from his satchel and held them up with a grimace.

"Good. Let's go—quickly."

We all snuck behind the tapestry together, but I acted first. With my magic, I pulled the water pooling on the floor and flattened it across her mouth to prevent the sound of screaming from alerting the others. Breena held Maisie down long enough for Rory to tie her hands behind her back in a tight fisherman's knot.

Horror flicked across Maisie's eyes, but when I sang, "Remember us," in a hypnotic tone, her expression slackened.

"We're not here to hurt you, Maisie. In fact, I believe you've already been hurt enough. We know the diluted pool harvested our magic, that Isla sent you there to have yours taken too. Why?"

Maisie looked just past her nose to the water still wrapped her mouth like a bandage.

Right.

Straightening my spine, I fixed my piercing gaze on her so she couldn't catch onto the fact that I didn't know what I was doing. "If you even try to scream, it goes right back on."

The hybrid nodded her head in desperate agreement, so I let the water covering her mouth slither to the side, staying right on her cheek in case I needed to shut her up again.

"I'll tell you everything if you promise to get me out of here. Out of these damned caves."

I looked over my shoulder to see Breena giving me silent approval. "We'll help you escape. Now, tell us quickly."

"Full bloods like you rarely come to the caves anymore, so we've had to resort to taking turns in the siphoning pool. I-I wasn't supposed to go again so soon, but Isla caught me talking to you and—"

"It was a punishment."

"Yes, and not an uncommon one. Most of us in the caves are young. We grew up on land, and some were even raised within these very walls. Sure, they feed us lavish foods and fill our stomachs with wine, but not all of us have the choice to be here, and the ones who do are the very ones giving out punishments."

"Like Isla," Zellia whispered.

"Isla is just a puppet. Her strings, and the three others just like her, are all pulled by a woman named Tinelle. You met her when you first arrived. She, uh, she was the one who did the test on you, to make sure you were both sirens," she said. When she caught my confused stare, she continued, "Yes, the really old one, but don't let her looks fool you. I'm sure you both know how powerful elders are. There's a reason they lead our pods, and Tinelle is no exception."

"Are they here now?" Breena asked, glancing over her shoulder as if Tinelle herself was breathing down her neck.

"They are. Every evening, they send us off to our rooms and stay in the main cavern to channel magic from the siphoning pool. They should be mid-ritual right about now, so if you're going to make a move, you better be quick about it."

The five of us all stared at each other; then, the water still clinging to her cheek slithered away, and Rory cut her free of his ropes. When Maisie sat up in bed and rubbed at her red wrists, Zellia reached forward and closed her eyes. At first, Maisie flinched, but when Zellia blew a soft song onto the hybrid's irritated skin, she relaxed and watched as the redness faded.

When Zellia was done with her simple healing song, my eyes darted around Maisie's face as I asked, "Will you come with us?"

Maisie knew her way around these tunnels better than we ever would, and she had firsthand access to how things worked around here: the siphoning pool, the ritual, the leaders.

"You promised to get me out, but if I help you, I need you to get rid of the five sirens keeping us here. I want *all* of us to be free. My friends need your help too."

"You have our word," I said.

Maisie straightened her spine then lifted herself out of bed. "Well then, I know another way into the main cavern. Follow me."

When the selkie clan and my pod rejected our requests for help and Breena was wounded, I'd begun to think I'd be facing Tinelle and the other hybrids alone. Now, I crept through secret tunnels with a healthy Breena, the fisherman who captured us, my younger sister, and a hybrid we'd turned to our side. While they weren't all warriors, I was relieved to have them.

Maisie led us, and we all wound through tunnels lit only by cracks in the walls that bled candlelight from neighboring caverns. The tunnel was on a steep incline, and the muscles in my legs burned as we ascended. I glanced over to Zellia, who squeezed Rory's hand as she led him along the dark path, the human's eyes a poor fit for this environment.

For a moment, my mind slipped to all the dark places I tried desperately to avoid. Thoughts of failure swirled through my mind, images of what would become of my mother if Zellia and I were unable to ever return to her. One wrong move tonight, and that might just be our reality.

When Maisie paused at an opening in the rocks, so did the rest of us. She held a pale finger up to her lips then motioned us forward. One by one, we crept through the opening and funneled out onto a landing overlooking the main cavern. My ears perked up as I heard chanting emanating from below.

Maisie knelt behind a ledge, still wearing nothing but her

nightgown as her knees rested on cold stone. Part of me felt bad that we'd pulled the girl out of her bed and hadn't even given her a second to throw on something more substantial. I forced myself out of any guilt and focused on the task at hand.

Breena and I kneeled next to Maisie, Rory and Zellia hanging back due to the lack of space on the ledge. The three of us peered over the rocks to get a better look at the source of the chants. Sure enough, that decrepit siren and her four puppets gathered around the siphoning pool, their arms raised.

"Our magic is somewhere in that pool," I said to Maisie, just loud enough that she could hear me over the ominous sound of chanting.

"So is the magic of a lot of other sirens."

The diluted pool they harvested the magic from was directly under us, so close that I could spit in it.

Breena stuck her head out a little farther over the ledge, peering down at the five sirens below. "How long do we have before they stop their ritual?"

Maisie slowly pushed herself off the ledge, her face cast in shadows as she whispered, "From the looks of it, we only have a few minutes. Whatever your plan is, it's best to do it fast."

Breena and I exchanged glances, and Maisie's lips twitched before dropping into a scowl.

"Please tell me you have a plan. You have a plan. right?"

Zellia's movements next to us caught my eye, offering me brief respite from Maisie's disapproving glare. My sister waved us over, so we met her back in the darkness of the tunnel.

"What's going on down there?" Do you think we could do some damage from up here?"

"If we could get Breena closer to them, she'd be able to smash the runes in the pool, but from up here, the only thing I can think to do is create waves so intense, they crack the stone. Still, there's a good chance that won't work."

Rory blinked several times before saying, "How close are the women to the ledge? Are they directly under it?"

"Most of them are, yes. Why?" Breena asked.

"I might have an idea." Rory reached into his satchel, dug around pieces of cut rope, and pulled out four glass vials.

"What are those?" Zellia asked, peering down at the vials that glistened in the cave's dim light.

"Payment." A smirk crept onto the fisherman's face. "I didn't mend my neighbor's dress for free, you know."

"The old hag gave you those? What do they do?" Breena's eyes widened with a vicious excitement. Depths, she was so cute when her violent side crawled out.

Rory held up each vial at a time, all of them different colors and viscosities. "In the green vial is acid, the light blue is a transformative potion, the milky one, well, this one is just a laxative..." He trailed off, slipping that one back in his satchel with a sheepish smile. "And the purple one is a hallucinogen."

I reached forward and ran my nail down the light blue bottle. "Tell me more about this one."

CHAPTER TWENTY-EIGHT
A VILLAINOUS VIAL

Breena all but giggled as she climbed back onto the ledge, the light blue vial in her grasp. When she popped the cork, she did so with a steady hand to avoid getting a single drop of the potent potion on her skin. I couldn't see the women below, but I knew my little selkie aimed at each one of them strategically before dripping undetectable drops upon their heads.

Just as we all thought she was in the clear, the rock ledge Breena leaned against cracked under her weight and crumbled down to the hybrids. Breena scrambled back, but the chanting below was quickly replaced by shrieks and hisses.

"You!" Tinelle screeched. Alarm prickled across Breena's face, and my body lunged forward before I thought any better of it. The old woman's head swung to me now that I was in her view, and if her movement had been any sharper, she might've broken her own neck.

"And you! Why are a siren and a selkie together, slinking around my cave?" she croaked. I pulled Breena in close to me, using my body to shield her from the elder siren. The woman's vision shot from us to the pool, her eyes bulging and red, her boney fingers twitching, as if itching to call on her magic.

"We know who you are, Tinelle!" I shouted, my chin raised high despite the women standing far beneath me. "And we know what you've been doing with that precious siphoning pool of yours. Your time stealing magic from sirens is over, as is your time destroying our sea."

Tinelle released a sickly chuckle, motioning to the other sirens standing with her, Isla included. "As you can see, I have more than a few willing participants. Borrowing your magic was simply a pleasant, and much welcomed, surprise."

"*Willing* participants?" Maisie made the mistake of joining us on the landing, staring down at the women below with hatred smeared across her tense features. "Don't pretend that any of you subject yourselves to that pool or that the rest of us are willing."

Isla's face went impossibly pale as she stared up at Maisie, but she didn't utter a word.

"You're a very important piece of the puzzle, dear. You all are," Tinelle sneered, the shriveled skin of her face scrunching further.

Breena leaned into my hair and hissed, "What point is there fighting with this woman? Just end her already."

Her muscles tensed beneath me, her feet stepping towards the ledge. I shook my head and held her back, counting on that blue vial to prevent bloodshed. If the potion worked, these women would be incapacitated within minutes without having to add their deaths to my conscience. I also couldn't let this woman slip through my fingers before understanding her twisted mind. Never knowing her reasoning behind all of this would surely eat me alive, chipping away at me through time.

My heart pounded in my ears as emotion slipped to the surface, raw and painful. "You take and you take, all for what? To kill the sea? To punish the sirens you once shared a home with? I don't understand!"

"Of course you don't! You were born with a song and a pretty little mask to keep you safe. Not all are so lucky. Some of us had a human parent who wanted us dead, all because they couldn't keep their hands off our mothers. Monsters, they called us," Tinelle spat. "We were finally getting somewhere in our war when your pod sank the Ever Wanderer. But then you gave up, gave in to the humans, leaving us hybrids with the burden of finishing the job you couldn't."

Her snarls sent me staggering back a step, the soles of my shoes grinding into the broken stone of the floor. Breena gripped my arms to hold me upright, my skin withering in pain as she forgot her strength. I forced my throat to relax, making it possible to shout back at the elder, "Gave up? We lost half of our pod that day! We didn't give up—we aimed to preserve what remained of our home."

My gaze shifted to where Zellia and Rory edged closer to the tunnel's entrance. With a snap of my wrist, I waved them away. Tinelle and the others couldn't see where they lurked in the shadows, and that was an advantage we needed to preserve.

My sharp gaze bore back into Tinelle. The woman tapped her wooded cane on the stone beneath her, splashing the thin layer of water coating its surface. "The only way to preserve our kind is by getting rid of the humans all together. Hybrids will never be able to live in peace until that day, and if we had to reignite the war by bringing the sirens to their desperate, starving end, then so be it."

The air began to buzz around me with Tinelle's magic, but I wasn't finished with her.

"You risked destroying us for a bit of payback?" I scoffed. "You're more delusional than I thought."

Maisie winced and whispered, "That wording was a mistake."

The puppet women all stared at their leader, fear licking up their faces like flames as they waited for Tinelle to make her move. The elder's face twitched as the cavern began to tremble around us. I could feel the water in the pools, the moisture coating the walls, and what loomed above us in the stone all vibrating, ready to erupt.

Maisie held onto a rock jutting from the ledge, gripping it for dear life as the entire place shook. "They must have completed their chant! No individual siren could do this."

She didn't need to clarify what "this" was. Each one of us could feel the power hanging heavy in the air. My jaw tightened as I realized they were using my very own magic against us, Zellia's and Maisie's too.

"Hold on," I said, and the four of them took my words literally, grabbing onto anything sturdy they could find. "This is *our* magic. I doubt a single one of them stepped foot into the siphoning pool, so we should have just as much claim over the power shaking these walls as they do, if not more."

"You're right!" Maisie shouted over crashing rock and the swirling pools below, a spark of hope igniting in her eyes. "Try tapping into it!"

I gripped onto Breena as I closed my eyes, and she held me equally as tight. If I couldn't keep an eye on her in this mess of crumbling rock, the very least I could do was feel her skin on mine, warm and brimming with life.

When my eyes squinted shut, I focused on the familiar hum of my magic, homing in on the sensation coursing through my body, zinging right to the edge of my fingertips. I caught the whispers of my magic dispersed through the air like mist, mixing with more magic that did not belong to me. I hoped Zellia and Maisie also caught glimpses of their power and grabbed hold of it.

Just when I sensed mine was almost within reach, Breena's grip on me loosened. She was getting ripped right out of my arms, the sound of her grunts tearing my eyes open. As I saw a giant hand made purely of water drag Breena off the stone ledge, I fought to channel every ounce of control, to not break my concentration on my magic. The hand tossed her squirming body onto the ground next to the siphoning pool—mere feet from the craggy old Tinelle.

Without thinking, I threw myself in the line of fire, closing my eyes and refocusing as another massive hand closed around my waist. Zellia screamed out, alerting the hybrids to her presence.

"Just stay alive for five more minutes!" Rory yelled out as the hand lifted me into the air. My own hands grabbed onto the fingers that wrapped around me, my magic pulsing and mingling with the fragments of my claim on it. My eyes flew back open as the hand became mine to control.

I was set down with a gentleness not extended to Breena only moments ago. I locked eyes with a seething Tinelle as the hand sloshed to the ground at my feet before reforming in front of Breena, who still lay crumpled on the floor. The watery appendage helped the selkie up until she was able to stand on her own, the sight alone enough to send a broken roar through the elder siren.

It wasn't until I heard screams rip through the air above me that I realized only Tinelle and one other hybrid remained. The three other women must have found Zellia, Rory, and Maisie in the tunnel, because my sister's shouts were unmistakable.

Something dull and wet hit the side of my face, shaking me back into focus. I blinked twice as my eyes darted to Breena as she used her incredible strength to fend off Tinelle's attacks.

Water beads formed in my hands, and I called for a deeper control of the monstrous hand. The power zapped through my bloodstream as I stole more and more magic in the air from Tinelle, taking as much as my body could contain before she could use it against my selkie.

Tinelle's attacks appeared weaker, the water forms she hurled at Breena growing progressively smaller and slower. The other siren was already charging toward me, hands raised, fingers squirming. Taking in a lung-filling breath, I screeched, targeting my song directly at her as loud as my lungs would allow. She threw her hands over her ears, her knees buckling as she collapsed onto the damp rock beneath her.

Above me, Rory and Maisie fought sirens one-on-one, Maisie with her magic and Rory with a green vial of acid. He uncorked it with wide, desperate eyes, splashing the contents onto the siren approaching him. She screamed and fell out of view as her hair began falling from her head.

"Please! Stop!" Isla's pleas echoed off the cavern walls, and my attention swung to her. Zellia gripped Isla's outstretched arm with a wicked grimace, the hybrid's once milky skin turning dark with rot.

"Zellia!" I screamed, pulling her attention off Isla. "Don't do this."

My sister's song ceased as she peered down at me in confusion, offering Isla a brief release. The hybrid used it to her advantage and swung at Zellia. Before her attack could land, Rory blew purple dust into her sky-blue eyes.

Isla's arm dropped as she stumbled away from Zellia in shock. Blinking rapidly, the woman's face froze before her mouth cracked into a smile—not one of malicious intent, but one of pure awe. She wandered over to the stone wall, running her fingers over it before leaning into its embrace.

The hallucinogen. Atta boy, Rory.

Before I could see what the intoxicated woman did next, Breena's grunts pulled my attention back to her and Tinelle. The selkie was holding her own against the quickly tiring old woman. I reclaimed much of the power she'd stolen, as did Zellia. I only hoped Maisie was able to obtain as much as we had.

Breathing deeply, I focused on the power building within me, staring down my target and preparing to unleash myself onto her. Just as my lips began to part, a dozen women came barreling into the room.

Breena and I stared at each other, uncertainty filling our gazes. Even Tinelle halted as her pod flooded the cavern. At first, they didn't seem to know which direction to go, who to attack. When they saw Maisie up on the landing, fighting the remaining puppet alongside Rory and Zellia, the hybrids, all disheveled and dressed in nightgowns, charged at us.

No, not at us. At Tinelle.

Trapped, furious women closed in on their leader, looking as if they were ready to beat the woman to death. Just when I thought Tinelle would surely meet her end at the hands of her pod, she suddenly disappeared. At first, I thought the woman had fallen, but then, the hybrids all began backing away, forming a circle where their leader once was.

Breena and I parted the crowd while we searched for any trace of Tinelle. Only when a young woman pointed to the ground did we realize our plan succeeded.

"For the love of all things salty," I muttered, a laugh bubbling up in me.

"The potion actually worked..." Breena processed what was happening, and I blinked several times to ensure my fatigued eyes weren't playing cruel tricks on me.

"We could use a hand!" a familiar voice echoed from above. I cranked my neck to see Zellia waving me down, standing next to a smiling Rory and a haggard-looking Maisie. She pinched glass between her fingers, the curious piece shimmering in the air above her.

Breena leaned into my side as she asked, "What does she have?"

"I have no idea," I admitted, attempting to get a better look. Curling my fingers inward, I used the rest of my magic to send a stream of water up to the landing, forming a slide from them to us. Zellia was the first to test my magic out, sitting upon the waterslide and riding it down until she landed at my feet.

She jumped up and wrapped her arms around me, relief flooding me as I felt my sister whole and alive in my arms. When she pulled away, she shoved a clear vial towards me. Inspecting it, I noticed three tiny sea snails clinging to the walls of the glass.

"I think there's room in there for two more, don't you?" Chuckling, I took the vial from between her pinched fingers. I was more than happy to do the honors, walking over to the circle of hybrids and peeling two more sea snails off the damp, stone floor.

one where Tinelle had disappeared, and the other where her puppet had fallen.

Breena let out a relieved laugh, and right as I popped the cork back onto the vial, she pulled me into her. Her lips found mine, and I had to fight back the urge to utterly devour her. My arms were shaking and sore, my buzzing magic slowly fading, fatigue taking its place, but I would always be energized by her and her kisses.

"Well, now what?" Maisie asked. Breena and I pulled back from each other just slightly, our gazes meeting one last time before we detangled ourselves all together.

Murmurs filled the cavern, dazed sirens glancing around at each other, us, and the vial in my hand. I twirled the glass in my fingertips, part of me tempted to smash the fragile thing right onto the ground, but a new, blossoming part of me clung to it, willing to preserve the life within.

"Rory? I'll take that dagger now," Breena said, holding out her hand with a lethal smile. Rory reached into his satchel and pulled a weapon free, its sharp tip protected by a stout leather sheath. We all watched her, unsure what the selkie's plan was with the deadly object. She freed the blade then took her time inspecting the glinting silver metal.

Striding right over to the diluted pool, she jumped into the tepid water without hesitation. I watched as she traced her inspecting fingers over the stone for harvesting runes. When she found the first one, she lifted the dagger into the air before slamming it down onto the stone, chipping the symbol apart with each powerful strike.

Reaching my hand out to Rory, he obliged by offering me a dagger. I joined Breena in the pool, attempting to destroy the next rune, though my arms were betrayed by my weakened state. Making no more than a few grooves into the stone, I slammed the blade through the water one last time, but to no avail. A frustrated grunt escaped my lips as my hands dropped back to my sides.

Breena slowly reached under my arms, taking the dagger from me. She didn't pull away like I thought she would, lingering behind me as she whispered, "Wrap your fingers around mine."

Doing as she asked, I watched as she guided my hands through the water, bringing the sharpened blade back to the stone. Scrape by scrape, we destroyed the rune together, her face buried in my neck as we did. She whispered sweet words into my ear, promises of freedom. I didn't attempt to hide the tears that trailed down my cheeks as we went, my heart swelling with love and pride. When the rune was no longer legible, the tip of the blade was gone, and I felt as though I could finally breathe again.

Water splashed around us, and we realized we had company. Zellia, Rory, Maisie, and a few other young women all climbed into the pool, various weapons in their hands, some sharp and others blunt. They worked feverishly, slamming their array of weapons into the stone, filling the water with sediment and dusty particles.

A few minutes later, not one rune remained. The cavern filled with excitable chatter and relieved laughter, the sounds echoing off the walls a beautiful song of unbridled relief.

"What will you do now?" Zellia asked before leaning back on the velvet cushion behind her and taking a sip of wine. "You're free to go anywhere, do anything."

Do I hear a hint of jealousy in her tone? I thought to myself, wondering if my sister's time on land was starting to get to her. Only hours ago, she stared longingly at the sea, but I knew all too well how quickly those feelings could change.

Maisie popped a berry into her mouth and tilted her head to the side in thought. I'd expected the hybrids to flee as soon as their captors were morphed into sea snails, but here they were, lounging with us around the pools and raiding Tinelle's wine collection.

"These caves have been our home for so long, many of us don't have anywhere else to go and no means to get there even if we had a destination in mind. I think I'll stay here for a little while, clean up the bedchambers and make this place a true home, not just a place to be kept," Maisie said. "Isla spoke so much of comfort and peace, but they rarely provided us with it. I think it's finally our turn to create that peace and comfort for ourselves."

"That's very honorable of you," Breena said, reaching her goblet of wine out toward Maisie in toast. "To whatever our new futures hold."

We all cheered to that, the sound of clinking metal and bottles ringing through the air as we celebrated with the stolen wine. I trailed kisses over Breena's cheeks and jaw, and she giggled in my arms, wine sloshing over the side of her goblet.

"Defeating your enemies gets you in quite the mood, hmm?" Breena hummed low in my ear.

I replied by nipping her bottom lip and whispering, "So does the thought of having a lifetime of moments just like this with you. Laughter, freedom, and delicious fucking food. You and me, selkie, a force to be reckoned with."

CHAPTER TWENTY-NINE
ANOTHER DAY, ANOTHER DEAL

"Are you sure you don't want to keep them?" Breena asked, leaning on the railing of the Indigo Tide. "We could put them in a dark and dusty cupboard."

"Depths, no," I said, holding up the vial of snails with a chuckle. "I don't need their bad energy. They can spend the rest of their days in the very place they tried to destroy, every new day a reminder of their failure."

"It's better than they deserve, you know." Rory emerged from behind me, tossing a disgusted glance at the snails.

"I do, but it gives me great satisfaction knowing the witch's potion is permanent. These wicked women will remain bottom feeders, never able to threaten families, hold sirens hostage, or stir up chaos ever again. The most they'll do is eat algae and avoid getting eaten themselves," I said. "I can live with that."

And the truth was, I could. No one was going to lose their life again because of these women, and that was victory. I was delighted by the sound of the cork popping out of its vial and the plop of each of the five snails hitting the surface of the water.

I couldn't help but smile, feeling like my father could finally rest, as could all the fragments of sea glass that called out to me for revenge over the last three years. While I'd never know which of the Ever Wanderer sailors ended his life, I can live knowing the women who attempted to rekindle the war my father died trying to end are now, well, sea snails.

"I'm proud of you," Zellia said, giving my arm a pinch. "No more death. No more hunting for food, or for answers, for that matter."

"How do you—"

"Sid, do us both a favor." She laughed and shook her head. "Let's not pretend you're coming with me. I know where your heart lies and where it should remain."

I stared at my sister, my mouth agape. "You know I'm staying?"

"I do, and I'm happy for you. You deserve peace more than anyone I know. Just promise me you'll visit. Mom and I may not need you to hunt for us anymore, but I still need my big sister, and she needs her daughter."

"You have my word," I said, those same words getting caught in my throat as a sob slipped out. Pulling her into my arms, I stroked her silky hair with my palm, savoring every second. "I love you, Zel. And you better come back to land too. For Grandpa."

"You could never get rid of me so easily. For life, Sid. Even if we're apart, you have me for life."

I nodded, an ugly snot bubble popping on my face. Rory handed me a hankie, and I took it from him with a sheepish grin. This crying thing was something I was going to need to get used to. I promised Breena my truths, after all, and I would always keep my word to that woman. Always.

We said our goodbyes to Zellia, knowing this wasn't the last time I'd see her, not by a long shot. The ache in my heart lessened knowing our mother needed her more than I did, knowing Zellia was going home, where her heart belonged.

When Rory pulled free of Zellia's hugs, he handed my sister a large serrated blade. She grasped its hilt in understanding, aware that there was one last task to accomplish before she could take her leave. The captain of the ship held Zellia's hand as she climbed up onto the side of the ship, knife in hand. She turned back to look at me one last time before she dove into the sea.

Her head didn't pop back up until she was fully transitioned, her shredded dress floating on the surface of the water. Rory scooped the fabric up with a small net attached to a pole and plopped it onto the deck.

"Gotta get this back to my neighbor," he said with a shrug. "A little stitching, and it should be good as new."

Breena poked the destroyed dress with her foot. "I think you owe her a new one, captain. Zellia did a number on it. But hey, you could always use a few more rags, right?"

As the two of them bantered back and forth, I turned my attention back to the sea, watching Zellia work as she sawed at the netted enclosure. When the fish began pushing their way out, I grabbed Breena's hand and guided her to the railing.

We all watched in silence until every last creature was freed. Zellia popped back up and waved the knife in the air with webbed fingers. "That's one! Twenty-two to go!"

"You heard the woman," I said to Rory, motioning to his wheel. "Lead the way, captain."

The three of us watched the sun set over the horizon, pink streaking a blue sky, as we enjoyed each other's silence. When Rory, Breena, and I finally arrived in Barthoah, a new life for me and Breena would begin, one without the weight of starving families or impending war. One full of love and curiosity, of release and surrender.

A new life would start for Rory too, I suppose, now that there was no pressure on him to remain a fisherman or live a life at sea. He could start a mending business or become a witch's apprentice if he truly wanted. The world was at our fingertips, and it was our turn to decide what we wanted to create for ourselves.

Breena mindlessly played with the little white hairs on my forearm as I contemplated what our next move was. Yet again, we would arrive in Barthoah, and our plan ended right at the edge of the dock. This time, though, fear didn't cling to this notion—only wildly expanding anticipation and tiny minnows swirled in my belly.

Rory released a yawn, leaning a little too much into his wooden captain's wheel. We'd been out on the water all day, sunrise to sunset, pulling Zellia along as we traveled from one netted enclosure to the next. By the time we dropped her off above the Dreslee, her eyes were heavy with fatigue, but a certain sparkle still shined in them in the dimming evening light.

For a moment, I was tempted to join her. I was tempted to hug my mother and tell her everything was going to be alright now, but this moment would have to wait. Surely, I would see her and my home soon. I would swim with Mai and sunbathe in the Kilkov, but first, I had a life to build.

"What will you do when we arrive?" Rory asked what I was sure we were all thinking. Breena and I shared a glance, an uncertain smile lingering in each of our gazes.

Before I could open my mouth, Rory continued, as if he never meant for us to answer in the first place. "I've been thinking, you know. Ever since you two decided to stay, I've been exploring possibilities in my mind."

"What kind of possibilities?" Breena asked, too curious to let the man continue.

"Before my father passed, he grew very ill. He was unable to keep up with his home for many years, and despite my best efforts, the place fell apart. When he finally found rest, he left me his cottage and the Indigo Tide. While I made the Indigo Tide my life, I haven't been back to his cottage."

"You never visited?" I asked.

"Maybe one day, I'll be able to face my father's home, but I still have residual guilt waring within me that needs settling before I can return. Maybe after making further reparations to the sea," he admitted. "And by now, the cottage is surely overrun by nature. With everything going on with the hybrids and keeping my mother safe, there was no time, even if I could stomach the memories clinging to the place like dust."

"What would you say if I asked the both of you to fix up his cottage for me?"

"You want us to repair your father's home?" I clarified. My gaze trailed over the fisherman, his sun kissed face tight with apprehension.

"Well, the two of you have skills and no place to live, no source of coin. Seems like a rather fine opportunity to me."

A sigh rolled out a Breena before she tilted her head and said, "Rory, we couldn't—-"

"Look, the feckin' place is just sitting there! He cared for that cottage almost as much as he cared for the sea, and it's not right letting it crumble apart like it has. I want it to be loved, and who better to love it than you?"

A home just for me and Breena? No more lingering in strangers' homes, crashing on couches, or occupying spare beds. We could fix this place up how we wanted, whatever that may be, having a place to live and love in the process.

I swallowed a lump in my throat as Breena grabbed my hand. No words were exchanged between us, but there didn't need to be. Our eyes, the way we poured into each other, said everything we needed to know.

"You work on the sea and we'll work on the cottage?" Hope

crept through Breena's voice as she asked, and she squeezed my hand just a little too hard.

"Sounds rather fine to me." Rory nodded, a satisfied smirk creeping across his lips.

"So, it does," I said. "Well, captain, it looks like we have ourselves another deal!"

CHAPTER THIRTY
STONE BY STONE

The sheets underneath me were soft, but nothing compared to the suppleness of her skin. Breena writhed under my touch, but it was I who came apart, watching pleasure unfold across her face. It lingered on her sweat-slicked brow and parted lips, and it danced through the air on her praise. You'd think after months of this—lounging, laughing, and loving in our own bed— I'd have gotten used to it by now, but how did one truly ever get used to perfection?

"It's almost time!" a voice called out from downstairs, causing my relaxed muscles to seize. Breena whimpered, her large, dark eyes begging me to ignore that voice, and depths, did I want to.

"Be down in a minute!" I yelled back down to Zellia, regret in my tone. My sister had been back at the cottage for two whole days and had already taken over planning our housewarming party. After six months of cottage renovations, neither Breena nor I had it in us to host, but if there was going to be a party, Zellia would be the one to ensure all festivities went swimmingly.

Breena let out a heavy sigh then clicked her tongue on the back of her teeth. "You know you're just going to have to make up for this later, right?"

Her head plopped onto her pillow, accepting defeat for now. She ran the back of her hand across her forehead, and I propped my head up on her thigh. I could nestle into her for the rest of my life, but I suppose our guests would grow weary of our absence, wouldn't they?

"Little droplet, we've built our home stone by stone, and when we're done celebrating that feat, I will unravel you piece by piece. You have my word." Placing a kiss on the sensitive skin of her thigh, I gave her a little pat on the hip. "Let's go."

"We *do* have stunning new dresses to show off along with the cottage, do we not?" Breena asked. I nodded slowly with a smirk on my face as I helped pull her from our dangerously comfortable bed. "Fine. I will take that as my reason to vacate this room."

"Are our incoming guests not reason enough?" I asked with a lifted brow. Tousling the velvety sheets until they were smooth, I erased any history of our presence. I pulled two dresses from the wooden armoire, handing one to Breena and taking the other into our bathing chamber.

Breena called out from the other room, "They are! But can't a girl have a sleepy morning in bed with her mate?"

"She can, but the sun will be setting in a few hours," I chuckled. "We can hardly call it morning."

"Are you two almost ready?" Zellia called out again, pounding on the door this time. I popped my head out of the sun-lit bathing chamber to see Breena lacing up her bodice. One loop, two loops, and finished.

"Yes! Come in!" I called, stepping back out into the bedchamber. I smoothed my hands over the pink dress I wore and beckoned my sister in. She used the tip of her toe to open the door, but I could barely see her face. She hid behind a small wooden box with rusted hinges.

"You did not!" I said, rushing over to her to grab my box of sea glass. I set it on the ground, my dress pooling around me as I sat in front of it. Breena and Zellia's gazes were trained on me as I ran my fingers along the wood grain. "I can't believe you brought this back with you."

"You've had more than enough time away from that little box and everything within it," Zellia said, joining me on the floor. "All these pieces of glass, of Dad, they're yours. You should be the one to keep them."

I threw my arms around Zellia, pulling her into my chest, my heart so full of love that I could barely stand it.

"Okay, okay," she laughed, shaking me off. "You're welcome!"

Zellia glanced over at Breena as she pointed her thumb at me. "You know you're responsible for this, right?"

"Oh, I take full responsibility for your sister's mushy heart. It's my greatest achievement," Breena said with her hand over her chest. She peered over to me with a puffed-out bottom lip, and I simply shook my head at her.

"I'm ignoring both of you!" I said, hiding my smile. Zellia just laughed and played with the shell around her neck, back in its rightful place thanks to our grandfather. I was pleased to see her wearing it. While the jewelry used to represent everything I wasn't and couldn't be, now all I saw in it was our familial love, and how could I ever take that for granted again?

"Hello?" an older gentleman's voice called out. "Where are my ladies of honor?"

The three of us rushed down the wooden steps softened by carpet in a warm moss green. We entered the front hall where, one at a time, we all greeted our grandfather. Breena and I welcomed him, and he set down a few platters of food on our kitchen table. I breathed in the delicious, savory scents, and my mouth watered as he uncovered his dishes.

The man knows how to cook, I thought to myself as I snuck a freshly baked roll drizzled with oil and flaked sea salt. The salt made my tongue tingle as I licked my lips free of it.

My grandfather ushered Zellia and I to sit before the rest of our guests arrived. He held our hands as he said, "Listen, I don't know how to tell you this, but we need to redo both of your pendants."

"Redo them?" I asked, my palm flattening over the glass droplet resting on my chest. "Why?"

"Well..." Our grandfather released our hands to dig around in his sweater pocket. "They're in need of an upgrade."

When he held out his fist and uncurled his aged fingers, one by one, he revealed a porous red stone in his hand. My mouth fell open as I stared down at the object sitting in the middle of his palm. "Is that..."

"What we think it is?" Zellia finished for me.

A spark of hope ignited in my chest as he nodded his head. "It sure is. Took me a bit to find that elusive little rock."

Bloodstone.

"This must have cost you a fortune!" Plucking the stone from his hand, Zellia and Breena leaned in closer to me, staring at the unassuming rock. I traced its ridges and lines with my eyes in quiet astonishment, knowing what I held would change our lives forever.

Our grandfather chuckled and said, "What good is coin if you have no one special to spend it on?"

"I'll cancel this whole gathering and go to your shop if it means putting bloodstone inside this pendant. I'd redo this glass piece a million times!" I held up my droplet-shaped pendant between my thumb and pointer finger. My grandfather simply laughed and told us not to cancel our plans. He said there would be time tomorrow, that tonight was for celebrating. I had no doubt I could get in the celebratory mood with a bloodstone in my hand.

I fiddled with the stone while staring through the cottage windows to the icy sea crashing below. While I'd visited home a few times in the past few months, sirens like me, like Zellia, weren't meant to make the trip from land to sea so frequently. With this bloodstone, I could jump into the sea right now, swim with my selkie in our natural forms with nothing but peace. I could visit

Maisie and the other hybrids in the caves and swim in their pools. It was only months ago I felt as though I had the entire world at my fingertips, but that feeling was nothing compared to the freedom I had now.

Breena stood behind me, wrapping her arms around my shoulders. She leaned in close to my ear and whispered, "Dearest siren, I believe you and I have a date with the sea."

"I come bearing gifts," Rory said as he entered his father's cottage with his mother in tow. Both he and Evina glanced around the front hall, as if it had been the first time they'd graced it, but we all knew otherwise. Breena and I managed to restore all that made this cottage so special, every cozy nook and stained-glass window. We may have had to strip some of the crumbling stone, replace rotten wooden beams and the flooring, but we hoped Rory still recognized its familiar character.

A proud smile crossed Rory's face as his gaze crept across each stone, each painting, every lit candle. My chest swelled, feeling as though we did his father's home justice and, in doing so, healed just a little piece of our human friend's heart. I supposed both of our fathers now lived within these warm, loved walls.

He took me and Breena in for a bear hug, each of us tucked under his arms, trays still in each of his hands. He whispered his gratitude into our hair, and I wept like a baby into his shoulder.

For the love of all things salty, Zellia was right. I am pure mush.

"You did good, girls," Evina said, patting us tenderly on the backs before wandering off to find my grandfather. Breena and I pulled away from Rory as my sister came barreling around the corner. Zellia rushed over to the former fisherman to see what kind of tasty treats he held. She shooed us away as she peeled back the cotton cloths on his dishes. He laughed as she peeked inside, his cheeks brightening with each hearty chuckle.

Zellia came to visit me often, and Rory always kept a bonnet shell on his person in case she needed to reach him. Without fail, he would pick her up from the Dreslee every time she summoned him. The two had grown close over the months, but I also think Rory liked the excuse to be back out on the water. After we defeated the hybrids, he was quick to say goodbye to his life as a fisherman, and many of his former crew did the same. For the past several months, he's been pondering his true passions, and somewhere along the way, he became a transporting service for sea fae.

Rory's second most frequent customer entered sometime shortly after, a beautiful selkie woman on his arm.

"Niven! Nehra!" Breena cried out. "You made it!"

Breena ran over to her older brother and his new mate, embracing them both with equal measure. We quite liked Nehra. Breena had known her since she was just a pup, but Niven had never expressed romantic interest in her until after Breena decided to stay in Barthoah. Breena suspected he never would have settled down with a mate while she was still in the Selkie Cove. Life in our new home seemed much easier on Breena, knowing that, in her absence, Niven finally felt free to live a life for himself. As the older sister, Niven and I were alike in that way.

My grandfather and Rory's mother chatted in two high-back chairs as he stoked the fire raging in our central hearth. The summer days were long gone, replaced by biting winds and snow I had yet to get used to. The warmth of my selkie helped ease my transition, and depths, did that woman love the snow. She claimed her blubber kept her nice and warm, but I didn't have the heart to tell her humans don't have blubber. The biggest fib I held onto was allowing her to believe otherwise, so I'd say my conscience was clear.

I joined Wallace and Evina in the sitting room, and Breena brought over a tartan blanket, a goblet of cranberry mead, and a plate full of warm, savory food. I could get used to this life. Never would I let a day pass where Breena didn't know how grateful I was for her and just how damned loved she was. Here, in this room, surrounded by family and friends, it was impossible not to feel the love. When they all returned to their homes and were blowing out their candles for the night, I would still be by her side, and unlike the candles, my love would never dim.

ACKNOWLEDGMENTS

Thank you to my darling fiancé, who encouraged me through all the ups and downs writing this book. This story took longer to craft than I anticipated, and you were there to listen to all my rants and celebrate every little accomplishment. This is now the fourth book of mine that you have read and lended that beautiful brain of yours to polish. I am grateful for every note, every correction, and every joke you left in the comment section. I can't wait to marry you next month!

Thank you to my parents, who have been supportive of my writing long before I published my first novel.

Mom, you have been a huge part of my editing process for each book, and I will always appreciate the time you have put into helping make my books as great as they can possibly be. Not only have you assisted in the creation of my stories, but you help me get them out to my readers. You've spent countless hours with me in my office, wrapping up books and preparing them to ship off to people all over the world. I couldn't have gotten nearly as many books out into the world as I have without you!

Dad, thank you for helping me with the business side of Eighty-Eight Butterfly house, and ensuring things run smoothly. From finances, to taxes, to random business laws, I am grateful to have you to lean on!

ABOUT THE AUTHOR

Marissa Serrao is the author of The Seeking, a YA portal fantasy series, and Love X Magic, an NA sapphic romantasy collection.

As a child, Marissa lived in a world of fantasy, befriending mythical creatures

and building many magical kingdoms inside her mind. It wasn't until years later that she revisited her love of fantasy worldbuilding and took it to the page, where she could invite others to explore the magic with her.

You can find Marissa at home in Charlotte, North Carolina sneaking in as many moments as she can to write each day, surrounded by her partner, furry kids, and far too many houseplants.

CONNECT WITH MARISSA

@authormarissaserrao

TikTok: https://www.facebook.com/authormarissaserrao/

Instagram: https://www.instagram.com/authormarissaserrao/

Facebook: https://www.facebook.com/authormarissaserrao/

YOUR GUIDE TO THE LOVE X MAGIC COLLECTION

Between Mischief & Magic

- A drunken demon, a princess who lost her magic, and a deal to save them both...
- Vibes: Cozy Cottagecore, Grumpy X Sunshine, & Slow-Burn
- Coziness: 4/5
- Spice: 1/5

Between Salt & Serenades

- A stubborn siren, a stranded selkie, and a deal to save the sea...
- Vibes: Seaside Adventures, Natural Enemies to Lovers, & Forced Proximity
- Coziness: 2/5
- Spice: 1.5/5

www.ingramcontent.com/pod-product-compliance
Lightning Source LLC
Chambersburg PA
CBHW022102310726
48972CB00007B/1845